Faith of My Fathers

SPENCER COUNTY PUBLIC LIBRARY
210 WALNUT
ROCKPORT, IN 47635-1398

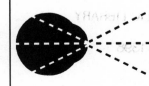

This Large Print Book carries the
Seal of Approval of N.A.V.H.

CHRONICLES OF THE KINGS, BOOK 4

FAITH OF MY FATHERS

LYNN AUSTIN

THORNDIKE PRESS
A part of Gale, Cengage Learning

Detroit • New York • San Francisco • New Haven, Conn • Waterville, Maine • London

GALE
CENGAGE Learning™

Copyright © 2006 by Lynn Austin.
Scripture quotations identified NIV are from the HOLY BIBLE, NEW INTERNATIONAL VERSION®. Copyright © 1973, 1978, 1984 by International Bible Society. Used by permission of Zondervan Publishing House. All rights reserved.
Thorndike Press, a part of Gale, Cengage Learning.

ALL RIGHTS RESERVED
Thorndike Press® Large Print Christian Historical Fiction.
The text of this Large Print edition is unabridged.
Other aspects of the book may vary from the original edition.
Set in 16 pt. Plantin.
Printed on permanent paper.

LIBRARY OF CONGRESS CATALOGING-IN-PUBLICATION DATA

Austin, Lynn N.
  Faith of my fathers : chronicles of the kings / by Lynn Austin.
    p. cm. — (Thorndike Press large print Christian historical fiction)
  ISBN-13: 978-1-4104-0823-5 (hardcover : alk. paper)
  ISBN-10: 1-4104-0823-X (hardcover : alk. paper)
    1. Manasseh, King of Judah — Fiction. 2. Bible. O.T. Kings — History of Biblical events — Fiction. 3. Israel — Kings and rulers — Fiction. 4. Large type books. I. Title.
  PS3551.U839F35 2008
  813'.54—dc22   2008012711

Published in 2008 by arrangement with Bethany House Publishers.

Printed in the United States of America
1 2 3 4 5 6 7 12 11 10 09 08

Dedicated to my friend
Catherine Pruim.
God must have known I would need
a special friend like you.

The Lord is my strength and my song;
he has become my salvation.
He is my God, and I will praise him,
my father's God, and I will exalt him.

EXODUS 15:2

PROLOGUE

"Come on, Joshua, just tell me the main points," twelve-year-old Manasseh pleaded.

"You didn't read any of the Torah lesson?" Joshua asked.

The look of horror on his face annoyed Manasseh. "You're such a goody-goody! It's not like I broke one of the Ten Commandments or anything. I just didn't get around to reading it."

"Rabbi Gershom is going to be furious when he finds out," Joshua said, his face solemn.

"So? Who cares what that old tyrant thinks. He can't do anything about it. I'm the king of Judah, remember?

"You'll feel his wrath, believe me. He can make you feel guilty without even raising his voice."

"If you tell me what the passage is about before he gets here, he'll never know."

"Oh, he'll know —" Joshua began, but

Manasseh tapped his finger on the scroll impatiently. "All right, all right," Joshua said with a lopsided grin. "But just this once . . . and only because you're my friend, not because you're the king." He unrolled the Torah scroll and found his place. "The passage we read yesterday told about the curses that God will send on us if we abandon Yahweh's covenant, but this part says if we turn back to God, He'll restore our fortunes and have compassion on . . . Hey, you're not even listening."

Manasseh had risen from the bench and crossed to the tiny room's only window. He opened the shutters, bringing in a gust of cold air. The window faced east, with a view of the Mount of Olives across the Kidron Valley.

"That's because you're boring me to death," he told Joshua. "I don't see why we need to study all these ancient rules and regulations, anyhow."

"Because they're part of God's Word. We —"

"Oh, spare me the lecture! You're as bad as Rabbi Gershom." It irritated Manasseh that his friend showed such a keen interest in all this stuff. To Manasseh it was as dry as old bones. "What else does it say?"

"This verse sums up Moses' entire speech

to the Israelites: 'I have set before you life and death, blessings and curses. Now choose life, so that you and your children may live. . . . For the Lord is your life, and he will give you many years in the land he swore to give your fathers.' "

"But He didn't do it," Manasseh said softly.

"What did you say?"

"Nothing." He was reluctant to voice the bitterness he felt, even to his best friend. Manasseh had been thinking of his father, King Hezekiah, who had been faithful to Yahweh — more faithful than all of Judah's kings since David. But God hadn't given him a long life. Hezekiah's life had ended abruptly, five months ago, at the age of fifty-four.

"Look! The sun is shining!" Manasseh said. The gray clouds that had muffled the late winter sky for days suddenly parted to reveal a small patch of blue along with the blinding sun. He turned to his friend. "It's an omen. Come on, let's go."

Joshua stared at him in surprise. "Go where?"

"Who cares! Anywhere but here." He pulled Joshua's hand away from the scroll, and it rolled up by itself. "Come on, Ox. Let's get some fresh air."

"But the rabbi will be here any minute. I don't think we should —"

"You're so predictable. Don't you ever get tired of playing by the rules? I do!"

"But we can't just walk away from our lessons."

"Why not? Who's going to stop me? I can do whatever I want, and right now I want to go outside and enjoy the sunshine, not stay cooped up with a bunch of ancient scrolls. And you're coming with me."

Joshua lumbered to his feet, knocking the bench over, reminding Manasseh why he had nicknamed him Ox. Thirteen years old, Joshua was tall and gangly, and although he seemed to grow a little taller each night, he never grew any fatter. Manasseh, at twelve, was still built like a child, slender and small-boned. Joshua always stood stoop-shouldered beside him, as if embarrassed to stand a head taller than the king.

Manasseh peered out of the doorway, looking both ways, then motioned for Joshua to follow him toward the back stairway.

"Where are we going?" Joshua asked again. "Shouldn't we find somebody to escort us if we're going outside?"

"We're going alone. I want to escape from this place, and I don't want any servants hanging around us."

"But —"

"Shh! Follow me. And pick up your feet when you walk. You sound like an entire troop of soldiers."

"Sorry."

Manasseh crept through the harem, passing his mother's closed door. She was still in mourning for her husband. The only person allowed to visit her from outside the palace was Joshua's mother, Jerusha. But the rain had kept even Jerusha away for the past few days.

He continued through the nursery, passing the room that had been his before he became king. Manasseh had been reluctant to move into his father's huge rooms, unable to accept the fact that his father was gone and would never use them again. At first the king's chambers had been filled with Hezekiah's presence and with his familiar scent — a combination of the incense from the Temple that permeated all his clothes, the fragrant soap he used to wash his hair and beard, and the aloe balm he massaged on his hands every morning. But Manasseh hadn't been able to stop his father's scent from slowly fading away, along with the memory of his voice and his reassuring touch.

Manasseh had almost made it through the

nursery without being seen when he passed his younger brother's open door. Amariah looked up from his reading.

"Hey, where are you two going?"

"He probably heard your big feet," Manasseh whispered to Joshua. "Walk faster."

"Wait for me!" Amariah hurried into the hallway, following along behind them. "Where are you going?"

"Never mind. You're not invited."

"I thought you had to study Torah with Rabbi Gershom."

"Get lost."

"Can't I come with you?"

"No!" Manasseh turned and gave Amariah a shove that nearly sent the ten-year-old sprawling to the floor. "Go back to your room! And you better not tell anyone you saw us or you'll be sorry. Understand?" Amariah nodded fearfully and retreated to his room.

"Why can't he come with us?" Joshua asked.

Manasseh didn't answer. He didn't need to give a reason — he was the king. He had been slowly realizing that fact for the past five months and had started doing whatever he pleased, gradually testing his authority. When no one questioned his decisions, he'd grown more daring. But today would be his boldest action — abandoning his boring Torah lessons to escape from the palace. No one could punish him for it, either. Joshua's father, Eliakim, served as his guardian and as the palace administrator until Manasseh was old enough to govern the nation by himself. But even Eliakim didn't have the authority to discipline the king.

He hurried down the flight of stairs that led to the palace courtyard, his feet skipping like a mountain goat's, while Joshua plodded along behind him, gripping the railing. Manasseh smiled as he opened the outside door. He was the king. He was free!

Huge puddles spanned the courtyard and more water ran in streams down the steep streets, washing the city clean. Manasseh dodged most of them, but Joshua's sandals were soon soaked. No one stopped the boys as they continued past the armory and the guard tower. The courtyard where they practiced their military training resembled a lake. They headed toward the Water Gate, which still bore that name even though the Gihon Spring had been closed for many years. The scent of almond blossoms and damp earth filled the wintry air as the wind tried in vain to chase away the clouds.

"Come on, Ox. I'll race you to the bottom." Manasseh sprinted down the steep ramp, well ahead of his friend. To slow an invading army's momentum, the road curved first to the left, then to the right before leveling off at the bottom. Manasseh savored the freedom of the wind in his hair and the power in his pumping legs as the ground raced past. He easily reached the olive grove first and flopped down on the wet grass. Joshua staggered up a few minutes later, breathless, and sank down on a low stone wall nearby.

"You win, Manasseh."

"That's because I'm the king. You're not supposed to beat me."

"No, it's because you're faster than I am." Joshua was still puffing hard from the race. His lungs made a rasping sound like a shutter hinge blowing in the wind.

Manasseh stared at the meadow, where he knew the spring had once flowed. "Too bad my father buried the Gihon Spring. I could use a drink of water." An olive grove and half a dozen almond trees coming into bloom surrounded it now. He tried to imagine how the spring would have looked with serving girls lining up to lower their jars into the clear water, but it was too difficult to picture — as difficult as picturing his father's face.

"Do you miss your father?" Joshua asked suddenly. Manasseh glanced at his friend, wondering how he had perceived his thoughts, then turned away. Across the Kidron Valley, clouds gathered above the Mount of Olives once again. The small patch of sunshine overhead wouldn't last much longer.

"What do you think, Ox," he answered sullenly. He knew he wasn't supposed to grieve forever. To continue to mourn was to doubt God's wisdom, the high priest had told him.

"Well, if it were my father — I guess I would miss him a lot," Joshua said. "I don't know how I could stand it."

"Then what makes you think I want to talk about him?" The dampness from the ground began to seep through Manasseh's robes. He stood, brushing off the loose grass, and sat on the wall beside Joshua. The cold stones weren't much drier than the ground.

"Don't you need to talk about him, though?" Joshua asked. "Otherwise, if everyone is afraid to say his name around you, after a while won't it be like he never existed? I would hate that. It would be much worse if everyone just *forgot* my father."

"No one around here is likely to forget

King Hezekiah, the greatest king since David. This valley is where the miracle happened. Yahweh answered my father's prayer and 185,000 Assyrians died in the night." Manasseh's voice had a mocking tone, almost as if he didn't believe the story. Joshua stared at him in surprise.

But Manasseh believed the story all right. It was the greatest achievement of his father's reign and the event that worried Manasseh the most. How would he ever live up to such a spectacular performance? He was Hezekiah's son. The nation expected even greater miracles from the heir to such a great king. But what if God didn't listen to Manasseh's prayers?

"If it was my father," Joshua said, "I wouldn't miss him because he's a famous man — the palace administrator and all that. I'd miss him because he's my abba."

A flood of longing overwhelmed Manasseh, and he jumped to his feet, hurrying down the path so that Joshua wouldn't see his sudden tears. He remembered how his father would remove the heavy mantle of his reign at the end of the day and for a few moments he wouldn't be the king of Judah anymore; he would be Manasseh's abba. He missed the way his father looked at him, the pride and the love he saw in his eyes, and the pressure of his strong hand on his shoulder. Then Abba would listen patiently to his childish tales as if they were the most important news he had heard all day.

Yes, I love him and I miss him and it's just not fair, Manasseh longed to shout like an angry child. *Abba was too young to die! He loved God and he obeyed all His laws, and I don't understand why God punished him — why He punished all of us — by taking him away!*

But Manasseh didn't shout. He was the king of Judah, not a twelve-year-old boy. There would be no childish tears and questions.

By the time Joshua caught up with him, Manasseh had his emotions under control. "Why are you still puffing like a long-distance courier?" Manasseh asked him.

"I don't know. . . . I can't . . . catch my breath."

"Is it one of your breathing attacks?"

"Almond blossoms . . . They give me trouble sometimes."

"Are you all right?"

"Yeah . . . in a minute." Joshua stopped and bent over double, resting his palms on his thighs as he struggled to exhale.

Manasseh had seen his friend have attacks like this before, since the boys had grown up together. He tried to act concerned, but secretly he enjoyed witnessing his friend's weakness. Joshua was superior to Manasseh in almost every other way: brighter in his academic studies, able to memorize long Torah passages, quicker with the answers to the rabbi's questions about the Law. Joshua had his father's brilliant intellect, and every aspect of the nation's government fascinated him. One day he would take Eliakim's place as palace administrator, serving in Manasseh's court. That was why their fathers had decided to educate them together. Only in their military training, which required the speed and physical agility that Joshua lacked, could Manasseh outshine his friend. Joshua was old enough to take part in the Temple services, too, beside his father. But even though Manasseh would soon be old enough, as well, he would never be able to stand on the royal platform and worship beside his own father.

At last Joshua stood upright and started walking again. "It's clouding over," he said, still wheezing. "I think it's going to rain."

"So what? I don't care if I get wet. Do you?"

Joshua shrugged off the challenge and ran his fingers through his hair in a gesture so much like Eliakim's that Manasseh couldn't help grinning.

"What? What's so funny?"

"Nothing, Ox."

It would be natural for Joshua to take his father's place someday, seated at the king's right hand, continuing his father's work. But when Manasseh thought about taking his own father's place, sitting on King Hezekiah's throne, his smile vanished.

They reached a fork in the road. One path led in a winding route up the Mount of Olives; the other curved to the right and eventually veered back toward the southern gates of Jerusalem. The sun was gone, now, and the air had turned cold. Manasseh felt a few drops of rain and turned right.

"Alms . . . alms for the blind . . ." An old woman sat in the middle of their path, calling out to them in a feeble voice. Her gray hair, matted like a bird's nest, stuck out from beneath her widow's shawl. Her lined face reminded Manasseh of a dried fig, and the thick, gray film that covered her eyes turned his stomach. She stretched out her hand, as gnarled as an olive branch, and grasped Joshua's robe as they passed by.

"Kind child, can you spare a mite for a poor blind widow?"

Joshua stopped and looked down at her, his face filled with concern. He patted his sides beneath his outer robe. "I'm sorry. I didn't bring my silver pouch."

Manasseh grew impatient. "Come on, Ox. It's starting to rain."

"Wait — do you have any silver with you? I'll pay you back. The Torah says, 'He who is kind to the poor lends to the Lord.' "

Manasseh heaved a sigh to let Joshua know how aggravated he was, then dug out his money pouch. He chose the smallest silver piece he could find and bent to place it in the woman's outstretched hand, careful not to touch her. But she suddenly grabbed Manasseh's wrist in a viselike grip with her other hand and drew his palm close to her face until it was only inches from her filmy eyes.

"Open your palm, boy. I'll read your future for your kindness."

"No, don't let her do it!" Joshua cried. "The Torah says —"

"Calm down, Ox. It's only for fun. It doesn't mean anything. Go ahead, old woman. Tell me all about my future." He gave Joshua a sharp look, warning him to keep quiet about his identity. The woman would have no idea she was studying the king of Judah's palm. She pulled it closer to her face and moved her head from side to side as she examined it.

"Ah . . ." she said, her voice hushed with awe. "This is a hand that will wield great authority one day! You will hold the lives of many people in this hand!"

"You shouldn't let her do this," Joshua mumbled, shuffling his feet.

"Oh, be quiet. What else do you see, old woman?"

"I see a long life with many sons. And power! Enormous power! You are destined for great renown, boy!" She seemed reluctant to release his hand, as if some of his power might rub off on her while she held it.

"Okay, let's go now," Joshua said. But Manasseh grabbed his friend's gangly hand and thrust it beneath the woman's face.

"What about his future? Read his, too."

"No! I don't want her to!" He tried to pull free, but Manasseh and the old woman pried his palm open and held it tightly. She pulled it close to her eyes and studied it for a moment, then suddenly dropped it as if it had burned her.

"What? Tell me what you saw," Manasseh said. The old woman shook her head fearfully and motioned for them to get away from her. "We're not going until you tell us what it said," Manasseh insisted.

"Danger!" she cried, still shooing them

away. "Great danger!"

"My friend is in danger?"

"No! He is a great danger to *you!*" She fixed Manasseh with her blind-eyed stare, and he couldn't turn away. He stood frozen, pierced by her voice and her filmy eyes. "Your lifeline and his take opposite paths. Warring paths. The authority belongs to you, but he will be much more powerful. The forces that are in him will be too strong for you!"

"She doesn't know anything," Joshua said. "Let's get out of here."

"He's not your friend, boy!" she told Manasseh. "He's your enemy! He'll try to destroy everything you do!"

"The Torah says, 'Do not turn to mediums or seek out spiritists, for you will be defiled by them'!" Joshua shouted at the woman. He grabbed Manasseh's arm and pulled him back the way they had come, breaking the old woman's spell. The rain was falling hard now. "I'm sorry I made you give her the silver," Joshua said, shivering. "She's evil."

"But how did she know my future? How did she know about all my power?"

"She doesn't know anything! She said I'd have more power than you, and you know that's not true. You're the king, not me."

24

Manasseh recalled the fear he had seen in the old woman's scaly eyes as she looked into Joshua's hand and the way she had dropped it as if it were a hot coal. He stared at his friend as if at a stranger, then quickened his pace.

"Don't look at me like that, Manasseh. You know I'm not your enemy." Joshua was panting as he hurried to walk beside him. "She's lying! We're best friends, aren't we?"

"That's what I used to think." Manasseh broke into a run as the rain suddenly poured down. Joshua couldn't keep up with him.

"Manasseh, wait for me!" He began to cough, trying to expel the air from his lungs so he could draw another breath. "Wait!"

Manasseh ran on, the rain stinging his face, until he could no longer hear Joshua's footsteps or his wheezing breaths behind him.

When he reached the first bend in the steep ramp Manasseh finally stopped and looked back. Joshua stood in the pouring rain near the almond grove. He was bent double again, coughing and gasping for air.

"Wait . . ." he called. "Help me . . ."

Manasseh had only seen Joshua this sick twice before, and both times he had been bedridden for days afterward. The rain and

25

cold air might make the breathing attack worse. Joshua was his best friend — his only friend — and Manasseh knew he should go for help. Joshua's father would know what to do. But then Manasseh would have to see the tenderness and love in Eliakim's eyes when he gazed at his son.

"Please . . . help me. . . ." Joshua's voice sounded weaker.

Manasseh turned away from him and slowly walked up the hill to his palace as rain and tears coursed down his face.

■ ■ ■ ■

PART ONE

■ ■ ■ ■

Hezekiah rested with his fathers. And Manasseh his son succeeded him as king. Manasseh was twelve years old when he became king, and he reigned in Jerusalem fifty-five years. His mother's name was Hephzibah.

2 KINGS 20:21; 21:1

1

"Wait here," King Manasseh told his servants. "I would like to be alone for a few minutes."

"Yes, Your Majesty."

He left his entourage of palace guards and servants standing by the cemetery entrance and walked forward alone, toward his mother's tomb. It was the close of a warm, spring day, just after the evening sacrifice, and Manasseh knew he would have only a few more minutes of twilight. Once night fell he would need a torch to make his way among the tombs. The graveyard was deserted and peaceful; the mourning doves in the distant trees grieved with him.

At twenty-one, Manasseh had grown into a handsome man. His long, narrow face seemed sculpted from costly stone, his straight nose, square forehead, and jaw skillfully wrought by an artisan. He had inherited Hezekiah's broad shoulders but not his height or strong frame. Like his mother, Hephzibah, he was slender and light-boned, with her thick dark hair the color of olive branches and her brown eyes flecked with gold. His lean body was muscular beneath his linen robes; he still trained every day with his military tutor in order to stay strong and agile. For his size, Manasseh had become very difficult to beat in hand-to-hand combat.

He reached the tomb he had hewn for his mother out of the cliffside and stopped. Hephzibah had died two years ago tonight. In a way it seemed like only yesterday that they had shared their evening meal together, yet when he tried to remember her smile or the sound of her singing, it seemed as if she had been gone forever. He stretched out his hand to touch the enormous block of stone that sealed the tomb, wishing he could reach for his mother and find her there. The stone felt warm, still holding the memory of the sun's heat. He pressed his forehead against it and closed his eyes.

When he finished reciting the prayers for the dead, Manasseh turned to leave. As he did, his foot kicked something lying on the ground in front of him. He bent to examine it in the twilight and found a small bouquet of wilting blossoms, wrapped in a roll of fine parchment. He recognized the writing as the beautiful calligraphy sold by the Temple scribes. He tilted the pages to catch the fading light and read the words:

Praise the Lord, O my soul;
all my inmost being, praise his holy name.
Praise the Lord, O my soul,
and forget not all his benefits . . .

He didn't need to read the rest to recognize his mother's favorite psalm. She had sung the words and haunting melody to him nearly every night when he was a child until he, too, knew it by heart. Sorrow engulfed him from the unexpected memory. When he realized that Joshua's mother, Jerusha, had probably placed it there, he tasted the bitterness of envy, as well. Both of Joshua's parents still lived, and even his elderly grandfather, Hilkiah. Manasseh had grown up beside this large, close-knit family — Eliakim and Jerusha, Joshua, his older brother, Jerimoth, and their sisters, Tirza and Dinah. Yet he always felt as if he stood outside, gazing through a window at the kinship and love they shared. Manasseh and his younger brother, Amariah, were very different from each other and had never been close.

He tucked the flowers inside the parchment again and left the bundle where he found it. But as he rose to his feet, he glimpsed a faint flicker of light among the tombs farther back in the cemetery. He walked a few steps in that direction, searching for the source of the light, but the graves looked dark and shadowy. Then he crouched and peered between the markers until he spotted it again: a single lamp, well-shaded. It might be necromancers. They sometimes defied the Law by practicing divination in cemeteries, consulting the dead in occult rituals.

His guards at the entrance were all looking the other way to give him privacy. If he shouted for them, he would probably scare the culprits off. The thought of surprising the criminals and making the arrest himself excited Manasseh. He pulled his dark outer robe closed and belted it so his pale under-tunic wouldn't be visible in the dark and give him away. Then he crept quietly toward the light.

He was lithe and agile, and he moved silently among the tall cedars, crouching occasionally to keep the lamp in sight. He was close now. He could hear someone mumbling in a singsong voice, but the words sounded like nonsense.

Only one shadowy figure knelt beside the newly buried grave. His bent head was a ball of woolly hair and beard, surrounded by a halo of light from the lamp. He had sacrificed three pigeons and cut them in two, separating the halves. Now he was drawing symbols in the patch of dirt between them as he mumbled incantations. Manasseh's heart thumped with excitement. He had all the evidence he needed to condemn the man. He quietly circled around him, then stepped out of the shadows in front of him.

"What are you doing?"

The man gasped and leaped to his feet. "Stay back!" He pulled a knife from inside his robe and swirled his foot in the dirt to erase the symbols he had drawn.

Manasseh's heart leaped faster. He had never considered that the necromancer might be armed, even though he had seen the slaughtered pigeons. The palace guards were too far away; the man could kill him before they could run to his rescue. He cursed himself for his foolish mistake.

"Easy, now . . ." Manasseh said as he sized his opponent. The man was a few inches taller and about twenty pounds heavier than Manasseh. He didn't look particularly strong and was at least ten years older than he was. But this wasn't a training exercise. The man must realize he would be condemned to death, and he probably wouldn't hesitate to use his weapon.

"You can't escape," Manasseh said. "My soldiers have you completely surrounded." He watched the man's eyes, waiting until he glanced sideways for a moment, and then Manasseh seized his chance. He grabbed the man's wrist with his left hand and punched him as hard as he could in the midsection with his right. The man expelled all the air from his lungs with a grunt. Then Manasseh kicked the legs out from under him and brought him to the ground, slamming his wrist against a rock until he dropped the knife. He planted his knee in the man's diaphragm and picked up the knife, holding it to his throat.

"I suggest you don't resist me."

The man nodded, his eyes fearful. His chest heaved as he strained to get his wind back. After a moment, Manasseh stood.

"Tell me your name."

"Zerah son of Abner."

"Sit up slowly, Zerah, and take off your belt. Slowly! Now put your hands behind your back."

Zerah gasped in pain as Manasseh tied his hands together. He had probably broken

Zerah's wrist when he'd slammed it against the rock. Manasseh pulled the knot even tighter until Zerah cried out.

"What were you doing here in the cemetery?" Manasseh asked as he walked around in front of him again. Zerah didn't answer. "Do you know who I am?"

"Yes."

"Then you know that you have to answer me." Zerah stared at the ground near Manasseh's feet. "Very well, then," Manasseh said. "Here's something to think about."

He bent to retrieve a small jug he spotted lying among Zerah's things. He removed the stopper and sniffed. As he suspected, it contained extra oil for the lamp. He dropped the lid on the ground and dashed the oil all over Zerah's face and hair. It ran down the front of his tunic, soaking it. Manasseh tossed the jar aside into the darkness and bent once more to pick up the lamp. He held it close to Zerah's round, shiny face. Zerah's eyes were narrow and close set, giving him the appearance of being cross-eyed. He had a large, rounded nose and full lips, as sensuous as a woman's. But his most prominent features were his thick eyebrows, arched like twin peaks above his eyes.

Manasseh relaxed now that he was in control and savored the rush of exhilaration that surged through his veins like strong wine. "Now, I think you'd better tell me what you were doing here, Zerah son of Abner."

"Seeking guidance," Zerah replied after a moment. His voice was surprisingly calm.

"From the dead?"

Zerah nodded slightly. "From their spirits."

"Even though it's against the law? You must have known you were breaking the Law of Moses, as well as the laws of Judah."

Zerah's eyes flared as if Manasseh had fanned a bed of coals. "It may be against the laws of Judah, but it's *not* against the Law of Moses!"

"You seem quite certain of that."

"My father is a priest. And so am I."

"I'm not familiar with any Temple priests named Abner. Nor do I recall seeing you in service. You're over age thirty?" Zerah nodded. "When were you ordained?"

"My father was a priest in Samaria and a prophet, as well. We're descendants of the prophet Zedekiah, who prophesied for King Ahab and Queen Jezebel. My family fled to Judah when the Northern Kingdom fell to Assyria, during your father's reign."

"So you're a priest of Baal."

"Baal . . . Yahweh . . . the same god with

many names."

"Oh no, Zerah. They're not the same at all. I've studied the Torah and —"

"You studied the Torah with the phony Temple priests. They only taught you what they wanted you to know. They kept the hidden things from you."

"What hidden things?"

"The Secrets of the Ancients . . . the Wisdom of Abraham . . . the ability to read signs and omens. And to foretell the future."

"Only Yahweh knows the future."

Zerah gave a short laugh. "That's what your Temple priests want you to believe so they can stay in power. If they can make you depend on them, they can control you."

"You're crazy."

"Am I, King Manasseh? Why is it that the rulers of all the other nations in the world are priests as well as kings, but you're not allowed to share the priests' power? Other kings have access to the hidden mysteries, but you can't even enter your own Temple sanctuary."

"Of course not." Manasseh spoke with indifference, but Zerah's words had struck a raw nerve. He was the king, yet Yahweh's priests made him feel like an outsider in his own Temple.

"It wasn't always that way, you know,"

Zerah continued. "The rulers of our nation used to be priests. Surely you've read of Melchizedek, King of Salem, who was also a priest of God Most High? Our father Abraham acknowledged his kingship and his priesthood by paying him a tithe. And Melchizedek blessed Abraham in return."

Manasseh recalled the story, but it sounded different, somehow, when Zerah told it. The Temple priests had been Manasseh's teachers. Their interpretation of the Law was all that he knew. He sat down on a large stone in front of his prisoner. "But that was before we received the Law at Sinai."

"Yes! Exactly! This ceremony you interrupted tonight is the purest form of our faith — the way our fathers Abraham, Isaac, and Jacob worshiped. It's all recorded in the first Book of the Torah. Abraham took a heifer, a goat, and a ram, each three years old, along with a dove and a young pigeon. He cut them in two and arranged the halves opposite each other." Zerah gestured with his head to show how he had done the same thing. "Then the spirits appeared to Abraham at night and foretold his future. How his family would be slaves in Egypt. How they would be delivered during the fourth generation. And how he would go to his fathers in peace and be buried at a good old age."

"I know the story."

"Then why is it against the Law when I do it? Father Abraham performed the same ritual to divine his future."

"The Torah says, 'Do not practice divination or sorcery.' "

"That's from the laws of the priests, not the laws of our forefathers. Abraham worshiped under the stars. He could read their mysteries. God commanded him to study the heavens. 'Look up . . . So shall your offspring be.' "

Again, Manasseh couldn't argue with him. Everything Zerah said could be found in the Torah.

"The stars prophesied his future," Zerah continued, "because Abraham knew how to read their mysteries. But Abraham never worshiped the god you call Yahweh. That's what the descendants of Aaron named the god they control. Abraham worshiped Elohim."

"What's your point, Zerah?"

"My point is that the phony priests and false prophets have stolen your power. The Torah says, 'The secret things belong to the Lord our God, and the things revealed belong to us and to our children forever.'

But they have deliberately outlawed the ancient mysteries, keeping them to themselves so they could control your kingdom. Just like they controlled your father."

Manasseh stood. "No one controlled my father!"

"That's what you think. They made him destroy all of the high places where every man could go to offer his own sacrifices and seek the wisdom of Abraham. Now the priests make us come to *their* Temple, offer *their* sacrifices, so we're under *their* control. We're told we can't worship God without them, and they make us recite empty rituals, devoid of power. This isn't the worship our ancestors knew. Then the priests put a curse on your father."

"They did *what?*"

"They cursed him! The God of our ancestors gave us the power of blessing and cursing. He told Abraham that whoever he blessed would be blessed and whoever he cursed would be cursed. Read it for yourself. Abraham knew the secret incantations, and so do your priests. That's how the man who calls himself a prophet cursed your father."

"You mean Rabbi Isaiah?"

"Yes. He knows how to read the future, and he knows all the ancient omens and signs found in the stars. He even has power over the heavenly bodies. Didn't Isaiah once make the sun roll backward? Isaiah used the same spell our forefather Joshua used when he made the sun stand still. Isaiah is a powerful man, Your Majesty. He deceived your father all of his life in order to hold him under his control. He would only reveal the future to him piece by piece. Then he cursed him."

"Why would Isaiah curse my father?"

"He wanted to make sure King Hezekiah died before you came of age. That way they could control you and train you to believe all their lies, too."

"You're lying."

"Am I? How long was your father ill before he died?"

Manasseh remembered the shock of his father's sudden death, how it seemed as if he was alive and healthy one day and wrapped in a shroud the next. He was too stunned to answer. Zerah leaned forward.

"Isaiah told your father he would live fifteen additional years, and the king died fifteen years later, to the very month. I know the ancient curses, too, King Manasseh. But my priesthood is outlawed by those who want to control you. I can read your future as well as Isaiah can. You were born under the sign of the lion, into the tribe of the lion. They know you are doubly blessed with the power of kingship. That's why Isaiah keeps you under his control."

"I haven't seen Rabbi Isaiah in years."

"He's controlling you, nevertheless, through your palace administrator, Eliakim. They have long been allies, even under your father. Isaiah used his power to secure the palace administrator's job for Eliakim."

"That's not how it happened. Isaiah prophesied that Eliakim would . . . Oh no . . ." He sank down on the rock again, seeing the truth in what Zerah had said, remembering the story his father had told him about Eliakim's rise to power. It was true — Isaiah and Eliakim had always been close.

"And now that Eliakim is old and nearing retirement, they're conspiring to replace him with his son."

"Joshua? But I've always known that Joshua would take Eliakim's place."

"No. They've always *told* you that he would. But shouldn't the king choose his own palace administrator?"

Manasseh transferred the knife to his other hand and wiped his sweating palm on his thigh. He suddenly remembered the blind woman in the Kidron Valley and what she had prophesied about Joshua and himself: *"The authority belongs to you, but he will be more powerful."*

"How do I know you're not making all this up?"

"Ask them. Ask Rabbi Isaiah. Do you believe he saw the future for your father and grandfather?"

"I know he did."

"Then ask him to tell your future. He knows what it is right now, but he won't tell you because then he can't control you. He'll refuse to do it, and when Isaiah defies you, ask your palace administrator to back you up. Make him choose between the two of you. Eliakim will side with Isaiah, not with you. So will his son and successor. They're all in this conspiracy together, along with the priests and Levites."

"I don't believe any of this," Manasseh said, but his voice was trembling.

"No? Doesn't Eliakim have a daughter? What family did she marry into?"

Manasseh knew the answer. As a close friend of the family, he had attended Tirza's wedding a year ago. But he wouldn't say the words aloud, unwilling to face the truth.

"She married into the high priest's family," Zerah answered for him. "They are all involved in this plot." Manasseh could only

43

stare at him, too stunned to speak. "You don't have to take my word for it," Zerah said after a moment. "I challenge you to put them all to the test. See if what I'm telling you isn't true. If I'm wrong, then I'm not a prophet. You can execute me for worshiping the God of Abraham. But if I'm *right,* then you'd better take control of your kingdom before it's too late."

Manasseh stood in the silent graveyard as crickets chirped and bats flitted between the darkened tombs. A sliver of moon had risen above the hills, but dark clouds suddenly washed across it, blotting it out, just as the turmoil rampaging through his soul seemed to erase every truth he had ever known. He didn't want to believe this crazed man he had found muttering among the tombstones, but all the stories Zerah had quoted from the Torah had been true. Manasseh had read the account of Abraham's night vigil. He remembered how Abraham, Isaac, and Jacob had each prophesied over their sons, telling them the mysteries of the future, secrets that for some reason had been denied to Manasseh.

"Do you know what my future is?" he asked Zerah.

"I could seek it for you through the stars and other omens. I could tell you . . ." His eyes flickered up to the moon that emerged, briefly, from behind the clouds. "I could tell you, for instance, that the new moon is rising in your sign. That means that the stars will be favorable for romance, for finding the woman who was destined to be yours."

Manasseh gave a short laugh, well aware that his palace harem was still empty. Choosing the one wife he was allowed to marry under the Law was a delicate process, Eliakim had informed him. Eliakim hadn't permitted Manasseh to make a selection yet, warning him about controlling his youthful lust.

"Do they even decide who you will marry, King Manasseh?" Zerah asked in a mocking voice. "I'm not surprised. There are many, many things they are hiding from you, secrets they never want you to learn."

"Name one," Manasseh demanded.

"Did they tell you that your mother worshiped our true mother goddess, Asherah?"

"That's a lie! How dare you slander my mother! She would never do a thing like that!"

"But she did. She worshiped Asherah faithfully until they imprisoned her and forbade her to do it."

"Idolatry is against the law! She wouldn't ⎯"

45

"Against *their* law. Why don't you ask Eliakim if it's true? But first make him swear an oath to tell you the truth."

Manasseh's entire body trembled with anger. "Stand up!"

"Am I under arrest for telling the truth?" Zerah asked.

"Start walking! That way — toward the entrance." Manasseh followed Zerah, carrying his lamp and his knife, leaving the dead pigeons and Zerah's other belongings to the night scavengers.

Once he returned to his palace chambers, with Zerah safely locked in the guard tower, Manasseh found that the eerie confrontation in the graveyard continued to haunt him. Like the severed sacrificial birds, he felt divided — between believing what he had always thought was the truth and believing Zerah's interpretation of it.

He had never consulted Isaiah about his future, but he was certain the rabbi would reveal it to him if he asked. Why wouldn't he? Isaiah had prophesied for King Hezekiah and King Ahaz before him. A shiver passed through Manasseh when he recalled Zerah's accusation that Isaiah had cursed his father. *Fifteen years. To the very month.*

"Would you like me to prepare your bath,

Your Majesty?" his valet asked.

"No. I want you to summon the palace guards for me. Send them to Rabbi Isaiah's house to fetch him. I would like to talk to him. Then light all the lamps in the throne room."

Isaiah wasn't masterminding a conspiracy to control him and his kingdom, Manasseh assured himself. But he needed to settle the questions in his mind tonight. Then he could execute Zerah for his lies and sorceries at dawn.

Manasseh received his first shock as soon as Isaiah arrived: the old rabbi entered with Eliakim by his side. *"They have long been allies,"* Zerah had said. Before Manasseh could issue an order, Eliakim took his usual seat at the king's right hand.

"Why are you here, Eliakim? I didn't summon you." Manasseh tried to keep his voice even and not show his surprise or the trickle of suspicion that shivered through him. Eliakim was always crowding him, always interfering in everything Manasseh tried to do, as if not trusting him to run the kingdom by himself.

Eliakim spread his hands innocently. "I often visit the rabbi in the evenings. He's kind enough to answer some of my ignorant questions from time to time. It's a rare privilege to bask in his wisdom and knowledge."

"I'm sure it is," Manasseh replied. "In fact, that's why I've summoned him." He shifted to face Isaiah, who stood patiently before his throne. The old prophet's hair and beard had turned completely white over the years, and he looked shrunken, his skin yellowed like an ancient parchment scroll. But his eyes were alert and Manasseh sensed the latent power concealed beneath his calm exterior.

"Rabbi, I'm well aware of how you prophesied during my father's reign, as well as my grandfather's and great-grandfather's reigns. Now I would like you to do the same for me."

"*Tonight,* Your Majesty?" Eliakim interrupted.

"Yes. I've been negligent in establishing a relationship with you, Rabbi Isaiah. But like Lord Eliakim, I would also like to tap the wealth of your wisdom and insight."

Isaiah pinned him with unnaturally keen eyes, as blue as the summer sky. "No, you don't. You want to know the future."

The rabbi's bluntness startled Manasseh, but he hid his surprise. "I'm only asking for the same consideration you showed my father."

"Prophecy doesn't work that way —" Eliakim began, but Manasseh cut him off.

"I would like the rabbi to answer, not you."

"Eliakim is right," Isaiah said. "Prophecy isn't fortune-telling. I can't predict the future."

"Didn't you once foretell Eliakim's future?"

Eliakim sat forward, his mouth opened to protest, but he caught himself.

"How old were you, Eliakim, when the rabbi foretold that one day you would sit here, in this very seat?"

"Your Majesty, it wasn't —"

"Just tell me how old you were." Manasseh forced himself to stay calm, to allow events to unfold by themselves.

"It was the night after my thirteenth birthday, Your Majesty."

"Amazing! And here you are, some fifty years later, just as Isaiah said you would be. That sounds like a very accurate prediction of the future, wouldn't you say?" Neither man replied. Manasseh turned back to Isaiah. "Rabbi, I've heard stories about all the events that happened before I was born. Didn't you also accurately predict that our nation wouldn't be invaded by the Assyrians at the time that Israel fell? And also that Sennacherib's forces would die by God's sword, not by man's?"

"I didn't foretell any of it. God did."

"But wasn't my father able to choose his course of action and govern the nation based on those predictions? By listening to your wisdom and foreknowledge, wasn't he better able to make sound judgments?"

"It wasn't by my wisdom that he —"

"Yes or no, Rabbi?"

Isaiah sighed. "Yes. Your father wisely heeded God's Word —"

"Then, that's all I'm asking. Tell me God's Word so I can do the same thing."

"I can't foretell the future. God has sometimes allowed me to catch a glimpse of it — to see a tiny thread in the fabric of His tapestry. And when He has, I've shared that glimpse with your father. Your grandfather never wanted to see what God revealed."

"Well, unlike King Ahaz, I'll listen to you, Rabbi. You may tell me everything that God has revealed about my future. Unless you have something more important to do tonight."

Isaiah clasped his hands in front of him and shrugged. "I don't know your future, Your Majesty. You choose the pattern yourself, and it's up to you how it will be woven."

The rabbi's words made Manasseh angrier. He struggled to keep his voice reasonable. "But are you willing to consult God for me? To go home and pray and perhaps return in a day or two with an answer?"

"You have God's Law, Your Majesty. It tells you everything you need to know about your future. If you obey it, you will prosper and live long in this land. You and your children after you. If you reject His law, you will die."

Manasseh was no longer able to control his anger. "Is that what happened to my father? Did he die so young because he rejected God's law?"

"No. Yahweh would have taken your father's life fifteen years earlier. You would have never been born. But in His infinite mercy and love, God extended King Hezekiah's life beyond his time."

"And how did you know that would happen, Rabbi? How did you know the exact length of time he would live?"

"God revealed it to me."

"Then it seems to me that we are talking in circles. You *can* predict the future, and in fact, you *have* predicted the future. I don't care how or what means you've employed to do it in the past; I just want you to use those powers for me, as well."

"But I have no power."

"Then how did you make the sun move for my father?"

"I didn't —"

"Eliakim, did you see the sun move backward?"

"Your Majesty, this is —"

"Yes or no, Eliakim."

"I saw the shadows move, yes."

"When Rabbi Isaiah prayed?"

"Yes, but —"

"Do I need to rouse old Shebna from his bed as a second witness? Did he see the sun move, too?"

"Shebna saw it, too," Isaiah replied.

"Good. Then we have established that you do have powers, Rabbi. Now my next question is, why are you refusing to use those powers for my benefit? Why do you want me to remain ignorant of my future?"

"If God reveals anything about your future to me, Your Majesty, you have my word on oath that I will tell you."

"Ask them under oath," Zerah had challenged. Manasseh drew a deep breath and gripped the armrests.

"Did my mother worship Asherah?"

Manasseh's question froze the two men into utter stillness. Eliakim seemed to have stopped breathing.

"Do I need to invoke an oath to learn the truth?"

"No," Isaiah said quietly. "I'll tell you the truth. For a time, yes, she did worship Asherah."

"Was she imprisoned for it?"

For the first time that night, Isaiah wouldn't meet his gaze. "She was banished from the palace and confined to your father's villa."

Manasseh turned to Eliakim. He was staring at the floor. "Why didn't you ever tell me?"

"It was something your mother was ashamed of. I didn't think she wanted you to know, or she would have told you herself."

"Liar! That's not why! What else haven't you told me?"

Eliakim looked up, not at Manasseh but at Isaiah, and the look they exchanged confirmed Manasseh's growing conviction that everything Zerah had told him was true. There was a conspiracy to control him, and these two men were deeply involved in it. He began to tremble, the way he had trembled in the cemetery as he had crept up on Zerah and disarmed him.

"Rabbi, I'm a reasonable man. I would like to give you one final chance to think things over and decide whether you're going to withhold your powers from me, powers that Eliakim has testified that you possess. In the meantime, I can't allow you to roam freely when there's a chance you'll turn against me. I'm going to ask Eliakim to escort you to the palace prison for the night, and maybe by morning God will reveal something to you. Prison worked quite well for Joseph. He saw the Egyptian Pharaoh's future very clearly after serving some time in jail. Eliakim, take him there. Now."

Eliakim stood. "Your Majesty, I . . . I can't put Rabbi Isaiah in prison."

Manasseh felt his stomach roll over in dread. "Why not?"

"Because he hasn't committed a crime."

"Refusing to obey the king is a crime."

"But he's not refusing to obey, Your Majesty. Your request is impossible to obey."

"The rabbi and I have reached an impasse, Eliakim." Manasseh heard the deep trembling in his own voice and felt it in his shaking limbs. This was the final test. "Which one of us are you going to support?"

Perspiration beaded on Eliakim's pale forehead. "Your Majesty, may I please explain —"

"No. Just answer my question. Which one

of us are you in agreement with?"

"But this is all just a terrible misunderstanding of —"

"Which one!"

"I . . . I have to side with the rabbi because —"

Manasseh groaned and passed his hand over his face. Eliakim had been like a second father to him. He didn't want to accept the truth that Eliakim had long been involved in a conspiracy against him. He wanted it to be just the delusion of a crazy man who talked to spirits.

"Your Majesty, please . . . can't we talk this over and —"

"I'm not listening to your advice anymore, Eliakim. It's time I started discovering the truth for myself. Guards!" The two sentries standing outside the throne room door rushed inside. "Put both of these men in the palace dungeon so they can't conspire with anyone else." The guards hesitated, staring at the condemned men in surprise. "Lord Eliakim and Rabbi Isaiah have both refused to obey my orders," Manasseh told them. "Are you refusing, too? Do you want to join them in prison?"

"No, Your Majesty." The guards each gripped one of the prisoners, but Manasseh sensed their reluctance.

"When they're safely locked away, assemble all of the soldiers assigned to the night watch and bring them here."

Again, Eliakim and Isaiah exchanged looks as the guards led them away. Manasseh tried to read what he saw in their eyes but couldn't. His stomach churned with shame and revulsion. How could he have been so naïve all these years, blindly trusting everything Eliakim said and did? Had the entire kingdom known what a fool he had been? It was time for him to grow up and begin to run the nation on his own.

When the night guards trooped into the throne room, Manasseh was immediately suspicious of them. Where did their loyalties lie? Were some of them part of this conspiracy, too? The only way he would ever know was to issue an order and see how they responded.

"I'm sorry to say that I've uncovered an elaborate conspiracy tonight," he told them. "Two men who I thought were my friends — Rabbi Isaiah and Lord Eliakim — have turned out to be my enemies." He paused to let them digest this information before continuing. "I know it may seem hard to believe, but tonight they proved it with their actions. They will be given a fair trial, of course, but in the meantime I want half of you to search Rabbi Isaiah's house for evidence. Bring me every document you find, and make sure you search for hiding places, as well. I want the rest of you to go to Eliakim's house and do the same thing. Bring all the documents to me."

Manasseh had to pause to regain his composure. His stomach churned as he considered the final step. It was difficult enough to believe that Eliakim was involved — but surely not his son Joshua, not Manasseh's trusted friend since childhood. For the second time that night he remembered the blind woman's prophecy: *"He's not your friend . . . he's your enemy."*

"Eliakim has a son named Joshua. Arrest him and bring him to me. Remember, all of these men are traitors to the kingdom. Treat anyone who tries to help them as my enemy, as well."

2

"So, my child, they left you behind to baby-sit your old grandfather, eh?" Hilkiah's round, wrinkled face beamed mischievously.

"Oh, Grandpa, you know that's not true." Dinah plumped the pillows behind her grandfather's head and tucked the blankets around him. Hilkiah's bed had been moved to Eliakim's old workroom on the main floor. Now that he was in his eighties, it had become too difficult for Hilkiah to climb the stairs.

"No? Then why is such a pretty young girl like you staying home with an old man like me? Where are all your suitors?"

"I don't have any suitors yet, Grandpa."

He chuckled merrily. "Oh yes, you do. You have dozens of them, but they're all afraid to approach your father — the king's mighty palace administrator — and ask for your hand." His voice was serious, but his eyes twinkled in the lamplight. Dinah sat on the bed beside him and hugged him.

"You're teasing me, Grandpa."

"No, I'm not. Your suitors troop in and out of my shop every day just to ask about you. They know I'm your grandfather, you see, and they think I'm less fearsome than Eliakim. Ask your brother Jerimoth. He'll tell you the same thing. Your suitors have tried to talk to him about you, too, but he gets annoyed with them. He tells them they're wasting his time. He's there to sell cloth, after all, not serve as a matchmaker."

"I can't ask Jerimoth because he's not home. He went to Heshbon with your caravan, remember?"

"That's right. And where did everyone else disappear to tonight? I suppose your father is still at the palace."

"No, he went to see Rabbi Isaiah."

"And your mother is with your sister in Anathoth. Still no word about Tirza's baby?"

She shook her head. "They promised to send a messenger as soon as the baby is born. I hope they don't forget."

"My little Tirza . . . a mother," Hilkiah said with a sigh. "I can't believe it. Only yesterday I was bouncing her on my knee out in the garden. Wouldn't you much rather be with your sister when her first baby is born instead of sitting around here

59

with your old grandfather?"

"Mama wouldn't let me go. She's afraid if I see what childbirth is like I'll never want to get married."

Hilkiah laughed. "Jerusha is a very wise woman."

"I won't have to worry about babies if Abba never lets me get married." She took Hilkiah's plump hand in both of hers and held it to her cheek, feeling the soft texture of his skin, loving every wrinkle and age spot.

"You're his youngest, Dinah. His baby. It's hard for Eliakim to let you go. But once he gets young Joshua settled down, your day will soon follow. You're only eighteen, after all. Hardly an old maid."

"But Joshua wants to marry my best friend, Yael, and she's a few months younger than I am."

"Is that where he disappeared to tonight?"

"Yes. If he keeps eating dinner with them, Yael's father won't have any money left for the wedding."

Hilkiah laughed. "I daresay your brother is love struck. But that's nothing compared to the way your father was. You never saw a man more in love than Eliakim."

Dinah knew what was coming. She had heard the story countless times but never grew tired of it. It was fun to imagine Abba acting silly with love for her mother. And it was so romantic to dream about a suitor loving her that much.

"Your father used to be handsome, you know, before his hair grew thin on top and his beard turned gray. Your brother Joshua reminds me a lot of him at that age, with his unruly black hair and mournful eyes. He's tall like your father, but Joshua is even thinner than Eliakim was, if that's possible. And, of course, your mother was such a beauty. Who could blame him for being smitten with her? But I daresay you're even more beautiful than your mother, Dinah."

"You're just saying that to cheer me up."

"No, no, my child. You know I don't lie. You're so slender and delicate, like fine porcelain. And that perfect face . . ." He held it in his hands as if he were appraising a precious jewel. "No wonder the suitors are lining up. One look into those dark eyes of yours and they're lost. No, your father won't give you away to just any man. Only —" Loud pounding on the front door interrupted him.

"The messenger!" Dinah cried. "Tirza's baby!" She jumped up and ran to answer it before the servants did.

"It's going to be a boy," Hilkiah called

after her.

But when she opened it, a dozen palace guards stood outside. Before Dinah could speak, the guards pushed past her and forced their way into the house.

"If you're looking for my father, Lord Eliakim, he —"

"We want his son Joshua," the captain said. "Is he here?"

"Why do you want Joshua?"

The captain gripped Dinah's arms and forced her to sit on the bench by the door. "If you stay here and keep quiet, nothing will happen to you, girl." Then he nodded to his men. "Search the house."

They spread out in all directions — upstairs, down the hall into the living areas, into the kitchen and servants' quarters, out into the courtyard, and into her grandfather's bedroom. It sounded as if they were tossing the house upside down, searching it. She heard Hilkiah's startled voice in the next room.

"Who are you? What are you doing in here?" A moment later a soldier dragged him into the hallway in his nightclothes and stood him in front of the captain. Dinah jumped to her feet.

"Leave my grandfather alone!"

"Hush, Dinah. I'm all right." Hilkiah nodded for her to sit down again, then turned to the captain. "Why don't you tell us what you're looking for, and then you can be on your way?"

"We're only interested in Joshua ben Eliakim."

"My grandson? Why?"

"If you tell me where he is, you'll be free to go."

"What's wrong? Has something happened?"

"Do you know where he is or not, old man?"

Dinah knew her grandfather wouldn't lie. It was her fault for placing him in this dilemma. She had told Hilkiah where Joshua was.

"My brother is King Manasseh's best friend!" she cried. "He'll execute all of you when he finds out about this!"

The captain ignored her. "Are you going to tell us, old man?"

"Not unless you give me some more information than —"

"Hold him." One of the soldiers seized Hilkiah from behind and pinned his arms behind his back. The captain untied the small wooden club strapped to his belt and rammed it into Hilkiah's stomach. Dinah screamed. She threw herself in front of the captain to shield her grandfather.

"No! Stop! Don't hurt him!"

The captain flung Dinah aside. "Someone come in here and hold this girl," he called. Another soldier ran in from the living room and grabbed Dinah, clamping his hand over her mouth. She struggled in vain to free herself.

"Now tell me where your grandson is."

"No . . ." Hilkiah moaned.

"Come on, old man. You're wasting my time."

Dinah watched in horror as the captain clubbed her grandfather again and again. *Please, God! Make them stop!* Hilkiah doubled over, groaning helplessly.

"This is your last chance," the captain warned. When Hilkiah didn't answer, the captain bludgeoned him in the head until blood poured down his face. The soldier holding Hilkiah let go, and he slumped to the floor.

"Can you still hear me, old man?" the captain asked. Hilkiah curled into a ball, moaning in agony.

"Maybe this girl knows something," the soldier holding Dinah said. The captain turned to her.

"Do you want to watch your grandfather die?" He gave Hilkiah a vicious kick. "I'm

64

going to ask you the same question I asked him. Where's Joshua ben Eliakim?"

Dinah had no qualms about telling a lie to save her grandfather's life. She waited until the soldier eased his hand off her mouth. "He's at the palace with King Manasseh."

"No, he's not," the captain said. "And this is what will happen every time you lie to me." He crouched beside Hilkiah and lifted his head, then smashed it against the stone floor, again and again.

"Stop!" Dinah screamed. The soldier quickly covered her mouth. She felt her legs buckle beneath her, but the guard held her suspended in the air, her legs dangling uselessly. She was going to vomit all over his hand. *Dear God, where was Abba? Where were all the servants? Why didn't somebody help them?*

Her grandfather lay sprawled on the floor, unmoving. A dark puddle of blood slowly spread beneath his head. His robes were askew with his tunic bunched up around his knees, and his bare legs looked pale and shriveled. Dinah moved instinctively to cover him, to tuck his robes around him so he would be warm, but the soldier held her tightly in his grasp.

"I'll kill you next, girl. Where is your

brother?"

She felt the hand uncover her mouth. "Help me!" she screamed. The captain grabbed her throat with both hands and choked off her cries. He squeezed tighter and tighter until Dinah's lungs felt as if they would burst. She felt the pressure building in her head. Her vision turned gray, then faded to black. She writhed in the soldier's arms as the terror of suffocation overwhelmed her. One second before she would have fainted, the captain loosened his death grip. Dinah drew a deep, gasping breath.

"This is your last chance," he told her. "Next time you die. Where is he?"

Dinah couldn't think. Who were these murderers? Why did they want Joshua? If she didn't tell them where he was, she would die. But if she told them, Joshua would probably die. They meant to kill all of them.

Hilkiah uttered a faint groan, and the captain turned and kicked him again. They were waiting for her answer. But Dinah couldn't remember any words or how to string them together into sentences. She tried to talk, but all that came out was a babbling moan of terror.

Her killer's hands circled around her throat again and squeezed. She couldn't breathe. His fingers were crushing her windpipe. Time slowed as stars of light exploded, then swam through her tears. In the eternity before the world went black, Dinah knew she was going to die.

"God of Abraham, what is going on? This can't be happening." Eliakim tried to pace, but the prison cell was too small. He could take only three steps before he had to turn and walk back again. The stone floor was rough and uneven beneath his feet.

The jail was little more than a crude hole, carved in the bedrock beneath the palace, with an iron door bolted across the opening. It smelled damp and musty, like ancient tombs and decaying bones. With no windows and no lamps or torches, it was blacker than a moonless night. It reminded Eliakim of the Siloam tunnel, and he tried not to panic at the thought of being buried alive. He couldn't see Isaiah, but he knew that the prophet sat on the floor, just a few feet away. The thought comforted him.

"This can't be happening," he said again. He had repeated the phrase a dozen times in the long hour since Manasseh had imprisoned them.

"Eliakim," Isaiah said with a sigh, "why don't you sit down. It's going to be a while until morning."

"I'm sorry, Rabbi, but it's all so crazy! What on earth is going on? What is King Manasseh thinking? How long is this temper fit of his going to last? He won't keep us down here all night, will he?"

"Are you asking me to tell the future, too?"

Eliakim heard the irony in Isaiah's voice and smiled in spite of himself. "Well, it would be nice to know what's going to happen next, Rabbi."

"God alone knows. We'll have to rest in Him. Come, Eliakim. Sit down."

He stumbled toward Isaiah's voice, his hands outstretched in the darkness. He found the opposite wall and felt his way down to the floor, sitting for the first time since the soldiers put him in the cell.

"Not very comfortable, is it?" Isaiah said.

"No. Are you warm enough, Rabbi? It's freezing in here."

"I'll be fine."

Eliakim folded his arms and tucked his hands in his armpits to warm them. "Now what?"

"Now we wait."

"I want to believe that this is all a terrible mistake. That Manasseh will listen to reason in the morning, but —"

"I know. Uncertainty is the enemy of our

faith." Isaiah heaved a deep sigh. " 'In that day I will summon my servant, Eliakim son of Hilkiah. . . . He will be a father to those who live in Jerusalem and to the house of Judah. I will place on his shoulder the key to the house of David. . . . I will drive him like a peg into a firm place.' Do you remember when I told you that?"

"How could I ever forget it?" Eliakim said softly.

"There was more," Isaiah said. "I never told you all of it. I'm sorry."

Eliakim waited for what seemed a very long time. He didn't know why, but his heart had began to pound. When Isaiah finally spoke, his voice sounded hoarse.

" ' "In that day," declares the Lord Almighty, "the peg driven into the firm place will give way; it will be sheared off and will fall, and the load hanging on it will be cut down." The Lord has spoken.' " Isaiah's robes rustled, and Eliakim knew the rabbi was wiping away tears.

Eliakim struggled to comprehend the words of the prophecy: they meant he would fall from power. Is that what was happening to him? Had Isaiah known this day would come? Eliakim groped in the darkness for Isaiah's shoulder and rested his hand on it.

"I'm glad you never told me, Rabbi, but

thank you for telling me now."

"The Lord showed me so much for King Jotham, King Ahaz, King Hezekiah. But Yahweh has shown me nothing of King Manasseh's reign, and I don't know why."

"Can't we do what Manasseh asked? Can't we pray and ask God to give us something to appease him? Maybe He'll show us His plan for Manasseh."

"I think this is His plan."

"You mean, to be falsely accused and imprisoned? But why?"

"I don't know. If it's His will to save us, then God will show me what Manasseh wants to know. If not . . ."

Eliakim groaned. "I've been trying to think back over the past few days, to remember something that might have happened to set Manasseh off like this, but I can't think of anything that's relevant. I stood beside him at the Temple this morning and again tonight. He held court today as usual. Nothing out of the ordinary happened. I went home for dinner to see if there was any word on my daughter's baby and —"

"So you're going to be a grandfather, Eliakim?"

"I already am." Eliakim knew that Isaiah was trying to distract his thoughts to help pass the time, and he decided to play along.

"My older son, Jerimoth, and his wife have a baby girl. My daughter Tirza is married to a priest, so of course she's hoping for a son, and —"

Eliakim heard footsteps descending the stairs. The cell gradually began to grow lighter as the torches drew near. He sprang to his feet. "Oh, thank God!" He helped Isaiah to his feet, and they felt their way toward the cell door as three soldiers came into view. The one in front carried a torch, while the other two carried what looked like a heavy sack between them. Probably some bedding. That meant he and Isaiah would be left down here all night.

"Stand back!" the first soldier shouted. "Turn around and face the wall with your hands over your heads."

As they obeyed, Eliakim glanced at Isaiah's face. He looked calm, but his eyes were tired, his face ashen. His robes were covered with rotting debris from the cell floor. Eliakim heard the soldiers struggle with the heavy beam barring the door, and then he heard the hollow squeal of rusty metal as the door swung open. There was a soft thud as the sack fell to the floor; then the door groaned shut again and the bar slammed into place. Eliakim quickly turned around to examine the bundle before the light disappeared again. But the mound wasn't a sack of bedding straw. It was his father.

"Abba! God of Abraham, no! It's Abba!"

Eliakim sank to the floor and lifted his father into his arms, cradling him. Hilkiah moaned softly. Isaiah crouched beside them. Then the light was gone again, the cell as dark as pitch. Eliakim felt his father's face with his fingertips; it was swollen and sticky with blood. Eliakim didn't want to believe that Manasseh would involve Hilkiah in this nightmare.

"Abba, what happened to you?"

"Eliakim?" he whispered.

"Yes, Abba, I'm here."

"I can't see."

"That's because there's no light in here." Eliakim's sleeve began to grow damp where his father's head rested against it. He touched Hilkiah's hair with his other hand. It was matted and soaked with blood. "Dear God, Abba! Who did this to you?"

"Soldiers . . . They wanted Joshua."

"Joshua? What for?" Hilkiah moved his head slightly as he shook it. "Was Joshua home? Did they arrest him, too?" Eliakim asked.

Hilkiah shook his head again. "I . . . didn't tell . . ." His voice was slurred, as if he talked out of only one side of his mouth.

Eliakim gently squeezed his father's right hand. "Can you feel this, Abba?" Again, Hilkiah shook his head. But then he lifted his left hand to his ear as if to swat away a fly. Eliakim touched his father's ear to see what was bothering him. The side of Hilkiah's head was slick with blood, but there was no wound. The blood was coming out of his ear.

"Eliakim . . . I'm dying. . . ." he mumbled.

"No, Abba, you're not! Don't die! Oh, dear God . . . !" He gently lifted Hilkiah into Isaiah's arms and scrambled to his feet, banging his fists against the cell door. "Jailer! Somebody!" he cried. The sound of his voice and pounding fists echoed in the tiny cell, bouncing back at him, deafening him. "My father needs a physician! Have mercy on him! He's an old man! He's done nothing wrong! Please!"

He heard no reply, no footsteps descending the stairs.

"Rabbi? Am I dying . . . for a righteous cause?" Hilkiah asked.

"Yes, my friend," Isaiah said. "You've played a very important part in Yahweh's eternal plan. You've lived your life faithfully, never compromising with evil. And you've raised your son and your grandchildren to do the same. Soon, now, you will stand in

God's holy presence."

Eliakim knelt again and gently took Hilkiah from Isaiah's arms. He wanted to clasp his father tightly, but he was afraid he would hurt him.

"It's so . . . hard to think . . ." Hilkiah whispered. "Say prayers with me, Eliakim. 'Hear O Israel . . .' "

" '. . . Yahweh is our God. Yahweh alone. You shall love —' " Eliakim's throat tightened, and he couldn't finish. In the darkness beside him, Isaiah continued to pray while Hilkiah whispered some of the words along with him.

" 'The Lord is my shepherd, I shall not be in want. He makes me lie down . . .' "

" '. . . lie down . . .' "

" '. . . in green pastures, he leads me beside quiet waters, he restores my soul.' "

" '. . . my soul.' "

"Abba . . . Abba, no!" Eliakim wept. "Oh, God of Abraham, you have the power to heal him! Nothing is too hard for you! I pray that —"

"No, son." Hilkiah's fingers touched Eliakim's lips. "Don't pray. Let me go home."

"No, Abba! I can't! Not like this!"

"Let me go . . . home to . . . Yahweh."

" 'Even though I walk through the valley

74

of the shadow of death,' " Isaiah murmured, " 'I will fear no evil, for you are with me.' "

" '. . . with me . . .' "

" 'Your rod and your staff, they comfort me.' "

Eliakim closed his eyes and wept as Isaiah and Hilkiah continued to recite, his father's voice growing weaker and weaker.

" 'Surely goodness and love will follow me all the days of my life, and I will dwell in the house of the Lord forever.' Amen." Isaiah finished the psalm. He rested his hand on Eliakim's shoulder. "I'm sorry, son. He's gone."

Eliakim buried his face on his father's chest. "But why?" he cried. "I don't even know why. . . ."

When Dinah opened her eyes, she was lying in a strange bed in a room she didn't recognize. Her neck felt bruised and swollen. She remembered the soldier's hands around her throat, choking off her life, and she cried out.

"Shh . . . it's all right, Dinah. They're gone now." She struggled to sit up and was startled to see King Manasseh standing beside the bed.

"My grandfather! They hurt my grandfather!"

75

"Shh . . . he'll be all right. I promise you," Manasseh said. He sat down on the edge of the bed.

"Oh, thank God." She began to weep, and Manasseh pulled her into his arms to comfort her. She felt his hand stroking her hair as she wept against his chest. After a while she dried her eyes and sat up again, ashamed of what she had done. It wasn't proper for an unmarried woman to be in a man's arms, even if he was practically a member of the family. "I'm sorry, Your Majesty. I shouldn't have done that. But I was so scared."

"I know. It must have been a terrifying experience for you."

She looked into his eyes, and her heart quickened. King Manasseh was so handsome, his brown eyes so unusual, as if they contained flecks of topaz. Like all of her friends, Dinah had often dreamt that she would one day marry King Manasseh.

"They wanted Joshua, Your Majesty. They said they would kill my grandfather and me if we didn't tell them where he was. But I don't know why they wanted him. What did he do?"

"I'm still trying to find out the truth myself." He held her shoulders, and she felt the warmth of his hands through her clothes. "Dinah, I can't find Joshua, either.

Do you know where he is?"

"Yes, he went to Yael's house to talk to her father. He wants to marry her."

Manasseh looked relieved. "Good. Now listen, Dinah, I need you to answer some questions for me so I can help your brother. All right?"

"I'll try."

"Has your father always had a close relationship with Rabbi Isaiah?"

"Yes, for as long as I can remember."

"And Eliakim knows the high priest quite well, too?"

"They often share a meal together. Tirza is married to his son. Why?"

"And Joshua knows both of these men?"

"Yes, but they can't be the ones who are after him. They —"

"This girl Joshua wants to marry. Who is her father?"

"His name is Amasai. He's one of the chief Levites, an expert on all of the priestly laws."

Manasseh's face went pale. He sat very still, poised like a predator about to strike his prey. Suddenly he stood and hurried to the door. He flung it open, and Dinah stared in horror at the captain who had beat her grandfather and nearly choked her to death.

"That's him!" she screamed. "That's the man who —" Manasseh turned to her, and when Dinah saw his face she knew she had made a terrible mistake. She had betrayed Joshua.

"He went to the home of Amasai, one of the chief Levites," Manasseh told the captain. "Hurry!"

The king closed the door again and leaned his back against it. "I'm sorry, Dinah, but I finally realized tonight that your father has been making a fool of me for many years. And so has your brother."

"I don't understand. You and Joshua are closer than brothers. Abba has been like a father to you."

Manasseh didn't seem handsome to her anymore. The dark look on his face as he slowly walked toward the bed terrified her. Her instincts screamed at her to run, but she knew she couldn't possibly escape. She began to whimper.

"I want to go home. Please . . . please let me go home." Manasseh shook his head. "Are you going to kill me?" she asked.

"No, Dinah. Why would I kill you?" He stopped beside the bed and traced her cheek with his finger. "You've grown into a very beautiful woman. Do you know that? Who has your father been saving you for? Certainly not for me." He took off his outer robe and let it drop to the floor, then sat on the bed again.

Dinah shivered all over with fear. "I haven't been promised to anyone, Your Majesty. If you ask Abba, I'm sure he'll let you marry me. He'll be glad to arrange a betrothal." She would say anything to keep him away from her. For the second time that night she felt like she might vomit.

"I don't need to ask your father, Dinah. I'm the king, remember? I can have whatever I want."

"Please . . . not like this. We have to have the wedding first. And say our vows. And —"

"There's no time for all of that." He smoothed her hair away from her face. "We were destined for each other, Dinah. Besides, I'm told that the stars are favorable for me tonight."

Joshua stood on Amasai the Levite's front doorstep and bowed to him in respect. "Thank you again, sir. Good night, sir." As soon as Amasai went inside and the door thumped shut behind him, Joshua grinned and raised his fist in the air with a shout of triumph. Finally! After months of waiting, Yael's father had agreed to their betrothal.

He had set a date for their wedding.

Beautiful Yael, with her soft brown eyes and hair the color of embers. She would finally be his wife. No more proper distances between them. No more clinging chaperones or formal good-byes at the door. Joshua would be able to kiss her ivory skin, hold her in his arms. But how would he ever wait three more months?

He started walking the familiar route home, completely unaware of his surroundings, his feet moving by memory. His imagination raced ahead to their future — standing beside Yael under the wedding canopy, sitting beside her at the marriage feast, leading her to their bridal chamber.

In a daze of happiness, Joshua rounded the corner and collided with someone in the darkness, nearly knocking the man off his feet. "Are you all right?" he asked. "I'm sorry. I wasn't watching where —"

"Master Joshua!"

"Maki, is that you?" In the dim light, Joshua recognized his grandfather's servant. "What are you doing here? Is it Tirza's baby?"

"You must follow me, Master Joshua," he whispered breathlessly. "Hurry!"

Fear filled Maki's wide eyes. He gripped Joshua's arm and pulled him into a narrow alley between two houses. Then he started to run at a fast trot, hauling Joshua along behind him. The lane was so dark Joshua couldn't see his own feet, and he stumbled over garbage and loose stones, stepped in water and raw sewage. The stench nauseated him as his sandals skidded on the slimy pavement. Had Maki gone crazy? They weren't headed home. They were going in the opposite direction.

"Maki, slow down a minute. You're hurting my arm."

"I can't! We must hurry!"

As his eyes adjusted to the darkness, Joshua noticed that Maki was not dressed. His feet were bare, and he wore only his linen undergarment. "Maki, why on earth are you — ?"

"Shh!"

Joshua was growing breathless from exertion. He felt as if a heavy stone were settling on his chest, making it difficult to breathe. If he ran like this much longer, he would have a breathing attack. They jogged north through the back lanes of Jerusalem along the western side of the Temple Mount until they finally reached the Sheep Gate. Maki stopped in the shadows.

The gate across the open square from them was closed and barred for the night.

Four soldiers stood watch. Maki uttered a curse. "We're too late!" He gripped Joshua's other arm and started pulling him back the way they had just come.

"No, wait. Stop," Joshua said, his lungs wheezing. "I can't run anymore. I have to rest."

"Not here, Master Joshua. It's not safe. Come on."

Joshua had no choice but to stumble after him again, through the narrow streets. He had never been in these back alleyways in daylight, much less at night, and it occurred to him a second time that Maki must have lost his mind. But Joshua was too tired and too winded to fight him. Besides, he had never been very good at physical combat.

Finally Maki stopped at the door of a ramshackle house that was little more than a crude shack. He put his fingers to his lips, warning Joshua to be silent, then opened the door. Joshua obeyed, saying nothing, but it was impossible to silence his raspy breaths or stifle his coughs. It felt as if more stones were being piled on his chest, pressing down.

Inside the single-room hovel, three people lay asleep on straw pallets spread across the floor. Joshua heard a gasp and one of the figures, a teenaged girl, sat up.

"It's all right," Maki whispered. "It's me."

"What — ?" she began, but Maki cut off her words.

"Shh. Don't light the lamp. Is the cistern empty?"

"Is the cistern — ? No, there's about a cubit of water in it."

"I'm sorry, Master Joshua. You'll have to get wet."

"Maki, I'm not crawling into anyone's cistern until you tell me what's going on. Where are we?"

"It's better for you if you don't know."

"I need to sit down." Joshua glanced around the room as his eyes adjusted to the gloom. He spotted a rough, three-legged stool beside a homemade table and sank down on it. The girl sat trembling on her pallet a few feet away from him with the blanket drawn up to her chin. She looked as confused as he was. The two smaller figures, who Joshua assumed were children, remained asleep.

Gradually the tightness in Joshua's chest began to ease. His mind cleared as the panic that always gripped him during a breathing attack died away. He looked up at Maki and saw that he was shivering. As Joshua removed his own robe and draped it around the servant's shoulders, Maki's eyes filled with tears.

"Maki, for goodness sake, tell me what's wrong."

"I don't know, Master Joshua, I don't know." His teeth chattered together like blocks of wood. "The king's soldiers burst into your house — dozens of them. They tore it apart, searching."

"For what?"

"For you, Master Joshua."

"For me? That's crazy!" Now he was certain that his poor servant had suffered a breakdown. He had to calm the man, get him into bed. "Do you have any strong wine?" Joshua asked the girl. She shook her head. "Maki, that doesn't make sense. King Manasseh wouldn't send soldiers to tear our house apart if he wanted to find me. I work in the palace. I was there all day. I . . . Maki, for heaven's sake, what's wrong with you?" The servant had covered his face with both hands. He was sobbing.

"His blood was all over the floor when they dragged him away, Master Joshua! They just walked through it like it wasn't even there! They left footprints in it!"

The girl scrambled out of bed and ran to Maki. "Shh, Abba . . . shh . . ." she soothed. She held him, rocking him like a baby.

Dread closed around Joshua's heart like a

fist. He carried the stool to Maki and eased him down on it, waiting until he finally stopped sobbing. "Can you try to start at the beginning?" Joshua asked quietly.

Maki nodded and drew a shuddering breath. "I was in bed, almost asleep, when I heard the soldiers crashing around. I got up, clothed like this." He looked down at his bare feet and thin undergarment. "The king's guards were running all through the house, ransacking it."

"The king's soldiers? Are you sure?"

"Yes. Palace guards."

"Go on."

"They were taking all of your father's papers and shoving them into sacks, knocking stuff over, breaking things."

"Why?"

Maki shook his head in bewilderment. "I don't know why. When I heard Lady Dinah screaming, I ran to the front hallway. I saw Master Hilkiah lying on the floor, and the captain . . . the captain was smashing Hilkiah's head against the stones! He just smashed it again and again!"

God of Abraham, this couldn't be true. Maki had dreamt the entire thing. He must have had some sort of nightmare that had made him go crazy. This had never happened. But Maki's horror seemed too real for a mere nightmare.

"Then the captain started choking Lady Dinah. He put his hands around her throat, and he said he would kill her if she didn't tell him where you were. But she wouldn't tell him, and so he just kept choking her and choking her until all the life went out of her."

Joshua needed to sit down to absorb this incredible story, but there was no other seat in the house. He leaned against the rickety table, praying that none of it was true.

"They dragged Lady Dinah and Master Hilkiah away. The captain told his men to take their bodies to King Manasseh. That's when they trampled through his blood and —"

"Maki, are you *sure* they said King Manasseh?"

"Yes," he answered, wiping his eyes.

"But it doesn't make sense."

"There was a lot of confusion — soldiers everywhere — so I crept up to the roof when no one was looking and climbed down the outside stairs."

"And you came to find me?"

He shook his head. "First I went to Rabbi Isaiah's house to find Master Eliakim. But there were soldiers at the rabbi's house, too, doing the same thing, tearing it apart."

"Did you see my father?"

"He wasn't there. Neither was the rabbi. Only soldiers. You are in great danger, Master Joshua. You must hide where no one will find you. There's a cistern beneath the house." Maki stood and gripped Joshua's arm again, pulling him toward the corner.

"Wait, Maki. Not yet. I need time to think."

Maki covered his face and began to weep again. "I've worked for Master Hilkiah since I was a boy. He was so kind to me. Such a godly man. They didn't have to do that to him. They didn't have to kill him and trample through his blood like he was a dog!"

Joshua let Maki's daughter soothe him. He walked across the room to a small window in the front of the house and peered out between the rough boards of the shutters into the darkened street. Everything was calm and quiet. No soldiers ran through the street ransacking houses and killing people. There was no reason for them to do it. Joshua had talked to King Manasseh only a few hours earlier. It was the anniversary of his mother's death. He was going to visit her tomb. Joshua could recall nothing out of the ordinary, certainly nothing that would cause the king's soldiers to break into his house, ransack it, and then kill his grand-father and his sister. But something had upset Maki. Joshua couldn't imagine what. He heard a scraping sound and turned to see the servant pushing off the lid of the cistern.

"Listen, Maki," Joshua said calmly, "I think I should go home and —"

"No, you can't go home! Master Hilkiah died to protect you. You must hide. If they capture you, then he died for nothing. That's why I'm helping you. I'm doing this for Master Hilkiah!"

"I'm sorry, but I just can't believe your story, Maki. There's no reason for any of it to happen. King Manasseh is my friend. Abba and I work with him. Maybe if I went to the palace and talked to him I could straighten this out and —"

"If you walk out of that door, Master Joshua, you are a dead man."

"I'll be careful to —"

Suddenly the servant leaped at him, and before Joshua could react, Maki wrestled him to the ground. He was more than a head shorter than Joshua and old enough to be his father, but the servant fought with the strength of a desperate man.

"I can't let you leave this house," Maki said as he tied Joshua's hands behind his back and dragged him toward the opening. "You must get into the cistern. Now!"

Dinah lay on the bed, unmoving. Manasseh had finally left her. Now she wanted to die.

The carved bed was inlaid with ivory and spread with fine perfumed linens, but the sheets made her cringe, as if they crawled with scorpions. She trembled at the feel of them beneath her skin. She stood up, nauseated with shock and pain.

The room was dark, but Dinah didn't search for a lamp. She could hide better in the darkness. She groped her way around the room and found a mikveh, half full of water, behind a latticed screen. The water was cold, but she sank into the bath and began to wash. She was filthy, so filthy. If only she could wash away the memory of him, but the horror was beneath her skin, inside her soul, and no amount of scrubbing would cleanse it. She thought of her mother and began to sob. Mama had been raped, too. But that man had been a stranger, not a trusted family friend. Dinah wasn't sure which was worse.

When she could no longer endure the frigid water, she climbed out and dressed again. Maybe Manasseh would let her go home now. Abba would hold her in his arms to comfort her and tell her everything would be all right. But she knew that her life would never be the same. She had been disgraced. No one could marry her now except Manasseh, and the thought of marrying him made her want to vomit.

She tried to open the door, but it was locked. So were the window shutters. Dinah curled up on the window seat, hugging her knees, shivering with cold and fear. She closed her eyes tightly, hoping the memory of what he had done to her would fade away, but it wouldn't. She couldn't make it stop happening over and over again in her mind.

"God of Abraham, please help me," she wept. "Please, please help me."

3

King Manasseh had slept poorly, his sleep disturbed by restless dreams of intrigue and conspiracy. He didn't know who to trust in his nightmares, as one by one his faithful servants and friends turned against him, plotting to stab him or strangle him while he slept.

As soon as it was light, Manasseh dressed and began to sort through the scrolls and documents his soldiers had confiscated from Isaiah's house. He separated them into piles on the table in front of him, laboring to make sense of them. On one pile he placed the prophecies that had already been fulfilled: words of warning to King Ahaz; Eliakim's rise to power; the destruction of the northern nation of Israel; the promise of deliverance from Sennacherib's forces. The size of the pile and the startling accuracy of Isaiah's predictions stunned him. He had never realized how truly powerful Isaiah was.

A second pile held oracles against other nations: Philistia, Moab, Damascus, Cush, Edom. Some of these predictions had already been fulfilled. Others, like the final destruction of the dreaded Assyrian Empire, had not.

On a third pile he placed prophecies that peered ahead into the distant future. These described the cataclysmic devastation of the earth itself and talked of a future kingdom in which the wolf would live with the lamb, and the lion would eat straw like the ox.

Ox — the soldiers hadn't found Ox. Manasseh still called Joshua by his boyhood nickname, even though he had finally outgrown his adolescent clumsiness. The fact that Ox had gone into hiding, successfully eluding the king's soldiers, proved that he was indeed part of Isaiah and Eliakim's conspiracy. Manasseh didn't want to believe that his trusted friend would betray him, too, but now that Ox had vanished, Manasseh had no choice.

He found only one prophecy that might foretell his own future. In it Isaiah warned King Hezekiah that some of his descendants would be carried off to Babylon at a future time. But it seemed unlikely that one of those descendants would be Manasseh. Babylon was no longer a major world power. The Assyrians had conquered the city several years ago and demolished it. Manasseh placed the scroll on a pile with a host of other confusing predictions that foretold the destruction of Jerusalem and the captivity of his nation, not by the brutal Assyrians, but by the Babylonians.

Next Manasseh picked up a small scroll made of much finer parchment than all the others. As soon as he unrolled it, he recognized his father's distinctive handwriting. Across the top Isaiah had written, *A writing of Hezekiah king of Judah after his illness and recovery.* The parchment contained a psalm, written by his father in the style of their famous ancestor, David.

Manasseh had never seen the poem before or even known such a psalm existed. Stunned, he began to read. He heard Hezekiah's voice in the words, saw his expressions and gestures between each line. When Manasseh finished reading, his eyes were wet with tears. This priceless legacy from his father belonged to him, not to Isaiah. Why did the rabbi have it among his scrolls? How had he managed to steal it from the palace?

Manasseh laid it aside, determined to

unravel Isaiah's complicated conspiracy, and he began to reread all of the prophecies that might hint of intrigue. In some passages the rabbi spoke of deliberately causing confusion: *"Be ever hearing, but never understanding; be ever seeing, but never perceiving"* and *"Bind up the testimony and seal up the law among my disciples."* But what worried Manasseh the most were references to a mysterious servant — *"my chosen one in whom I delight;"* a child who would *"reign on David's throne"* and be worshiped as *"Wonderful Counselor, Mighty God."*

Who was this servant? When had they planned for this coup to take place? Manasseh remembered the day the blind woman had looked into Joshua's palm. *"The authority belongs to you, but he will be much more powerful."* Could their intended usurper be Joshua?

Manasseh still planned to offer Isaiah and Eliakim a fair trial, of course, allowing them the opportunity to present evidence in their defense. But before that took place, he needed to question the strange man he had found murmuring in the cemetery last night. Perhaps Zerah had additional proof to back up his accusations.

The guards brought Zerah to the king's

chambers with his wrists and ankles in shackles. He tried to bow, but the ankle chain was too short, making it difficult for him to rise again without a guard's help. His forehead was damp with perspiration, his lips white with pain.

"Are you ill?" Manasseh asked.

"It's my wrist. I think the bone is broken. I've been suffering all night."

"Send for one of my physicians," Manasseh told his servants. "Tell him to bring bandages and a splint." The guards hauled over a bench for Zerah to sit on while he waited for the royal physician.

"I've begun to investigate your accusations of conspiracy, Zerah. You were correct when you predicted that Isaiah would refuse to reveal my future. Also, that my palace administrator would support him."

"I'm not surprised, Your Majesty."

"But the soldiers who searched both houses found only vague references to a conspiracy." He gestured to the piles of scrolls on the table in front of him.

"They are supremely clever, Your Majesty. Any evidence that might condemn them would be cleverly hidden among the words of innocent-looking documents."

"A code?"

"Exactly."

"Then let me read one of them to you: 'For to us a child is born, to us a son is given, and the government will be on his shoulders . . . Of the increase of his government and peace there will be no end. He will reign on David's throne. . . .' "

"Vague words, but their intent is clear, King Manasseh. They planned to replace you with their own man."

Manasseh stood and walked a few steps to his window, turning his back on Zerah, unwilling to reveal how upset he was by Zerah's interpretation. "You should also know," he said, striving to keep his voice steady, "that the soldiers found no mysterious books of incantations or magic spells, nothing to prove that Isaiah put a curse on my father."

"Did you find anything that belonged to your father among Isaiah's things?"

Manasseh felt as if all the blood had drained from his body as he remembered the psalm his father had written. He whirled to face Zerah. "Yes. Why?"

"In order to invoke a curse, Isaiah would have needed something that belonged to his victim. Something very personal."

"I found a psalm my father wrote after he nearly died. It was in his own handwriting."

Zerah nodded. "It would have given Isaiah

power over him."

Manasseh was grateful for the interruption when the royal physician arrived. He needed time to absorb this news.

"Where would you like me to treat him, Your Majesty?" the physician asked.

"Do it here. Unshackle him." Manasseh sank into his seat again, watching in silence as the doctor carefully examined the prisoner's wrist. Zerah uttered only a faint moan as the doctor realigned the bones, but he appeared pale as the doctor affixed the thin wooden splint to his wrist with bandages.

"How did you break your wrist?" the doctor asked as he worked.

Zerah glanced up at the king. "It happened during my arrest."

When the physician finished, he took a square of linen and tied Zerah's arm in a sling. "It won't be possible to shackle his wrist for a while, Your Majesty."

"The shackles are no longer necessary," Manasseh said. "You may remove the ones on his ankles, as well."

After the doctor left, Zerah bowed low to Manasseh once again. "I am very grateful, Your Majesty."

"Can you decipher this code for me? I need proof of their conspiracy."

"You won't need to decipher it in order to

convict your enemies. The rabbi's own words will witness against him. I've heard his so-called prophecies. He preaches things that contradict the Laws of Moses. May I show you?" Zerah gestured to the scrolls piled in front of the king.

Before Manasseh could reply, the shofar trumpeted from the Temple Mount, announcing the morning sacrifice. "I'll have my servants carry these to Eliakim's office," Manasseh said. "You may take all the time you need to read through them."

"How many blasphemies do you require in order to convict him, Your Majesty?"

"The Torah requires two witnesses for the death penalty. But find three, an extra one for good measure."

"Very well, Your Majesty."

" 'I cry to you, O Lord . . . Listen to my cry, for I am in desperate need.' " Joshua paused to shift positions. His back and neck ached from standing bent in the cramped cistern, but if he stood straight, he would hit his head on the stone lid that sealed him in. He needed to rest his legs for a while. He lowered himself into the water, careful not to slip on the slimy stone floor as he had done earlier that night. When first lowered into the cistern, Joshua had panicked and, with his hands tied behind his back, had nearly drowned before righting himself in the water.

Joshua knelt, the icy water reaching to his chin. But if he sat down, it would cover his head. He shivered in the darkness. " 'Set me free from my prison that I may praise your name.' " He finished reciting the psalm of David for the forty-second time. Or was it the forty-third? He had lost count.

Would this long night never end? He tried to doze to help pass the time, but his shivering always awakened him, along with the continual struggle to breathe. His air passages had swollen shut, allowing only a thin stream of air in and out. Each breath whistled like the night wind through tree branches. He recited to stay calm, aware that panicking would only make the breathing attack worse.

" 'I cry aloud to the Lord,' " he prayed, starting at the beginning again. " 'I lift up my voice to the Lord for mercy.' " He twisted his hands, trying in vain to untie himself so he could push the stone lid off. His wrists chafed from rope burns. Maki had tied his hands too tightly. Joshua had tried repeatedly to push the lid off with his back and shoulders but, although he had to bend his neck when he stood, he couldn't quite get his back under the stone, even standing on his toes.

Was he imagining it, or was the cistern growing a little brighter? Perhaps the new day had finally dawned and the light was filtering through the channel that brought rainwater into the cistern. He thought about calling for help but couldn't draw a deep enough breath to yell.

Joshua could no longer kneel in the chilly water. He stood again and wiggled his toes, which were growing numb. What had gotten into Maki? And why didn't Yahweh help him?

As if in answer to his prayer, Joshua heard the scrape of stone as the cistern lid slid to one side. The light of early dawn blinded him. He looked up, squinting, and saw Maki's dark face and his silver hair and beard.

"Master Joshua, I will feed you some food now. Then you must hide again."

"No, Maki, please! I'll die if you don't get me out of here!" The effort to talk made Joshua cough — deep, wracking coughs that came from low in his chest. His lungs had started to fill with fluid. He hadn't had an attack this serious since Manasseh had stranded him in the almond grove in the pouring rain when they were boys. The fever that followed had nearly killed Joshua.

"Please, Maki, don't leave me in here."

"But it's not safe to come out yet."

"Abba, look at him — he's shivering. He's sick." The young woman they had awakened last night appeared in the semidarkness behind Maki's shoulder. "We have to get him out of that cold water."

"Yes! God of Abraham . . . please!" Joshua begged.

Maki stared at him for a moment as if deciding. "All right. Help me lift him, Miriam." They grabbed Joshua beneath his armpits and strained to pull him out. His chest and stomach scraped along the rough plaster walls.

"I'm too heavy . . . untie me . . . let me climb out."

"I can't untie you, Master Joshua, until I'm certain you won't try to run away. Nathan, Mattan, come help us." Two small boys, about six and eight years old, appeared behind Maki. They couldn't possibly lift him out, but they bent over the cistern to help, tugging on Joshua's soaked clothes. Joshua used his legs to push, and after several minutes of heaving they finally succeeded in pulling him from the cistern. He lay on his side on the dirt floor. His drenched robes turned the dirt to mud in a puddle beneath him. He wanted to thank them for saving him, but a spasm of coughing overwhelmed him and he couldn't talk. The pain in his chest was agonizing.

"He's shivering, Abba," the girl said. "We have to get him out of his wet clothes."

"But there's nothing else for him to wear."

"Wrap my blanket around him until his clothes dry. Let him sit by the fire."

Joshua lay on the floor, helpless, while they talked about him as if he couldn't understand. "Untie me," he begged, but he could say no more because every time he tried to talk he started coughing again.

"Turn around while I undress him, Miriam. It's not decent for you to help." Maki tied Joshua's ankles together with another piece of rope as the girl turned her back. He briefly untied Joshua's hands and stripped off his wet clothes, then quickly tied him again. Joshua was too weak to take advantage of his moment of freedom. Maki wrapped a filthy, tattered blanket around him and dragged him over to the hearth.

Gradually, Joshua began to feel the fire's warmth. His every breath was audible, like a prolonged gasp. "Maki . . . why?"

"I told you why, Master Joshua. The king's soldiers are searching for you. It isn't safe. You must hide."

"How long . . . are you going . . . to keep

me here?"

"I don't know. I need to find a way to smuggle you out of Jerusalem."

Despair engulfed Joshua like the cold waters of the cistern. No one knew where he was. How would they ever rescue him? Maybe he would die here in the hands of this madman before Abba could find him. He shivered with cold and the beginnings of illness while the two ragged boys stared down at him as if he were a captured animal in a cage. He felt like an animal, too, lying naked beneath the blanket, bound hand and foot, stripped of his dignity as well as his clothes. He was an important court official, the future palace administrator. He wanted to weep at the injustice and at his own helplessness.

"Maybe he's hungry, Abba. We should give him some food." The girl was twisting his clothes, wringing the water out of them onto the floor. Maki pushed Joshua into a sitting position, propping him against the side of the hearth, and then held a piece of bread near his mouth.

"Here. You must be hungry, Master Joshua."

"He needs something warm, Abba. I'll heat up the broth." She finished wringing Joshua's robes and hung them on a rope suspended above the fire. As they began to steam dry, the smell of wet wool gagged Joshua. He couldn't eat the bread.

"Are you doing this for the ransom money, Maki? Abba will pay any price if you just —"

"How dare you accuse me of coveting your money! I risked my life to save you. I'm putting these children's lives in danger, too."

"But it doesn't make sense. Why would someone want to kill me?"

Maki's face went rigid with anger. "Once again, Master Joshua, I will tell you everything I know. The soldiers broke into your house, searching for you. They killed your grandfather and your sister. They didn't tell me why. This morning I returned to your house before dawn, hoping to get my clothes and a pair of sandals, but the house is still surrounded by soldiers. I didn't dare go in. Then I went to your brother's house, but it's well-guarded, too. The same with Amasai the Levite's house. Soldiers everywhere."

"And all of them are waiting to arrest me, I suppose."

"You still don't believe me?"

"How can I believe you? There's no reason for anyone to arrest me!" Joshua's outburst triggered another coughing fit, and it was several minutes before he could stop. The girl knelt in front of him with a bowl and a spoon, waiting to feed him. The fragrant broth smelled of leeks and garlic, and Joshua suddenly realized how hungry he was. He let her feed it to him, careful to eat slowly and not burn his mouth. The soup soon warmed him from the inside.

The room grew brighter once the sun rose above the surrounding hills, and Joshua got his first good look at this girl who called Maki "Abba." She was in her midteens, he guessed, and very thin, but he saw a woman's body beneath her coarse, ragged robes. Her swarthy skin and dark hair looked like they could use a good washing with strong soap. He hoped she didn't have lice. Her oval face was very plain, marred by a dark mole on her cheekbone beneath her left eye. But she had been kind to him. He clung to the hope that once her father left the house she would help him escape. He struggled to recall her name. He thought Maki had mentioned it. Yes . . . it was Miriam.

"Thank you, Miriam," he said when the bowl was empty. He tried to catch her eye, but she kept her gaze averted as she rose to give some of the broth and chunks of bread to the two boys.

When the shofar sounded for the morning

sacrifice, Maki cursed. "If I had a robe to wear, I could go to the Temple. Maybe I could learn something that would help you."

"Here, take my robe, Abba," Miriam said. "And you can wear Master Joshua's sandals." There was nothing feminine about the ragged outer robe Miriam wore. It might have once belonged to a man. She was about the same height as Maki, and it fit him well, but Joshua's sandals were much too big for Maki's feet. He fastened them on anyway and shuffled to the door.

"Keep the door and window closed," Maki told her. "If anyone comes, hide Master Joshua in the cistern again. And don't leave the house for any reason. Understand?"

"Yes, Abba."

"I'll be back as soon as I can."

Joshua glimpsed a pale blue sky and thin, high clouds as the door opened briefly, then slammed shut again. His only hope of freedom was to befriend Maki's children. Maybe he could talk them into setting him free.

"Miriam, may I have a drink of water?" he asked. She didn't reply. Instead, she gave the water dipper to the older boy, and he held it to Joshua's lips. The boy was a filthy little urchin, the kind that Joshua had seen trying to rob money pouches outside the Temple gates and stealing fruit from the vendors in the marketplace. He looked as though he had never had a bath or a decent meal in his life. "What's your name?" Joshua asked him.

"Nathan."

"How old are you?" The boy shrugged. "Listen, Nathan, my wrists are getting sore. I think your father —"

"He isn't my father!" Nathan's hands balled into fists. He stood poised as if for a fight.

"I'm sorry . . . I think *Maki* tied this rope too tightly. My fingers are growing numb. Can you loosen it for me?" Nathan shook his head, his face sullen. Joshua tried again. "Is that your little brother? What's his name?"

"He's Mattan." The younger boy's dark eyes were infected, the corners and lashes crusted with mucus. He had a large, running sore on his leg that looked as if it wasn't healing properly.

"What happened to your leg, Mattan?"

"He burned it when he fell on the hearth," Nathan answered.

Their stubborn faces told Joshua that his plan to befriend them wasn't working. He decided to appeal to their greed instead.

"Listen, I had a silver pouch when I came in here. Maki must have taken it when he stripped off my clothes, but I have more silver at home. A lot more. I work for King Manasseh. Do you know who he is?" They stared at him, unblinking. "Well, I work for him. So does my father. They'll give you a great deal of silver if you untie me and —"

"Stop talking or we'll put you in the cistern again," Miriam said.

"Please, Miriam, I don't know why your father is doing this to me, but you must realize that it's wrong to hold someone prisoner. Can't you help me? Now that he's gone, can't you —"

"Nathan! Mattan!" she said sharply. "You have chores to do." They obeyed immediately, leaving Joshua alone by the hearth. No one spoke as the boys rolled up their bedding, then drew water from the cistern to rinse the dishes. After a while the girl approached to add more wood to the fire.

"Miriam, why won't you help me?" Joshua asked. She shifted his robes on the clothesline and rehung them to finish drying. A moment later he heard her grinding grain between two stones. Joshua closed his eyes and tried to doze, the warmth of the fire bathing his face.

After what seemed like a very long time,

Maki returned. Without a word of greeting, he crossed the room and stood looking down at Joshua, his face grim. "Your father wasn't at the sacrifice this morning. When is your brother due back from Heshbon?"

Joshua hesitated, unsure if he should tell Maki or not. But perhaps he could win his freedom by cooperating. "He'll probably get home late today. He won't want to travel tomorrow, on the Sabbath."

"Then I must leave immediately and try to meet up with him along the way. If I don't warn him, he will walk into their trap. May I borrow some of your silver to buy a decent pair of shoes?"

"Take as much as you need."

"If the rumors are true, Master Joshua, then I've learned two things. First, someone warned Lord Shebna that he was also in danger and he has fled the country." The regal face of the Egyptian Shebna, one-time tutor and palace administrator, flickered in Joshua's memory.

Maki paused, biting his lip, the look of anguish on his face so genuine that Joshua almost believed it was real.

"And the second thing?"

"Your father and Rabbi Isaiah are in the palace dungeon."

4

Eliakim knew the long night had finally ended when he heard the Temple shofar sounding faintly in the distance. His father's body, which he still clutched in his arms, had grown stiff and cold, his blood crusted hard on Eliakim's clothes. Sometime during the night, Isaiah's whispered prayers had gradually grown fainter until he had drifted to sleep. Eliakim knew by the sound of his breathing that he hadn't awakened yet.

Eliakim hadn't slept. The darkness in the cell had penetrated his soul, settling in his heart beside his unanswered questions.

"I will drive him like a peg into a firm place," Isaiah had once predicted. *"All the glory of his family will hang on him."* But there had been more to that prophecy: *"The peg driven into the firm place will give way . . . the load hanging on it will be cut down."* Eliakim caressed his father's cold face in the darkness, trying to memorize its contours, try-

ing to comprehend why God had made Hilkiah suffer for his son's fall from power.

As that firm peg, Eliakim knew that all the weight of his family had hung on him: *"its offspring and offshoots — all its lesser vessels, from the bowls to all the jars."* That meant not only Eliakim's father but his children. And his grandchildren. He closed his eyes.

"Heavenly Father, I won't bargain with you for my own life. I'll accept in faith whatever you've willed for me. But I plead with you — as one father to another — I plead with you for my family. For Jerusha. For Jerimoth. Joshua. Tirza. Little Dinah. I know that they're innocent of whatever madness the king has accused me of. He has already murdered Abba — let him murder me, too, if he must. But please, not my wife and children. Not their little ones . . ."

Eliakim had no idea how long he prayed. In his world of utter darkness, time no longer held any meaning. Eventually Isaiah awoke and convinced Eliakim to lay his father's body aside. Then they knelt together and recited morning prayers. The familiar words lifted Eliakim's sorrow for a moment and transported him to the Temple. In his mind he saw the dazzling golden roof and sacred vessels, smelled the aromas of incense and roasting meat. For a brief time the universe made sense again, reflected in the order and beauty of the sacrifice, echoed in the harmony of the music. But when their prayers ended and Eliakim opened his eyes, he faced his dark prison cell once again.

When the palace guards descended the stairs with torches, the light was as blinding as the noonday sun. The guards hauled both men to their feet and fastened shackles to their wrists and ankles. When Eliakim tried to walk, he discovered that the shackles were connected by a short chain. Squinting into the glaring light, Eliakim recognized one of the guards.

"Levi, thank God it's you. Please tell me what's going on." Levi wouldn't answer. Eliakim had known the guard for almost twenty years. Despair tightened around his heart.

"My father is dead," Eliakim said softly. "I don't care what you believe about me, but you know that Hilkiah was a righteous man. Promise me that you'll give him a decent burial." Levi didn't answer, but when Eliakim met his gaze for a moment, he saw Levi's silent promise that he would do it.

As they climbed the narrow, ladderlike stairs from the dungeon, Eliakim's eyes gradually adjusted to the light. Several times he had to hold on to Isaiah to prevent him from falling. Like himself, the rabbi was weak from cold and hunger. The soldiers led them to the waiting area, outside the throne room.

"Will we be allowed to bathe and change our clothes?" Eliakim asked. His robes, like Isaiah's, were covered with filth from the dungeon floor and stained with Hilkiah's dried blood. The chamberlain was a man Eliakim had known since he first came to the palace as King Hezekiah's engineer, but he wouldn't answer Eliakim or look at him.

The doors finally opened and they were led inside the throne room. The great hall was packed with nobles and elders. The entire court had been called to witness their trial. Eliakim's friends and colleagues — men he had worked with closely under Hezekiah and now Manasseh — were seated in their usual places. But in the unnatural silence that hung over the assembly, Eliakim glimpsed their enormous fear and horror. He was on trial for proclaiming Isaiah's innocence; any man who spoke up in their defense would join them in the dungeon. He scanned the room carefully but didn't see his son Joshua. His absence offered Eliakim a ray of hope.

Isaiah bowed before King Manasseh. But Eliakim rebelled at the thought of bowing to Hilkiah's murderer. He looked Manasseh in the eye and saw distrust and suspicion. Where had they come from? How had these seeds, which Eliakim had never realized were there, sprouted and grown to such enormous proportions so quickly?

"I charge you both under oath, by the Living God, to tell this court the truth," Manasseh said.

"I do so swear," they answered.

"We'll begin with you, Rabbi. The chamberlain will show you some scrolls that were found in your house. Do you recognize them?"

Isaiah glanced through them briefly. "Yes, they are mine. I wrote them." He appeared calm and poised. Eliakim wished he could have even a small measure of the prophet's peace instead of the intense anger and fear that pounded through him.

"Then you will recognize that all of these prophecies have already been fulfilled — with amazing accuracy."

"Yes, they have."

"Then do you still deny under oath and before my court that you possess the power to foretell the future?"

"I possess no such power, Your Majesty.

Only Yahweh knows the future. I am merely His vessel. A bowl may hold the food that gives life and strength to the body, but the bowl has no power in itself."

Manasseh shifted uneasily on his throne. Eliakim knew he was nervous. The king had never tried such a serious case on his own before, without Eliakim or Shebna to help him prepare for it. But the seats on either side of the king, places either he or Shebna had occupied for over thirty years, were empty. Where was Shebna?

"I want you to look carefully at this next pile of scrolls," Manasseh continued. "Are they yours?"

"Yes, they are."

"One of them predicts the downfall of Assyria, another the destruction of Jerusalem. These prophecies haven't been fulfilled yet, have they?"

"No, Your Majesty, they haven't."

"Will you please tell this court when they will take place?"

"I can't. I don't know when."

"You can't, Rabbi? Or you won't?"

"Your Majesty, when you send one of your servants on an errand, bearing your message, you reveal only the message you have entrusted the servant to deliver. He doesn't know the mind of the king or what Your

Majesty has planned for the future."

Anger and frustration hardened Manasseh's face. Eliakim knew the young king lacked the experience and maturity to deal with Isaiah's quiet wisdom.

"Rabbi, you once told my father this: 'Some of your descendants, your own flesh and blood who will be born to you, will be taken away and they will become eunuchs in the palace of the king of Babylon.' Am I one of those descendants?"

"I don't know, Your Majesty."

"You're lying! You saw the future so clearly during my father's reign. Do you expect me to believe you when you suddenly claim blindness during mine?" Isaiah didn't reply. "Give him the next scroll," Manasseh ordered. "Tell the court what it is, Rabbi, and who wrote it."

"It's a psalm, written by King Hezekiah."

"Is it an original or a copy?"

"An original. This is the king's handwriting."

"I never saw my father's psalm until today, Rabbi. There is no copy of it here in the palace. Did you know it existed, Eliakim?"

He glanced at the parchment Isaiah held in his hand and recognized Hezekiah's handwriting. "No. I never saw it before either."

"Why did you steal this from my father?"

"I didn't steal it," Isaiah answered quietly. "Your father gave it to me."

"Why?"

"I don't know why," Isaiah said with a long sigh. "He wrote it right after his illness, the time he nearly died. He gave it to me on the first morning he was able to get out of bed when I accompanied him to the Temple. He asked me to keep it for him. And so I have."

"Did you put a curse on my father?" A hush suddenly fell over the hall, as if every man held his breath. "First you told my father he would die, then you suddenly changed your mind and told him he would live fifteen more years. How would you know the date of his death, to the very month, unless you were the one who cursed him?"

The outrageous accusation seemed to stagger Isaiah. Several long moments passed before he could answer. "Yahweh's hand rested on Hezekiah from the time he was a small child and God rescued him from Molech's flames. I loved Hezekiah like a son. I could no more curse him than I could curse my own son."

"And is it your own son who you're plotting to place on my throne, Rabbi?"

Isaiah seemed to sway slightly as if rocked by Manasseh's words. "I don't know what you're talking about."

"Or perhaps it's Eliakim's son?"

A stab of fear ripped through Eliakim's composure. *Not Joshua. Please, God, don't involve Joshua in Manasseh's delusions.*

"Show them the next scroll. Who is this servant of Yahweh who will sit on David's throne?"

Isaiah's hand trembled as he took the scroll. "He's the promised Messiah, Your Majesty. The seed of the woman who will save the world from their sins."

"Do you deny that this king will sit on the throne of David?"

"No."

"When will this happen?"

"Only Yahweh knows when the Messiah will come."

Manasseh gripped the armrests of his throne until his hands turned white. "I will offer you one final chance, Rabbi. Will you prophesy for me as you did for my forefathers? Will you reveal my future?"

"I can't, Your Majesty. I don't know what your future is."

"Eliakim, you've heard his refusal. Do you still wish to defend him?"

"What you've asked him to do is impossible, and I —"

"As my palace administrator and most trusted advisor, tell me — is Isaiah justified in refusing my direct order?"

Eliakim's limbs began to shake, not with fear but with anger. Manasseh was twisting Isaiah's words. The rabbi wasn't receiving a fair trial. "He is justified, Your Majesty. Only Yahweh can do the impossible."

Manasseh's face seemed to turn to stone. "Show the rabbi the last three scrolls. Are those your words, Rabbi? Written in your own writing?"

"They are."

"And have you spoken these prophecies publicly, as well?"

"Sometimes, yes."

"Then I accuse you before all these witnesses of uttering teachings that contradict the Laws of God!"

Again, the entire assembly seemed to catch its breath. Eliakim could hear his heart pounding in his ears. The sentence for blaspheming the Torah was death.

"Number one, Rabbi. Did you write these words: 'I saw the Lord seated on a throne, high and exalted'?"

"Yes."

"But the Torah says, 'No one may see God and live.' "

"I know it does."

"Then why did you make such a blasphemous claim?"

"Because it's true." A murmur of surprise swept through the crowd. Manasseh leaned forward, perched on the edge of his throne.

"Number two. Did you write these words: 'Seek the Lord while he may be found; call on him while he is near'?"

"Yes."

"Even though it is written: 'The Lord our God is near us whenever we pray.' Have you never read that?"

"I have."

"Then you knew you were uttering blasphemy?"

"I spoke the words Yahweh told me to speak."

"Finally, then, did you tell my father that God would add fifteen years to his life, so that he would die at age fifty-four?"

"Yes, Your Majesty."

"Even though Yahweh promised our forefathers in His Word, 'I will give you a full life-span'?"

Isaiah stared at the floor for a moment as if deep in thought. Eliakim had often witnessed the surging power of God as it flowed through the rabbi whenever he prophesied. He expected that power to fill

Isaiah now, blasting Manasseh's lies and accusations into dust. But when Isaiah finally looked up, his eyes were sad, defeated. He was simply an old man, bound in chains.

"I could give a good answer to all of these charges, Your Majesty, but I won't. It would only compound your guilt."

"*My* guilt!"

"Yes. It's better for you to sin in ignorance than in willful rebellion against God."

Manasseh stood. "Eliakim, you've heard these charges against Rabbi Isaiah and how his words have blasphemed the Torah. How do you find this defendant?"

"I find him not guilty! But *your* guilt is written all over these robes I'm wearing!" Eliakim rushed toward Manasseh, but the chain between his ankles tripped him, dropping him to his knees with a jolt of pain. He continued to shout as he struggled to stand. "This is my father's blood! You murdered an innocent man, and if you condemn Isaiah to death, you will be murdering one more!" He was close enough to see that Manasseh's entire body was shaking.

"Your own testimony in front of all these witnesses has condemned you both to death!" Manasseh said. "I hereby confiscate all of your property and condemn you both to be publicly executed the morning after the Sabbath. In addition, I sentence Isaiah to be tortured until he confesses to causing King Hezekiah's death. Now take them both out of my sight!"

Eliakim stared defiantly into the terrified faces of his friends and colleagues as the soldiers hauled him away. He couldn't help hating them for their cowardice.

Once again the soldiers led him and Isaiah down the treacherous stairs, into the black pit beneath the palace, and left them there, still wearing their shackles.

Why was this happening? Why hadn't Yahweh intervened to save them? This may indeed be part of God's plan, as the rabbi said, but like a weaver standing too close to his tapestry, Eliakim couldn't see how it all fit together.

5

Jerimoth paused at the crossroads where the road from Heshbon intersected with the Way to Beth-Horon. The animals needed a brief rest, and then the caravan would ford the distant Jordan River and cross into Judean territory. He was almost home.

His trip to Moab had been enormously successful. Jerimoth could hardly wait to see his grandfather's face when he saw what excellent deals he had made. At age twenty-eight, Jerimoth had everything a man could wish for — a lovely wife, a healthy daughter, a prosperous business that he loved, working as a cloth merchant like his grandfather and great-grandfathers before him. Jerimoth loved the challenge of making shrewd investments, the delicate art of haggling over prices, the battle of wills to see who would be the first to concede their price. Abba and Joshua lived with their heads in the clouds, occupied with politics and government, but

Jerimoth had more in common with his grandfather. Hilkiah understood the lure of the marketplace. He had taught Jerimoth everything he knew, then made him a full partner in the business when Jerimoth had married three years ago.

He bore a physical resemblance to Hilkiah, as well — short and stocky with twinkling brown eyes — even though he had been named for his maternal grandfather. Jerimoth's black hair was already growing a little thin on top, his forehead a little high, his waist a little plump, thanks to the pampering of his sweet wife, Sara. After being away from home for almost two weeks, he was eager to return, eager to hug her and his two-year-old daughter, Rachel, with the dancing eyes and soft, black curls.

The caravan had rested long enough. It was time to get his drivers back on the road. The day promised to be hot, and Jerimoth knew the men would be content to rest under the palm trees all day if he let them. He didn't take much notice of the lone figure hurrying up the road until the man called his name.

"Jerimoth! . . . Master Jerimoth!"

It was Maki, his grandfather's servant. The man had worked for Hilkiah since before Jerimoth had been born.

"What brings you so far from home, Maki? Nothing's wrong, is it?"

Maki was breathless and perspiring heavily in the afternoon sun. Jerimoth led him to the palm tree he had been resting under and offered him a drink of water. He thought it odd that Maki carried nothing with him, no water or provision bag. Why would Hilkiah send him on such a long journey un-equipped?

Maki drank great gulps of water, then eased off his shoes and poured some on his blistered feet. The sandals appeared to be brand-new. No one in his right mind would walk all the way from Jerusalem in unbroken shoes.

"What's wrong, Maki?" Jerimoth asked, crouching beside him.

"Master Jerimoth, I know that what I'm going to tell you will sound crazy." He spoke slowly and deliberately, as if to a small child. "But you know of my undying loyalty to Master Hilkiah. You must believe me." His hazel eyes stared so intently that Jerimoth felt a wave of fear.

"Of course I'll believe you."

Maki drew a deep breath. "For reasons I cannot know or imagine, King Manasseh has turned against your family. If you go back to Jerusalem, your life will be in great danger."

"In danger? How can this be?"

"I have been doing what I can to save your family, but . . ." He stared down at his lap, twisting the corner of his robe in his hands. "But my efforts haven't always been successful."

"What do you mean?" Jerimoth's heart hammered against his ribs.

"To make sure you would believe me, I brought this message from Master Joshua." He reached into the folds of his cloak and produced a jagged potsherd. The cryptic message read, *Follow Maki's instructions.* It was signed, *Joshua.*

"What instructions? What do you want me to do?" Jerimoth asked.

"You must leave your caravan here. It will surely give you away if you bring it back to Jerusalem. The only way I can safely smuggle you into the city so that we can rescue your family is if we trade places. I will be the rich master returning home from a business trip. You will be my servant."

Jerimoth's legs ached from crouching. He stood and leaned against the trunk of the tree as he tried to comprehend the unsettling news. He had known Maki all his life. The man served as a valet to Hilkiah, working beside him in the shop, caring for him at home now that Hilkiah was semi-retired. Jerimoth had known Maki to be loyal and hardworking but never imaginative. He was fairly certain Maki couldn't make up a story like this. He stared at the potsherd in his hand. Why would Joshua use something so crude? They had plenty of parchment at home.

"But, Maki, how? Why? You have no idea what this is all about?"

"No, Master Jerimoth, I don't. But you must believe me!"

"I do believe you. I'm just trying to think. . . ." He swatted absently at the flies buzzing around him as he tried to make sense of Maki's story. A short distance away the mules grazed leisurely, their tails swishing. His drivers dozed beneath the palm trees. The peaceful scene made Maki's story seem like a tall tale, but the oozing blisters on his feet offered the most compelling evidence of his sincerity.

"All right. We'll have to go back to Beth-Jeshimoth and rent some temporary storage space for these goods. Then we can trade clothes and start on our way." He saw relief on Maki's face and tears in his eyes as he turned his face away.

Jerimoth grasped Maki's elbow and helped him to his feet, but he didn't release it right away. "What about my wife and daughter?"

"They are unharmed, Master Jerimoth."

Finding safe storage space in Beth-Jeshimoth took longer than Jerimoth hoped and cost him too many daylight hours. By the time he paid the disgruntled mule drivers and started home on foot, it was late in the day.

Maki proved to be a convincing actor as he played the part of Jerimoth's rich master. His silver hair and close-cropped beard looked very distinguished and his nut-brown skin glowed with Jerimoth's expensive oil. Jerimoth's new robe fit Maki well, but the threadbare cloak he had swapped it for smelled as if it had never been washed.

Jerimoth's anxiety grew to enormous proportions as he contemplated Maki's story. He had the urge to run all the way home, but the journey was uphill and Maki was limping painfully. They were still several miles from Jerusalem when the sun began to set, marking the beginning of the Sabbath. Jerimoth wanted to weep in frustration. The Law forbade them to travel any farther.

With a knot of fear in his stomach, he passed through the city gates of Michmash and began to search for an inn. They would have to spend the night here. And all day tomorrow.

Eliakim gripped the bars of his prison cell and stared out into the blackness, his eyes straining for any pinpoint of light. He knew from the distant shofars that the Sabbath had begun. Unless Yahweh provided a miracle, tomorrow he would die.

"Talk to me, Eliakim." Isaiah's voice echoed in the void behind him. "The darkness is bad enough — let's not make it worse by enduring it in silence." Eliakim slowly turned around and leaned against the bars.

"I have no idea what to say."

"Well, we can always talk about our doubts and our fears. Yahweh knows them all anyway."

"I can't believe you struggle with doubts, Rabbi."

"Nonsense. Of course I do. In fact, right now I'm wondering what I might have done differently to avoid involving you."

"I think it's the other way around. I was responsible for training Manasseh. I raised him after King Hezekiah died. I think I must have failed somehow, to —"

"Don't lay his guilt on yourself, Eliakim. You raised Manasseh faithfully, according to God's Law. But once he became an adult it was up to him to choose whether or not he would follow God's teaching. He alone is responsible for his actions."

Eliakim nodded, then realized that Isaiah couldn't possibly see him. He groped in the darkness toward Isaiah's voice and sank to the cell floor to sit beside him.

"I'm so worried about my family. Jerusha . . . my children. There wasn't any warning. I didn't have a chance to make sure they were safe. If Manasseh would kill Abba, then . . ."

"Have you committed your family to God? Have you placed them in His hands?"

"Yes."

"Then leave them there. Don't take the burden on your own shoulders again. No matter what happens, they are safe in Him."

Eliakim closed his eyes, fighting his tears. "Joshua is only twenty-two. He has an entire lifetime ahead of him. Lately he's been half-crazy in love with Amasai's daughter." Eliakim managed a small smile, remembering Joshua's mournful yearning. "I know we're not supposed to play favorites with our children, but Joshua is very special to me. He died in my arms when he was a baby . . . and I breathed my own life into him. He was a miracle baby, born while the Assyrian army surrounded Jerusalem. He has always been so bright and quick, so sincere about following God's Law, so eager to live righteously. Ever since he was a child he wanted to work for the king — to follow in my footsteps. I had no idea that following my path would lead him here."

"Eliakim, your son isn't here in prison with us. If King Manasseh had arrested him, don't you think that he would be?"

The thought comforted Eliakim for the moment. "Are we really going to die tomorrow?" he asked.

"As the psalmist has written, 'All the days ordained for me were written in your book before one of them came to be.' If this is our time, Eliakim, Yahweh is ready to receive us."

"The king must have gone crazy, accusing you of cursing Hezekiah. Where did he get such an insane notion? Is Hezekiah's son really capable of . . . of torturing you to death?"

"We'll learn the answer tomorrow."

Eliakim ran his fingers through his thinning hair. "Are you afraid to die, Rabbi?"

Isaiah let out a long sigh. "Yes, I fear the pain of death — but not death itself."

Eliakim leaned his head against the stone wall. "Am I wrong to pray that Manasseh won't go through with this?"

"No, I'm praying the same thing."

"I've known Manasseh since he was a baby. I rejoiced with his father and mother when he was born. I watched him grow and mature. How can he accuse me of conspiring against him? I've worked my entire life to build this nation so that he would have something to inherit. I don't deserve this, and neither do you."

"Do you hate him?" Isaiah asked.

"I . . . I hate what he's doing to us."

"Can you forgive him, Eliakim?"

"I —"

"No, don't answer right away. Search your heart first." Isaiah laid his hand on Eliakim's arm. "King Manasseh brutally murdered your father. He twisted our words and our motives so he could falsely accuse us and condemn us to death. Tomorrow morning he will execute us. Do you wish for revenge? Do you want to see Manasseh pay for what he has done to us and to your father?"

"God, help me," Eliakim whispered. "Yes."

"Yes," Isaiah echoed. "Yes, so do I." For a moment neither of them spoke and a deep silence filled the underground cell.

"But we must forgive him," Isaiah said at last. " 'The Lord is compassionate and gracious, slow to anger, abounding in love.' As His chosen people, we bear His image. We, too, must forgive."

"How, Rabbi?"

"We must not wish for vengeance. 'Will not the Judge of all the earth do right?' Don't let Manasseh rob you of a lifetime of righteous living by hoarding hatred for him in your heart. There is no place for evil in the presence of a Holy God. Can you imagine yourself standing before Yahweh's throne tomorrow, asking for His grace, with the ugliness of hatred staining your heart? We must kneel before Him and confess our sin of unforgiveness, confess our hatred and our desire for revenge. Then we must let go of it, asking God to remove it from our hearts. We must choose to cancel the debt of justice that Manasseh owes us. If we do that, you and I will be free. We can go to our Father in peace. We can behold Him face-to-face."

Deep in his heart Eliakim clung to the hope of a miracle. Maybe God would change Manasseh's heart. Maybe he and Isaiah would be spared.

It would be easy to forgive Manasseh if forgiving him would allow Eliakim to return to his home and to his family; if he could lie down tonight beside Jerusha again, watch Joshua marry the girl he loved, hold his new grandchild in his arms. If he could continue living the full life he had lived until two days ago, Eliakim would find it much easier not to wish for revenge. But to trust God in the darkness, when the dawn might bring his death . . . this was the most difficult thing Eliakim had ever done. He knelt in his prison cell beside Isaiah and pressed his forehead to the stone floor.

" 'Search me, O God, and know my heart,' " he whispered. " 'Test me and know my anxious thoughts. See if there is any offensive way in me, and lead me in the way everlasting. . . .' "

Miriam sat on the floor of her shuttered house and sorted through the basket of barley to remove the twigs and stones. It seemed strange that the grandson of Abba's wealthy master lay propped against her hearth with his wrists and ankles bound, wrapped in her blanket. She hoped he wouldn't start talking again or trying to bribe Nathan into setting him free. Nathan might do anything for a price. But Miriam believed her father's story. Abba wouldn't lie to her. She would keep Joshua tied until Abba came back.

It worried Miriam that Master Joshua wasn't breathing right. He sounded as if he had just run up a steep hill and couldn't catch his breath. Miriam stole glances at him from time to time as she rinsed the barley and cut up leeks to make their meal. Sometimes he was watching her, too, and it embarrassed her. She had given Abba her outer robe, which left only her undertunic. She tried to stay on the opposite side of the room so he couldn't see her. It was dark with the window shuttered. Mattan or Nathan could give him water.

But when the barley was ready, Miriam had to go near him to put the pot on the fire to cook. She knelt beside him warily and poked the coals to rekindle them, then added another stick of wood and made a place for the pot among the embers.

"Miriam, please help me." His voice was a weak whisper.

"Are you hungry?"

"Let me go home."

His face was flushed, and he was sweating. Maybe he was too hot by the fire. But no, he was shivering. She touched his brow.

"You have a fever."

"I need a physician."

"I can't pay for a physician."

"I can . . . my family can. Please . . . send one of your brothers to get my father."

"Abba said your father is in the palace dungeon."

Joshua moaned and shook his head from side to side. "He's not . . . can't be. . . ."

"My abba doesn't lie."

He closed his eyes in defeat, then seemed too weak to open them again. Forgetting her fear and embarrassment, Miriam studied him up close. He would be very handsome if he weren't so pale and ill. Dark circles rimmed his eyes like bruises. Without thinking, she brushed his curly black hair off his forehead. It felt soft and clean, not greasy and matted like her own hair. But he was burning with fever. What if he died? She couldn't let him die. Abba had risked his life to save him. Her father was depending on her. Miriam had once nursed her brothers through a terrible fever. She knew what to do.

"Nathan, draw another basin of water from the cistern," she ordered. "Mattan, bring me every clean rag you can find." The man moaned as she gently eased him down, resting his head in her lap. "Now, both of you go gather some eucalyptus branches. We need to burn them to freshen the air."

"But it's the Sabbath," Nathan said. "We'll get in trouble if we're caught gathering wood on the Sabbath."

"Then don't get caught." Her brother enjoyed the thrill of danger. Miriam knew he would get the wood.

After they left, Miriam spent the next hour patiently bathing Master Joshua's face and arms and chest with cold water from the cistern. He slept fitfully, and his coughing came from deep in his chest. As she worked, she learned every feature of his aristocratic face by heart: his wide, high forehead; his thick, gently arched brows; his full lower lip; his curly, black beard. When he briefly opened his eyes, she saw that they were so dark she could barely tell where the black centers began and ended.

She had never been so close to a man before, except for Abba. The men Mama brought home were usually drunk, and Miriam stayed away from them, especially after one of them had tried to paw her. She studied Master Joshua's hands as she bathed them, admiring his long, perfect fingers and immaculate nails. They were smooth rich-man hands, not chapped and rough like her own. She knew from the lavishly embroidered robe and fine linen tunic hanging on the rope above the hearth that he was telling the truth when he said his family had money. What would it be like to be a rich man's wife?

Before long the boys returned with eucalyptus branches bundled inside their cloaks.

They threw them on the fire, filling the room with a pungent aroma, cleansing the air in the stuffy shack. After Miriam had bathed Joshua's body in cool water for a long time, his fever seemed much better, his breathing easier. She finally moved his head off her lap and rose to tend the fire and stir the barley broth. His eyes blinked open.

"Yael?" he whispered. "Don't go, Yael."

Had he forgotten that her name was Miriam? Or was he calling someone else — maybe his wife? She felt a stab of jealousy that she couldn't explain or understand. She knelt beside him again and tenderly caressed his cheek. "I'll be right back."

Miriam hurried outside for a few more sticks of firewood, not wanting to be away from him for too long. Suddenly she thought of her mother's many boyfriends. Miriam had never understood what drew Mama to them or why she would leave her children alone for weeks at a time to go away with them. But now Miriam felt an inexplicable attraction to this man and wondered how she could convince Master Joshua to take her away with him when he left.

She went back inside and tended the fire, stirring the broth so it wouldn't burn. Then she knelt beside him again and lifted his

bound hands in hers. He opened his eyes.
"Yael?"

"It's all right," she said. "I'm right here."

6

When Eliakim Heard the king's soldiers descending the stairs, fear gripped him. Heart-pounding fear. He couldn't speak, couldn't catch his breath. His limbs trembled like a man with palsy, and he had to lean against the wall in order to stand. He helped Isaiah to his feet, and they huddled together, blinking in the blinding torchlight.

The soldiers unlocked the door and herded them out of the cell. Eliakim's knees could scarcely hold him, making it difficult to climb the steep, uneven stairs.

He emerged from the lower darkness to palace hallways awash in golden sunlight. The dazzling brightness made his eyes water after nearly two days of total blindness. Eliakim could have walked sightlessly through these familiar corridors without the soldiers leading him. They took him as far as the throne room doors and stopped.

While he waited to be summoned inside, Eliakim remembered the first time he had approached these forbidding doors. He had been awestruck to be summoned by King Hezekiah, astounded to learn that he would work for him. Eliakim thought of all that he and Hezekiah had accomplished together: building the walls, digging the tunnel, confronting the Assyrians, reforming their nation. Hezekiah had become his closest friend, yet now his son — only a few years younger than Hezekiah had been when they first met — was accusing Eliakim of treason and betrayal. He couldn't believe it. Surely Manasseh wouldn't go through with this. He wouldn't execute his father's trusted friends.

The double doors swung open. The soldiers led Eliakim and Isaiah inside. The throne room was empty except for King Manasseh, seated on the throne, and a cross-eyed stranger with his arm in a sling who sat beside him in Eliakim's seat.

Manasseh seemed so young and insecure to Eliakim; his fine features were permeated with uncertainty. After two days of blindness, Eliakim's eyes seemed to suddenly open and he saw that the king was a deeply troubled young man. What was Manasseh so afraid of?

He looked small and lost on Hezekiah's enormous throne. Manasseh had inherited Hephzibah's slight frame and would probably never reach his father's imposing stature. Suddenly Eliakim understood the true root of the king's paranoia. Manasseh would have to live up to Hezekiah's stature in the eyes of his nation. That explained his desperate need to know his future and to learn if Yahweh would perform miracles for him, too.

If only Eliakim could sit down with him, talk calmly to him, convince him, somehow, that all of life was a walk by faith. King Hezekiah had experienced fear and doubt and failure, as well. Eliakim wanted to reassure Manasseh that if he leaned on Yahweh in faith, he would be able to build confidence in himself. He stepped forward.

"Your Majesty, I —"

"Silence! I'm sick of your interrupting me, taking over for me, running the nation for me! You won't speak until I tell you to!"

Eliakim saw then that his own experience and wisdom had multiplied Manasseh's insecurities. He should have stood in the background more, offered his opinion less often. And it had probably made matters worse that Eliakim's son Joshua had consistently surpassed Manasseh in all of their studies together. Could fear and jealousy explain why Manasseh had turned against Eliakim's family so suddenly?

"God knows I have no wish to execute either of you," Manasseh began, "but I cannot allow Isaiah to use his considerable powers against me. I am forced to conclude that anyone who refuses to work for me is working against me."

Eliakim resisted the urge to interrupt again. This was all a ridiculous misunderstanding, not a crime punishable by death. But he held his tongue.

"I'll offer you one last chance to change your mind, Rabbi Isaiah. Will you prophesy the future for me as you did for the kings before me?"

Isaiah met the king's gaze. "I don't know your future, Your Majesty."

"Then I condemn you to death!"

Fear shot through Eliakim. Manasseh was going to go through with this. He was actually going to execute them.

"You can spare yourself additional torture, Rabbi, by confessing to the fact that you killed my father by putting a curse on him."

"I did no such thing, Your Majesty. I loved and respected your father as my own son."

Manasseh looked ill. Eliakim could see that he was afraid to go through with this but equally afraid not to. The king turned to the man seated beside him as if for reassurance and whispered something; then he faced Eliakim again.

"Do you still find Rabbi Isaiah innocent, Eliakim?"

All the air seemed to rush from Eliakim's chest to make room for his wildly pounding heart. It would be so easy to declare Isaiah guilty and save his own life. But it was so much more difficult to do the will of God. Eliakim swallowed the lump of fear in his throat.

"Isaiah is innocent, Your Majesty."

Manasseh closed his eyes. "Execute them both."

Eliakim swayed as his knees went weak. He was going to die. A jolt of sheer terror rocked through him, shaking him. He looked up at this selfish boy-king whom he had raised and loved; he waited until their eyes met.

"I want you to know that I forgive you, Manasseh."

"Forgive me! For what? You're the one who should be begging for forgiveness! You're the traitor, the liar . . . the murderer! Take him out of my sight!"

Eliakim couldn't move. Two soldiers gripped his arms and led him through the doors. His movements felt jerky, uncontrolled. Eliakim was ashamed of himself for being so fearful, but he couldn't help himself. He was going to die.

They hauled him outside. Dazzling sunlight seared his eyes, blazing with white light and heat as if the sun had moved closer to the earth during his time underground. He continued forward, propelled by the soldiers on either side of him, stumbling because of the chain that connected his ankles. The guards were marching him faster than his feet wanted to go.

After only a moment, it seemed, they passed through the gate, leaving the city. A crowd had gathered, summoned by the executioner's pounding drum. Hundreds of eyes stared at him curiously. Did they recognize him? Surely they would recognize Isaiah. But clothed in filthy robes that were stained with Hilkiah's blood, Eliakim knew he and Isaiah both looked like beggars.

They stopped when they reached the execution pit. Eliakim shuddered when he saw the torture Manasseh had devised for Isaiah. He would be strapped between two planks of wood and slowly sawn in half. The soldiers were already removing Isaiah's chains in preparation.

Eliakim's hands shook as he held them

out for the soldiers to remove his shackles. They pushed him against the whipping post and tied him to it, his face scraping the scarred wood. Someone ripped his robe down to his waist, laying his back bare for lashing. Isaiah stood a few feet away from him.

"Rabbi?"

Isaiah turned to him. An expression of profound peace radiated from the rabbi's face, flowing, it seemed, from his very soul. Eliakim caught a glimpse of the Eternal One's peace.

"Yahweh," Eliakim whispered. Instantly the peace of God filled him, as well. Yahweh was beside him — no, *inside* him — shielding him with His love.

"Make your confession," the guard ordered. "Everyone who confesses will have a share in the world to come."

Eliakim closed his eyes and leaned against the post. " 'Hear, O Israel. Yahweh is God — Yahweh alone.' "

When the Sabbath ended, Jerimoth rose at daybreak to finish the steep climb to Jerusalem. With his head covered and his eyes lowered, he followed a few paces behind his grandfather's servant, Maki, pausing every so often to switch the bulky provision bag to his other shoulder.

Maki had been unwilling to give Jerimoth any additional information about his family's safety, promising to tell him everything once they were in Jerusalem. Jerimoth hadn't pressed him. For now, the less he knew the more clearheaded and calm he could act.

They decided to enter the city by the Damascus Gate. It would be busy this time of day, and they could blend in with the crowd. But as they drew near they saw a huge crowd pouring from the city, their voices a roar of excitement.

"What's going on?" Maki asked a passerby. "Where is everyone going?"

"To the execution."

Maki swayed slightly and his face grew pale. Then he continued walking, faster now. The king's execution grounds were just outside the gate. They would have to pass by them. Jerimoth hoped they could slip through the gates unnoticed in all the excitement.

As they neared, Jerimoth was surprised to see people already turning away from the spectacle. Usually the common people lingered long at these grisly affairs, savoring every gory minute. But judging by their faces, this execution had proved to be too much for the mob. It must be a particularly brutal one.

"Wait here," Maki told him. "I'll go see."

Jerimoth didn't know what drew him, but he ignored Maki and followed closely behind him. Maki elbowed his way to the pit and stopped, peering between the spectators. Suddenly he whirled around again, turning his back so abruptly on what he had seen that he collided with Jerimoth.

"Maki . . . what?"

"God in heaven! Don't look!"

The two men struggled with each other as Maki tried to turn Jerimoth around and push him away. Jerimoth continued to move forward, a terrible foreboding in his racing heart. The crowd in front of them turned to view this new commotion, and as they parted, Jerimoth suddenly understood why Maki didn't want him to see.

In a pool of blood too horrible for words, Rabbi Isaiah lay dead. A few feet away, another man had been stripped to the waist and lashed to the pole. The soldiers had just finished scourging him with a whip and his back lay open, bloody and raw. When they cut the leather thongs, the man crumpled to the ground. Then the soldiers began pelting him with stones. The condemned man looked up and Jerimoth froze in horror.

It was his father.

"Ab— !" he started to scream, but Maki cut him short with a slap to his face.

"Insolent servant! I said we're leaving! Now come!" Maki gripped Jerimoth's arm and dragged him away. Jerimoth's feet stumbled drunkenly beneath him.

He couldn't think, couldn't speak. He didn't know what to do. He had to stop them. He had to help Abba. What had they done to him? God of Abraham . . . *Abba!*

Maki towed him through the winding streets and back lanes into a stinking ghetto of slums and shacks. But Jerimoth didn't see any of it. His eyes were blind to everything but the terrible image that was burned on his heart: the look of agony on Abba's face . . . the bloody lash marks on his back.

"I'm sorry, Master Jerimoth," Maki wept as he half-carried him through the filthy streets. "We were too late. God in heaven, I'm sorry. I'm so sorry. . . ."

When Joshua awoke he was still lying in front of the fire with his hands tied. Miriam bent over him, laying a cold compress on his forehead. The air smelled of eucalyptus.

"You're awake," she said. "I think your fever has finally broken."

"I feel much better." Joshua remembered

149

how his fever had begun to rise shortly after Maki left, and he'd been filled with despair, certain he would die in this stinking hovel. "Did you take care of me?" he asked. She nodded shyly. "Thank you. How long have I been sick?"

"Two days. Would you like some broth?"

"Yes, please."

She turned to fill a bowl from the pot of soup near the flames. "Who is Yael?" she asked with her back to him.

"Yael? Why?"

"You were calling her name."

Yael. If this ordeal ever ended, he would see his lovely Yael again. In three months' time she would be his wife. Her father had finally agreed. The embers on the hearth beside him glowed deep red, the color of her hair. Joshua remembered his dream now. He must have felt Miriam's hands bathing his face to cool his fever and dreamt it was Yael. He rolled onto his side and sat up with the blanket wrapped around him like a cocoon. Someone had untied his ankles.

"Did Maki come back?" he asked.

"Not yet."

Joshua was thoroughly sick of this one-room hut with its uneven dirt floor and musty smell. He was tired of staring up at crooked ceiling beams that were so rotten that mud and straw from the roof trickled down every time the wind blew. How could anyone stand to live here? He longed for his own home, where the large rooms allowed light and air to stream in and sweet-smelling linens covered the ivory beds. Even his servants' quarters were cleaner than this shack.

Suddenly the door opened and Joshua's brother stumbled inside. "Jerimoth!" he cried out. "Thank God you're here!"

Jerimoth didn't reply. He didn't seem to notice Joshua at all but stared straight ahead, as if in a trance. He looked very ill, his face blanched of all its color. Then Jerimoth's face twisted with anguish and horror. He crumbled to the floor beside Joshua like a wall of blocks built by a child and cried out from the depths of his soul. It was a savage howl of incomprehensible sorrow and staggering grief. His pain shuddered through Joshua.

He felt his own hands fall free as Miriam untied them. Joshua embraced his brother, covering his body with his own as if he could shield Jerimoth from whatever had hurt him. Everyone in the room fell silent, caught in the horror of Jerimoth's piercing cries. Joshua gripped his brother tightly, fearing he would shake apart with the force of his agony.

Gradually Jerimoth's cries grew weaker and died away into silent weeping. Joshua gripped his brother's shoulders, the rope still dangling from one of his wrists, and made his brother meet his gaze.

"Jerimoth, tell me."

"It was Abba . . ." Jerimoth's hoarse voice sounded like a small child's.

Joshua's heart pounded faster. "Tell me."

"They killed him, Joshua. He's dead."

The room began to whirl as it had when Joshua lay ill with fever. He gripped Jerimoth's shoulders as if to hang on for balance. "Who killed him?"

"King Manasseh. He executed him. I . . . I saw Abba. He . . ." Jerimoth collapsed again, unable to finish.

Maki had also come through the door, closing it behind him. Joshua looked up at him, his eyes imploring the servant to say it wasn't true. But Maki's grief-stricken face confirmed Jerimoth's words. The servant grabbed the front of his robes — Jerimoth's robes — and tore them again and again.

"How do you know this, Maki? Tell me everything."

Maki's voice was barely a whisper. "When we got to the city gate, we saw a crowd gathering to watch an execution."

"Abba's?"

Maki nodded. "He was being scourged. Afterward . . . the soldiers stoned him to death."

A cry of anguish, twin to the one Jerimoth had uttered, rose inside Joshua, but he choked it back. His father couldn't be dead. Abba would always be there — wise, strong Abba. He was the pillar that supported their entire family. How could he be dead? "You witnessed this, Jerimoth? This is true?" Joshua breathed.

"Oh, God of Abraham!" he wept. "Yes . . ."

Joshua knew, then, that everything Maki had tried to tell him for the past three days was also true. Manasseh's soldiers had ransacked his house. They had beaten his grandfather to death and trampled through his blood. They had strangled Dinah for refusing to betray him. They were searching for him, to arrest him. Maki had indeed risked his life to save him. Abba, beloved Abba, was dead. The horror of the truth overwhelmed Joshua, but unlike his brother, he wouldn't weep, wouldn't cry out.

"But why? God of Abraham, why?" he whispered.

"The king also executed Rabbi Isaiah," Maki told him. "The written charge was blaspheming the Torah —"

"No! Not Abba!"

"And treason against the king."

"Never! Abba would never commit treason! It's all lies!"

He turned to Jerimoth, but his brother was prostrate with grief, his face pressed into the dirt, unaware of anything but his pain. Joshua had once witnessed a public execution, and the image of the prisoner's bloody back, the sound of the screams and the stones pelting his body, had tortured Joshua's soul for days. If that man had been Abba . . . To do that to Abba . . .

"Manasseh will pay for this," Joshua said. "If it costs me my life, Jerimoth, I swear I'll get revenge for what he did to Abba."

7

The commander of Manasseh's execution squad bowed before him. "They're both dead, Your Majesty," he said quietly.

"Did Rabbi Isaiah confess?" Manasseh asked.

The commander stared at the floor and shook his head. He seemed strangely subdued, as if the task had affected him deeply. He was a seasoned professional. There was no excuse for this behavior.

"What's wrong with you?" Manasseh demanded.

"Your Majesty, I'm accustomed to executing violent criminals. The rabbi was a very old man. It was hard for me to —"

"Are you questioning my decision?"

"No, Your Majesty. You wouldn't have issued the orders unless you had proof of his guilt."

He was speaking the correct words, probably from fear, but everything about the commander's demeanor told Manasseh that the man had performed the task against his will. Manasseh wanted him out of his sight. "You are dismissed," he said.

The commander started to leave, then turned back. "We removed this from Lord Eliakim's finger . . . after . . ."

Eliakim's official signet ring lay in the soldier's open palm. The sight of it gave Manasseh a start. For as long as he could remember, he had seen that ring on Eliakim's finger. It had been part of him. The image of the soldiers wresting it from his dead, limp hand made Manasseh shudder. He wouldn't touch it.

"Give it to the chamberlain. Tell him to put it in the treasury until I choose a successor." He thought of Joshua, Eliakim's chosen successor. "Have they found Eliakim's son yet?"

"No, my lord. We haven't found Lord Shebna, either."

"I want you to double the guard here at the palace until we root out all of the conspirators. Run security checks on everyone who enters, including the servants. Then double all the guards at the city gates. Check every load entering or leaving the city. You must find Eliakim's son Joshua. He's at the heart of this conspiracy, and I won't rest until he is captured."

After the commander left, Manasseh sat alone in the huge, echoing throne room. The seats on his right and his left were empty, the usual crush of petitioners strangely missing.

What had he done? Shebna and Eliakim had occupied those seats, guiding and counseling Manasseh since the day he'd become king. He couldn't rule the entire nation by himself. But he couldn't promote any of his other advisors until he learned who else was involved in this conspiracy. Not knowing whom to trust, he sent for his brother, Amariah. It seemed to take him a long time to arrive.

Amariah finally entered the throne room with his shoulders slumped, his head bowed. His fearful hesitancy infuriated Manasseh. His brother had always been too passive, too content to sit and strum on a lyre all day, composing songs, instead of drilling with the palace guards or maneuvering for his rightful position on Manasseh's court. He was a few inches taller than Manasseh, but wiry and slender, with the sensitive facial features of a child. His curly dark hair had their father's coppery highlights, and his beard probably would, too, once it finished growing in.

"Sit down," Manasseh ordered. He gestured to Shebna's seat on his left.

Amariah obeyed, staring silently at the floor.

"Say something!"

Amariah finally looked up. "Why did you kill him, Manasseh?"

"Are you part of their conspiracy, too?"

"You know I'm not. It's just that whenever I think of Abba, whenever I picture him in my mind . . . I see Lord Eliakim beside him."

"You're such a fool! Don't you realize how that compounds his guilt? He sat here in a place of trust, but he abused that trust! He conspired to kill our father!"

"I have a hard time believing that," Amariah said. He spoke so softly that Manasseh barely heard him.

"Then you're an even bigger fool than I thought. Doesn't God's Word promise long life to those who serve God and obey Him? Who was more faithful than Abba? Why would God take Abba's life?"

Amariah didn't reply. He stared at Manasseh for a long time before speaking. "What are you going to do now? Who's going to take Eliakim's place?"

"Someone I can trust, obviously. Can I trust you? My own brother?"

"I don't want the job, Manasseh. I've

never wanted —"

"I know! You have no ambition at all, do you? You've always been content to sit back and let an outsider like Joshua take your rightful place. He isn't even of royal blood."

"That's because Joshua has the talent and the intellect for it. I don't."

Amariah's weakness angered Manasseh. "You're shirking your responsibilities. You've always been able to get away with it as long as Eliakim and Shebna and Joshua were around to take over, but you're King Hezekiah's son, too. It's time you took some responsibility. I'm making you my secretary of state."

"Are you crazy? What do I know about being the secretary? I'm only nineteen! I haven't even finished my studies! Shebna held that position since before we were born!"

"Well, there's no better way to learn than by experience. Move into Shebna's office. Start with all the unfinished business he left behind."

"I can't do it, Manasseh. I'm not qualified to —"

"Oh, grow up! You have our father's blood in your veins. That's all the qualifications you need."

Even with his brother beside him, the day

seemed endless to Manasseh and much too quiet without the usual business to attend to. Icy fear, like a rare winter snowstorm, had blanketed the entire city, settling over everyone, bringing the nation to a standstill. Manasseh wondered how long it would take for the fear to melt away and life to return to normal.

When it was time for the evening sacrifice, Manasseh walked up the hill with his brother. He always felt like a stranger at the Temple, with little to do except watch the priests perform the ceremony for him. Tonight the feeling bothered him even more than usual. As king, he should enjoy equal status with these priests. Instead, he stood as an observer, like all the other men. Only the royal platform set him apart and raised him a few feet above the crowd. The rabbis had taught him that he was also a sinner, no greater in God's eyes than anyone else, but their reasoning didn't seem right to Manasseh. He remembered what Zerah had said: The kings of other nations were also priests.

When the high priest himself emerged from the Temple side chambers to conduct the evening sacrifice, Manasseh was instantly suspicious. Today wasn't a feast day or a new moon. But when the high priest began to recite the liturgy, a shiver of dread passed through Manasseh's veins.

" 'The wicked plot against the righteous
and gnash their teeth at them . . .
The wicked draw the sword and bend the
   bow . . .
To slay those whose ways are upright.
But their swords will pierce their own
   hearts,
and their bows will be broken.' "

Manasseh turned to his brother. "Who are they talking about? Who are they accusing of wickedness?"

"I assume it's your enemies. The men you executed."

Manasseh wasn't convinced. His uneasiness continued to grow, swelling inside him like fermenting wine, until the high priest recited the final verses:

" 'Wait for the Lord and keep his way.
He will exalt you to inherit the land . . .
But all sinners will be destroyed;
the future of the wicked will be cut off.' "

Manasseh didn't wait for the benediction. He stepped off the platform and strode down the royal walkway to where his guards were waiting. "Arrest them," he said.

"Arrest who, my lord?"

"Every priest and Levite who participated in that service."

Joshua huddled in front of the hearth beside his brother. With the window tightly shuttered and the door closed and barred, the only light in the darkened room came from the fire. He had sent Miriam and the boys to the market so he would have some time alone with Jerimoth and Maki.

Joshua's lingering fever made him light-headed, and he longed to give in to sleep. But the shock of witnessing Abba's brutal death had paralyzed Jerimoth, leaving the task of family leadership to Joshua.

Jerimoth couldn't stop shaking, even though he sat close to the fire. Joshua hated to pile more tragedy on his brother's shoulders, but he had to be told about the other deaths. Joshua wrapped his arms around him.

"Jerimoth, I hate to do this to you —"

"Is it my Sara . . . or . . . or the baby?"

"As far as I know, they're still safe." He drew a shaky breath. "But Maki said that on the night they arrested Abba they . . . the soldiers murdered Grandpa . . . and Dinah."

Jerimoth clung to Joshua and wept like a

small child. "But why? Why is Manasseh doing this to us?"

"I don't know. Nothing makes sense. I've relived my last few days at the palace again and again, but I can't recall anything that would explain what Manasseh has done. I wish I could confront him and demand an explanation, but that's impossible."

Joshua had shed no tears. Instead, he'd channeled all of his emotions into the reservoir of his anger and hatred. It was growing very deep.

"Jerimoth, listen to me. We can't give in to our grief until we find a way to save what's left of our family. Mama is still in Anathoth at Tirza's house. Your Sara and Rachel, and my Yael, are here in Jerusalem. We need to leave the city as soon as possible. We have to decide where we'll go, what we'll do, how we'll live."

At last Jerimoth released his grip on Joshua and wiped his face with shaking hands. "Yes, yes . . . you're right."

"We've lost everything. Maki says Abba's house, your house, and Grandpa's booth in the marketplace are all under guard. It isn't safe to go back for anything. I had only a few pieces of silver with me. Do you have any?"

"I don't know . . . a small amount."

"We have to start all over again, Jerimoth. We have to rebuild Grandpa's business with what's left."

"I don't see how. It's impossible. We would need investment capital and —"

"But we *have* to. It's a matter of survival. Think, Jerimoth. Think about what you need to do. Don't dwell on . . . on this morning anymore. We have to take care of the women and children." He watched his brother struggle to control his emotions and saw him dig into his inner resources of strength.

"The goods I just purchased are in storage in Moab," Jerimoth finally said. "They're worth a fair amount. And I have business contacts . . ."

"Good. You need to concentrate on Grandpa's business so we can survive once we're safely out of the country."

"Where will we go?"

"To Moab. Or maybe to Egypt. Someplace that isn't an Assyrian province."

"I think I can find a place for us in Moab. But if the soldiers are guarding my house, how will we —"

"I've been working on a plan. Maki, will you come here for a minute, please?" The servant got up from the stool by the table and squatted beside them in front of the hearth. "We both owe you our lives, Maki. I wish we could reward you somehow, but —"

"It isn't necessary. I owed your grand-father my life, Master Joshua. Maybe now I have repaid him. If there was one thing Master Hilkiah believed in, it was helping those in need."

Memories of his grandfather tugged at Joshua, threatening to pull him down into grief and despair. He remembered Hilkiah's twinkling eyes and easy humor, his quiet humility and generosity, his deep faith and love for God. Hilkiah didn't deserve to be beaten to death. If only Joshua had stayed home that night instead of going to Yael's house. If only he had taken care of his grandfather instead of leaving him and Dinah alone. Joshua would probably be dead along with Abba, but at least his grandfather and his sister might still be alive.

"Have you made any plans, Maki?"

"No, Master Joshua. I have no plans."

"Is this your family? Can you stay here until you find work?"

Maki poked at the logs in the fire, trying to coax the embers to life. He wouldn't meet Joshua's gaze. "Miriam is my daughter. Nathan and Mattan have other fathers." When a dry piece of wood finally caught fire, he looked up. "I never wanted anyone to know about her, especially Master Hilkiah. He was such a godly man, and I was ashamed of my sin. Miriam's mother and I were never married."

"Where is Miriam's mother?"

Maki shrugged. "Who knows. Ever since Miriam was old enough to take care of the boys, her mother has come and gone as she pleased. I have always supported my daughter, but most of what her mother gets is spent on wine. That's why they live like this."

"You should have told my grandfather. He would have given Miriam a job in the kitchen or —"

"I wanted to ask him, but Miriam wouldn't leave her brothers."

"I'm sure my grandfather would have cared for them, too."

"I know he would have, but the boys resent me. They'll have nothing to do with me. Maybe it's because I've looked after Miriam all these years while their own fathers . . . Well, I don't think they even know who their own fathers are." He turned away again, poking aimlessly at the fire. "The funny thing is, I started my life just like them. My story is identical to theirs. I also made a living by robbing vendors in the marketplace. But I got caught when I was ten years old and sentenced to fifteen lashes. Master Hilkiah paid my fine, and I was spared." Maki laid down the stick and wiped his eyes with the back of his hands. "He was so much more than my master and employer. He was a father to me. When they killed Master Hilkiah . . ."

Jerimoth laid his hand on Maki's shoulder. "I'm sorry," he whispered. "I knew my grandfather loved you, but I never realized how much you loved him."

Joshua wondered how much more they had never known about their grandfather. "Will you help us, Maki?" he asked after a moment. "We need to save the rest of our family and escape from Judah, somehow. I know I'm asking a lot and I have no way to repay you at the moment, but I swear —"

"I'll help you. The only payment I ask is that you take Miriam with you."

"But we have no place to go and not even a shack like this one to live in."

"Any house will be better than this one. If I don't get Miriam away from this place soon, her mother will sell her into the same way of life that she lives."

"Her own daughter?" Jerimoth asked.

Maki nodded grimly. "She tried to sell her once before, but I stopped her in time."

Jerimoth moaned. "Of course, Maki. We'll take both of you with us."

Joshua knew that his brother was right, but the burden of responsibility he already carried was much too heavy. Now it would grow heavier still. He had been trained for a position of leadership in the palace, but he had never imagined that leadership would be like this. "I thought you said Miriam wouldn't leave her brothers," he said after a moment.

Maki gazed at him solemnly. "No, Master Joshua. She won't."

Joshua quickly calculated the number of people he and Jerimoth would have to provide for: their mother, their sister Tirza, her husband, and their new baby, Jerimoth's wife and daughter, his fiancée, Yael. That was already nine people. Maki, Miriam, and the two boys would make thirteen. How would he escape with that many people, let alone support them all? Most of them were women and children. But Joshua knew he could never get out of Jerusalem safely without Maki's help.

"The four of you are welcome to come with us," he said at last. "My plan is to help Jerimoth's wife and daughter escape first, then Yael. As soon as we're all out of the city, we'll quickly make our way to Anathoth and rescue Mama and Tirza before word spreads about the first escapes."

Jerimoth laid his hand on Joshua's arm. "Not Yael. We must leave Yael here."

"What are you talking about? She's going to be my wife! I can't leave her behind anymore than you could leave Sara!"

"Listen to me. Your betrothal was never official. Yael has no legal connection to you. She isn't in danger."

"I love her! I won't leave without her!"

"If you love her, you'll let her stay here, where she's safe. You're a wanted man, Joshua. What kind of a life can you offer her?"

Joshua sprang to his feet and walked the few steps to the other side of the room. He was so tired of hiding in this filthy house, so weary of the darkness and confinement. How could he imprison Yael, too? The life of a refugee would be no life for her. He couldn't ask her to give up her beautiful home, all of her servants, her elegant clothing, and plentiful food. Until a few days ago he could have given her a life of wealth and ease. Now he would have to add Yael to the growing list of people he had loved and lost — people Manasseh had snatched away from him. So much sorrow, so much loss.

Jerimoth stepped up behind him. "If I

could leave Sara here and know that she would be safe, that she would be provided for, I would do it, Joshua."

"I swear I'll come back for her," he said quietly. "As soon as we're settled. As soon as I can make a home for her, Yael is going to be my wife."

Miriam shifted the small basket of food to her other arm as she hurried home from the market with her brothers. She had to get back before Master Joshua left. Now that his older brother had arrived, the time when they would leave drew closer and closer. She couldn't believe that only a few days had passed since Joshua had burst through her door in the middle of the night, gasping for air. Or that only yesterday she had nursed him through his illness, bathing him with water to cool his fever.

She had memorized his face in the firelight and secretly combed her fingers through his curly black hair while he slept. She had held his smooth hands in hers and imagined being his wife, feeling those hands caressing her face. He had been kind to her. He had called her by name.

Miriam had never met a man like Master Joshua before, so refined and aristocratic. He certainly wasn't like the men her mother brought home. No matter what, Miriam had to find a way to go with him when he left. Her mother had begun to teach her how to win a man's love. The idea had always repulsed Miriam until Master Joshua had burst into her life.

When she opened the door and saw him seated cross-legged by the hearth, she breathed a sigh of relief. His older brother still wore the sorrowful look of a lost child, but Master Joshua had never shed a tear, showing the same inner strength and courage he had shown when battling his illness. It was one of the reasons she loved him. Abba motioned for her to join them, and she sank to the floor beside Master Joshua.

"Miriam, they've offered to take us with them," Maki said. "All of us, if we'll help them."

Miriam's heart leaped. She turned to Joshua. "What do you want me to do?"

"Help our family escape. It will be dangerous, but —"

"No! We're not going anywhere!" Nathan cried. "We can't leave Mama!"

Miriam scrambled to her feet to confront her brother. "Mama doesn't care one bit about any of us, and you know it! You should have heard how she cursed when she found out she was pregnant with you and

171

Mattan. And she has run off and left you alone with me ever since you were born. Why should we stay here with her? So she can have someone to beat when she's drunk? Did you already forget how she pushed your brother into the fire for spilling his broth? Show him the burn on your leg, Mattan. Remind him what our mother is really like!"

As Mattan shrank back into the shadows, Miriam regretted hurting him with her words. But she had to convince Nathan. She couldn't let Master Joshua leave without her.

"I'm leaving this place, Nathan, and so is Mattan," she said. "If you're smart, you'll come with us."

The room was silent for a moment after her outburst, then Master Joshua stood and quietly walked over to where Nathan stood sulking by the door.

"Nathan, I'll need your help if my escape plan is going to work. I'll try to pay you back, somehow, when —"

"I don't need any rich man's money to survive."

"What do you need, then? Tell me, and if I can provide it I'll —"

"I don't need anything."

"Except a father?"

Joshua's question caught the boy by

surprise, and for a moment Nathan was unable to disguise his pain. Miriam knew how much he longed for someone to call Abba. She often heard him crying late at night after her father had visited her. Nathan didn't even know who his father was. Their mother probably didn't know, either.

"You shut up about my father!" Nathan shouted.

"I just lost my father," Joshua said quietly. "He was the most important person in my life. I know how much a father means to a boy. I'll try to be a father to you if you'll let me."

"What about Mattan?" Nathan asked sullenly.

Jerimoth rose from his place by the fire and rested his hand on Mattan's head. "I will be Mattan's father."

Tears burned in Miriam's eyes. It could be a dream come true for all of them if only Nathan would lay aside his stubbornness and allow it to happen. She dug in her basket and pulled out the small packet she had nearly forgotten.

"Nathan, look. This is balm for Mattan's leg. Master Joshua gave me the money to buy it for him."

Joshua took it from her and knelt beside Mattan as he opened it. "This will help your leg heal faster. May I put some on you?"

Mattan drew back in fear. "Will it hurt?"

Jerimoth pulled up the stool and sat down. "It might hurt a little," he said. "But I'll hold you so you won't be afraid."

Miriam saw tears in Jerimoth's eyes as he held out his arms, waiting. Mattan hesitated. He had never known the comfort of a father's arms as she had. He was probably afraid to trust these two men who might be gone again in a day or two like all the others.

"Come on, Son," Jerimoth said gently. Mattan flew into his arms, clinging to him.

Miriam's own father reached for her hand as she brushed the tears from her eyes. But a moment later she heard the front door slam, and she saw that Nathan was gone.

8

Joshua crouched in the shadows between the two stalls in the marketplace, studying each face in the milling crowd, searching for Jerimoth's wife, Sara. She should be easy to spot. She would be carrying her baby, Rachel. And she would be flanked by the two palace guards who accompanied her to the marketplace every day. Maki had watched her movements for days. She would soon pass this way.

Joshua squeezed his hands into fists, willing them to stop shaking. He had never been more afraid in his life. He had devised this plan. He was placing all these people's lives at risk, as well as his own. He had tried so hard to anticipate everything that could possibly go wrong and to think of alternative courses of action, but what if he missed something? What if someone panicked?

He wished he could pray. He longed to cry out to God for help so he wouldn't have to face this ordeal alone. But the heavens had turned to stone for him. God hadn't helped Dinah or his grandfather. He had closed His ears to Abba's cries. Why would God listen to him?

Timing. It would all depend on perfect timing. Joshua trusted Maki and Miriam. They realized their lives were at stake and would be cautious, but he still worried about Nathan. The boy had finally agreed to help, but only after making it clear that he was doing it for Miriam's sake alone. Jerimoth, who had more experience as a father, had fared much better in winning Mattan's trust. But little Mattan was so young, so vulnerable to fear. They were all hiding in the empty market stall behind Joshua, waiting for his signal. There was no sign of Sara.

When Joshua realized he was holding his breath he slowly exhaled. He started to rake his fingers through his beard, then stopped when he felt the dusty ashes. He had coated his hair and beard with them in an attempt to disguise himself as an old man. He was wearing Miriam's tattered robe. He dried his sweating palms on it.

Were the others as frightened as he was? Joshua had already decided that if the soldiers captured any of them he would give himself up. He couldn't allow one more innocent person to suffer because of him.

Suddenly he spotted Sara. She walked slowly, holding little Rachel by the hand. The toddler took wobbly, uneven baby steps in her tiny sandals. Joshua recognized the palace guards walking on either side of Sara. And they would certainly recognize him. He had taken his military training with these two men, sparred with them, laughed with them. Would they help him for friendship's sake or betray him for fear of King Manasseh? He couldn't take any chances. No one had helped Abba.

Joshua ducked inside the empty market stall where the others waited. "Get ready. Here she comes. And be careful, I know both of the guards."

Maki nodded and hurried out of the stall, walking down the street toward Sara. Would she recognize him in Jerimoth's robe and realize what they were trying to do? Joshua felt for his weapon, Miriam's kitchen knife, which Maki had sharpened on a whetstone. Joshua hoped he wouldn't have to use it. Then he crept back to his lookout post in the shadows.

"Officers! Help me! I've been robbed!" Heads turned at the sound of Maki's shouts, and a crowd quickly gathered. Sara and the guards stopped walking. Joshua ducked inside the booth again and signaled to Miriam and the two boys. He saw Jerimoth close his eyes, his lips moving in silent prayer as he sat and waited.

"They took all my money!" Maki cried. "Go after them! They went that way!"

The guards didn't take the bait. Instead, they began to argue with Maki. Joshua was too far away to hear their words. He saw Miriam and the two boys snaking silently through the crowd toward Sara.

Maki's face turned red with rage. "You can't let them get away with this! Go after them, I say, or I'll report both of you!"

At last one of the guards took off after the imaginary thieves, running down a side street in the opposite direction. Maki remained with the other soldier, arguing loudly to divert his attention. He slowly positioned himself between the guard and Sara. Joshua saw Miriam creep up beside Sara. They began inching away.

"Faster . . . hurry . . ." he whispered. The crowd was starting to lose interest and drift away. Joshua left his lookout and returned to the abandoned booth just as Mattan and Nathan rushed into the hiding place. Nathan was struggling to carry baby Rachel. She squirmed to free herself, to howl in protest, but Nathan held his hand firmly over her mouth until he dropped her into her father's lap. Jerimoth clutched her to himself.

"Shh, it's all right, Rachel. Shh . . . your abba is here." Jerimoth hugged her fiercely for a moment, then he released her and began tearing off her clothes and shoes. Mattan smeared her dark, silky curls with oil while Nathan rubbed her body with a mixture of mud and ashes. Moments later, she no longer resembled a spoiled rich baby but a filthy urchin like the two boys. Jerimoth barely had time to kiss her sooty cheek before the boys darted out of the stall with her again, heading for the city gate and freedom. Seconds later, Sara tumbled in beside Jerimoth, clinging to him, weeping.

Joshua returned to his lookout post and watched as Miriam, now wearing Sara's blue head scarf, slowly walked down the central street of the marketplace. He saw the soldier straining to keep an eye on her, while Maki continued to shout. "What's this city coming to when hoodlums and thieves roam in broad daylight, robbing innocent people?"

Miriam was twenty yards away from the guard now, wandering in the milling crowd. He looked worried. He finally pushed Maki aside and elbowed his way forward to catch up with her.

"Wait! What about my money?" Maki shouted. The soldier ignored him.

Jerimoth tugged on Joshua's sleeve. "Come on. We're ready to load the cart."

"Just a minute." Joshua watched as the soldier finally caught up to Miriam and whirled her around. Then panic filled the soldier's face when he discovered that he had followed the wrong woman. He released Miriam and darted through the square, grabbing every women in a blue head scarf and peering into her face. He hadn't suspected Miriam. He had let her go. That was all Joshua wanted to see.

Jerimoth had already helped his wife climb into the deep pushcart they had bought with the last of Joshua's silver. She huddled there, waiting. "Hurry, Joshua, get in!" Jerimoth whispered.

"Wait. Not yet . . ." Miriam hurried into the booth the same moment as her father, pulling the blue scarf from her head. "Give it to me," Joshua said. He removed a shard of broken pottery from his pocket and folded it inside the fabric.

Jerimoth grabbed it away from him. "What is that? What are you doing?" Before Joshua could stop him, his brother unwrapped it to examine the potsherd. On the smooth side,

Joshua had scratched a drawing of an ox. "Are you out of your mind?" Jerimoth cried.

"I want Manasseh to know it was me! If he's going to annihilate our family for no good reason, I want him to know that *I* won this round, not him!"

"This isn't a game, Joshua! The soldiers can describe Miriam and Maki. They'll realize they were involved. Their lives are more important than playing a stupid game!"

"Manasseh has to understand that I'm fighting back! He led Abba to his death, and no one lifted a finger to help him! I want Manasseh to know that I'll fight him until the day I die!"

Maki pushed between them. "Shh . . . You must lower your voices."

"Let him leave the scarf here if he wants to," Miriam said. "It's important to him. I don't care if the soldiers remember me or not." She took the scarf from Jerimoth and wrapped the potsherd inside it again, then laid it in the middle of the floor. "We need to go."

Joshua removed his outer robe and curled up inside the cart, wedging himself on all fours on top of Sara, protecting her. They piled small sacks of grain and baskets of fruit and vegetables on top of them until the cart was heaped high and the occupants were well-hidden. Then Joshua's world turned dark as they covered the entire load with goatskins.

"Can you breathe?" he whispered to Sara.

"Yes. I'm all right." He hoped he wouldn't start to cough.

Jerimoth grunted and the cart began to move. He would play the servant's role once again along with Miriam, pushing the two-handled barrow; Maki would be their master. The cart rumbled toward the city gate.

Joshua's body soon began to ache from the cramped position. His foot was falling asleep, but he didn't dare move it. The load on his back felt heavy, and he hoped he wouldn't crush Sara. He guessed by the way the cart kept screeching to a stop, then lurching forward again, that the streets were crowded.

At last he heard soldiers shouting orders. The cart rumbled to a stop. They must be at the gate. Maki had scouted all of the gates and reported that the soldiers were stopping everyone who left the city and inspecting every load. Joshua's plan would succeed or fail right here.

"What's in the barrow?" he heard someone ask.

"Market goods," Maki answered. "But

why the traffic jam? What's the problem?"

"We need to inspect your load."

"You've never seen produce and grain before? Or is it the quality of my goods you're concerned with?"

"We have to make sure you're not smuggling anyone out of the city."

"Smuggling someone! You're joking, right?"

"Haven't you heard about the plot against King Manasseh?"

"No, I haven't."

"The king already executed two of the conspirators. We're looking for the rest of them."

"You're not going to make me empty my entire cart! I have a long journey home. I'll never make it there by sunset at this rate. And tomorrow's the Sabbath."

"The other choice is to let me run my spear through your load."

"But what if you rip a bag of grain? I'll be spilling my supplies all the way home!"

"It's up to you, sir."

Joshua's heart tried to pound out of his chest. He could feel Sara shaking beneath him.

"I have a third alternative," Maki said quietly. "I'll give you a half-shekel of silver to lift the cover and take a quick look so I can be on my way."

"I can't do that, sir."

"A full shekel, then. Have mercy on my servant here. The sun is already getting hot, and he has to push this load over the Beth-Horon Pass." The soldier didn't reply.

That shekel was the last of Jerimoth's money. Now they were broke. Joshua tried taking slow, even breaths so he wouldn't cough. Then sunlight streamed through the cracks above him as someone removed the goatskins.

"The others might be watching," the guard mumbled. "I have to pretend to spear your load."

"My grain is on the bottom. Be careful."

Suddenly the tip of a razor-sharp spear sliced into Joshua's left shoulder. He clenched his teeth to keep from crying out.

"All right. Move along," the guard said.

The cart quickly rumbled forward again. They were moving downhill. Then the jostling motion changed as they left the cobblestone pavement of the city ramp and moved onto the dirt road leading away from the city.

They had made it. They were safe.

Gradually, the first numbness of shock wore off and excruciating pain began to radiate down Joshua's shoulder and arm from the spear wound. The back of his tunic grew warm and sticky. He was losing a lot of blood.

"Are you all right?" he whispered to Sara.

"Yes. Are you?"

"I'm fine." But he wasn't. Each jolt of the groaning cart sent shivers of pain through him. *Please hurry,* he silently pleaded. Instead, the cart drew to a stop again. He heard the muffled sound of a baby crying, then Nathan's voice.

"Can you spare a crust of bread? My sister hasn't eaten all day." Joshua knew the road must be crowded with travelers since the boys were continuing their charade.

"Can you handle a cart, boy?" Maki asked. "I'll give all three of you something to eat if you help my servant push this down the mountain and over the next pass."

The cart began to move again, lurching, jostling downhill, pitching Joshua forward against the front of the cart until the pain in his shoulder was agonizing. He closed his eyes, hoping the whirling dizziness in his head would stop. The baby's screams added to the tension. They should be almost to the hiding place Maki had found. He said it wasn't far. *Hurry!*

The road surface changed again. Now they were crossing rugged, uneven terrain.

The jerking motion sent stabs of pain down Joshua's left arm and his back until he could no longer stifle his moans. Suddenly the cart bumped to an abrupt stop. The load on top of him grew lighter as Maki and Jerimoth lifted the cargo out. Then they reached in for him.

"Joshua! You're bleeding!" Jerimoth cried. "Sara . . . ?"

"I'm all right. But my baby . . . my poor baby. Give her to me."

With Maki's help, Joshua stumbled out of the cart and sank down on the grass. He was only dimly aware of Jerimoth's family huddled together, weeping for joy. The burning pain in his shoulder overshadowed everything else.

"Open your tunic. Let me see the wound," Miriam said. She knelt beside him, holding a skin of wine from the cart. He tried to do what she said, but it hurt too much to move his arm. She gently peeled his bloody tunic off his shoulder. Joshua gasped as she poured some of the wine into the wound. "Here. Drink some." She pressed the wine-skin into his hand and watched as he took a few swallows. "I have to stop the bleeding," she told him. "It's going to hurt."

Joshua gritted his teeth as she pressed her hands on his back to hold the wound closed.

"Is it very deep?" he asked.

"About an inch. But it's a clean wound, not ragged. It should heal well. Abba, do you have anything I can use for a bandage?"

Sara unwound her sash. "Here. Take this."

"Just hurry," Joshua said. "We have to get to my sister's house before Manasseh's soldiers do."

"Praise God, everything else went well," Jerimoth said, exhaling. "Mattan, you've done a splendid job with your new sister. Come, let me introduce you properly." The little boy beamed as he edged closer to where Jerimoth sat beside his wife. The baby had finally stopped crying, but the occasional sob still shuddered through her.

"Sara, my love, we have a new son," Jerimoth said. "His name is Mattan. He . . . Sara, why on earth do you feel so . . . so lumpy?"

"It's your silver and gold, Jerimoth. When the guards weren't looking I sewed every piece I could find into my dress."

"It's much too dangerous," Jerimoth said. "I can't let you put Nathan at risk. That's final."

Joshua grabbed his brother's arm as he started to turn away. "You know what happened in the marketplace. The whole plan almost fell through because the guards wouldn't chase an imaginary thief. But if they see Maki being robbed, it'll be different."

"And what if one of the soldiers catches Nathan? What then?"

Joshua didn't want to think about that possibility. He glanced over to where Nathan and Mattan sat with Miriam, near the cart.

"Why don't we ask him, Jerimoth. Let him be the one to decide."

Maki joined them as Joshua explained the plan to Nathan. The boy sneered with contempt at Jerimoth's concern. "I'm not afraid of any soldiers. They haven't caught me yet, and they're not about to."

"But you know your way around the back alleys of Jerusalem," Maki said. "This is different. This is a strange city, and —"

"They'll never catch us. Right, Mattan?"

"Don't involve Mattan," Jerimoth said. "He's too young to —"

"Who gave you the right to tell us what to do?" Nathan shouted. "We don't need you. You need us! My brother and I can take care of ourselves."

"We're wasting time," Joshua said. "If Nathan's willing to do it, then it's settled."

They left Miriam, Sara, and the baby hidden among the bushes with the cart and made their way to their sister's home in Anathoth, a half mile down the road. The wound in Joshua's shoulder throbbed dully, and he tried not to use his left arm, keeping it pressed against his chest so it wouldn't start bleeding again.

They soon reached the crooked street where Tirza and Joel lived. Their house was jammed into a modest neighborhood beside a dozen homes just like it. Two guards stood in a meager patch of shade out front, talking. Joshua had planned this rescue for the noon hour, when the sun was hot, so the street would be deserted.

"Everyone ready?" he asked. "Do you remember what to do?"

"Let Mattan stay here," Jerimoth begged. "Please, he's just a child. Why involve him in our family's mess?"

"We have no choice," Joshua said angrily. "I don't see anyone else racing to our family's defense, do you?"

Nathan folded his arms across his chest as if squaring for a fight. "Mattan and I aren't afraid."

Joshua wasn't fooled by Nathan's bravado. Fear raced through his own veins, colliding with the heavy stone in his stomach. The others must be trembling, as well. "Just be careful," he told Nathan.

Jerimoth rested his hand briefly on Mattan's head. "Yahweh go with you, son." While Maki and the boys left to stage the robbery on the street in front of the house, Joshua and Jerimoth ducked down the alley toward the rear of the house.

The simple four-room home was all that Joel and Tirza could afford until Joel entered the priesthood at age thirty. That was still four years away. Until then, Joel's job was to study the Torah with the other scholars, memorizing the multitude of priestly laws and regulations. Joshua knew that his father had been supporting them financially. But the young couple's life was about to change forever. He wondered how much help Joel would be in a fight.

Joshua's mother, Jerusha, was inside, too. Did she know about Abba? Or about Dinah and Grandpa? He dreaded the moment when they would have to tell her. For now, he pushed all distracting thoughts from his mind, concentrating on what he had to do next.

He peered over the wall at the tiny paved courtyard behind the house. He expected to find another guard by the rear door, but the yard was deserted. The rear window was shuttered against the sun's heat, but the door stood open. He watched it for as long as he dared, scanning the bushes and neighboring yards. He saw no guards anywhere. Time was short. He pulled Miriam's kitchen knife out of his belt. It was more suited to chopping vegetables than attacking armed soldiers, but it was their only weapon. He doubted if Maki or his brother could use a sword, even if they had one. They were cloth merchants, not warriors.

"Stay here," he whispered to Jerimoth. "I'll signal when it's safe."

Joshua climbed over the wall and ran toward the house, crouching low. No soldier appeared out of ambush. He listened for a moment by the open door. Everything was quiet. Too quiet. He had the terrible feeling he was walking into a trap.

He signaled to his brother and watched him clamber over the wall. Jerimoth's face was very pale and beaded with sweat. His breath came in quick gasps. Jerimoth must be even more terrified than Joshua was, with a wife and daughter to worry about.

"Count to twenty, then follow me inside," Joshua told him. "You find Tirza and Joel. I'll look for Mama. Ready?" Jerimoth nodded, wringing his hands.

Joshua slipped through the open door into a storage area, his knife poised in front of him, expecting a guard to jump him from the shadows. He saw earthenware jars stacked along the walls but no guard. The room smelled of grain and olive oil. He heard a newborn baby crying inside the house.

A moment later, Jerimoth ducked through the door behind him, his eyes wide, expectant. Joshua nodded to reassure him, then made his way down the narrow passage toward the living area.

Move quickly. Find the women. Get out, he told himself.

Joshua found the entire family seated on the floor around the table, eating their noon meal: Mama, Joel, and Tirza, rocking a fussy newborn in her arms. The soldier who should have been guarding the back door sat eating with them. He tried to scramble to his feet, but Joshua moved faster, forcing the guard to sit down again, pressing the kitchen knife against his throat.

"Sit down. Don't move. Lay your hands flat on the table," Joshua commanded. The soldier was very young, only seventeen or eighteen years old. That explained why he had foolishly left his post and allowed himself to befriend his hostages. Joshua was grateful when he surrendered without a struggle.

Mama, Tirza, and Joel didn't move either.

They stared at Joshua in stunned surprise. "Can you travel?" he asked Tirza. She nodded. "Then get your things. Hurry!"

They all followed Jerimoth, leaving Joshua alone with the guard. He could hear his family hastily gathering their belongings in the other rooms. He reached into the folds of his robe and pulled out another potsherd inscribed with an ox. He had to use his left hand to do it, and the movement sent waves of pain down his back and shoulder. But the agony was well worth the triumph he felt. He shoved the plates aside and laid the emblem in the middle of the table where the soldiers were certain to find it. Then he looked around for something he could use to tie up his prisoner.

"They'll kill me for letting you get away," the young guard said, his voice shaking.

"I doubt that. But if you had been at your post, I might have had to kill you."

"If I had been at my post, you never would have gotten this far."

"Listen, I don't know what they told you, but we aren't traitors. We haven't committed any crime. The king's charges against my family are completely false."

"Are you going to kill me?" the guard asked.

"I'm not a murderer. I'll find something

to tie you with and —"

"Not in here. Please. Don't let the others know I left my post."

"All right. I have no quarrel with you. Get up." Joshua lowered the knife and took a step back to give the guard room to stand. He glanced toward the door to see if Jerimoth was ready, taking his eye off his prisoner, and in that brief moment the guard reached for his sword.

"No, *don't!*" Joshua shouted.

The boy didn't listen. He continued to pull his weapon from its sheath. In an act of pure instinct, Joshua thrust his knife into the boy's stomach, twisting it in and up, as he had been trained to do, in order to pierce his heart. He had practiced the maneuver on a sack of straw countless times, but living flesh felt horribly different.

The young soldier cried out and jerked away from Joshua, dropping his sword. Joshua's knife snapped in half, leaving the blade inside the boy. Joshua held the bone handle with the stump of blade in his hand. He threw it on the floor, then looked up at the guard in horror.

Blood. So much blood, everywhere. It poured from the boy.

The soldier sank to his knees. He tried to talk, but his words came out in a strangled gurgle. His eyes pleaded with Joshua to help him, not to let him die. He held both hands over his stomach, trying to stop the bleeding, trying to hold everything inside.

"No, wait . . ." Joshua begged. "I'm sorry. I didn't mean to . . ."

If only he could stop all the blood, take the knife blade out of the gaping wound, help this boy somehow. Joshua eased him to the floor. The guard was only a kid. He was weeping, afraid to die, his eyes wide with fear.

"Oh, God, forgive me . . ." Joshua begged. "I . . . I didn't mean to . . ."

The boy twitched in his arms, gasping, dying.

Jerimoth rushed in the room, then stopped. "Joshua . . . what happened?"

"He went for his sword . . . I should have disarmed him first. Oh, God . . . Oh, God!" Joshua remembered the horror of pushing his knife into a living person and shuddered.

"Never mind, Joshua. We need to go."

"But I can't leave him. He's still alive . . . he's —"

Jerimoth grabbed Joshua under his arms and dragged him to his feet. "Joshua, get moving! Now! Before it's too late!"

Joshua felt dizzy as his brother pushed him toward the passageway. His hands were sticky with blood. He was going to be sick.

Jerimoth paused for a moment to peer out the front window. "I wonder if Maki . . . No!" he cried out. "They caught Mattan!"

The terrible words penetrated Joshua's paralysis. He shoved Jerimoth aside to look. A soldier stood in the middle of the street with little Mattan struggling in his arms.

Joshua knew it was his fault. He should have listened to Jerimoth. He never should have involved the boys. A rush of angry strength surged through Joshua's veins like strong wine. He picked up the dying soldier's sword and ran out of the front door, his only thought to save Mattan.

"Help me!" Mattan screamed.

Maki was pleading with the guard. "Let him go. He's only a boy. It's all right, let him go."

The guard looked up as Joshua rushed toward him, sword in hand. "Joshua! It's *you!*"

Mattan wriggled free from the stunned guard's grasp and fell to the ground. Maki reached to help him up.

"Run! Both of you, *run!*" Joshua shouted, then realized his mistake. The guard needed only a fraction of a second to comprehend that they were all working together.

Joshua's legs weren't moving quickly

enough. He tried to get to Maki in time, but before he could, the soldier drew his sword and ran it through Maki's body.

"No! *Maki!*"

Joshua turned into a madman then. Ignoring all his caution and training, he leaped at the guard, slashing wildly, his only thought to kill this man for what he had done to Maki. He felt nothing, saw nothing, blinded by fury and grief.

When he became aware of his surroundings again, Joshua found himself standing in the middle of the street, his hand fused to a sword. Blood dripped from it. The dead guard lay at his feet, stabbed dozens of times.

At the edges of his vision, Joshua saw people emerging from their houses. Mattan had disappeared, but Maki lay curled in the dirt, moaning. Joshua threw his weapon down and lifted Maki in his arms. Pain knifed through Joshua's shoulder as his wound ripped open again, but he didn't care. He began to run, carrying the servant in his arms.

Joshua ducked between the houses, ran down back streets, cut through alleyways, running on and on. He felt the warmth of Maki's blood soaking him and ran faster. He couldn't let Maki die. He had to find

Miriam. She would know how to stop the blood.

Joshua ran until he reached the outskirts of the city; then his legs buckled beneath him and he crumpled to the ground, gasping for air. Maki cried out in pain as they fell together.

"Hang on, Maki," Joshua begged. "Hang on . . ." Joshua tried to stand, tried to lift him again, but his legs wouldn't hold him.

"No . . ." Maki moaned. "Leave me here."

"I can't let you die! Please, God. *Please!*"

"Listen." Maki clutched Joshua's wrist with amazing strength. "Miriam," he whispered. "Take care of my Miriam."

"I will! I promise. I swear!"

Maki's grip went slack again.

Joshua held him in his arms and wept as he watched his servant die.

Joshua hid Maki's body beneath a clump of bushes beside the road. He had no time, no way to bury him. He needed to get back to the others. They must get out of the country. He stumbled through the underbrush, afraid to take the road that was slowly filling with afternoon traffic.

Joshua cursed himself for all the mistakes he had made. He should have listened to Jerimoth and not involved the boys. He should have disarmed the young guard right away. He should have waited before rushing outside to save Mattan. Maki might have persuaded the soldier to release the boy. It was his fault that Maki was dead. The servant had risked his own life to save Joshua and his family, and this is how he had repaid him.

Joshua allowed tears of guilt and regret to fall as he pushed on, jogging as fast as he dared. One more obstacle to their freedom remained. They had to cross into Moab before word of their escape reached the border outpost.

As Joshua stumbled into their hiding place, his mother rushed toward him. "Joshua! Dear God — look at you! Are you all right?" She ran her hands over his body, his face.

"It's not my blood, Mama."

When she was convinced that he was all right, she clasped him tightly in her arms, weeping. "I was so worried! Thank God, thank God!"

Joshua glanced quickly around the little grove. Everyone was there, even Nathan and Mattan. Then his eyes met Miriam's.

"Where's my father?" she asked.

He couldn't look at her. "I'm sorry, Miriam. . . . He's dead."

"No! He isn't dead! He isn't!" She rushed at Joshua, beating him with her fists. "It isn't true!"

Joshua didn't try to defend himself. He allowed her to beat him, welcoming the blows. Her father was dead because of him. So were the two soldiers — one killed brutally and the other one dead because of Joshua's foolish mistake. He had never witnessed death up close before, but today he had seen it, felt it, caused it. Death was so final. So irreversible. He understood, now, about Abba. About Dinah and Grandpa. He grieved for all of them and for himself.

Jerimoth pulled Miriam away and tried to take her in his arms. "Miriam, we must go. We must cross the border before the soldiers catch up with us."

She twisted free from him. "Come on, Nathan," she said. "We're going home."

Joshua grabbed her arm. "Miriam, you can't —"

"Don't tell me what I can do. I curse the day Abba ever dragged you through our door. He would still be alive if it weren't for all of you."

"Let her go, Joshua," Jerimoth said. "She's right, this isn't her battle."

"You can't go back there," Joshua said.

"How will you live?"

"We'll manage. We got along fine before *you* came."

"You'll end up making a living like your mother."

"What do you care?" she asked bitterly.

Joshua grabbed her hand and pressed it against the front of his robe, which was soaked with Maki's blood. "The last words your father spoke before he died were about you. I held him in my arms, and I swore to him that I would take care of you. I owe him my life, Miriam. If you want to go back to Jerusalem, then I have to go with you."

Miriam's legs gave way, and she sank to the ground in a heap. "Abba . . ." she wept. "I want my abba." She was too young to be facing such tragedy. Joshua felt a wave of pity for this sad little urchin. He crouched beside her.

"Please come with us, Miriam," he said gently. "Your father wanted you to have a better life. That's why he agreed to help us."

"Yes, please, Miriam," Jerimoth said. "Think of your brothers."

She dried her tears with dusty hands, leaving streaks of dirt on her face. "All right," she said at last.

"Get in the cart, Joshua," Jerimoth said. "I'll divide everyone into three traveling groups, like you planned."

All at once, the shock and trauma of the day caught up with Joshua. He felt so shaky and weak-kneed that Jerimoth had to help him into the cart. He lay alone in the cramped darkness, covered with all the worldly goods they possessed, wondering why life no longer made any sense.

Yahweh was supposed to guard the steps of those who loved Him. He was supposed to reward the righteous and punish the wicked. A week ago it had all seemed true. A week ago life had made sense. Now the world was spinning out of Yahweh's control.

Joshua's best friend had turned against him for no reason. His father, grandfather, and sister were all dead — three innocent people. Joshua had killed three more innocent people today. His family was destitute and fleeing for their lives. Where was Yahweh in all of this? How many more people would have to die before God set things right again?

The Temple in Jerusalem seemed far away — part of another world of reason and purpose. Away from God, away from His sanctuary, the world was filled with murder and chaos. As the cart jolted down the road toward the border, Joshua wept until he fell into an exhausted sleep.

He awoke again when the cart came to a stop, and he rubbed his swollen eyes. Sunlight no longer filtered through the cracks. He felt the weight on his back growing lighter as the grain and produce were lifted off, then his brother reached in to help him climb out. Joshua could scarcely move. His muscles had grown stiff, like the dried blood on his clothes. Millions of stars filled the night sky.

"Where are we?" he asked.

"In Moab. We're safe, Joshua. All of us."

9

"I want to hear the entire story in your own words," King Manasseh demanded. He glared at the three guards who stood trembling before his throne.

The first soldier drew a shaky breath. "My partner and I were in the marketplace, guarding the woman and her child, when a well-dressed man ran up to us, shouting that he had been robbed. We refused to help him at first, but he was so insistent that I finally decided to chase the thief."

"If you didn't witness this crime, how did you know who you were chasing?"

"I didn't know, Your Majesty."

"Yet you abandoned the conspirator's wife, whom you had been assigned to guard, and ran after an invisible thief?"

"I trusted my partner to keep an eye on her." He glanced accusingly at the soldier beside him.

Manasseh addressed the second guard.

"So. If you had enough sense to stay with your prisoner, how did she get away?"

"Your Majesty, the man who claimed he had been robbed caused a huge scene. In all the excitement someone switched places with her. When I saw her moving away I followed her, but it was the wrong woman."

"And where is this other woman?"

"She vanished, Your Majesty."

"What a pair of fools!" Manasseh shook his head in disgust, then turned to the third guard. "Why did you leave your post?"

"They used the same trick, Your Majesty. I saw two street urchins robbing a very well-dressed man of his silver pouch. My partner and I chased them. The thieves were only boys. I figured we would catch them in no time. My partner caught the smaller one and carried him back to the house. I kept chasing the other kid."

"Did you catch him?"

"No, Your Majesty. He was too quick for me, so I returned to my post." He wiped the sweat from his brow and swallowed. "By the time I got back, my partner was dead. I can't even describe what they did to him. It was inhuman. They also killed the soldier who'd been guarding the back door. Everyone in the house escaped."

"Can you describe any of these terrorists?"

"The same man posed as the robbery victim both times. Dark complexion, silver hair and beard. Some caravan drivers found his body along the road outside of Anathoth. I think my partner must have wounded him — there was blood on his sword. But no one seems to know who the man was."

Manasseh's frustration mounted. "All three of you knew Joshua ben Eliakim. That's why you were assigned to guard his family. Will you swear to me that you didn't see him? That none of you helped him?"

"Yes, we swear!"

"And you found no evidence at all that would identify who was behind this?"

The soldiers exchanged looks. "When we searched the marketplace we found this. It was wrapped inside the woman's head scarf."

"And I found one exactly like it inside the house in Anathoth. It's just an ordinary potsherd, but it has a picture on one side. It looks like some sort of cow or bull. . . ."

All the blood in Manasseh's veins seemed to stop flowing. "Give it to me." He stared down at the drawing of an ox. He had seen it before, countless times. Joshua would scribble the picture in the margins of his notes or doodle it on a clay tablet when he was bored. They had joked that one day they would have the design made into a signet ring.

Manasseh handed it to his brother, seated beside him. "Now do you believe that Joshua is part of this conspiracy?"

"It's Joshua's ox," Amariah murmured.

When he was in control of his emotions again, Manasseh turned back to the three trembling soldiers. "Joshua's nickname is 'Ox.' You were this close to him, and you let him escape. For that, I sentence all three of you to death."

As Manasseh watched the soldiers being dragged away, his fears began multiplying rapidly. Joshua was too clever for him. He had outsmarted Manasseh's best soldiers. Where would he strike next?

"But I don't understand," Amariah said. "Who could have killed those two soldiers? Joshua hated military training. He was almost as bad at combat as I was. He could never kill anyone, especially two armed soldiers."

Manasseh knew his brother was right. But that led to an even more frightening conclusion — someone was helping Joshua. Someone powerful. How could Manasseh win back the advantage?

"Find Zerah ben Abner," he told his chamberlain. "Bring him here to me at once."

"How's your wrist?" Manasseh asked as Zerah bowed before him.

"It's healing well, thank you."

"I need your help, Zerah. I need guidance — a word from God about what I should do. But I can't go to the Temple priests. You were right, they're working for my enemies."

"I would be honored to help you, Your Majesty. What would you like me to do?"

Manasseh hesitated, wary of doing anything that might violate the Torah. He wished he was more confident in his knowledge of the Law, but he had always relied on Joshua to remember the finer points.

"I'm not sure what I should do," he began. "But like King David, I have an enemy. I fear he may be seeking my life."

"I understand, Your Majesty. And you should do the same thing King David did. Invoke God's curse on him."

Manasseh struggled to disguise his shock at such an outrageous suggestion. Beside him, Amariah shifted uncomfortably in his seat. "Who is this man?" Amariah asked. "Why are you listening to him? You shouldn't get involved with this stuff. The Torah says —"

"Excuse me, Prince Amariah, but you've been misled about what the Torah says." Zerah's intense, commanding gaze silenced the prince. "Many of David's psalms are curse formulas. For example, these words: 'May those who seek my life be disgraced and put to shame; may those who plot my ruin be turned back in dismay. May they be like chaff before the wind, with the angel of the Lord driving them away; may their path be dark and slippery, with the angel of the Lord pursuing them.' "

"I don't want any part of this," Amariah said. He started to rise.

"Sit down!" Manasseh ordered. "You'll stay until I tell you to go." He turned to Zerah. "How can I enlist Yahweh's help without going through the Temple priests?"

"I am a priest, Your Majesty. A true priest. I know the curses as well as the high priest does. I will perform the ceremony for you. But I'll need some information first. Do you have something I can write on? I'll need to take notes."

Manasseh felt relieved to receive help against his enemy. Joshua was too clever for him, too formidable a foe to fight alone. He seated Zerah beside him in Eliakim's chair and had parchment and ink brought to him.

"Now, tell me about your enemy, Your Majesty. Start with when he was born."

"He was born in the springtime, in the first month. Just before Passover." Zerah stopped writing and looked up in alarm. "Is something wrong?" Manasseh asked.

"That means he was born under the sign of the ram."

"Is that significant?"

"It might confirm my suspicions, Your Majesty. He might be the promised son Isaiah referred to in his prophecies. You see, Abraham's promised son, Isaac, was also born under the sign of the ram. That's why the ram caught in the thicket could take his place."

Manasseh leaned back on his throne, taking a moment to digest this upsetting news. Had Joshua been educated beside him all these years so that he could usurp his throne? He wondered when they planned for this coup to take place. "What else do you need to know?" he said at last.

"Was he born before or after the spring equinox?"

"Let me think. . . . It must have been after because he was eight days old on the day of the Passover feast. He always bragged that he was circumcised on Passover."

"So he received the sign of the covenant on the day of our national liberation," Zerah mused to himself. "That's more than a co-incidence. That would have been a powerful sign to them. And Passover would have meant a full moon. He would have been born between the equinox and the full moon, two more very powerful signs." He looked up at Manasseh again. "You must understand, Your Majesty, that the position of the moon and stars at the time of his birth are very important omens. Isaiah surely knew all of these mysteries, too. Were there any unusual circumstances surrounding his birth? These would be crucial elements in foretelling his future."

Manasseh felt a wave of dread. He had heard the story of Joshua's birth so many times he had grown sick of it. Now it terrified him. He folded his hands on his lap so Zerah wouldn't see them shaking. "He was born on the day the Assyrians first surrounded Jerusalem. He came almost a month prematurely."

Zerah stopped writing again and stared at Manasseh. "Yet he lived?"

"He lived. That's why he was named Joshua — 'Yahweh saves.' On Passover night he stopped breathing. His father breathed his own life into him."

"Yes, of course. It all fits. Lord Eliakim had powers, too. You did well to eliminate him before he used them against you."

"One more thing, Zerah. Joshua was born backward — feet first."

Zerah laid the parchment on the small table between them. "I won't lie to you, Your Majesty. You are wise to fear this enemy. These are all very powerful omens. Any one of them would be daunting, but in combination . . ." He shook his head in awe. "I may need to enlist the help of my fellow priests. I don't know how to ask this, but in order to invoke God's power on your behalf, we'll need a place to worship."

Deep uneasiness filled Manasseh. "What are you saying? Do you want to use the Temple?"

"No, the sanctuary is under your enemies' control at the moment. We need permission to worship on the high places again."

"Will you be worshiping Yahweh?"

"Yes, of course. But we'll worship Him the way Father Abraham did."

"All right. I'll cancel my father's decree forbidding worship on the high places."

Amariah stared at him. "Manasseh, you can't —"

"Shut up! You have no idea what kind of powers we're up against!" He turned to

212

Zerah again. "Will you need anything else?"

"I'll need something that once belonged to him, something personal."

"The guards can direct you to his house. Take whatever you want out of it. In fact, since I've confiscated all of his family's property, you may move into his house if you want to."

"Thank you, Your Majesty. That's very generous of you. One more thing, though. I'll need to know your enemy's greatest weakness, where he might be most vulnerable to attack with a curse."

"You mean physical weaknesses?"

"We can start with those, yes."

Manasseh smiled as relief flooded through him. "That's easy. He suffers from attacks where he can't catch his breath. He nearly died from such attacks once or twice."

"Good. Then he isn't invincible."

"And there's one other area where he's vulnerable. His family is very important to him. They are very close-knit. He helped his mother, his sister, and his brother escape, along with their families. He snatched them right out of my soldiers' hands."

"Family ties can be a powerful motivator, Your Majesty."

"Yes, but he didn't rescue his younger sister. I have her here in my palace."

Amariah nearly jumped from his seat. "Dinah? You brought Dinah here? Manasseh, why?"

"I've made her my concubine."

Amariah moaned.

"A wise move, Your Majesty. Very wise," Zerah said. "This union with your enemies will be a source of great power for you. It will be difficult for Joshua ben Eliakim to seek the destruction of your heirs if they are also his nephews."

As the sky grew bright with stars, Dinah began to tremble. It was almost time. Manasseh would be here soon. If only she had died with her grandfather.

Dinah knew it was a great sin to kill herself. But surely God would forgive her for not wanting to live this way. This wasn't life — this was torture. All alone, day after day, locked in this room. How long had it been now? She should keep track of the days, making a scratch on the wall like other prisoners did. But every day was the same as the last. The servants brought three meals, the sun rose and set, Manasseh returned.

In all this time, no one had spoken to Dinah. She had begged the servants to say something so she could hear another voice besides her own, but they silently hurried in and out of her room, staring at the floor in fear, eager to leave again. They were as terrified of the king as she was. Manasseh hadn't spoken to her since that first terrible night either. He knew Dinah had grown up in a boisterous family with plenty of noise and laughter and love, and he was trying to break down her resistance with silence. If the torture didn't end soon, Dinah feared she would go insane.

When she peered between the slats of the shutters she could glimpse the world beyond her window, a world of blue sky and white clouds and soaring birds. She knew she was on the second floor of the palace because she recognized King Ahaz's clock tower in the courtyard outside her window. On days when the sun shone she could watch the shadow crawl up and down the spiral stairs. Night would follow when it reached the bottom, and Manasseh would return. If only he would kill her. Then God would welcome her to paradise.

Where was Abba? Didn't he know Manasseh was holding her here? She looked for her father every day among the officials in the palace courtyard below her window, but she never saw him. Dinah was afraid for him. Abba would never allow Manasseh to do this to her. He would die before he would let any harm to come to his children. Either Abba didn't know where she was or something terrible had happened to him.

What would he tell her to do if he were here? Dinah closed her eyes and tried to picture him coming through the door. Abba — so tall and distinguished-looking with the waves of gray in his rumpled hair and beard. He would smile at her and she would see the tender love in his dark eyes. Then he would take her hands in his and kiss the top of her head. *My little Dinah,* he would say. *Hush, now. Don't be afraid.* He would hold her in his arms and calm her fears with words from the Torah, the way he used to do when she was a little girl, frightened by a thunderstorm or the wind or the darkness.

"God will never leave you nor forsake you, Dinah. He is our refuge and strength. Therefore we will not fear, though the earth gives way and the mountains fall into the heart of the sea."

But the earth had given way. Manasseh, the king of Judah, had taken her captive. Dinah was only eighteen, but she would have to stay with him, living in this room for the rest of her life. There was nothing anyone could do.

If she thought about it for too long, despair would swallow her alive. She had to think about her mother. Mama had once been captured, too. Hers had also been a life sentence. But Mama had escaped. Yahweh had helped her. Maybe if Dinah prayed, maybe if her family was also praying, Yahweh would help her escape like Mama had.

Dinah fell to her knees in front of the window seat and cried out to God for help. She was still on her knees when she heard the door being unfastened. Manasseh was here. She dried her eyes and stood up. Praying had calmed her fears, giving her peace and determination. She knew what she must do. She would play Manasseh's game, making him think he had worn her down and won her love. Maybe then he would allow her more freedom. He would remove the locks and allow her to leave the palace. Eventually Yahweh would provide an opening, and she could escape. Tonight she would take the first difficult step toward freedom.

The door opened and Manasseh stepped inside, closing it behind him. Instead of shrinking away from him as she had always done, Dinah walked toward him and bowed in submission. "Good evening, Your Majesty." She tried not to gag on the lump of revulsion in her throat.

When he pulled her into his arms and kissed her, she didn't resist. She allowed her body to relax and circled her arms around him as she returned his kiss. After a moment he released her and held her by the shoulders.

"Do I sense a change in your attitude toward me, Dinah?" He wasn't speaking loudly, but his voice sounded like thunder in the room after a week of silence.

"Yes, my lord," she whispered.

"This is much better, Dinah. Come, let's sit over here and talk for a while." He led her to the couch and sat beside her, holding her hands. His touch made her skin crawl.

Dinah hadn't expected such immediate results from her prayer, but it gave her hope. Yahweh had heard. He would help her.

"Why the sudden change of heart?" he asked.

"I . . . I'm so lonely, my lord. I miss my family."

His face turned cold, his eyes dangerous. "I'm your family now. We're a family — you and I. The Torah says that a man and woman must leave their father and mother and cleave to one another. Do you remember hearing that?"

"Yes, my lord. I'm sorry. I've treated you badly."

"Are you really sorry, Dinah? Prove it. Show me how you feel about me and our new life together." He leaned back against the couch cushions, waiting, a smirk of superiority spread across his face. Once again, Dinah hated him. She saw his wish to control her, to humiliate her. How badly did she want her freedom?

Beyond her shuttered window, the moon and stars beckoned Dinah to break free, to live again. She whispered a silent prayer, then took Manasseh's arrogant face in her hands and kissed him.

10

Miriam knelt beside the river, rubbing soap into the wet cloth, then rubbing it gently against a stone to scrub out the stains. Lady Jerusha knelt beside her, struggling to wring out the swaddling cloths that Miriam had already washed. It was not a task for a rich lady.

"Let me do that for you, Lady Jerusha. You don't need to —"

"That's kind of you, Miriam, but I can do it. I used to be much better at washing clothes, but I'm a little out of practice. It's time I relearned."

It was so hard to believe that Lady Jerusha wasn't a rich lady anymore. In the two weeks since they had arrived in Moab, Jerusha had shown no anger or bitterness over the way her life had suddenly changed. Instead she had joined Miriam in all the work, doing tasks her servants had once done. And Lady Jerusha had been so kind to Miriam, so gentle with her, comforting her after Abba died. She understood Miriam's sorrow. Jerusha had lost her husband, her daughter, and her father-in-law.

Once, Miriam heard Jerusha crying softly in the night and had tried to comfort her in return. "I was thinking of Eliakim," Jerusha said. "I remember how cold his feet always were in the winter when he came home from the palace. I used to let him warm them against mine. It's funny how you remember such simple things about the people you loved."

Miriam understood. She remembered the way Abba's silver hair and beard felt beneath her fingers. He used to tease her when she was a little girl, telling her it was made from real silver. She didn't want to believe that Abba was dead. He had always wandered in and out of Miriam's life unexpectedly, and she had learned not to depend on him too much, never knowing when he would come or go. Now she tried to pretend that he had just gone away again, that he might come back for her at any moment. But she couldn't quite do it. The stain she'd scrubbed from Master Joshua's clothes had been Abba's blood.

With the laundry finished, Miriam waded into the river in her tunic to bathe and wash her hair. Lady Sara was trying to wash Rachel, who squirmed and fussed in the cold water. Miriam had been watching these rich ladies closely, imitating them. She was learning to keep herself bathed and clean, to scrub her hair until it shone, and to comb all the tangles out so it looked pretty. Maybe then Master Joshua would notice her.

Miriam was sorry for the way she had treated him when he'd told her Abba was dead. But she still didn't understand what he'd meant when he'd offered to go back to Jerusalem with her. Should she have done it? Would Joshua really have lived with her and taken care of her? He no longer acted as if he remembered his promise to Abba. He paid no attention to Miriam at all. But Master Joshua had wept when Abba died. That must mean something. She hadn't seen him weep for his own father.

Miriam was glad she had decided to stay with Joshua's family. She wished Lady Jerusha was her mother. She never treated Miriam like a servant but talked to her the same way she talked to Lady Tirza and Lady Sara. Miriam's real mother probably hadn't even discovered she was gone.

Miriam squeezed the water out of her hair as she waded out of the river, then wrapped herself in her new robe. Abba had bought it for her with Master Joshua's money so she could act as a decoy for Lady Sara. It wasn't a rich lady's robe, by any means, but it wasn't one of the ragged hand-me-downs she'd always worn, either. She had never owned a robe as fine as this one and certainly never one that was brand-new.

"Let me help you, Lady Sara," Miriam said. Little Rachel had finally grown accustomed to the cold water, and now she wanted to play in it instead of getting dressed. Miriam had already proven adept at handling the spoiled baby.

"Yes, we should start for home before it gets dark," Jerusha said. Miriam gathered the wet laundry and piled it into a basket. Then she and Jerusha carried it between them as they walked back to the small mud-brick house they'd rented.

Together they hung the laundry up to dry, draping it on the ropes the men had strung outside the house. The lines were always in use, usually draped with long lengths of swaddling cloth that Tirza used to diaper her baby son. He was a colicky child, and Tirza was always exhausted from rocking and nursing him. She was grateful when Miriam offered to wash his clothes.

Through the open window Miriam heard the mumbling, singsong chant of the men as they recited evening prayers. They swayed and bobbed in rhythm as they prayed. Since she had never been to the Temple in Jerusalem, she had never heard such prayers before. Tonight the men were praying to find work. Ever since arriving in Moab they'd spent every day trying to find jobs. So far they'd had no luck. Master Joel had studied to be a priest back home. Miriam wondered why he didn't look for work at one of the many temples here in Heshbon. And Master Joshua had worked for the king of Judah; was there no king in Moab?

By the time Miriam finished hanging laundry, the evening star twinkled above the neighbor's roof. She went inside and began unrolling her bedding. Everyone went to bed as soon as it grew dark, since they couldn't afford oil for the lamps. She stole glimpses of Master Joshua as she worked. The men always closed their eyes when they prayed.

She unrolled Lady Jerusha's mat beside her own, then helped Mattan and Nathan arrange theirs on the opposite side of the room beside Joshua's mat. Jerusha hung a blanket to divide the two sides of the tiny room. This house was much too small for eleven people, but it was all they could afford.

The married couples slept in two cramped storage rooms with curtains hung over their doors for privacy. Miriam envied Sara and Tirza. She saw the tender way their husbands treated them, especially Master Jerimoth. He couldn't help touching Sara's hand or her shoulder whenever he was near her or slipping his arm around her waist, as if he needed to draw an essential nutrient from her in order to live. Was it because of the babies? If Miriam gave Joshua a baby, would he treat her that way, too?

The men finished their prayers and said good night, but Miriam tossed on her pallet for a long time, unable to sleep. She heard the soft voices of the married couples as they talked together in the darkness, and she felt an unbearable loneliness. She wanted to belong to someone — to be held and cherished in the cold, dark night. Is this how her mother had felt? Had the nights been lonely for her, too?

"Miriam, figure out what you want in life and grab it," her mother had once told her. *"Don't wait for good things to come to you because they never will. You have to grab what little happiness you can from this miserable life."*

That's really all Miriam wanted: just a little taste of happiness.

Lady Jerusha was already asleep beside

her. Miriam rose quietly from her pallet and crept across the room past the dividing curtain.

Master Joshua slept on his back with his arms bent above his head. She stood for a moment, gazing down at him, but his face looked no less troubled in sleep than it did when he was awake. *Don't wait,* her mother's voice seemed to say. Miriam knelt and lifted the blanket to lay beside him.

"Miriam . . ."

She whirled around at the sound of her name. Lady Jerusha stood beside the curtain.

"Come back to bed, Miriam," she said gently.

"I . . . I was just making sure he had a blanket." Miriam realized immediately that Jerusha would never believe her, and she was sorry she had compounded her guilt by lying. What would happen to her now? Would Lady Jerusha throw her out of the house? Miriam was so ashamed for getting caught that she wanted to run out of the door and never come back. But the night was cold, the city dark and unfamiliar. Besides, she had no place to go. Shaking with fear, she crept to her mat and lay down again, turning her back to Jerusha.

After a moment, she felt Jerusha's light

touch on her shoulder. "Miriam?"

"I know what you must think of me, Lady Jerusha — that I'm no better than my mother."

"I don't think that at all. I think you're a lonely young woman who just wants someone to hold her and love her."

Miriam began to cry. How had she known?

Jerusha gently rubbed her back. "It's not your fault, Miriam. I'm sure no one ever taught you that what you wanted to do was wrong. But Yahweh's Law says we must not sleep with someone unless we're married to him. Your body is a gift that you will give your husband someday. God wants you to save it for him."

"I thought . . . if I slept with Master Joshua — if I gave him a baby — he would want to marry me."

"If he slept with you, he would have to marry you, that's true. But someday he might resent the way you tricked him into it, and for the rest of his life he might feel trapped. Is that the way you want him to feel about you?"

Miriam shook her head. "Are you going to tell him what happened?"

"Of course not. Nothing happened."

"But you're going to send me away."

"Why would I do that?"

"Because now you know what kind of a person I really am, and you're all so religious and so good and —"

"You're wrong, Miriam, very wrong. I'm not a good person. But I am a forgiven person, and there's a world of difference between the two."

"I don't believe you would ever do anything wrong, Lady Jerusha."

"No? The truth is that for a time I chose to stay alive by living the same kind of life your mother lives."

Miriam whirled around to face her. "I don't believe you. You're nothing like my mother."

"That's because God changed me. He worked two miracles, Miriam. He forgave me for the choices I made, and He gave me a second chance, with a godly husband who loved me, even though he knew how I had lived."

"Master Joshua's father?"

Jerusha nodded, biting her lip. "Miriam, I know how lonely and unloved you must feel right now, especially with your father gone. But Yahweh will be a father to you if you'll let Him. And just like a real father, He will provide for you, give you guidance and advice, and He'll love you more than you've ever been loved in your life. His word promises that if you delight yourself in the Lord, He will give you the desires of your heart."

Miriam stared. "You mean Master Joshua will marry me?"

Jerusha gently brushed a lock of hair off Miriam's face. "When I was not much older than you are, I thought the desire of my heart was a man named Abram — a simple country farmer like my abba. But God knew so much more than I could ever know. And God gave me Eliakim." In the dim light, Miriam saw tears glisten in Jerusha's eyes.

"I think the desire of your heart, Miriam, is to find a husband who loves you and who will stay with you and take care of you for the rest of your life. Am I right?"

Miriam nodded tearfully, remembering all the men who had come and gone in her mother's life, sleeping with her for a time, then disappearing when they grew tired of her. Even Abba hadn't loved Mama enough to marry her and make a home with her.

"Only Yahweh knows whether or not that man is Joshua. You must learn to trust God, Miriam. He will provide what's best for you."

11

Dinah sat on the edge of her bed and wept. She had just vomited her breakfast. Now she knew for certain that she was pregnant.

According to the tiny scratches she'd made on the wall every day, more than a month had passed since Manasseh captured her. All the other signs of pregnancy were there. This bout of morning sickness confirmed her fears.

God of Abraham, why now? Why this?

Her plan to win Manasseh's trust had been going so well. She could move freely through the rooms of the harem but still not beyond them. Her shuttered windows opened now, even though iron bars prevented her from climbing out or jumping to her death. But her greatest achievement had been convincing Manasseh to bring her presents of gold and silver jewelry — earrings, bracelets, necklaces. She hoarded these pieces to use as bribes and to finance her flight to freedom. Yes, everything had been going so well. Until now.

If she didn't find a way to escape before her pregnancy began to show, she would surely be confined to the palace once Manasseh learned of it. But the prospect of escaping within the next few months seemed hopeless.

Dinah had a vague plan to pay a caravan driver to smuggle her out of the city, but she had no idea where she would go after that. Where was the rest of her family? Were any of them still alive? She never saw Abba or Joshua among the nobles and officials milling in the courtyard below her window. She feared they were dead.

Now she was going to have a baby. Manasseh's baby. It was true that she hated him, but there was no doubt in Dinah's mind that this was her baby, too. The child would be part of her family — part of Abba and Mama, part of Jerimoth and Tirza and Joshua, part of Grandpa Hilkiah. She and her baby would escape together somehow and continue her family line. No matter what, she would never allow Manasseh to shape this child into his own image.

As another wave of nausea swept over her, Dinah sank to her knees beside the bed. *God of Abraham . . . please! Show me what to do.*

Help me and my child escape from this terrible place!

Sweat plastered Joshua's tunic to his back and dripped off his forehead. He wiped it out of his eyes with the keffiyeh, which was wrapped around his head, then crouched to tie the bundle of grain he had just cut. His back ached from bending with the sickle all morning, but he couldn't rest until noon. His Moabite employer had taken a risk hiring him without any experience, and Joshua had to prove himself if he hoped to stay on for the threshing after the harvest.

Joshua was still unaccustomed to hard labor. He fell exhausted onto his pallet each night after sunset and never moved until dawn. Then he would rise, say morning prayers with Jerimoth and Joel, and walk the mile and a half to the fields to work. But he was grateful for this grueling struggle for survival. It gave him little time to dwell on why Yahweh had abandoned him and his family.

He glanced over his shoulder toward the far side of the field where the women walked behind the reapers, gleaning the kernels of grain left behind. Jerimoth's wife, Sara, worked slowly after fainting on her first day in the hot sun. Her soft hands were unaccustomed to the sharp, bristly stalks and were already riddled with fine cuts. Beside her, Miriam was able to do twice as much work with her strong back and nimble, work-hardened hands. But the sight that broke Joshua's heart was seeing his mother bending in the field.

"Mama, stay home and help Tirza with the babies," he had begged. She wouldn't listen to him.

"I was born a farmer's daughter," Jerusha said. "I'm not ashamed to work in the fields." But it was difficult for Joshua to imagine his mother as a farmer's daughter. He had known her only as the wealthy palace administrator's wife, gowned and perfumed and seated among the other nobles' wives at palace banquets. She had presided over a busy household of servants who cleaned and cooked and scrubbed clothes for her. To see her on her knees grinding grain between stones or bending in the broiling sun to scavenge for wheat aroused emotions inside Joshua that frightened him: anger, hatred, and the desire for revenge, all directed at Manasseh. Bitterness, resentment, and devastating disillusionment, all directed at God. The painful words of David's psalm had become his unending refrain: *"My God, my God, why have you forsaken me?"*

The workers on either side of Joshua advanced ahead of him. He bent and swished the sickle through the wheat, hurrying to catch up. The dust and chaff made his lungs ache, but he knew he had been fortunate to find any work at all. It had been obvious to all the farmers they had approached that Joel and Jerimoth knew nothing of farm labor. Young and strong from his military training, only Joshua had been deemed fit for hire.

"You concentrate on reestablishing Grandpa's business," he'd told Jerimoth. His brother had poured himself into the task, spending long hours in endless negotiations, plotting business ventures and mergers, angling for a loan on the goods he had in storage in order to purchase more. Joshua had neither the knowledge nor the nerves for the rigors of the marketplace. He was better off earning their daily bread through physical labor until Jerimoth's market risks had time to reap interest. Joshua had faith in his brother. He had to. His faith in God had died with Abba.

Joel, their brother-in-law, had been distraught when he was rejected as a field hand. How would he support his wife and newborn son? Jerimoth had finally set Joel up in business at a small table in the market-place, soliciting work as a scribe. Joel spent his days reading and copying contracts, letters, and other documents for anyone who would hire him. The few pieces of silver he earned helped pay their rent. He was also teaching Nathan and Mattan how to read and write.

Joshua turned around to check on the women again. Mama looked tired but all right. Sara was wilting fast. He worried that she might be pregnant again. Miriam was working hard enough for all of them. The women could rest after tomorrow, on the Sabbath. For Joshua it would be a workday like any other. There were plenty of Moabites willing to work if he didn't. It would be the first time in his life that Joshua had knowingly violated the Torah, but their survival was at stake. He wondered what Abba would have done. *"My God, my God . . . In you our fathers put their trust . . . They cried to you. . . ."*

Finally the foreman signaled to stop work for the noon meal. Joshua wiped his gritty brow again and tossed his sickle onto the pile with the others. He walked stiffly across the field to where the women were laying out their lunch. He made a point of joining them every day to let the other workers know that he was their guardian and protector.

Jerusha walked forward to meet him with a skin of water. For the third time that morning, the words of David's psalm echoed in Joshua's mind: *"You brought me out of the womb; you made me trust in you even at my mother's breast. . . ."* My God . . . why?

"Thanks, Mama."

"You look tired, Joshua." She brushed the dusting of chaff off his beard and eyebrows. It made him look old, gray-haired. He wondered if he reminded her of Abba. Maybe she was using the weariness of hard labor to crush her memories, as well.

Miriam opened the bundle of food and passed barley buns to everyone. "Here, Master Joshua."

"Miriam, I told you not to call me that! Look at me! Do I look like anyone's master?" He regretted his harsh words as soon as he said them, but Miriam didn't seem to mind. As he held out his hand for the bread, she examined the blisters on his palm from gripping the sickle.

"Your blisters have broken open. Do they hurt?" she asked.

"I'll have calluses soon. Then it won't matter." As he took the bread and began to eat, Miriam removed her head covering. He glanced around to see if any Moabites were watching. "Miriam, it's indecent to —" She tore off a narrow strip from one edge. "What are you doing?" he asked her.

"Hold out your hand." For a young girl, she had an insistent way of taking charge that made everyone listen. Joshua held out his hand. Within moments, Miriam had deftly wrapped the cloth around his blistered palm, securing it around his thumb and wrist so it wouldn't slide. As she tied the ends he noticed that her own hands were rough and scratched from the stubble. "Too tight?" she asked him.

"It's fine." He turned away from her and went to sit beside his mother. He avoided Miriam as much as he possibly could. Seeing her reminded him of Maki's death and his own stupid mistakes. Remembering filled him with unmanageable guilt.

When the break ended, Joshua crossed the field again to join the other men. He surveyed the work they had done and calculated how much was left to do — at least three more days' worth, he hoped. When he saw the foreman walking toward him, he felt a wave of uneasiness.

"Can I have a word with you, Jew?" the man asked.

"Yes, my lord." The foreman worked bare-chested like the other Moabites, and his bronzed arms and chest were heavily muscled. He was probably in his mid-thirties, and Joshua had heard that he lived a rough-and-tumble life among his workers, breaking up their fights with his own fists, celebrating with them with strong drink after the harvest. The foreman lived in a modest home on the edge of the landowner's property, overseeing his crops and herds year round. Joshua had never met the rich landowner. He lived in a lavish house in town.

"I notice you eat with those three women every day," the foreman said.

"Yes, we're all one family."

"Is one of them your wife?"

"I'm not married."

"I've been watching the little dark-faced one, the one doing all the work. I'm wondering if she's available."

"To work for you?"

The foreman laughed. "In a manner of speaking. I meant as my concubine."

Hot anger blazed through Joshua at this insult to his family. He choked it back, remembering that his family no longer had stature in anyone's eyes. Besides, if he threw a punch at this brawny man, he would likely end up with several broken bones and a few missing teeth. Joshua needed this job. He must answer shrewdly.

"As you know, my lord, we are Judeans. Our customs are very different from —"

"You're in Moab now, Jew."

"Yes, my lord, that's true. However, our religious beliefs require a contract of marriage before —"

"All right, then, I'll marry the girl. She appeals to me. I'll make any arrangements you want. I'll even see that you're hired for the threshing. After that, the grape harvest. Who knows, as my brother-in-law you could work for me full time."

"But I understood that you were already married, my lord."

The foreman shrugged his burly shoulders. "So? It happens that I am. But I make a good living. I assure you that I can support two wives quite well."

The second insult hit Joshua harder than the first. He wasn't able to afford even one wife, and his own mother had been reduced to gleaning. "I can see that you do well, my lord," he mumbled.

"My first wife has only given me daughters. I would like to have a son."

"With so many beautiful Moabite women, I'm surprised you would choose a foreign wife — and one who is Jewish."

The foreman grinned, and Joshua didn't like the look of it. "I have my reasons for choosing a Jew," he said. "But you haven't answered my question. Is the girl available or not? And at what price?"

Joshua recalled Maki's death grip on his wrist, the strangled plea to take care of Miriam. Right now, Joshua's own future looked pretty hopeless. How could he take care of Miriam? The foreman's offer would certainly give her a better life than gleaning and subsistence in an overcrowded shack, better than the life she had lived in Jerusalem. But she was so young — probably no more than fifteen or sixteen. And so thin. Still, this was an honest offer of marriage, even if it was polygamous.

"I really cannot give you an answer, my lord," Joshua said at last. "My older brother is the head of our family. I will tell him about your offer tonight."

The foreman grinned. "Good. I'll be waiting for his answer."

When the day finally ended, Joshua walked back to town with the women. He ate the simple evening meal of bread and lentils and still felt hungry when he rose from the table. The heavy field labor created an appetite that these meager portions couldn't quite satisfy. Yet the meal would have to suffice. They had three men, four women, and four growing children to feed.

As Joshua experienced true hunger for the first time in his life, he wondered how he had ever taken food for granted. Against his will, he thought of all the lavish meals he had eaten in the palace banquet hall, all the platters heaped with scraps that went to waste. He couldn't remember the last time he had eaten meat. Yes, he could — it was at Yael's house, the night his privileged life had come to an end.

He joined his brother and Joel in one corner of the room to recite evening prayers. Yahweh knew that Joshua wasn't really praying, that he was only reciting memorized words. But the ritual seemed to give comfort to the other two men. Afterward, Joshua told them about the foreman's marriage proposal.

"Is he an honest man? A God-fearing man?" Jerimoth asked.

"We didn't discuss religion," Joshua said. He heard the edge of bitterness in his voice. "He's a Moabite. But he can offer Miriam a better life than we can."

"Do you think her father would have approved of him?"

"I don't know! You knew Maki better than I did! You worked with him every day!"

Jerimoth's brow furrowed with concern. "You're tired, Joshua. Maybe we should discuss this another time."

"No, listen. I'm sorry I lost my temper. But we need to talk now. He's waiting for your answer."

"*My* answer?"

"You're the head of the house now."

Jerimoth sighed and rubbed his eyes. For a moment Joshua glimpsed the enormous strain Jerimoth was under. Joshua's work might be backbreaking, but Jerimoth's was nerve-racking. He was taking heavy financial risks with what little gold and silver they had managed to smuggle out.

"In that case," Jerimoth said at last, "I think we should ask Miriam."

"Ask Miriam? Are you out of your mind?"

"Why?"

"Her father wouldn't ask her opinion! Did Abba ask Tirza's opinion before her betrothal?"

"Actually, your father did ask her," Joel said quietly.

"That's unheard of."

"I know. But your father loved his daughters. Tirza's happiness was important to him."

Joshua turned away to hide his grief at this painful reminder of their father and the

242

love he had lavished on all of them. "Go ahead. Ask Miriam, then," he said.

Jerimoth called her over. Joshua knew she had already heard every word they'd said. In a house this small, it was impossible not to.

"Miriam, you've seen this man Joshua works for?" Jerimoth asked. "You've heard that he has asked to marry you?"

"Yes, I heard."

"What do you wish to do, my child?" She stared at the dirt floor, kneading her hands.

"What about my brothers? Will they come, too?"

"We'll have to talk to this man and come to some sort of agreement about the boys. But as you know, I've grown very fond of Mattan. Both boys have become invaluable to my work in the marketplace. I would hate to lose them. Still, it's up to you, Miriam."

"I . . . I don't know . . ."

"Joshua, can you tell us anything more about this man that might help Miriam decide?" Jerimoth asked.

Joshua couldn't look at either of them. "I should probably tell you that he's already married."

"Married!" Jerimoth shouted.

"Miriam would be his second wife. His first wife has only given him daughters."

243

"Absolutely not!" Jerimoth said. "It's out of the question!"

"Why?" Joshua asked. "He can well afford two wives."

"You may go now, Miriam," Jerimoth said. "I'm sorry we bothered you with this."

"Don't you understand?" Joshua asked. "I'll probably be fired if we turn him down!"

"Then we'll have to trust God for another job."

"That's easy for you to say! You have work!" Joshua strode outside, banging the rickety door behind him. He dodged around the sodden laundry, forever hanging on the line, and sat down on a low step leading out of their yard. The evening breeze felt cool after the stuffy air in the overcrowded house, but it brought the nauseating smell of sewage from the filthy street. These Moabites had worse sanitary habits than the poorest Judeans. Joshua's entire family had been sick from drinking the water at first.

After a few minutes, Joshua heard the door open and close behind him. He didn't turn around. "Go away, Jerimoth. I want to be alone."

"I'm not Jerimoth," his mother said. "May I stay?" She began to knead his aching shoulders. It felt good.

"You heard our discussion?" he asked her.

"Yes, I heard."

"And what do you think Miriam should do?"

"I agree with Jerimoth."

"But how are we going to survive? You know how difficult it was for me to find work!"

"Yes, but you would have this job only until the season ends. Miriam would have to live with this man, and his jealous first wife, for the rest of her life."

"It would be a better life than the one we're giving her."

"Are you so sure of that? You're comparing this life with the one *you* knew."

He whirled to face her. "Well, don't you, Mama? Sometimes everything seems so hopeless that I can barely stand it! I sleep and work, and work and sleep, just so I won't have to think about my old life. But I can't help it — I want it back! All of it! And I want to know why God let me survive when I was a baby, why He called me to a life of service beside the king, why He trained me and prepared me for it, then ripped it all way from me! What did we do to deserve this suffering? What did Abba do that he deserved to die?"

"I understand how you feel, Joshua." His mother had tears in her eyes as she touched his cheek. "You know the story of my life. You know those aren't empty words. I do understand."

He fell into her arms, clinging to her. "I'm sorry, Mama."

"Hang on to Yahweh, Joshua. Cling to Him, just like you're clinging to me. Even in the darkness. Even in the times when it seems like He has forsaken you. Because He hasn't forsaken you. 'Where can I flee from your presence? If I make my bed in the depths, you are there.' That's where we are now — in the depths. But hang on to God, son. That's what all of us must do."

"But why is this happening? I need to know *why*."

"When the Assyrians captured me my suffering seemed pointless, too. But God did have a reason. And I've chosen to trust that He has a reason for this suffering as well. I will thank Him for all that He has given me, not curse Him for all that I've lost."

"But it's so hard to do that."

"Yes, Joshua, it is. But I know that deep in your heart you desire to serve Yahweh. When serving Him meant years of discipline and study and learning, you poured yourself into it willingly. I used to fear that you would ruin your eyesight, reading all those scrolls by lamplight. Now Yahweh has asked you to bend your back all day, cutting grain. Can you do that job for Him with the same willingness? Without letting bitterness and resentment grow in your heart?"

"Why should I bother? Look how God rewarded Abba for serving Him."

"Your father was willing to serve God as an engineer when it meant laboring in a suffocating tunnel. He was willing to serve as secretary of state when it meant being persecuted by Prince Gedaliah and Lord Shebna. He gladly served as palace administrator during the most dangerous time in King Hezekiah's reign, confronting the Assyrians face-to-face. And I know that if God asked Eliakim to die at Manasseh's hands in order to fulfill His purpose, then your father gave his life willingly."

An image of the brutal execution pit came to Joshua's mind, merging with an image of his father's face. No, this time what Yahweh had asked of Abba had been too much. Joshua buried his face in his mother's shoulder. "Mama . . . I miss him so much!"

Jerusha gripped him tightly. "I know, son. I know."

■ ■ ■ ■

PART TWO

■ ■ ■ ■

[Manasseh] did evil in the eyes of the
Lord . . . He rebuilt the high places his
father Hezekiah had destroyed . . .
Manasseh also shed so much innocent
blood that he filled Jerusalem from end to
end. . . .

2 KINGS 21:2–3, 16

12

"Unclear? What do you mean the omens are unclear?" Manasseh stared at the sheep's liver lying in the bloody basin and wished he knew how to read the signs himself. Zerah rinsed the blood off his hands, then dried them on a towel.

"I'm sorry, Your Majesty, but something is blocking our vision."

"Well, can't you remove it? You know I don't like to begin the day until you've read the omens for me."

"Only you can remove the blockage, Your Majesty."

"Stop talking in riddles, Zerah. I have work to do, and I need guidance. Just tell me what the problem is."

Zerah rested his hands on his hips. "Very well. The full picture is blocked because you are controlled by the narrow traditions you grew up with. My priests and I are forced to function with our hands tied."

"But you told me this would work. Before I built this altar, you said I could continue to attend the Temple sacrifices like I've always done, then walk across the courtyard to you for the omens."

"I thought it would work, Your Majesty, but I see now that the old rituals are holding you back from all that God has for you. They're blocking your path to true knowledge and preventing me from guiding you properly."

"I won't give up the daily sacrifices and the feasts, Zerah."

"I'm not asking you to. You don't have to give up anything or change anything — simply move beyond it. You can have all of this and so much more," he said, gesturing broadly.

"That's why you're here. I've already told you I gain more from your daily rituals than I ever did from the other sacrifices. Now you're telling me it's not working?"

"You're still limiting your experience to one mountain, one Temple, one sacrifice," Zerah said. "God is in everyone and everything, not just in this Temple. All is spirit. You must be willing to move beyond this experience and seek the mystical oneness of all things."

"More riddles! What are you talking about?"

"Tell me, do you feel united with God after your daily ritual over there?" Zerah asked, pointing to Yahweh's altar. "Do you really *experience* God?"

"I didn't know I was supposed to experience anything."

"No. You simply do it because you think the Torah says to do it. But isn't the goal of worship to experience union with God?"

"I suppose so," Manasseh said grudgingly.

"Your Majesty, you will never experience that union until you worship God in all of His fullness. Listen, the Torah says, 'God created man in his own image . . . male and female he created them.' If we are made in His image and we are male and female, then God must be both male and female, too. True worship acknowledges both. Authentic worship includes Yahweh's female counterpart."

"Now you're asking me to worship Asherah?" Manasseh asked in astonishment.

"Call her Asherah or call her whatever you want. But those are the words of your own Torah — 'male and female.' You can't deny what Scripture says."

Like most of Zerah's words, these sounded dangerously close to blasphemy. Yet everything Zerah said always contained a familiar ring of truth. The priest confused Manasseh, leaving him afraid to believe his words and equally afraid not to believe them. Manasseh had been told all his life that it was wrong to worship Asherah. Now he didn't know what to think.

"I need proof, Zerah. A sign that you're speaking the truth about Asherah."

"*You* are proof, Your Majesty. Living proof. Your father would only worship Yahweh, and he went for years without a son. After your enemy Joshua was born, they set your mother free from prison to worship Asherah. Nine months later *you* were born. What Yahweh never gave your father, Asherah gave your mother."

A terrible desolation filled Manasseh at the reminder of his mother's sin. Hephzibah had worshiped Asherah. Isaiah had admitted it. But was worshiping Asherah really a sin? If what Zerah said was true, then his mother had merely worshiped God in His fullness.

"Suppose I decided to include Yahweh's female counterpart in my worship. What would I have to do?"

"Your Majesty, you are still too bound by the old ways of thinking. I'm not sure you're ready to hear the truth or accept it."

"Don't patronize me! I wasn't completely brainwashed by the priests."

"All right, but I caution you not to react immediately to what I tell you. Allow yourself time to think about it before you cry blasphemy."

"Get on with it!"

"Very well. Since God is both male and female, the physical union between the sexes symbolizes our union with God. Therefore, it is a sacred sacrament that must be practiced by everyone in order to find oneness with God. Your priests forbid it, naturally, because they want to remain in power. They don't want anyone to find God except through them. So they've filled you with guilt. But can you deny the way you were made? Can you deny your natural instincts and passions? God created us this way. And God saw everything He created and called it 'good.' He intended physical union to be a part of the way we worship Him."

Manasseh struggled to conceal his shock. He'd heard of these ungodly rituals involving male and female prostitutes. "But that's how pagans worship," he said. "The Torah says —"

"No. Only the priestly laws say it's wrong. Abraham had more than one wife. Jacob had at least four women."

Manasseh shook his head. "I'm sorry. I can't absorb all of this."

"That's why I warned you to give it time. But as long as you are already shocked, I may as well tell you the rest of it. True worship involves sacred union with both aspects of God. Male and female. Think about it."

Manasseh suppressed a shudder of revulsion. "Do you expect me to throw out everything I've been taught?"

"Of course not. You can't. Your old worship system was built entirely upon a foundation of guilt: sin, confession, sacrifice. You won't be free until you realize that sin is an illusion created to control you. There is no such thing as sin. Could good exist without evil? Don't we need to experience evil in order to understand good? Don't both good and evil operate inside of you?"

"Of course."

"Then when you deny what's inside you, when you deny what you were created to experience, you live a stunted life, crippled by guilt. Would a loving God expect that? Would He want you to deny the way He created you?"

"I just don't know —"

"You see?" Zerah said. "You have been brainwashed. Name one instance when Abraham offered a sacrifice for sin."

Manasseh tried to think of one, but it seemed like a long time ago that he had studied the Torah with Rabbi Gershom. And he had hated those lessons. The rabbi was too strict, the monotonous laws too boring. He had relied on Joshua to interpret everything for him. Just as his father had relied on the traitorous Eliakim.

"Get rid of the concept of sin, Your Majesty, and you will be free. The priests will have no control over you. The omens won't be blocked by your unbelief, and you will worship God in His fullness."

The more Manasseh thought about it, the more he saw how Isaiah had used guilt to control his father, making him a slave to the Temple rituals, a slave to his prophecies. At once Manasseh's idyllic image of Hezekiah shattered like broken pottery. Instead of seeing him as a strong leader, filled with a matchless faith, he now saw his father as a helpless figure, deceived and deluded by lies, tied to a powerless god who couldn't even grant him a son. All of his life Manasseh had feared not living up to his father's stature; now Zerah offered him a way to rise to even greater heights than Hezekiah.

"Come with me, Zerah," Manasseh said. He strode across the courtyard to where one of the chief priests was tending the altar fire. "Listen to me," he told the priest. "Tell your fellow priests and Levites that from now on Zerah and his priests are in charge of this Temple. He is the new high priest with full authority over everything. All of you will serve him. Do you understand?"

The priest looked at Manasseh in fear and confusion. "We can't do that, Your Majesty. We —"

"But you *will* do it — or die. Along with your wives and your children. And if any of you tries to leave Jerusalem or to shirk your Temple duties, I will hunt you down and destroy you like dogs."

Miriam knelt in the courtyard by the hearth, coaxing the coals into flames to heat a caldron of water for Joshua's bath. The men would be home for dinner soon. Jerimoth and Joel would arrive first and greet their wives and children with kisses. Joshua would soon follow. Miriam always made sure he had a warm bath to soak in and clean clothes to wear. It was what any good wife would do.

Taking care of Joshua the way Tirza and Sara cared for their husbands — washing and mending his clothes, cooking special foods for him, preparing his bath — seemed natural to Miriam. Each time she traced the imprint of his foot in the soft leather of his sandal or smelled the salty, outdoor scent on his clothes, her love for him grew stronger.

She knew that Joshua still struggled with his grief. His suffering seemed so much deeper than that of the others. After living in Moab for nine months, Miriam had yet to see him smile or hear him laugh. But she was certain that one day his sorrow would finally lift, and he would notice all the things she did for him. He would realize how much she meant to him, and he would return her love at last. Finally she and Joshua would be together.

The gate creaked open and Miriam looked up from her work. Joshua walked into the courtyard, looking tired and dusty. She ran to fetch him a drink of water.

"I'm sorry, my lord, but your bath water isn't warm yet," she told him. "I didn't expect you this soon."

"That's all right. I came home early on purpose. I need to talk to you."

Tears of joy sprang to Miriam's eyes. This was the day she had been waiting for. Joshua wanted to talk to her, alone. He stood close to her, his deep voice low and intimate.

"Miriam, you've taken good care of me these past months. I know I don't always remember to say thank you. I hope you don't think I'm ungrateful or that I take you for granted. If it weren't for you, my mother would have to work twice as hard as she does."

"I enjoy taking care of you, my lord." She looked up at him and their eyes met for a moment; then Joshua quickly turned away. She wished she knew what it was that always made him turn from her — shyness, or something else?

"Then you're happy living here?" he asked. "You would like to stay?"

"Of course. This is my home now. Your family is like my own."

"My family is very fond of you." He gazed into the distance, and Miriam glimpsed the suffering in his dark eyes. She felt herself being pulled deeper into his soul. She could help soothe away all the pain if he would let her.

"I wanted to talk to you first, Miriam, before telling the others, because this should really be your decision. I've been saving all the money I've earned for the past few months, and I finally have enough for a dowry. I don't earn a lot, but at least I can afford to support a wife now."

Miriam's heart raced with joy and anticipation. She moved a step closer to him, sensing that any moment he would reach for her. After all these months, she would finally feel his strong arms surrounding her. She would be able to hold his handsome face between her hands and feel the softness of his hair and beard, the way she had when he lay ill with his head in her lap.

"I need you, Miriam," he said. "Yael isn't used to washing clothes or cooking meals. Before I go back to Jerusalem to marry her, I need to know if you would be willing to work for us."

Miriam felt the shock of his unexpected words like a dash of cold water. He couldn't have hurt her more if he had run a knife through her heart. She turned away and sank to her knees to keep from falling, then poked at the fire so he wouldn't see her shame or the hot tears that filled her eyes. What a fool she had been, imagining that he would marry her. He thought of her as his servant. Nothing more.

"Of course I don't expect you to work for nothing," he said. "I'm willing to pay you a fair wage. And I think you'll like Yael. She's a gentle woman, kind and sweet."

Miriam pushed one of the logs deeper into the fire until the flames licked at her hand, burning her. She cried out in pain, letting Joshua think her tears were from the burn on her fingers, not the wound in her heart.

"Are you all right?" he asked.

"It's just a burn. Clumsy of me. If you would like your bath now, the water is hot."

"In a minute. You haven't answered my question. Would you be willing to work for Yael and me?"

Miriam nodded, knowing it was a lie. She wouldn't stay in his house. She couldn't bear to watch him with another woman. A dull pain throbbed behind her eyes from holding back the full force of her tears.

"Thank you, Miriam. And please don't say anything to the others about this yet. I have a few more plans to make before I tell them, all right?"

"Sure."

"You should go put something on your hand. It's hurting you. I can carry my own bath water."

Miriam turned her back to him and walked into the house, her unseeing eyes gazing straight ahead, her feet taking her by memory to the small room where she slept. She and the others had recently moved to a bigger house in a nicer part of town, and until today she had been so excited to have a room of her own that she hadn't cared that it was in the servants' quarters. Now she realized that she wasn't a member of this family. She never would be. Miriam buried her face in her blanket and sobbed.

After a long time, she sat up and dried her tears. She couldn't let the others know what a fool she was, falling in love with a man who would never love her in return. She poured cold water into a basin and splashed some on her face so no one would see that she had been crying, then she looked at herself in the bronze mirror hanging above the basin. Her nose was too big, the beauty mark on her cheek, loathsome. Her hair was plain brown, her skin a dull tan. Yael was kind and gentle and sweet, Joshua had said. Miriam remembered how his voice had softened when he'd spoken Yael's name, and tears sprang to her eyes again.

Miriam couldn't live here anymore. But she had no idea where else to go. Several months ago the Moabite foreman had wanted to marry her. Now she wished she had accepted his offer.

When Miriam heard Jerimoth's voice outside in the courtyard she went to her window and looked out. He, Joel, and her brothers had just arrived home from the marketplace. Mattan walked beside Jerimoth, holding his hand.

"I smell lamb for dinner, Abba," Mattan

said, gazing up at him. Jerimoth smiled and tousled the boy's hair.

"Yes, run and ask your mother if it's ready. I'm starved."

Jerimoth had kept his promise and had become a loving father to Mattan. Miriam's brother no longer resembled a ragged urchin but a strong, healthy six-year-old with a bright future ahead of him. Miriam knew she would have to leave Mattan behind if she went away. It would be cruel to tear him from his new home and the father he had grown to love. But her brothers were the only family Miriam had, and when she thought about leaving them she felt lost.

As she watched, she saw Joshua come outside to greet Jerimoth and Joel. His curly hair was still wet from his bath, and he wore the clothes she had washed and laid out for him. She would find his dirty tunic on the floor near the mikveh where he had dropped it, leaving it for her to pick up. She was only his servant.

Joshua said a few words to Nathan, but there was no warmth between them as there was between Jerimoth and Mattan. Nathan hadn't allowed himself to get close to anyone. He liked studying with Joel and had a remarkable aptitude for numbers, but

Miriam knew Nathan still stole from the other vendors in the marketplace. He did it for the thrill, since there was no longer any need. Miriam worried about him. Nathan wasn't happy unless danger edged his life. What would happen to him if she left? She saw no answer to her dilemma, and she began to cry again.

"Miriam, is something wrong?" She felt Jerusha's hand on her shoulder and quickly wiped her eyes. Over the past nine months, Jerusha had gradually filled the ache inside Miriam that Abba had once filled. Miriam loved Jerusha more than she had loved her own mother. Jerusha always talked to her as they worked together, and she was teaching Miriam the ancient stories of their ancestors, Abraham, Isaac, and Jacob. In return, Miriam listened as Jerusha talked about her husband, Eliakim. Miriam could see how much she missed him, how much she had loved him. But Jerusha's deep faith and trust in God always prevented her grief from overwhelming her. Miriam wondered what it would be like to have faith like Jerusha's, to have a God you could look to in trust, a God you could call "Abba."

"They're tears of joy," Miriam lied. "It makes me so happy to see little Mattan with Jerimoth."

Jerusha pulled Miriam into her arms and held her close. "I love you, my precious daughter. I lost my Dinah, but I thank God for bringing you to me."

13

The innkeeper dropped another log onto the hearth, sending a cloud of smoke and soot into the narrow, windowless room. They filled Joshua's lungs and throat, making his chest hurt when he breathed. He hated this dingy place, but since the foreman of his work crew had invited him here to share a drink after work, he couldn't refuse. The inn's low-beamed ceiling seemed to press down on him, suffocating him. He couldn't wait to finish this conversation and escape into the cool evening air. He sipped his cup of strong wine slowly, hoping the foreman wouldn't notice his distaste.

"I have to admit, Jew, I didn't think you could even lift a brick when you first asked for a job on my construction crew. But you've more than proven yourself in the last few months."

"Thank you, my lord."

"And you're an excellent leader, too. The

men respect you and work hard for you. That's why I've decided to make you my assistant on our next project. And any more of your handy little inventions would be welcome, too."

"I'm very honored, my lord. What is the next project?"

"I've been asked to make some improvements to the temple complex."

Joshua stared down at his drink. After nine months, he still had no answers from God on why He had rejected him, but Joshua wasn't sure he wanted to turn his back on God completely by building a temple dedicated to idols. When he remembered that his father's first building project for King Hezekiah had been repairing Yahweh's Temple, he felt ashamed of what he was considering.

"When would the work start?" he finally asked.

"As soon as this job is finished. Probably early next week. Why? Is there a problem?"

"A small one, my lord. I was planning to get married as soon as we're finished."

"Congratulations! That calls for a toast." The foreman signaled the innkeeper to refill their glasses. What little wine Joshua had drunk was already burning his stomach and making him dizzy, but he allowed his glass to be refilled.

"So," the foreman continued after they had toasted, "you'll need a few days off? A week, maybe, to spend with your new bride?"

"A bit longer, my lord. She lives in Jerusalem. I'll need time to travel there and —"

"Say no more. Take as long as you need. You're welcome to a job with me whenever you return."

"I'm very grateful, my lord."

Joshua knew he would need a steady job in order to provide for Yael. His lifestyle here in Moab still wasn't what she was used to, but he vowed to make something of himself in time. In the past several months he had already worked his way up from a common laborer to assistant foreman and discovered that he was much better suited to construction work than to farming. Joshua had a talent for engineering like his father, and his innovative ideas had already impressed his boss.

His family had moved into a nicer house on the outskirts of Heshbon, and there was room for Yael now. His brother's business was gradually prospering — Jerimoth could probably turn camel dung into gold — and they could afford the larger home in a better area of the city. Jerimoth had urged

Joshua to quit manual labor and do the accounting for his growing business, but Joshua was saving all his earnings for Yael's dowry. He could do Jerimoth's bookkeeping at night now that they had money for lamp oil again.

Joshua was only half listening as the foreman talked on and on about their next job. He had noticed a young man sitting at a table in the corner, and Joshua had been studying him while his boss talked. The light in the inn was too dim to see the man clearly, but he looked familiar to Joshua. He wasn't a Moabite, nor was he a Jew. Joshua would have guessed that he was an Egyptian, except he didn't know any Egyptians. The man's broad face was beardless and dark-skinned, his black hair thick and straight. He was a handsome young man, maybe nineteen or twenty years old, with a muscular build and strong, sturdy limbs. Joshua wondered where he had seen him before.

"Hey, Jew," the foreman said suddenly. "What's so interesting over in that corner? Why do you keep staring over there?" The foreman swiveled around to look where Joshua had been gazing.

"My lord, do you know that man sitting over there in the corner?" Joshua asked. "I don't know why, but he looks very familiar to me."

"He's a regular in this place. Maybe you saw him the last time we were here."

"Who is he?"

"I don't know, but he seems to have plenty of money and plenty of time on his hands. He spends a lot of both right there at that table."

The foreman talked about their work for a while longer, discussing which of their workers they would retain or fire. Joshua was still nursing the same glass of strong wine when his boss finally had enough to drink. Joshua rose to leave with the foreman.

"No, stay and finish your drink," his boss insisted.

When he was gone, Joshua carried his wine over to the table in the corner. "May I sit here?" he asked the familiar-looking stranger.

The young man looked up with glazed eyes. "Go ahead. I won't stop you." His words were slurred, and Joshua saw that he was thoroughly drunk.

"Excuse me for staring, but you look familiar to me," Joshua said. "Have we met before?"

"Beats me."

"What's your name?"

"That's the problem," he said, leaning forward. "I don't have a name."

"Well, where do you live?"

"Most of the time, right here. Although the girls in Asherah's temple know me pretty well, too." He grinned drunkenly, and Joshua was certain that he had seen that smile before, those straight, even teeth. Who was he? It was driving him crazy.

"You're not a Moabite. Are you from Egypt?" Joshua asked.

"Never been there in my life."

Joshua was about to give up and go home when he had a thought. "Have you ever been to Jerusalem?"

The young man's eyes filled with drunken tears. If the fellow was going to get weepy and sentimental, Joshua thought he'd better leave. "Never mind," he said, standing up. "Sorry for bothering you."

"Jerusalem was my home," the stranger said quietly, "but I had to leave."

Joshua sat down again. "Then we do have something in common. It was my home, too." Suddenly Joshua knew why the young man's broad smile and dark face looked so familiar. He did know him.

"You're Lord Shebna's grandson, aren't you?"

"I used to be, but not anymore. The old man deserted me."

"Deserted you? Where did he go?"

Shebna's grandson laughed and reached for his drink, nearly knocking it over. "I couldn't tell you — either Sheol or paradise, depending on how forgiving Yahweh felt that day."

"Lord Shebna is dead?" Joshua asked in surprise.

"Very dead." He slurped his drink noisily.

"I'm sorry. How long ago did he die?"

"Don't ask me. I don't even know what day this is."

"How long after you left Jerusalem was it?"

The young man laughed again, not a real laugh but one that was filled with irony and self-pity. "You should have seen the old man. We took his fancy Egyptian chariot, you know. He drove it like the demons were after him that night. Had to get out of town. Couldn't let King Manasseh arrest him. But when we got here he turned to stone."

Joshua waited for an explanation, but Shebna's grandson seemed to have lost his train of thought. "What do you mean?" Joshua finally asked.

"Huh?"

"You said Shebna turned to stone. What

did you mean?"

"Just like a stone. A statue. Couldn't move, couldn't talk, just lay there looking at me until he finally died. My grandfather had a tomb in Jerusalem, you know. Big, fancy thing with a pyramid on top. Never got to use it. I had to bury him here."

"I'm very sorry about your grandfather. I knew him. He worked with my father for many years."

"Good for him." The man swallowed the last of his drink and looked around for the innkeeper. "I need a refill. Want one?"

"No thank you. I've forgotten your name."

"Hadad."

"Let me walk you home, Hadad. Where do you live?"

"I live in Moab now."

"Great. That helps. Listen, Hadad, there's something I really need to know. Who warned you and Lord Shebna to flee that night?"

Hadad stared at him, bleary-eyed. "Who warned us?"

"Yes. I'm on my way back to Jerusalem soon, and I don't know who I can trust. It would help if I had even one name."

"I used to live in Jerusalem." Hadad's eyes grew moist again. Without asking, Joshua stood and hauled him out of his seat. He started leading him toward the door.

"Wait," Hadad said. "I need a refill. . . ."

"Come with me. I'll get you one." Joshua propelled him forward, half-carrying him through the city streets. Since Hadad couldn't tell Joshua where he lived, Joshua decided to take him to his own house.

"Do I know you?" Hadad asked as he stumbled along.

"I'm Joshua ben Eliakim. I remember you from our military training at the guard tower. You were a few years younger than me. I think you studied with Prince Amariah, didn't you?"

"Amariah was my best friend . . . but a lousy soldier," Hadad said. "The prince couldn't fight a pussycat."

They had no sooner entered the courtyard of Joshua's house when Hadad became sick. Joshua quickly stepped clear of him. Afterward, Hadad sank to the ground and passed out. Joshua was trying to decide what to do with him when Jerimoth came outside.

"What's going on out here, Joshua? Who is this? Why did you bring a drunkard home with you?"

"He's Lord Shebna's grandson."

"I don't care if he's my own grandson, we don't need him vomiting all over our house."

"I need to talk to him when he's sober, Jerimoth. I need to find out who warned him and Lord Shebna to escape from Jerusalem."

"Why? What difference does it make?"

"Because I'm going back there."

"Oh no, you're not. Have you been drinking, too?"

"I'm going back for Yael."

Jerimoth grabbed him by the shoulders and stared hard into his face. "Now you listen to me. This family is finally getting back on our feet again — finally putting the pieces back together and starting a new life here. You'll kill Mama if you go back there. If something happens to you, she'll never get over it."

"Nothing is going to happen to me. I'm going to sneak into the city, talk to Yael's father, give him the dowry I've saved, and bring Yael back here with me."

"No, Joshua. You're not."

"I love her, Jerimoth. She's all I've thought about these past months, the only thing that has kept me sane. You can come home to Sara every night. You can put your life back together because you have all the pieces. But part of me is still in Jerusalem."

"I won't let you do this to Mama."

"I won't tell her where I'm going. I'll say

that I'm traveling to Egypt with one of your caravans."

"I don't think you've thought this through. We have a modest lifestyle here but certainly not what Yael is used to. You're going to ask her to marry a bricklayer? You expect her to give up all her servants and scrub clothes for you down by the river?"

"She'll have Miriam for a servant."

Jerimoth stared at him. "Miriam isn't our servant!"

"Of course she is. Just like her father was."

Jerimoth was about to speak when Hadad moaned and tried to sit up. "Joshua, please get him out of here before he gets sick again," Jerimoth begged.

"In a minute. . . . Look, I don't want to argue with you, Jerimoth. I want to go back for Yael with your blessing. Can't you try to understand how I feel? When we lived in Jerusalem you worked in the marketplace, you sold your cloth, and you came home every night to your family. You still have all of those things. I was raised in the palace, I was educated with the king, I was training for a life in government . . . now I have nothing. I'm the most literate bricklayer in Moab. Am I supposed to marry a Moabite girl? Raise a bunch of halfbreed children? I love Yael!"

"Did you forget that you're still a wanted man? Manasseh has probably offered a nice reward for your head. The first person who recognizes you will have quite an incentive for turning you in. Besides, do you really think Yael's father is going to let her go with you? I know you love her, but you'll be putting both of your lives at risk. If you go back to Jerusalem, you'll be committing suicide."

Before Joshua could reply, Hadad finally managed to sit up. He looked around in a daze, then was sick again.

Jerimoth groaned. "See? I told you to get him out of here. Who's going to clean up this mess?"

"I will," Joshua said quietly. He gathered some rags and drew water from the cistern, then bent to clean up the mess Hadad had made. Jerimoth watched him in silence. The work helped diffuse some of Joshua's anger and frustration. When he finished, he wiped the vomit off Hadad's face and put his own cloak under his head for a pillow. Then he faced his brother again.

"I'm leaving for Jerusalem at the end of the week. Please help me, Jerimoth."

"I should help my own brother commit suicide?"

"No, you should help your brother rescue the woman he loves. I helped you rescue

Sara, remember?"

Jerimoth exhaled loudly. "Yes, yes, of course I remember. It's just that I saw what Manasseh did to Abba. I witnessed his savagery. . . . And I'd never forgive myself if I let him do the same thing to you."

Hadad was still unconscious when it was time for Joshua to leave for work the next morning. He asked the women to watch him and to do their best to keep him there until he came home. But as Joshua labored all morning, he worried that Hadad would disappear before he had a chance to question him. Unless Hadad returned to the same inn, how would Joshua ever find him again?

When it was time for the noon break, Joshua decided to run home and check on him instead of eating his lunch. He found Hadad sitting in a daze in the courtyard where he had spent the night, looking very ill. Miriam was kneading bread in the trough nearby before baking it in the outdoor oven. The tray of food she had given Hadad lay untouched. Joshua crouched beside him.

"How do you feel?" he asked.

"Terrible. But what do you care? Who in blazes are you, anyway?"

"You don't remember talking to me last night?"

"No." Hadad cradled his head and closed his eyes. "I could use a drink."

"Can you answer a question for me first?" Joshua asked.

"Buy me a drink and I'll tell you my whole life story."

"Hadad, who warned you and your grandfather to escape from Jerusalem?"

"Why do you want to know that? You the police or something?"

"Do you remember Lord Eliakim, the palace administrator who worked with your grandfather?"

"Sure."

"I'm his son Joshua."

Hadad laughed. "No, you're not. Joshua was a pale, skinny kid who hung around with King Manasseh. Kind of sickly-looking."

"Yes, that's me."

Hadad stared at him, squinting as if it hurt his head to concentrate. "Never. You're as brown as a Moabite and built like a slave-laborer."

"That's because I've been working like one ever since I escaped. But I assure you, I am Joshua ben Eliakim. Ask me something and I'll prove it."

"Look, I don't care if you're King Manasseh himself. I'm leaving now." Hadad tried to stand, but Joshua forced him down again.

"Wait. First tell me who helped you escape."

"I don't remember."

"Miriam, find me a piece of rope," Joshua ordered. She dropped the dough and disappeared into the house, emerging a moment later with an extra piece of clothesline. Hadad was moving and thinking too slowly to react before Joshua pinned him to the ground and tied his hands and feet.

"Hey! What do you think you're doing?"

"Making sure you stay here until I get home from work. Maybe your memory will improve by then." Joshua grabbed the food Miriam had set out for Hadad and gulped it down, then set off at a trot to make it back to work on time.

"Help!" Hadad cried. "Somebody help me!"

Oh no, Miriam thought. *Not this again.* She tried to ignore him as she finished baking the bread, but he was making too much noise. It would be a long time until Joshua came home from work this evening. She couldn't have this stranger yelling for help the entire time. She slid the last loaf into the oven and went over to sit beside him.

"Would you like something to eat?" she asked.

"No, you stupid girl. I would like you to untie me."

Miriam bristled. "Calling me a stupid girl is hardly going to win my sympathy. My name is Miriam. What's yours?"

"Hadad."

" 'Fierce'? You don't look very fierce to me. You look like a drunkard, and you smell like one, too. I should know; I've seen enough of them."

"But I'm a wealthy drunkard, and I'll pay you very well if you untie me. Do you know that your boss is a madman?"

"Why don't you just tell him who helped you escape?" Miriam asked. "Then he'll let you go free."

"Because I don't remember. I was drunk the night we escaped."

"Well, maybe if you think about it really hard, it will come back to you."

"It hurts too much to think," he said, closing his eyes. "I need a drink."

"I'll get you some water." She started to stand.

"No," Hadad moaned, "not water. I need a real drink."

"We don't have anything else," she said with a shrug. She sat down beside him again. "Look, why don't you tell me every-thing you do remember."

"Then you'll untie me?"

"Yes."

Hadad sighed and closed his eyes. "I was mad at my grandfather that night. We had a big fight, so I went out and got drunk."

"Do you remember what you fought about?"

"My name. The fact that I don't have one."

"I thought you said your name was Hadad."

"Not that name, you stupid girl — an ancestry, forefathers. I don't have a name because I'm illegitimate. My parents were never married."

Miriam felt her cheeks grow hot, as if she had opened the oven door. "Is that such a bad thing?" she asked. "Not having a name?"

"It is if you want to make something of your life — hold a position of honor and authority or marry into a respectable fam-ily."

Like Joshua's family. Miriam looked down at her rough, workworn hands. She was il-legitimate, too. No wonder Joshua thought of her as a servant. "I see," she mumbled.

"No, you don't. It was all my grandfather's fault. That's why I was so furious with him. He never married his concubine. So my father never had a chance in life, either. He died in a drunken brawl when I was five years old. I barely remember him. But my grandfather was this big-deal palace official. Worked for King Hezekiah. He was getting old, and he wanted to make amends for all the mistakes he had made in his life, so he took me in. I was his penance, his pity-project. He raised me in the palace. Educated me . . ."

"It sounds like a nice life," Miriam said, remembering her own life.

"It was. Until I started getting interested in women. That's when I learned that all of the noblemen's beautiful daughters were off limits to me because I didn't have a name."

"What about your grandfather's name?"

"Yeah — what about it! That would have done the trick, all right. Every nobleman in Jerusalem would have lined up for a chance to marry his daughter to Lord Shebna's grandson. He was the secretary of state! But the stubborn old man wouldn't do it. He refused to legally adopt me."

"Why?"

"Because then he wouldn't have anything to hold over my head, stupid. He told me, 'I am not pleased with the way you live your life, Hadad.' He wanted me to study harder. Drink less. Said I needed to *prove* myself first. I told him he could go to Sheol for all I cared."

"And you call *me* stupid?" Miriam asked. "You couldn't have wanted a name very badly or you would have done what he asked."

Hadad glared at her. He looked as if he would have slapped her if his hands had been free. "You're sure an impudent little thing, aren't you, girl?"

"I told you, my name is Miriam."

"Well, you certainly live up to your name — bitter and rebellious."

"My mother was bitter for having me. She thought that having a baby would make my father marry her, but it didn't."

"In that case, you should have a little more understanding for how I feel."

"No, I don't. Because I never had a wealthy grandfather to look after me and educate me. I wasn't offered any advantages like that. If I had been, believe me, I wouldn't have thrown them back in his face."

Hadad looked away, momentarily subdued by her outburst. "Well, it doesn't matter anymore. My grandfather is dead."

"I'm sorry."

"Me too. And not just because he never had a chance to adopt me. He was a decent man underneath all his stubbornness. Brilliant, too. He educated King Hezekiah and served as his advisor in the palace. He could have taught me a lot if I hadn't screwed up."

"It seems to me you're still screwing up."

Hadad's face filled with rage. He lunged at Miriam as if forgetting he was tied up, and nearly fell over. "You wouldn't be this outspoken if my hands were free!" he shouted.

"Well, it's true. You are still messing up. You've been lying here drunk all night and hung over all morning. Is that the only thing you can find to do with your life?"

"I don't have a life, you stupid girl. We had to flee Jerusalem or die. I left my life behind."

"So did Master Jerimoth and Master Joshua, but they've started all over again. Don't you ever work?"

"Why should I work? My grandfather smuggled out a ton of gold. Heaven knows, he never spent anything he earned on himself or his family. I figure he owes me at least that much."

"So you're going to get drunk every day and live off his money for the rest of your life?"

"Why not?"

"You said your grandfather was a decent man? Then it's a good thing he never gave you his name if this is how you've decided to live."

Miriam stood and went to take the bread out of the oven, leaving Hadad to shout curses at her as he struggled to free himself.

Joshua raced home after work, anxious to see if Hadad had remembered anything. He found him where he had left him, looking subdued and very hung over.

"It's no use," Hadad said, groaning. "I just don't remember anything. The last thing I recall of Jerusalem is fighting with my grandfather. I was drunk. He must have thrown me into the back of his chariot the night we left. I woke up here in Moab."

"But you told me last night that you remembered the ride. You said Shebna drove like the demons were after him."

"I did? Well, give me a drink and maybe I'll remember some more."

Joshua's frustration mounted. "Try to think, Hadad."

"I'm tired of thinking! Your servant girl has been badgering me about it all day!"

"Miriam has?" Joshua asked in surprise.

"Yes. She's sure an insolent little thing.

I'll bet the only reason you put up with her is because she's pretty."

"I don't find Miriam attractive," Joshua said. "Her mother was a prostitute. Listen, I'm going back to Jerusalem for my fianceé in a few days. That's why I was hoping you could give me the name of someone who would help me."

"I can't even remember what happened yesterday, let alone nine months ago," Hadad said. Joshua sighed and crouched beside him to untie his hands. "You're letting me go?" Hadad asked.

"I'm sorry for holding you prisoner all day, but I'll be taking a huge risk when I go back, and I was hoping to find at least one ally in Judah. I'm leaving at the end of this week. If you suddenly remember something, will you come back and tell me?"

"Sure. But I think you're insane to go back there. She must be some woman."

"Yes. She is." The thought of Yael made Joshua more determined than ever to rescue her and marry her, regardless of the danger.

"Do you want a word of advice?" Hadad asked. "Go back as a Moabite."

"What do you mean?"

"You've changed a lot in the last few months. You've put on muscle. You're not just pale skin and bones anymore. I didn't recognize you. So take the masquerade one step further. Cut your hair and beard like the Moabites do. You're so brown from the sun, you'll look just like one."

"But the Torah forbids us to cut the hair off the sides of our heads or clip the edges off our beards like the pagans do."

"True. And they would never expect Eliakim's son to violate the Torah, would they?"

"No, I guess they wouldn't." Joshua thought about how he had already been violating the Torah — working on the Sabbath, eating with pagans, planning to build a temple dedicated to idols. He felt ashamed.

"He's right, you know." Joshua whirled around at the sound of his brother's voice. He hadn't heard Jerimoth come out to the courtyard. "Your hair will grow back once you return here safe and sound," Jerimoth continued. "I think it's a good suggestion, Joshua. I can use my connections to get you a job with a Moabite caravan traveling to Jerusalem. It will be a perfect disguise."

Jerimoth's offer moved Joshua. For a moment he couldn't speak. "You're going to help me, then?" he asked.

"Of course. You're my brother."

14

Dinah screamed and writhed in pain. "I can't go on!" she cried. "I can't!" She had labored for hours, but the baby refused to come. She had never imagined such relentless agony, such unbearable suffering. The midwives and royal physicians hovered around her bed telling her what to do, yet she felt utterly alone. No one soothed her or held her hand. She wanted her mother.

"You're fighting against us, my lady," one of the midwives told her. "You're resisting the birth. Don't you want this baby to be born?"

Dinah didn't know the answer. The child had been conceived in violence, fathered by a man she hated, a symbol of Manasseh's mastery and ownership of her. And she had resented her pregnancy at first because it prevented her escape. Maybe she didn't want this baby to be born.

But no, the child belonged to her, too. He

was part of her, part of Mama and Abba. She just wanted the pain to end.

"Push!" the midwife told her. Dinah cried out as her body strained to force the baby from her womb. In a terrible burst of burning pain, it was finally over.

"It's a boy! A son!" someone cried out. "The royal heir has been born!"

Above the bustle of activity, Dinah heard her baby crying. "Let me see him," she begged. "He's mine." But the royal physician blocked her view as he bent to sever the umbilical cord. When he finished, the child was whisked away, no longer hers.

"The king has a son!" the midwife announced triumphantly.

Dinah lay back, exhausted and shivering, as the physicians turned all their attention to her son. Her role had ended. She didn't matter. "He's *my* son," she wept. "Please, let me hold my son." The midwife wrapped a blanket around Dinah, ignoring her pleas. Dinah closed her eyes and cried until she finally drifted to sleep.

She didn't know how long she had dozed, but the Temple shofars awakened her as they trumpeted the news: King Manasseh had a son.

"He isn't Manasseh's son," she murmured. "He's mine."

The midwife returned after Dinah awakened. "Would you like something to eat, my lady?"

"I want to see my baby. Bring him to me. He must be hungry."

"The wet nurse has already fed him."

"But that's my job!"

"No, my lady. Your job is to have more sons. That won't happen if you nurse him."

"I'm his mother! I want to take care of him!"

"You are the mother of the king's heir. The baby has dozens of servants to take care of him."

Dinah kicked the covers off and tried to get up. "I labored all day and night for him. I'm going to hold my baby!"

"No, my lady. Lie down. You'll injure yourself."

"Then bring him to me." She lay back against the cushions as the midwife hurried from the room. Dinah hoped she would bring him. She was much too weak to walk to the nursery by herself. Before long, the woman returned, carrying a small bundle. She hesitated for a moment, then laid the baby in Dinah's arms.

Dinah loved her son the moment she saw him. He was so tiny and precious, a perfect little boy. She brushed her lips against his soft, black hair and smelled his sweet baby scent. She had been so afraid he would look like Manasseh, but she saw no resemblance at all. The baby's complexion was pink, his wrinkled face still a little squashed from his struggle to be born. She wondered what Manasseh would name him.

"I'll call you Naphtali — my struggle," she whispered to him. She lifted his hand and kissed his tiny fingers. One day he would be the king and wield a scepter in that little hand. The royal blood of King David flowed through his veins.

"Is that your destiny, my little one? Will you be the king one day?" If she escaped with him, he would be just an ordinary man. Was it wrong to take Naphtali away from his future throne? Besides, where could they go? How would they live? Would Manasseh ever stop pursuing them, searching for his firstborn son? But maybe it was a greater wrong to leave him here for Manasseh to raise. Dinah felt so confused, so lost. Naphtali was the only family she had left.

A few minutes later the midwife returned. "Let me take him, my lady. You need to rest."

She kissed his forehead, holding him close. "Sleep well, little Naphtali," she whispered. "Grow strong."

Hadad went straight to the inn to get drunk again as soon as he left Joshua's house. It was the only way to make the pain go away. Why did Joshua have to stir up all those memories of his grandfather again? Hadad had been trying so hard to erase them all, especially the ones of their last night together in Jerusalem.

His grandfather had found out where Hadad had been spending his evenings when he should have been studying. Shebna had stood in the doorway to Hadad's room with his arms folded across his chest, his face revealing his anger and deep disappointment.

"There is something much more important than intellect or ancestry," Shebna had told him, "and that is moral integrity. Right now, you lack it. I will not give you my name so that you can contaminate it with filth like your father did."

Then came the memory Hadad wanted most to forget. "I hate you, old man!" he had shouted. "Why don't you admit it — you hate me, too!"

The anger on Shebna's face had transformed to sorrow. He lowered his head, speaking so softly Hadad had barely heard him. "No, I love you, Hadad. That is why I care enough to discipline you."

In the fifteen years they had lived together, his grandfather had never told Hadad that he loved him. But Hadad didn't respond to his grandfather; instead he had gone out to get drunk.

He wished he knew if Shebna had been able to hear him after he suffered his stroke. Hadad had tried to tell his grandfather that he didn't hate him, that he loved him, too. He'd begged Yahweh not to let Shebna die, to give him another chance to make things right. But he never got it.

After leaving Joshua, Hadad went on a drinking binge for the next few days to chase away the memories. In his sober moments, he wished he could remember something that would help Joshua. The man was insane to return to Jerusalem. He was going to get himself killed. At times he thought of the sharp-tongued servant girl, Miriam. She had asked him why he didn't make something of his life. But Hadad knew it was too late to change. He no longer needed to earn a good name. The only person he wanted acceptance from was dead.

And then, just as it seemed he was firmly mired in a life of drunken stupor, glimpses of his last night in Jerusalem returned.

"King Manasseh has gone crazy," his grandfather had said as he'd gathered their possessions that last night. *"We will not wait for the outcome of Eliakim's trial."*

Shebna had been a smart man, a survivor of palace intrigue and upheaval. As soon as he'd heard that Isaiah and Eliakim were in prison, he'd ordered Hadad to harness the horses to his chariot. They had left late that night.

And suddenly Hadad remembered who had warned them. He lifted his head from the table and looked around for the innkeeper, signaling to him. The man hurried over. Hadad was his best customer.

"Yes? You would like more wine?" the innkeeper asked. "I see that your cup is empty."

"What day is it?" Hadad asked.

"The last day of the week."

Hadad saw by the pale light coming through the open door that it was very early in the morning. He had slept at this table all night. With his head pounding like hammer blows, he pulled himself to his feet and laid a pile of silver on the table for the innkeeper. Then he stumbled through the door and down the street toward Joshua's house, hoping he wasn't too late.

Hadad never would have recognized Joshua when he met him in the street if Joshua hadn't been walking with his older brother. He had not only squared off his beard and trimmed his hair and sideburns, but he wore a band of cloth tied around his head and a sleeveless Moabite laborer's tunic, open to his waist. It revealed his strong chest and shoulders, bronzed by the sun. He had even tied a Moabite amulet around his neck. King Manasseh himself wouldn't have recognized him.

"Hadad!" Joshua shouted when he saw him. The sound echoed painfully through Hadad's head. Joshua gripped his shoulders to steady him. "Did you remember something?"

"Yes. I know who warned us that your father and Isaiah had been arrested. It was Prince Amariah."

King Manasseh heard the babble of petitioners' voices as they waited outside his throne room, but the responsibility of making so many important decisions no longer worried him. The omens had spoken favorably that morning; the guidance he had received from the starry hosts had been clear. He was ready to pronounce his judgments.

Zerah sat beside the king, dressed in the high priest's garments. The palace administrator's sash and keys were fastened across his shoulder. "Your Majesty, before we begin, may I speak with you alone for a moment?" Zerah glanced meaningfully at Amariah, seated on the king's left-hand side.

Manasseh guessed that Zerah wanted to discuss something religious. They both knew that the king's brother didn't agree with Zerah's new methods of worship. Amariah had argued with Manasseh about all the changes at first — the shrines on the high places, the altar for divination, the Asherah pole — but then Amariah had suddenly stopped arguing and withdrawn into himself.

"You're excused, Amariah," Manasseh told him.

"I'll be in my rooms if you need me." Amariah's shoulders were slumped as he shuffled from the throne room.

"I'm still worried about him," Manasseh said when he and Zerah were alone. "He's doing an adequate job as secretary of state, but he lacks enthusiasm for his work. He lacks enthusiasm for anything."

Zerah leaned back in his seat and combed his fingers through his woolly beard. "Don't worry. He's harmless. My people have been watching him for months now, and he's not involved in any conspiracies or rebellions. I think he's a coward, if you want to know the truth. He cries out in his sleep sometimes."

Manasseh frowned. "How closely do you watch him?"

"I do what needs to be done, Your Majesty. But I don't want to discuss Prince Amariah. He'll come around to our way of thinking eventually. It's you I'm concerned about."

A ripple of fear crawled up Manasseh's spine. Dread seemed to stalk him, but he didn't know why. "What's wrong?"

"As your priest, it's my job to intercede for you with God, to tell you how to stay in His favor. You don't have to do what I tell you, of course, but it's my duty to keep you informed." Zerah's startling brows arched meaningfully. "It concerns your son. Your firstborn. If you want power over your enemies and the patronage of God —"

"What are you saying? You're not going to tell me to sacrifice my son!" Manasseh stared at Zerah, horrified. This time he had gone too far.

"Not *sacrifice* him, Your Majesty. *Offer* him. There is a huge difference between the two. Offering Isaac was the defining moment in Abraham's life. God said, 'Now I know that you fear God, because you have not withheld from me your son, your only son.' This offering is the most awe-inspiring act of faith a man can make. And because Abraham was obedient, God said, 'I will surely bless you and make your descendants as numerous as the stars in the sky . . . Your descendants will take possession of the cities of their enemies.' Isn't that what you want, Your Majesty?"

Once again Manasseh felt as if Zerah had backed him into a corner. He was terrified to do what Zerah said and terrified not to. He couldn't deny the fact that his reign had been blessed since he'd started following Zerah's advice. And no disasters had struck him for deviating from the Torah, as he'd been taught to expect. But offering his firstborn seemed like too much to swallow.

"I can't forget my father's horror of child sacrifice," Manasseh said. "He condemned people to death for offering their sons. And he hated my grandfather for offering his sons to Molech."

"But don't forget, your father was offered and redeemed, just as Isaac was. God accepted King Ahaz's offering and blessed his reign with peace. Under Ahaz, our nation never knew the warfare we experienced during your father's reign."

"But the Torah clearly says not to do it."

"Are you certain of that, Your Majesty? I brought a Torah scroll with me so I could show you what it says. First, let me read about Abraham: 'Then God said, "Take your son, your only son . . . Sacrifice him as a burnt offering.' " You see? It was God himself who commanded Abraham. God instituted the ritual."

"But I remember reading other places in the Torah where it said —"

"You're right. Child sacrifice is mentioned in many other places. But I think you should read what it says for yourself."

Zerah had placed markers in the Torah scroll. Manasseh opened to them, one after the other, and read:

"Consecrate to me every firstborn male. The firstborn offspring of every womb among the Israelites belongs to me, whether man or animal."

"After the Lord brings you into the land of the Canaanites and gives it to you . . . you are to give over to the Lord the first offspring of every womb."

"Do not hold back your offerings . . . You must give me the firstborn of your sons . . . Let them stay with their mothers for seven days, but give them to me on the eighth day."

"All the firstborn are mine. When I struck down all the firstborn in Egypt, I set apart for myself every firstborn in Israel, whether man or animal. They are to be mine."

"Every firstborn male in Israel, whether man or animal, is mine."

Manasseh stopped reading. "I get the point, Zerah. But I also know that the Law commands us to redeem our sons with silver."

"That verse is found among the rules for the priests and Levites. 'The first offspring of every womb, both man and animal, that is offered to the Lord is yours. . . .' meaning the priests! Doesn't that sound like a contradiction, Your Majesty? God doesn't change His mind. Why would He say in a dozen places that the firstborn are His, then suddenly decide that they belonged to the priests? Tell me, who receives the silver when a firstborn son is redeemed?"

"The priests and Levites do."

"See what I mean? The priests not only profit financially but steal the power and blessings that are supposed to be yours when you offer your firstborn to God."

Manasseh kneaded his forehead with his

fingertips. He felt an ache deep in his stomach, as if fear had hatched from its shell to gnaw at him. "I just don't know if I can do this."

"It's not a disgrace to admit that your faith isn't strong enough, Your Majesty. God gives us the freedom to serve Him or not to serve Him. But do you want power? Do you want to earn God's favor and blessing?"

"Of course."

"Then you must give everything you have to Him in total devotion, like Abraham did. If you do, God will be obligated to you. And don't forget, you have an enemy in Joshua ben Eliakim. Will he offer his firstborn son to Yahweh?"

"Joshua? Never!"

"That gives you an advantage, then, doesn't it? Besides, your son is also his nephew. That gives you an even greater advantage."

"I'll have to think about this," Manasseh mumbled.

"That's fine. But don't forget what you just read — 'Let them stay with their mothers for seven days, but give them to me on the eighth day.' "

Manasseh closed his eyes to try to quell his nausea. "I won't forget."

15

Joshua hadn't realized how homesick he had been for Jerusalem until the caravan started the steep ascent to the city. He gazed at the familiar hills and the gleaming Temple on Mount Zion with a knot of emotion in his throat. He wanted to absorb all the wonderful, familiar sights and sounds, drinking them in like a thirst-crazed man, but he didn't dare. Once they passed through the city gate he had to be careful to keep his head down so no one would recognize him.

He spent the afternoon unloading the caravan goods at their destination in the marketplace. Then, as the day grew late, Joshua found himself anticipating the sound of the Temple shofar, timing it almost to the second by the descent of the sun in the west. When it finally trumpeted, he thought of his father. Going to the Temple had never become routine for Eliakim, and his face would change at the sound of the shofar to a look of joy, expectation, peace. Even on the last evening that Joshua had worshiped with him, his father had gone with anticipation, eager for his appointment with Yahweh.

The special fanfare also announced the beginning of the Sabbath. Joshua had planned this trip so that Yael would have an extra day to get ready before they left Jerusalem.

The other caravan drivers ate their evening meal and settled back with their wineskins, ready to drown out the weariness of their long journey and hard work. They invited Joshua to join them, but it was time for him to go to Amasai the Levite's house. On the Sabbath, his father-in-law would preside over the dinner table for the traditional meal with his family: his wife, his three sons, his daughter, Yael.

Joshua checked to make sure the letter he would deliver to Amasai was still in the pocket of his cloak. The sealed roll of parchment was blank inside, but it would provide an excuse to get Joshua past the servants and face-to-face with Yael's father.

He took a winding route to Amasai's house to make certain he wasn't being followed, approaching the large stone building from the rear. He stood in the shadows, watching the back door for a long time to check for guards. Then he circled around to watch the front. He had expected to see many lamps burning as the family welcomed the Sabbath, but the lights inside the house were few and dim. It almost looked as if no one was home.

When he was certain the house wasn't guarded, Joshua stepped from the shadows and walked toward the door, pulling the roll of parchment from his cloak. He wished he could silence his pounding heart and the rush of fear that surged through his veins. They made it difficult for him to think. It seemed to take a long time for the servants to answer his knock.

When the door finally opened, it wasn't a servant he faced but Yael's oldest brother, Asher. He was only a few years older than Joshua and they had known each other well, but Asher gazed into Joshua's face without recognizing him. "Yes? What is it?" he asked.

"I have a letter for Amasai the Levite." Joshua spoke in Aramaic instead of Hebrew.

"Let me see it." Asher reached for the scroll, but Joshua pulled it away.

"I must give it to Amasai in person."

"He isn't here. I'm his son. I'll make certain he gets it."

"May I wait until he returns?"

"No. Either give it to me or be gone."
Asher started to close the door, but Joshua
wedged his foot inside, preventing him from
shutting it.

"Tell me when Amasai will return."

"First tell me who sent you here."

Joshua saw the fear in Asher's eyes and
realized that their mutual suspicion had created an impasse. He would have to take a
chance and reveal himself. Joshua rested his
hand on his hip, close to the dagger he had
tucked into his belt. "Asher, look at me
carefully," he said in Hebrew. "I'm Joshua,
Eliakim's son."

Asher inhaled sharply. His eyes widened
in surprise. "It *is* you!"

"Is your house still under guard?" Joshua
asked. Asher shook his head. "Then let me
come in."

Asher seemed even more fearful now that
he knew who Joshua was. He stood frozen
in the doorway, dazed, until Joshua grew
tired of waiting and forced his way inside.

Yael. At last he was going to see Yael. She
would be seated at the Sabbath table, finishing her meal. He strode past Asher into the
house, but the dining room was dark, the
table empty. No one else was home. Asher
had closed the front door and followed
Joshua inside.

"Where's Yael? Where's your father?" Joshua asked.

"I guess you haven't heard. My father is dead. King Manasseh executed him, just like he executed your father."

Joshua's heart speeded up. "Was it because of me?"

"Only indirectly. Sit down, Joshua." Asher motioned to a chair and then slumped onto a bench nearby. But Joshua was too tense to sit. "After the king executed your father and Rabbi Isaiah, my father and the high priest were outraged," Asher told him. "Especially when they learned that no one had come to Isaiah's defense. They decided to send Manasseh a message through the liturgy at the Temple. Manasseh executed both of them for it."

"What about Yael?"

"The soldiers almost destroyed this place searching for you. They were convinced that we were hiding you somewhere. They guarded all of us for months, in case you tried to contact us. It looks like they gave up too soon."

A tremor of fear rocked through Joshua. "They didn't hurt Yael, did they?"

"No, but they made her life a living hell — watching her day and night, accusing her of helping you escape, threatening her with prison or worse. After they killed our father, she grew so nervous and fearful we were all afraid she would lose her mind. She wouldn't eat, wouldn't sleep. . . . It was pretty hard on all of us. So my brothers and I finally decided . . . well, we decided that the best thing we could do for her was to have her marry someone else."

Joshua leaned against the wall to keep from falling over as the room tilted. He wanted to cry out but could only utter one word. "Who?"

"Joshua, what difference does it make —"

"Tell me who she married!"

"One of the Levite musicians. Amos."

Joshua knew the man. He was a widower in his thirties with several small children to raise. Joshua had survived the loss of everything else in his life by focusing on his love for Yael. She was the reason he got up in the morning, endured hard labor all day, continued living. She had been the only thing God hadn't taken from him. Now Yael was beyond his reach, as well. Tears of anger and despair sprang to his eyes, but he forced them back. What had he done to deserve this? *My God, my God . . . why?*

Asher rose from his seat and touched Joshua's shoulder. "Listen, I'm sorry. We —"

He twisted away. "Leave me alone!" He needed to flee this house and its memories of Yael, and run as fast and as far as he could, but he had to wait until the strength returned to his shaking limbs. If he tried to walk now, he would fall on his face.

"Joshua, have you seen what King Manasseh has done to this country? Have you seen the abominations?"

Joshua didn't answer. Yael was married to someone else.

"First, the king reopened all the high places for worship," Asher told him. "Then, after he killed my father and the high priest, he wouldn't allow anyone to be ordained in their places. Instead he ordained a new priesthood and a new high priest. None of them are from the tribe of Levi."

Asher's words seemed to swirl around Joshua like a vapor that he couldn't quite grasp. "Why are you telling me this?"

"Joshua, the new priests are Sodomites. The king let them build altars in the Temple courtyard. They brought their sin and pagan worship into Yahweh's Temple. Manasseh is holding all of the real priests and Levites hostage. He's forcing us to perform the daily sacrifices and feast days side by side with his paganism. If we refuse, he says he'll kill all of us and our families."

Joshua shook his head. None of what Asher said was important to him. His life had been irrevocably cut off from this world, and without Yael, none of it seemed real to him anymore. None of it mattered. The room fell silent.

Then Joshua heard a new sound, and he imagined for a moment that it was Yahweh, laughing at him. But it wasn't laughter. It was weeping. Asher had covered his face.

"You can't imagine such darkness, Joshua! He made an Asherah pole. King Manasseh put an Asherah pole in the holy of holies beside the ark of Yahweh!"

Joshua didn't know this King Manasseh. This wasn't his boyhood friend. "Why are you telling me all this?" he asked again. "I don't work for him anymore. I have nothing to do with him."

"Please help us, Joshua. We've all heard how you helped your own family escape. Help us escape, too."

"Where is your God, Asher?" he asked bitterly. "Why doesn't Yahweh help you escape?"

Joshua turned and staggered out of the door. He no longer cared about soldiers or guards as he jogged, unheeding, down the middle of the street. Yael — he had to rescue Yael. They had forced her to marry a man she didn't love. He knew where Amos lived. He sprinted through the streets searching for the house, then pounded on the door until a servant answered. Joshua showed him the sealed letter.

"I have an urgent message for Lady Yael," he said. "Get her." The servant disappeared, leaving Joshua on the doorstep, panting.

It was so hard to breathe. He unsheathed his dagger and held it by his side. Yael loved him, not Amos. He would rescue her from this place and take her back to Moab.

A moment later Amos appeared, alone. He was older and fatter than Joshua remembered. "Yes? What is it — ?"

"The letter is for Yael! *Only* Yael!"

Amos nodded and turned to call behind him. "Yael, dear, please come here for a moment."

Then she was standing in front of him, exactly as Joshua remembered her — the flaming halo of dark red hair, skin like unblemished ivory, warm brown eyes that made his heart tremble.

"Yes?" she said in her soft, familiar voice. She stared at Joshua, but he saw no flicker of recognition in her eyes. Amos draped his arm around her shoulder, protectively.

She was waiting, but Joshua couldn't speak. Then, in a smooth, graceful gesture,

Yael rested her hand on her abdomen, on the perfect little shelf that the baby growing inside her womb had provided. Amos's baby.

Joshua could no longer control his grief. He turned and fled alone into the night.

Joshua ran blindly until his lungs heaved and he could run no longer. When he stopped to figure out where he was, he saw that he wasn't far from the central marketplace. He crept back through the dreary streets to the caravansary, numb and shivery with shock. The other drivers were either asleep or drunk by now and took no notice of him. He found a place to lie down and wadded up his cloak for a pillow, tucking his dagger beneath it.

But Joshua's pain wouldn't allow him to sleep. Like a river in flood stage, his sorrow overflowed its banks, drowning him in deep, black water, engulfing the remaining shreds of his faith. He was finished with God, and God was evidently finished with him. Yahweh had taken everything that mattered away from him. Joshua would never pray again. There was no need to. He had nothing more to say to God.

He couldn't stay in Jerusalem, but he didn't want to go back to Moab. How could he mumble phony prayers with Joel and Jerimoth every morning and evening? How could he bear to live with their happiness? But he didn't want to drown his grief in a glass of wine, either, as Hadad did. Joshua's only option was to continue traveling with this caravan, allowing it to take him wherever it led, wandering the ancient caravan routes through Egypt, Cush, Aram, and Philistia, outrunning his pain. A few hours before dawn, when exhaustion finally won the battle with sorrow, Joshua slept.

Someone shook him awake. "Joshua . . . Joshua, wake up."

His eyes flew open, and he was instantly aware of the fact that he was back in Judah. And that no one should have known his real name. Terror seized him. He had been caught! He grabbed his knife and scrambled to his feet, trying to focus on the shadowy figure who had awakened him. The man drew back in fear.

"Easy, Joshua. It's only me, Asher."

Joshua's heart continued to pound even after he saw that Asher was alone, unarmed. "How did you find me?"

"You were dressed like a Moabite, and this was the only caravan from Moab."

"What do you want?"

"We can't talk here," Asher whispered.

"Follow me."

Joshua remembered Jerimoth's warning that a reward might be offered for his capture. He might be walking into a trap. He braced his legs to run and glanced around, planning his escape route if soldiers suddenly appeared. The main entrances would be guarded. Maybe he could lose his pursuers in the back lanes of the marketplace. But how would he get through the city gates? He didn't have Maki to help him this time. As his heart crashed against his ribs, Joshua's raspy breathing raced to keep pace with it.

"I'm not going anywhere with you, Asher. Tell me what you want."

"It's Rabbi Gershom. He asked to see you."

"You told someone else I was here in Jerusalem?" Joshua's panic soared at the thought of a servant overhearing Asher.

"I only told the rabbi. You know you can trust him, Joshua."

Yes, Joshua knew that he could. Rabbi Gershom, his most demanding instructor, had taught the Torah to him and Manasseh for twelve years. He had demanded excellence, and Joshua had always worked hard to please him. Rabbi Gershom was wise, God-fearing, and exacting, and he could

315

make Joshua feel as if he had done something wrong even when he hadn't. But when Joshua did transgress, such as the time Manasseh had convinced him to skip their lessons and go for a walk, the grave look of disappointment on the rabbi's face had been much worse than any rebuke he might have given. Being ill with a breathing attack afterward seemed like a minor punishment compared to what Joshua deserved. Now, when he remembered what he had done to his hair and beard, his hand flew to his face self-consciously.

"Why didn't the rabbi come here with you?" he asked.

"He can't. He's too weak to walk. He's been bedridden for several months now. He's dying, Joshua."

Rabbi Gershom dying. The words made no sense. Gershom was a huge bear of a man, taller than Joshua's father, with a body like the trunk of an oak tree and thick, hairy arms and legs. Bushy black brows jutted over his dark eyes, eyes that pinned you like hot, iron nails. Even his voice roared, bear-like, as he thundered the words of God's holy Law. Joshua could never imagine Rabbi Gershom too weak to leave his bed. Asher might sooner ask him to imagine the Great Sea going dry.

"Please, Joshua. You would help the rabbi rest in peace."

Joshua realized that they were almost all gone — all the faithful ones of King Hezekiah's generation, the ones who had witnessed Yahweh's miracles: his father, Rabbi Isaiah, King Hezekiah, the high priest, Amasai the Levite, Lord Shebna, Joah the scribe, and now Rabbi Gershom. Who would take their places? Joshua thought of the next generation. Hadad was a drunkard. Asher trembled helplessly behind the walls of his father's house. Joel, the high priest's successor, was in exile, working as a scribe in Moab. Joshua himself labored in foreign fields and temples.

"All right," he finally said. "Lead the way."

A deep uneasiness filled Joshua as he followed Asher up the hill to Gershom's house. He lived just below the king's palace and the Temple Mount, not far from Joshua's old house. Joshua had avoided this part of town, fearing the memories. Flickers of winter lightning flashed in the deserted streets, but it was too far away to hear the answering thunder.

The rabbi's house was dark and shuttered. Asher led the way inside without knocking. A solitary oil lamp burned on a stand beside Rabbi Gershom's bed. He lay propped on

317

cushions with his eyes closed, but he opened them as Joshua entered the room. Joshua recognized the thick brows and gimlet eyes, but they were on the wrong face, the wrong body — on a man half the size of the bear-like Gershom. His dark, swarthy skin was as pale as parchment. Joshua stared, and Gershom stared back, until Joshua realized that the rabbi hadn't recognized him. He touched his sideburns as if he could make them grow back.

"I'm sorry, Rabbi. It's me . . . Joshua ben Eliakim."

"Yes, I see that now. Please, sit down." The rabbi's bed was a thick pallet of straw on the floor, covered with rugs. He motioned to a pile of cushions on the floor beside him, and Joshua sat down, cross-legged. Asher went out, leaving them alone.

"It seems we've traded bodies, young Joshua. You have grown strong and brown, while now I am the one who is thin and pale." He smiled slightly, and Joshua looked away to hide his sudden tears. He had never known Rabbi Gershom to smile, much less attempt a small joke. "So, my son. Now you have come back to us, a changed man."

Joshua cleared his throat. "I came back for my fianceé, but —"

"Asher has told me the story. I'm sorry."

The compassion in Gershom's eyes stunned Joshua more than the smile had. This wasn't the same stern man who had been his teacher for so many years. Gershom was a changed man. He reached for Joshua's hand and covered it with his own huge one. "But even in something as painful as this, Yahweh's will must be accomplished."

Joshua's face hardened at the mention of Yahweh. "I don't know if I believe in God anymore, Rabbi." He didn't care if he shocked Gershom or disappointed him. In fact, he hoped the rabbi would throw him out of the house. He could deal with Gershom's anger, but compassion and understanding from a man who was obviously dying was too painful to endure.

"Of course you believe in Yahweh!" Gershom said. "You wouldn't be this angry with Him if you doubted His existence."

Joshua realized that it was true. He wasn't angry at fate or at circumstances but at a Person — Yahweh. The God his fathers had trusted and worshiped and served. The God who had inexplicably abandoned him.

"I have every right to be angry."

"You're angry, Joshua, because Yahweh's actions don't fit your image of Him. The idol you've made won't do your bidding."

"But the Torah promises that if we observe

God's commandments we will live. 'He whose walk is blameless is kept safe.' My father —"

"Is your idol limited to one verse? Does that sum up all of your beliefs? Don't you see? Yahweh had to destroy your limited image of Him so you would worship Him as the sovereign God. We are put here to do His bidding, not the other way around."

Joshua didn't want to hear any of this. He wanted to leave. But even in the dim lamplight, Gershom's eyes and voice and words had pinioned him, and he couldn't move. The rabbi was forcing Joshua's feet to find their footing, to seek solid ground after floundering in bitterness and uncertainty for so long.

"I understand your anger, son. You have suffered a great deal for one so young. But that only means that Yahweh has a great purpose for your life."

"My life had a purpose before Yahweh abandoned me!"

"Every great man God has used first suffered adversity and seeming abandonment. Think of Jacob, running from Esau's death threats; Joseph, sold into slavery and unjustly imprisoned; Moses, fleeing Pharaoh's palace to tend sheep for forty years; or King David, hiding from Saul's jealous rages. Yahweh deals with our pride and our self-sufficiency through adversity. And, oh yes, my young friend, you had plenty of both. In adversity our intellectual knowledge becomes actual knowledge. You've learned these words . . . say them with me: 'Even though I walk . . .' "

" '. . . Through the valley of the shadow of death,' " Joshua recited, " 'I will fear no evil, for you are with me. . . .' "

"Yes, Joshua. And now that you and I are walking through that valley, we will learn if it is true. Adversity is the testing ground of our faith. God has to risk losing you forever to your anger and bitterness in order to have you for His true son. Anyone can believe and sing praises on the Temple Mount when the sun is shining, but true praise is sung in the darkest valley when the Accuser tells you to curse God for making you suffer so much pain. If you can still praise your Father's goodness, even in the darkness, then you are His son indeed."

Joshua stood, his body rigid with anger. "Then I guess I failed the test. I failed God and I failed you. Yahweh's risk didn't pay off. He *has* lost me!"

Rabbi Gershom laughed out loud. The sound of it — unexpected and unfamiliar

— stunned Joshua. He slid to the floor again.

When the rabbi's laughter ended, he wiped his eyes. "You fail to convince me, Joshua ben Eliakim. You have your faults, but being a quitter was never one of them. I've seen you wrestle with a difficult interpretation of the Law long after your friend Manasseh gave up — working late into the night, wasting gallons of lamp oil, so your father told me. But to give up on Yahweh before He gives you an answer for your suffering? I know you too well."

"You're right! I do have questions for God! Like, why did He allow Abba to die? Abba loved God. He served Him faithfully. Why — ?"

"Hold it. Stop right there." Gershom held up his hand, the stern teacher, once again. "You are not asking a valid question, and so Yahweh is not obligated to answer it."

"I have a right to know why Yahweh allowed my father to die!"

"No, you don't. You have no right at all. What Yahweh asks of your father is Eliakim's business, not yours. Just as it's none of your business why Yahweh has me lying here on a bed of pain, wasting away."

"He was my father!"

"Yes. And so was I."

Joshua clenched his fists, clinging to his anger like a drowning man clings to a plank. It was the only thing that kept him afloat, preventing him from sinking even further into sorrow and loss. God was taking everyone — his father, his grandfather, Yael, and now Rabbi Gershom. "I'm not supposed to ask why?" he said, his voice shaking.

"You may certainly question Yahweh, but ask the right questions, Joshua. Ask Him what He wants to teach you through this suffering. Ask which of your faults, like pride or self-sufficiency or self-righteousness, He's trying to purge from you. Ask which of His eternal qualities, like love and compassion and forgiveness, He wants to burn into your heart. Yes, go ahead, ask questions! Ask why He gave you the talents and gifts that He did — your excellent mind, your ability to lead others. Ask Him what He wants you to do with your life.

"Your friend Manasseh has been asking the wrong questions, as well. He also wanted to know why God allowed his father to die after all the good things Hezekiah had done. Yahweh longed to use Manasseh's grief to draw him to himself, to teach Manasseh to lean on Him as he had once leaned on his father. But Manasseh wanted easy answers.

He didn't want to wrestle with God, and so he answered the questions himself. He decided that Isaiah and your father had killed King Hezekiah. Now sin and bloodshed and suffering have multiplied from Manasseh's mistake. And he's still looking for easy answers. Instead of asking God how he should live each day, he's asking sorcerers and mediums what his future is going to be. Have you seen what King Manasseh has done to our nation?"

"I can't move around freely, Rabbi. It isn't safe."

"Manasseh practices all the sins of his grandfather, King Ahaz: idolatry, witchcraft, divination, sorcery. Sometimes I think, this can't be Hezekiah's son! How devastated that godly man would be if he saw the evil in his child's heart!"

Joshua choked back his shame. What would Abba say if he saw the hatred and bitterness in his son's heart? Joshua leaned his elbows on his thighs and rested his forehead in his hands. "What do you expect from me, Rabbi? Manasseh won't listen to me anymore."

"The Torah says, 'Can a corrupt throne be allied with you — one that brings on misery by its decrees? They band together against the righteous and condemn the innocent to death.' Earlier the psalmist also asks this question, 'Who will rise up for me against the wicked? Who will take a stand for me against evildoers?' "

"You expect me to oppose the king? How? I can't undo all the evil Manasseh has done. What do you want from me?"

"There's a scroll on that table over there. Can you reach it? Yes, that one. Now, unroll it and read it to me."

Joshua removed the linen covering and unrolled the scroll, recognizing the precise script of the Temple scribes. But it was a long scroll, much longer than any of the books of the Torah. He found the beginning and read, " 'The vision concerning Judah and Jerusalem that Isaiah son of Amoz saw during the reigns of Uzziah, Jotham, Ahaz and Hezekiah, kings of Judah —' " He stopped in amazement. "These are Isaiah's prophecies?"

"Yes. An entire lifetime of oracles. A few years ago Isaiah asked the scribes to make a copy of his original scrolls for safekeeping. I want you to take it with you when you leave Jerusalem."

"But why? What am I supposed to do with it?"

"Manasseh confiscated all of Isaiah's original writings. Keep this copy safe until all this madness ends."

"And then what?"

"A valid question. I expect Yahweh will tell you if you ask Him." Joshua laid the scroll on the bed beside the rabbi. "I can't take this. I'm not going back to Moab. I'm leaving for Egypt tomorrow with the caravan."

"So. You've decided to run away from God instead of running to Him?"

"I've tried, Rabbi! I've cried out to God for answers! He hasn't given me any!"

"With all that you've suffered, I suspect that your own cries of pain are still drowning out the voice of God. He's waiting for you to let Him shine the light of His presence in the darkness of your fear and grief. But you're not desperate for that light yet."

"You think I enjoy this suffering?"

"No, but you're still looking for a way to cure it yourself. You thought that coming back and marrying Yael would make you happy again, and it might have for a while. But the only thing that will ever make you feel whole again is a sense of Yahweh's presence in your life."

"He abandoned me, Rabbi, not the other way around!"

"That's not quite true. How earnestly did you seek God's presence before all this happened, when you had your old life?"

"I read the Torah, I prayed, I kept all the sacrifices, obeyed all the laws —"

Gershom's eyes pinned Joshua. "Did you have a daily sense of His presence? Or did you live in the afterglow of your father's and grandfather's relationships with God? Think about it. They brought an awareness of God into your life. They were the ones who impressed His commandments on your heart and talked about them when you sat at home and when you walked along, when you lay down and when you got up. When did you ever have to seek Yahweh's face before this tragedy happened? In whose strength were you living: God's or yours?"

Joshua rubbed his eyes. He was tired of this discussion. It was almost dawn, and he had a long journey ahead. He didn't want to hear any more. But the rabbi showed no sign of letting up on him.

"King David knew suffering like yours, Joshua. David's father-in-law gave his wife to another man, too. But David knew the secret of conquering despair. Of all the things he could have asked for — relief from his enemies, the restoration of his kingdom, his very life — what was David's request? 'One thing I ask of the Lord, this is what I seek . . . to gaze upon the beauty of the

Lord.' "

Gershom gently laid his hand on Joshua's lowered head. "Get still before Yahweh. Seek His face. Then wait for the Lord. Don't be impatient. Remember, Jacob wrestled with God all night until the sun rose, saying, 'I will not let you go unless you bless me.' "

"I've already lost everything. There is no blessing God could give me that would bring any of it back. What more does He want from me?"

"Ask Him. Then wait for His answer." The rabbi's strength suddenly gave out, and he sagged against the cushions and closed his eyes.

After a moment Joshua stood, his limbs cramped and stiff. "I should go now and let you rest."

Gershom opened his eyes. "Take Isaiah's scroll. There's a leather bag with a shoulder strap under that table."

"But what am I supposed to —"

"You'll find a use for the scroll someday. May Yahweh go with you, my beloved son." He smiled briefly and closed his eyes.

Asher was waiting for Joshua near the front door. "Thanks for talking to him," he said. "I know it will help the rabbi rest in peace."

Joshua wasn't sure if anything he had said

would ease Gershom's suffering, but he nodded anyway. "Take care of him, Asher," he said. Then he hefted the leather bag to his shoulder and they walked outside. Joshua was surprised to see how light the sky was, how fresh and clean the morning air smelled. The city's stones glowed rosy pink, reflecting the dawn sky. He had forgotten how beautiful Jerusalem was, and he swallowed a lump in his throat. When he left this time, he would probably never see Jerusalem again.

Joshua wondered what had become of his old house. His family had left everything they owned behind, all of his father's things, Hilkiah's things, a lifetime of precious possessions. It was only a few blocks away, but he wouldn't go past it. Better not to stir up any memories he couldn't handle. He would return to his caravan, help load the cargo, move on without looking back.

Asher was still beside him when they reached the main street that ran from the palace and Temple to the marketplace. Even before he reached the corner, Joshua heard the rumble of marching feet. Asher pushed him into the shadows behind the buildings.

"Wait here. It sounds like soldiers. Let me have a look first." Asher ducked around the corner, then returned a moment later. "Stay hidden. It's a royal procession — King Manasseh."

"Is he going up to the Temple?"

"No, he's coming this way."

"I have to see him." Joshua pushed past Asher and peered around the corner at the approaching procession. Dozens of palace guards surrounded the king, white-robed priests trailed behind him. "What are all the guards for?" he whispered to Asher.

"The king imagines all kinds of conspiracies against him. He won't go anywhere without guards."

"Where is he going?"

"I don't know."

"Well, there are priests with him and you're a Levite. You should know where —"

"Those are Manasseh's priests."

The procession was close now, and Joshua could see Manasseh clearly. More than nine months had passed, but the king looked the same. His handsome face was somber yet arrogant, his stride controlled, powerful, like a lion staking his territory. Except for the guards, Joshua saw nothing different about Manasseh, nothing that would explain why he had suddenly turned against Joshua and his family. Manasseh had been Joshua's closest friend his entire life. They shared twenty years of memories and confidences, laughter and tears. But this man was a stranger to Joshua: a murderer, a tyrant.

Joshua wanted to rush forward and demand an answer, then plunge his knife into Manasseh's gut in revenge for his father and his grandfather and his sister. A life for a life. But he had promised Jerimoth on oath that he wouldn't do anything foolish. Their mother was doing well, but she couldn't survive any more losses.

A moment later the king had passed by him. Crowds of curious townspeople followed the procession, and Joshua fell in step with them. Asher tried to pull him back.

"Someone might recognize you. It isn't safe."

"I want to know where he's going."

The procession passed through the marketplace and continued south, heading toward the Valley Gate. Joshua lagged farther and farther behind, wary of being trapped outside the gate in the narrow Valley of Hinnom. Except for the trampling feet and a few murmured whispers, the procession moved in silence. But suddenly, above the sound of marching, Joshua heard the faint cry of a baby.

Asher stood utterly still. "O God, no!"

"What's wrong? What's Manasseh doing?"

"He's going to sacrifice his son!"

"His son? Manasseh has a son?"

"They announced his birth eight days ago."

Joshua refused to believe it. Manasseh wasn't a pagan. They had studied the Torah together. The king knew that child sacrifice was evil. But in the distance a column of smoke slowly rose in the sky. Joshua heard the drums, throbbing their deadly cadence. The sound echoed off the jagged cliffs. He grabbed Asher's arm and started to run.

"Come on. We have to stop him."

"Are you crazy? You saw the guards. They'll kill you before you even get close to him."

"I don't care! I can't let him do this. I can't let him murder an innocent child."

"Joshua, don't — !"

Suddenly there was a loud shout and the drums rumbled like thunder. Then everything was still.

"It's too late," Asher whispered. "God help us all."

It wasn't just Abba and Grandpa and Dinah. They weren't the only innocent ones to die in Manasseh's bloodbath. How had Yahweh lost control of His nation? Why had he abandoned His chosen people to this evil man's reign?

"Listen to me, people of Jerusalem, listen!" Joshua recognized the man who stood shouting a few hundred feet away from them, outside the Valley Gate. He was one of the company of prophets, a disciple of Rabbi Isaiah. "Manasseh king of Judah has committed these detestable sins," the prophet shouted. "He has done more evil than the Amorites who preceded him and has led Judah into sin with his idols. Therefore, this is what the Lord, the God of Israel, says: 'I am going to bring such disaster on Jerusalem and Judah that the ears of everyone who hears of it will tingle. I will stretch out over Jerusalem the measuring line used against Samaria and the plumb line used against the house of Ahab . . .' "

Joshua and Asher saw the three guards hurrying up the road toward the gate, and so did the prophet. The crowd began to scatter. "Run!" Asher whispered. "Why doesn't he run?"

But the prophet continued to shout, undaunted by the approaching soldiers. " '. . . I will wipe out Jerusalem as one wipes a dish, wiping it and turning it upside down. I will forsake the remnant of my inheritance and hand them over to their enemies. They will be looted and plundered by all their foes, because they have done evil in my eyes and have provoked me to anger from the day their forefathers came out of Egypt until this day.' "

Before Joshua's startled eyes, one of the guards drew his sword and ran it through the prophet's body. The remaining crowd fled in fear as the man lay dying. His blood flowed, unavenged, in the dusty street.

Joshua took a final look at the dark funnel of smoke, curling toward heaven. Then he turned and ran up the hill to rejoin his caravan, determined to leave this godforsaken city forever.

16

Manasseh stared at the ceiling beams above his bed and remembered his son's cries — helpless, pitiful cries. He had almost called out to Zerah to stop the sacrifice. But then the drums had drowned out the sound, and in that emotional moment he had thought of Abraham, raising the knife high above his son Isaac, unwavering, unhesitant. Manasseh had renewed his resolve, watching in fatherly pride as Zerah approached the flaming altar with Manasseh's firstborn son in his hands. God would honor Manasseh's faith. God would intercede.

But no ram had miraculously appeared in the thicket. No divine hand had snatched his son from the altar. Manasseh had watched, paralyzed with horror, as the flames licked his son's small body, reducing him to ashes and smoke.

Now Manasseh lay alone in his room, too stunned by what he had done to move from his bed. He couldn't remember walking up the hill to his palace afterward. He didn't know if anyone had spoken to him or if he had answered them. He had locked himself in his chambers, alone, giving orders not to be disturbed.

He thought of his father.

A year before he died, Hezekiah had walked with Manasseh and Amariah down to the Valley of Hinnom. The boys had sat on the grass together while Hezekiah told them in a quiet voice how his brothers had died there. Then he'd told them how King Ahaz had plotted to kill him, as well. Manasseh remembered the tremor in his father's hushed voice as he'd spoken. He had seen tears in Hezekiah's eyes as he had placed his strong hands on Manasseh's shoulders and gazed steadfastly into his eyes. "You are my firstborn, Manasseh. You belong to Yahweh. But by His grace He allowed me to redeem your life with silver. You will live to serve Him and to take my place one day."

Manasseh had tried to ask his father questions about Molech's sacrifices, but Hezekiah shook his head. "I can't speak of it, son. I . . . I have no words. There are no words in any language."

Now Manasseh understood. The sacrifice today had penetrated his soul, becoming a visceral experience of sight and sound and smell beyond human description. Manasseh couldn't talk about what he had done, couldn't deal with it or rationalize it because he lacked the words. Yet the scene replayed endlessly in his mind.

He needed to get out of bed and go downstairs. He needed to take his place on his throne and run his kingdom. Guilt was merely a device of the priests, invented to control him. Sin was an illusion. He had earned power and favor with God through this act of faith. But Manasseh couldn't move. He couldn't speak. He had no words.

"You are my firstborn, Manasseh. . . . You will live . . ."

Why had he allowed his firstborn son to die?

"Where are you going, Lady Dinah?"

"To the nursery to see my baby. If I waited for him to be brought to me, I would never see him."

Dinah was tired of begging to see her son, tired of being told that the servants were busy feeding him or bathing him, or that he was asleep. As her breasts ached with the milk her baby should be drinking, Dinah hated Manasseh more than ever for denying her the role she was meant to play. But when she reached the nursery, Naphtali's crib was empty.

"Where's my son?" she asked the nurse.

"King Manasseh sent for him this morning, my lady."

Dinah went cold with fear. She imagined little Naphtali, so tiny and vulnerable, being placed in Manasseh's cruel hands. "He sent for him? Why?"

"He didn't say, my lady."

Then Dinah remembered. Today was the eighth day. Naphtali would be taken to the Temple to be circumcised and dedicated to God. It was the covenant ritual of her people.

"Please tell the nurse to bring him to me as soon as he gets back." He would need his mother to comfort him, to soothe away his pain and his tears.

The morning passed slowly, like a heavily laden cart rolling up a steep hill. "Have they brought my baby back, yet?" Dinah asked the servant who brought her noon meal.

"No, my lady."

Maybe Manasseh was holding a feast or a celebration for him. Even so, Naphtali was only an infant. He would need to be fed and to be put to sleep in his own bed.

Late in the afternoon, Dinah returned to the nursery. Surely they must have brought him back by now. They had neglected to tell her. But not only was Naphtali's crib still empty, but the blankets and linens had been stripped off of it, as well. And the shelves with his swaddling clothes were all bare. Was Manasseh hiding him from her?

Dinah ran through the corridors to the servants' quarters to find the nurse. The woman sat on her bed, her eyes red and swollen from weeping. Dinah knelt in front of her.

"My son . . . Where is my son?"

The nurse closed her eyes. "He's gone."

Dinah grabbed the woman's arms, shaking her. "What do you mean he's gone? Where did Manasseh take him?"

"To . . . to the Valley of Hinnom."

"No!" Dinah screamed. Her fingers dug into the woman's arms. "Why did you let him take my son? How could you give my baby to that monster? How could you let Manasseh kill my beautiful, perfect baby?" She wasn't asking the nurse — she was asking God.

"He . . . he's the king, my lady. How could we refuse him?"

The horrible impact of what Manasseh had done struck Dinah with brute force. She collapsed to the floor, screaming, tearing at her clothes and her hair. More servants rushed into the room, lifting her from the ground, carrying her to her room, laying her on the bed. Someone held a cup of wine to her lips. It tasted bitter with drugs.

"Drink it all, my lady. You've had a terrible shock." The wine made Dinah numb and dizzy, but it couldn't erase the image of Manasseh hurling their helpless child into the flames.

"O God, why didn't you save him?" she cried. "Why didn't you help him?"

"Don't leave her alone," she heard someone whisper. "Stay with her all night."

Dinah knew it was her own fault. She'd known how evil Manasseh was and what he was capable of doing. She should have protected her baby from him. She should have run away before Naphtali was born.

"I want to die," she moaned as she beat her breast. "Please let me die."

"Don't say such things, my lady." Her maidservant was weeping, as well.

"I have nothing to live for."

"You'll give King Manasseh more children."

Manasseh. She would have to spend the rest of her life with Manasseh.

"No. Oh, God, no. Please let me die."

"It's wrong for you to want to die, my lady."

Yes, the maid was right. It was wrong for Dinah to die now. First she had to kill Manasseh. He was a murderer. *An eye for an eye,* the Torah said. *Don't allow a murderer to live.* It was too late to bring Naphtali back, but Manasseh would be back. As soon as Dinah's forty days of purification ended, he would return to her.

The least she could do for her son was to avenge his murder.

"I think I'll lie down and rest for a while," Jerusha said, but Miriam knew that she was going to her room to pray for her son. Joshua had been gone almost two weeks. They had expected him to return days ago. Unable to disguise his concern, Jerimoth had finally told his mother the truth — that Joshua had returned to Jerusalem for Yael. Now, as each day passed with no word from him, Miriam watched Jerusha grow pale and thin with worry.

"Joshua is so much like his father," Jerusha had often told her. *"The way he stands and walks — even the way he runs his fingers through his hair. I look at him and I remember Eliakim."* Miriam knew that if Jerusha lost him, it would be like losing her husband all over again.

Miriam, too, feared for Joshua's safety.

She wished she knew how to pray, wished she could believe that God would listen to her. Her anxiety for Joshua lay like a heavy stone in her stomach. In spite of the way he had hurt her, Miriam hadn't been able to stop loving him. If they didn't hear from him soon, she would go back to Jerusalem herself to look for him.

Outside, the rain poured steadily down, making the house dreary and damp. Like the children, Miriam hated staying indoors all day. They had to use the indoor hearth for cooking, and it made the house stuffy with smoke. The afternoon seemed three days long.

Sara and Tirza napped along with their children, but Miriam couldn't rest. Instead, she tried to fill the endless hours of waiting with work — hauling water, grinding grain, washing or mending clothes. Tomorrow was the Sabbath. They would prepare all their food today so they wouldn't have to work tomorrow. She laid out the dishes on their best linen cloth. Then she began to knead the dough for the Sabbath loaf.

Suddenly she stopped and covered her face with floury hands. *O God of Abraham . . . Jerusha's God . . . I know that I'm not from a good family. I know I have no right to ask you for anything. But please help*

Joshua. Please bring him home safely. I don't even care if he brings Yael with him. I'll work for her. I'll cook and do her wash. But, please . . . for Jerusha's sake —

Miriam stopped when she heard the front door slam. She wiped the flour off her hands and went to see who it was. Jerimoth stood in the entryway, twisting a roll of parchment in his hands. His face was pale.

"Where's my mother?" he asked.

"In her room, resting." Miriam followed Jerimoth down the hall, not caring if she was invited or not, her fear for Joshua swelling inside her.

"Mama, look. It's a letter from Joshua," Jerimoth said, waving the parchment. "He's all right. He's safe."

The swiftness of God's answer to her prayer stunned Miriam. He really had heard! God had answered!

Jerusha closed her eyes as a tear rolled down her face. "Thank God, thank God," she whispered. Miriam pushed past Jerimoth to sit on the bed beside her. When Miriam looked up at Jerimoth again, his face was still grim with worry.

"What's wrong?" Jerusha asked him.

"Yael is married to another man. I can only imagine how devastated Joshua must be."

Miriam didn't have to imagine. She knew Joshua's pain firsthand. But what was devastating news for Joshua was the answer to her unspoken prayers.

"When is he coming home?" Jerusha asked.

Jerimoth exhaled. "The caravan he's with is traveling to Egypt and Cush. He said he's going with them. He needs some time alone."

Jerusha wiped her eyes. "Will he be safe, Jerimoth?"

"Yes, Mama. He was only in danger in Jerusalem. He'll be fine once he's out of Judah. In fact, it took some time for his letter to reach us, so he's probably in Egypt by now."

"May God go with him," Jerusha whispered. She took Miriam's hand in her own, then looked up at Jerimoth. "I pray that neither of you ever knows the helplessness of watching your children suffer."

Joshua plodded down the Egyptian road beside the camels, the sun beating down on his back from high above the metallic sky. The heat and humidity wilted his limbs as if they were new shoots. The leather bag with Isaiah's scroll grew heavier by the mile, and his back was soaked with sweat beneath it. As he walked, the carved finials on the end of the scroll staves rattled against each other, clattering endlessly, making his head throb. His blood pounded in his ears like the slow, deadly beating of the sacrificial drums. Joshua wished he had never gone to Gershom's house that night or seen what Manasseh had done at dawn.

In the distance on his left, the sky was growing dark with storm clouds. Jagged flashes of lightning speared the horizon as billowing thunderheads soared higher and higher like smoke from a furnace. The camels lifted their noses to the wind and whimpered as the thunder rumbled toward them.

"Move it! Let's go!" the lead driver shouted. "Maybe we can beat the storm to the next oasis."

Joshua prodded his two camels' flanks with his sticks, jogging to keep pace with them. But when he looked into the darkening sky and felt the first drops of rain, he knew they would never make it to shelter. There was no sign of the oasis on the horizon.

Suddenly a rain of pebbles, hard and sharp, struck Joshua's face and arms. "Hail!" the lead driver shouted. "Get the camels down before they panic!"

The frozen pellets, as large as date pits, stung as they hammered Joshua's skin. He yanked hard on the loping camels' reins, finally dragging them to a halt. The older of his two animals quickly dropped to its knees on Joshua's signal, but the biting hail had spooked the younger female. She backed up, twisting away from him, bellowing with fright. Just as he struck her legs with his staff to make her kneel, a loud thunderclap boomed above them. The camel reared. When she came down, her front leg struck a rut in the road and she fell on her side, her leg twisting beneath her. Joshua's stomach twisted with it as he heard the bone snap like a dry tree branch.

For a moment it seemed as if he stood apart, lifted outside himself, viewing the scene from far away. He saw the writhing camel, struggling in vain to stand, and the other drivers staring at him in silent disdain. The thick-necked Moabites, filthy with sweat and dust, seemed like little more than brute beasts to him, standing among their shaggy, foul-smelling animals. What was he doing here dressed like one of them, wandering aimlessly through foreign lands, ferrying goods that would be highly prized today, used up and tossed aside tomorrow? *"Utterly meaningless! Everything is meaning-*

less. What does man gain from all his labor at which he toils under the sun?"

"You fool!" the lead driver suddenly shouted. "You've killed her!" He gripped his staff like a bat and lunged at Joshua, cracking it against his forehead with all his strength.

The unexpected blow felled Joshua. For a moment everything went black. He lay sprawled in the dirt, stunned, his head ringing with pain, while hail stung him like a thousand angry bees. Then his vision cleared and he looked up in time to see the man coming at him a second time. Joshua quickly rolled out of the way and scrambled to his feet.

All at once, the helpless rage and fury that had been billowing inside Joshua for days burst forth, out of control. The Moabite's face blurred. He was no longer the lead driver, but King Manasseh, the man who was responsible for all of Joshua's sorrow and loss, a man who was capable of killing his own son. Joshua lowered his head and charged his enemy, knocking him to the ground. Then he pummeled him again and again with his fists, lashing out in hatred, expelling his pent-up anger and need for revenge. His fury raged like the thunder and hail around him.

By the time the other drivers managed to pull Joshua off, the Moabite was bloody and unconscious. When Joshua saw what he had done to the man, he nearly vomited. He would have killed him if the others hadn't intervened.

Someone untied Joshua's belongings from the injured camel and handed them to him. "Here, take your things and go. Hurry! Before he wakes up."

Trembling all over, Joshua bent to retrieve the bag with Isaiah's scroll. It had fallen from his shoulder during the fight. He used the hem of his tunic to wipe away the blood that streamed from his forehead into his eyes, then he started walking down the road in the direction they had just come, his feet sliding on slippery pellets of hail. He climbed a small rise but didn't look back when he reached the top. As he started down the other side, the hail changed to rain. Joshua lowered his head and walked into the wind, soaked and shivering.

He had left Jerusalem ten days ago, his home in Moab more than two weeks ago. If Joshua wasn't mistaken, tonight was the spring equinox, the beginning of a new year. But it wouldn't be a new beginning for him. He hadn't left his grief behind, he had merely shouldered it with the rest of his burdens, hauling it from Moab to Judah and now to Egypt. He might as well carry it home again.

Joshua planned his route back to Heshbon as he walked; he would follow The Way of the Sea north until he was out of Egypt, then cut across southern Judah below Beersheba, following The Way of the Arabah. That road intersected with The King's Highway in Edom, and he could follow it north for the last sixty miles to Moab. The trip would probably take two weeks. That would give him plenty of time to decide what he would do with his life once he was back in Heshbon.

He thought about his mother as he slogged through the rain, how she had escaped from the Assyrians and traveled alone for hundreds of miles through rugged terrain. Now, cold and alone in a strange land, Joshua recognized the fullness of her courage. *"My father's prayers were the only reason I made it home."* Whenever Jerusha told her story she always finished with those words. *"My father's prayers . . ."*

Joshua walked all afternoon without stopping. Eventually the rain ended and the sun blazed again from behind hazy clouds, steaming his clothes dry. The gash on his forehead had crusted shut, and he fingered the welt gingerly. His bruised knuckles had swollen, and they throbbed painfully as he walked, reminding him that he had nearly killed a man — reminding him that in his anger, he had already killed two others. Yet his rage still wasn't satisfied. Joshua knew it continued to smolder inside him, its deadly force building, preparing to explode once again. He wanted to be free from it before it took control of him, before he killed someone else. He wanted the dark clouds of depression that covered his soul to lift, but they seemed to grow heavier with each step he took.

He walked on, trying to remember carefree times of laughter and happiness, but all of his memories included Abba or Manasseh or Yael, and they only deepened his pain. Late in the afternoon, exhausted, Joshua stopped at an oasis to replenish his water supply. The rattling scroll staves had been driving him crazy all day, and he finally sat down on a stone wall near the well to see if he could find a way to muffle the sound. He opened the leather bag, lifted the scroll out, and unwrapped the linen cloth.

When he saw the scroll, Joshua stared in disbelief. He was certain it had been rolled to the beginning when he'd read aloud from it at Rabbi Gershom's house. He hadn't taken it out of the bag since then, yet now the scroll was divided almost equally between the two staves. How had it happened? Had it unrolled as he'd walked?

He pushed the two rolls apart to read from it. He should see the same words he had read to Gershom, *"The vision concerning Judah and Jerusalem that Isaiah son of Amoz saw . . ."* Instead, Joshua read these words:

"Why do you say, O Jacob, and complain, O Israel, 'My way is hidden from the Lord; my cause is disregarded by my God?' Do you not know? Have you not heard? The Lord is the everlasting God, the Creator of the ends of the earth. He will not grow tired or weary, and his understanding no one can fathom. He gives strength to the weary and increases the power of the weak. Even youths grow tired and weary, and young men stumble and fall; but those who hope in the Lord will renew their strength. They will soar on wings like eagles; they will run and not grow weary, they will walk and not be faint."

Joshua stopped, suddenly aware of a tender presence hovering near him. Often when he had studied late at night, his father would come to his room and stand silently in the doorway. Eventually Joshua would sense his presence and turn to see Eliakim watching him, his eyes shining with pride and love. That was what Joshua felt now — an unseen Father looking over his shoulder, watching him in love. Joshua held his breath. The babble of voices around him fell silent. He looked down at the scroll again, reading from a different column.

"I took you from the ends of the earth, from its farthest corners I called you. I said, 'You are my servant.' I have chosen you and have not rejected you. So do not fear, for I am with you; do not be dismayed, for I am your God. I will strengthen you and help you; I will uphold you with my righteous right hand.

"All who rage against you will surely be ashamed and disgraced; those who oppose you will be as nothing and perish. Though you search for your enemies, you will not find them. Those who wage war against you will be as nothing at all. For I am the Lord, your God, who takes hold of your right hand and says to you, Do not fear; I will help you."

As quickly as it came, the presence vanished. Joshua felt desolate when it did. He looked up, surprised to find himself seated on a stone wall by an ancient well in Egypt, surrounded by a swirl of activity and noise. The sun lay low in the sky.

Joshua returned the scroll to its bag and lifted it to his shoulder. Then he set out across the desert, like Jacob, to wrestle with his God.

17

King Manasseh stood on the royal platform after the evening sacrifice, surveying the latest changes that Zerah had made to the Temple precincts. Sculptures and artwork from the finest artisans adorned the new shrines and altars until the Temple Mount bore little resemblance to the stark, unadorned site the king remembered from his youth.

"Does everything meet with your approval, Your Majesty?" Zerah asked.

"It's magnificent. I can't understand why the Levites forbid us to express our natural creativity. I won't tolerate artistic censorship as long as I am king."

He stepped off the platform and strode across the courtyard with Zerah. His four bodyguards moved like hulking shadows, surrounding him. Manasseh passed the four-faced image that stood at the center of the courtyard, designed to depict the four faces on the throne of God. They looked in four directions, so that whichever entrance the people used, a face confronted them, reminding them that this Temple was God's earthly throne.

Manasseh rounded the corner near the Temple side chambers and stopped. "This is new. What is this roped-off section for and all these booths?"

"This is Asherah's sacred precinct," Zerah told him. "Every woman, married or not, must show her devotion to the goddess by coming here once in her life, to offer herself for service. She must sit within the sacred precinct, wearing a garland of string on her head as a symbol of sacrifice, while the male worshipers pass through the roped-off pathways to make their choice. Once a woman is seated, she cannot go home until a stranger throws a piece of silver into her lap and takes her into one of the booths for the ritual. The silver is her sacred offering to Asherah, along with any product of conception that may result. Afterward, she — What is it, Your Majesty? What's wrong?"

"Nothing." But Manasseh knew that his face had betrayed his disgust. Not only did this ritual contradict everything the priests had taught him about adultery and fornication, but it raised a very disturbing question that he wasn't certain he wanted answered. "My mother worshiped Asherah," he finally said. "Did she participate in this?"

Zerah hesitated, studying Manasseh's face. "I don't see how she could have, Your Majesty. The priests forbade it during your father's reign."

Manasseh told himself that the desolation he felt was only a remnant of the false guilt imposed on him by his upbringing. He must shed it once and for all. Even if his mother had lain with a stranger, she had been an adult, free to make her own decisions. The religious fanatics had no right to dictate morality or to condemn people for their choices. But he turned his back on Asherah's sacred precinct and headed down the royal walkway to his palace. His bodyguards and Zerah kept pace with him.

"Everything is ready for tonight's celebration, Your Majesty," Zerah told him. "We'll begin with a procession through the city to the Temple."

Against his will, a stab of superstitious fear knifed Manasseh in the gut. "Do we have to hold the ceremony in Yahweh's Temple?" he asked.

"What better place to meet with our God? I promise it will be the most awe-inspiring ritual you will ever witness."

Manasseh halted and turned on Zerah, suddenly angry. "You said the same thing about the sacrifice of the firstborn!"

Zerah folded his arms across his chest and met the king's gaze evenly. "And it was, Your Majesty. But the ritual of the spring equinox is the most important festival of the year, celebrated by our forefathers since before the time of Abraham."

A faint memory stirred in Manasseh's mind. "Didn't God tell Abraham to leave Ur of the Chaldeans and forsake the pagan rites of his ancestors?"

Zerah shook his head in disgust. "That's a lie. I can show you Torah passages to prove that Abraham celebrated this festival, just as we will tonight."

"I'd like to see them." Manasseh glanced around to make sure that his bodyguards were alert, then started walking again.

"On this night, God will preside over the council of heavenly beings," Zerah continued. "They will fix the destinies of mortals for the coming year, and once these are written on tablets, they cannot be changed. But at tonight's celebration, we'll have the opportunity to influence those decisions. As the stars come into alignment this sacred night, it is possible to coax the heavens to serve our wishes on earth. If we offer the proper sacrifices, we can win divine favor and sway the hand of God to our advantage."

"What kind of sacrifices?" Manasseh said, remembering his son.

"That depends on what you wish to ask of God. Libations of wine and oil bring bountiful harvests. A young bull assures virility. A ram, one year old, brings prosperity. A ram is an especially powerful offering, Your Majesty, since the sun will rise tomorrow morning in the sign of the ram."

"Isn't that the constellation that guides my enemy, Joshua?"

"Yes, but will your enemy pay homage to the heavenly hosts tonight?"

Manasseh gave a short laugh. "Not likely." He waited for his guards to open the palace doors and secure the hallways before going inside.

"Your Majesty, tonight we will also perform a special curse ceremony to break your enemy's power. Remember, his destiny will also be fixed tonight. We will direct his fate as well as our own."

"Then let's choose his destruction."

They walked in silence until they reached Manasseh's chambers. Zerah stopped him outside the door. "Your Majesty, our celebration will be a pale shadow of the revelry enjoyed in heaven as the new year is ushered in. I've tried many times to convince you that your Temple rituals have become stunted imitations of what they should be. Tonight I will prove it. God intended for us to celebrate with joy and revelry, with eating and drinking and dance."

"And orgies?"

"Of course. Wasn't God's first commandment to 'be fruitful and multiply'? Performing ritual union at the spring equinox will grant you great blessings and guarantee your nation bountiful crops. It will empower you. Why else do you think your priests forbid it?"

Manasseh smiled slightly, remembering the strict purity and harsh denial his teachers demanded.

"Don't forget, Your Majesty, you are the sovereign king of this nation. You have the absolute right to do whatever you please. You are accountable to no one."

Jagged rocks studded the desert floor in the place where Joshua stopped for the night. He spent several minutes clearing away the stones so he could lie down. A scorpion ran from beneath one rock and skittered out of sight across the sand. Joshua disturbed a sand viper beneath another.

As soon as the sun set, the desert temperature plummeted. Joshua pulled his outer cloak from his bundle of meager possessions and wrapped it around himself. The robe was made of fine lamb's wool, one of the few possessions he still owned from his former life in Jerusalem. He had been wearing it the night Maki rescued him. A royal design once decorated the hem and sleeves, but Joshua had plucked out the gold threads months ago and traded them for grain and olive oil in Moab.

Even wrapped in his warmest robe, Joshua felt the numbing cold. When he heard the distant cry of jackals, he decided to build a fire. He gathered an armful of brush and dry sticks and soon had a small fire kindled. A year ago he wouldn't have known how to start one without calling a servant to help him. His stomach growled with hunger, but Joshua had determined to fast and pray until Yahweh filled his inner hunger, until the darkness in his soul blazed with God's light.

Why have you allowed all this to happen, Yahweh? Why didn't you step in and prevent Abba's death? Or your prophets' deaths? I need to know why.

For a long time Joshua's mind was too cluttered to pray for more than a few minutes at a time. As his thoughts wandered, he remembered Rabbi Gershom's words: Manasseh also wanted to know why Yahweh had allowed his father to die after all the good things King Hezekiah had done. Joshua stared into the flames, remembering the day he'd learned that King Hezekiah was dead. But the memory that stood out in Joshua's mind was his own father's deep grief, not Manasseh's. His father had been the most important person in Joshua's life, and he had witnessed the events surrounding King Hezekiah's death through Eliakim's eyes, eyes that saw God's purpose and plan, by faith, in every circumstance of life. Joshua hadn't questioned King Hezekiah's death. But now he realized that his friend Manasseh certainly must have.

Manasseh had looked so young as he'd stood all alone on the royal platform, wearing his father's crown for the first time. Joshua remembered watching him with restless envy, knowing that one day he would stand beside Manasseh and they would rule the nation together. King Hezekiah's death meant that Joshua was closer to the day when all of his studies and preparations would end, and he could begin his life's work at last. But what had Manasseh felt as the high priest poured the anointing oil over his head? Fear? Anger?

Joshua had no idea. He was the young king's closest friend, yet Manasseh had never confided his feelings. He probably hadn't confided them to anyone or expressed the rage and doubt that Joshua now felt after his own father's death. In the past months, feeling abandoned by God, Joshua knew he had come perilously close to rejecting Yahweh forever. Is that what Manasseh had done?

Joshua stared up at the starry sky, then closed his eyes. Only two possibilities existed: light or the absence of light. If Manasseh rejected the Source of all light, then his sole alternative was to live in darkness. Joshua shuddered and stirred the fire, adding a few more sticks.

Manasseh now practiced divination and sorcery. He had erected an Asherah pole and altars to idols. He had sacrificed his firstborn son. But how had the darkness taken control of him and of their nation so quickly? The evil must have always been present, hidden in men's hearts as they'd merely pretended to worship God.

Joshua recalled one night during the spring equinox, years earlier, when King Hezekiah's soldiers interrupted an orgy on a high place used for Baal worship. All of the people involved had been refugees from the north. They had brought the pagan practices of King Ahab and Queen Jezebel with them as they'd fled from the Assyrians. Joshua and Manasseh learned of the arrests by accident, overhearing the soldiers' conversation in the courtyard one morning when they went for their military training. Perhaps their fathers shouldn't have sheltered them from the knowledge of such evils.

But those evildoers had been caught and punished. Justice had been served. If God was still in control, why did evil triumph now? Why had Yahweh allowed Joshua's father and Rabbi Isaiah to die? Why had the priests and Levites died for defending them? And what about Joshua's grandfather and sister Dinah? Their only crime had been trying to protect Joshua. Why hadn't God heard their prayers and saved them?

I need to know, Yahweh. I need to know why. *Why don't you judge evil? Why did you make scorpions and deserts and stones when you could have easily made this a fertile place with palm trees and streams? Is there a purpose in evil? I need to know!*

But God remained silent, as cold and distant as the stars that blinked in the darkened sky. The tiny pinpoints of light would disappear, mocking Joshua if he stared at them for too long.

After many hours, many unanswered questions, Joshua's eyes grew heavy. He closed them for a moment and fell into a restless sleep.

King Manasseh stepped from his sedan chair when the royal procession reached the Temple Mount and accepted the goblet of wine Zerah thrust into his hand. The Temple courtyards already pulsed with activity. Manasseh smelled the aroma of roasting meat and heard the sound of lively music and clapping nearby. He raised the cup and drank deeply, hoping it would lighten his mood.

Zerah studied him as he drank. "What's wrong, Your Majesty?"

"I had another argument with my brother. He refused to join me tonight."

"You were wise not to compel him. Amariah's unbelief would have disrupted the spiritual forces."

"First thing tomorrow I'm transferring him to an outpost in the Judean desert," Manasseh said. He drained his cup and handed it to his servant.

"Be patient with him, Your Majesty. Prince Amariah is young and of very weak character. Guilt still controls him."

"I don't care! I don't want him as my secretary anymore!"

"Listen to me." Zerah's voice was low, his dark eyes piercing, hypnotic. "Until you have a son to replace you, Amariah is the only heir to your throne. You need to keep him here where we can watch him. And where your enemies can never reach him."

Manasseh knew Zerah was right. He also knew he had to put aside his anger for tonight. He accepted the refilled goblet and began walking toward the music.

The night was cool and clear, the Temple Mount dimly illuminated by a few scattered torches so that the stars were clearly visible. Manasseh scanned the skies as he walked, but his guiding star in the constellation of the lion hadn't risen yet. Night was a much better time to worship, he decided, a powerful time. The sun felt too hot, too bright and searing, at Yahweh's sacrifices, making Manasseh feel naked and exposed beneath God's angry gaze.

The crowd parted to make way for him, giving him a front-row view of the musicians and the young women dancing provocatively before them. At first the sight shocked Manasseh. Men and women danced separately at Yahweh's festivals. But he forced himself to watch and found the spectacle both disturbing and arousing. When the song ended, Zerah steered him away.

"Come. This is the night to savor all of the sensory delights given to us by our Maker. But first, I have something for you."

Manasseh surveyed the priests' faces as he followed Zerah. None of them were from Yahweh's Temple. The musicians hadn't been Levites, either. "Did you banish Yahweh's priests and Levites from tonight's celebration?" he asked.

"Of course not. They were invited, but only a few of the younger ones chose to come." He led Manasseh into one of the side chambers used by the priests to change from their everyday clothes into sacred garments. Inside, a plain wooden box lay on the table. "Open it, Your Majesty."

Manasseh unlatched the fastenings and removed the lid. The high priest's breastpiece lay on a lining of purple cloth. It wasn't large, but even in the dim lamplight the twelve stones sparkled with rainbows of color. The embroidery work of gold, blue, purple, and scarlet seemed to breathe like a living thing.

"Magnificent, isn't it, Your Majesty?"

Manasseh had never seen it this close

before, only from a distance when the high priest wore it over his ephod on holy days and festivals. He was afraid to touch it. The breastpiece's pocket contained the mysterious Urim and Thummim, used by his ancestors for divination. "Why are you showing this to me?" he asked.

"Because you must wear it tonight."

"But only the high priest may wear this."

Zerah's face darkened with anger. Manasseh recognized its source as passion, not malice. "The king should be the high priest to his own nation! This breastpiece is rightfully yours! The Torah says that King David danced in an ephod when he moved the ark to Jerusalem and he wore this breastpiece, as well. He wore it every time he sought guidance, but of course the Levites deleted those facts from the record. David is your ancestor. You have a right to wear it, too."

Zerah lifted it from the case and slipped the golden chains over Manasseh's head. He felt the weight of it settle against his chest. After a moment, he fingered the twelve precious stones. "Magnificent," he murmured.

"Can you feel their power, Your Majesty?"

Manasseh watched the breastpiece pulse as it rested above his pounding heart. "Yes," he whispered.

"It is radiating energy into your body. The Levites know the mysterious power of each of these stones and crystals — ruby, topaz, amethyst, and all the rest. Their power belongs to you."

Manasseh's mouth felt dry. He took the goblet of wine from his servant and swallowed its contents in three gulps.

"Come, Your Majesty. A night of revelry awaits you, a night of new experiences and delights."

Outside, the fire in the bronze altar mesmerized Manasseh as he stared into its dancing flames. It was time for the priests to slay his offerings of year-old bulls and rams. The animals had been conceived during the fertility rites a year before; now he would offer back to Mother Earth the firstfruits of what she had given him.

While the offerings roasted, the priests began a frenzied dance around the altar to the pounding beat of drums and chants. They whirled faster and faster, moaning, screaming, their eyes rolling back in their heads, until they reached a near-lunatic state. Then Manasseh watched in horror as they drew knives and cut themselves, spilling their blood on the ground around the altar, splattering droplets of it on his own clothes and face as they whirled past him.

He backed away.

"The blood of man is sacred," he mumbled. "Life is in the blood."

Zerah gripped his arm to hold him in place. "Remember Cain and Abel, Your Majesty?"

"Of course I do!"

"Then surely you recall God's words to Cain after He rejected Cain's offering: 'If you do what is right, will you not be accepted?' What happened next, Your Majesty?"

Manasseh pried Zerah's fingers from his arm, angry with him for this childish grilling. It reminded him of his Torah teacher. "Cain took his brother out to the field and killed him!"

"Yes, Cain shed Abel's blood on the ground as a sacrifice, just as these priests are doing."

"Then why did God curse him?"

"Because he shed Abel's blood instead of his own."

"Well, I've seen enough of this. Get me something to wipe off all this blood."

"No, leave it, Your Majesty. It is holy. You must wear the mark of it as you talk to the spirits." He led Manasseh across the courtyard to the altar of divination. Dozens of white-robed priests followed, gathering in a circle around them. A woman stood beside the altar, wearing priestly robes and making circular motions with her hands as she wafted the burning fragrance of incense to her nostrils. The thick, cloying smell, along with all the wine he'd drunk, made Manasseh's stomach roll.

"A woman priest?" he asked.

"She's not a priest in the usual sense. She wears the robes because tonight, like the other priests, she will act as a mediator between man and God."

"You mean she's a medium?"

"That's right."

Manasseh looked around for his cupbearer and drank a few more gulps of wine to silence the alarms of his conscience. Zerah would have a logical answer to his concerns, he told himself. He always did. Hadn't King Saul consulted a medium, conjuring up Samuel from the dead?

This woman didn't look particularly threatening. She was small-boned, as Manasseh's own mother had been, and only about ten years older than himself. She wore no covering on her head, and her black, wavy hair, with one startling swath of gray, reached nearly to her waist. Her eyes were closed, and she chanted in a soft voice as she swayed to an unsung rhythm.

Suddenly her body went limp and she fell backward as if she had fainted. Manasseh moved to catch her, but Zerah stopped him. "Just watch."

She appeared to be asleep, except that, as Manasseh watched, the expression on her face slowly changed to one of deep concentration. Then her features began to twitch as if unseen insects crawled across her face. The movement increased, faster and faster, until her face transformed before his eyes into a different face. It was no longer soft and feminine but angular and hard — a man's face. She sprang to her feet, and even her stance was a man's: defiant, proud, her body controlled by a masculine spirit.

Manasseh stared, fascinated and terrified at the same time. He wanted to run but found he couldn't move, as if an invisible hand held him in place. When she spoke, the unearthly voice chilled Manasseh, like the sound of grinding stone when a tomb is opened.

"You seek to know what transpires in the heavenly council, King Manasseh?"

He tried to answer but nothing came out. He cleared his throat and tried again. "Yes . . . yes, I do."

"Your devotion and good works have not escaped the heavenly council's notice. The changes you have made during your reign have earned divine favor and, with it, divine power to succeed in all that you do. The spirit of your firstborn son, which you released from its earthly prison, stands present with the gods to intercede on your behalf. Your son's message to you is this: Beware — more than one enemy wishes to destroy you. If you make full use of your spiritual powers, you will prevail. But first you must break free from the chains of fear, forged in your past. They still bind you."

Her face twisted again as her body went rigid. Then she collapsed to the ground, convulsing wildly. Manasseh shrank back, his eyes riveted on the repulsive sight, certain that she writhed in her death throes. At last she went still.

"Is she dead?" he whispered.

"No. The spirit guide has left her, that's all."

Manasseh stared at her crumpled body for a few more moments before turning to Zerah. When he did, the intensity of Zerah's gaze as he stared into the king's eyes, the unchecked passion of his emotions, made Manasseh's heart pound. The familiar knife of fear twisted through him. "What's wrong?"

Zerah lunged at him, and before Manasseh

could respond, he gripped both of the king's wrists in his hands. "Shackled!" he cried.

"What are you doing to me?" The warmth of Zerah's hands seemed to burn Manasseh's flesh. Zerah's eyes, beneath his startling brows, danced like the flames of the altar fire.

"The taboos of your past still shackle you, my lord. But tonight, on this holiest of nights, power is available if you wish to break free." Zerah's hands slid from Manasseh's wrists to his hands, but his gaze never wavered as he entwined the king's fingers in his own. "Are you ready to move to a higher level of spirituality?"

Manasseh knew what Zerah wanted. He could only nod.

"Then come with me."

Joshua cried out in his sleep as the nightmare jolted him awake. Evil engulfed him like deep water, pulling him under, choking off his life. He sat up, gasping for air, his heart pounding against his ribs. He searched the darkness for the evil presence he sensed, but it slithered out of sight, eluding him. *Just a dream,* he told himself. *A dream.* But he couldn't stop shaking. His fire had burned out, and his cloak was insufficient against the desert's bitter cold. But the moon had already set and the night was too dark, the terrain too treacherous for Joshua to stumble around searching for more sticks. He curled into a tight ball and wrapped his cloak over his head, shivering as he tried to warm his body. There was little he could do for the rest of the night but pray, keeping fear and the elusive shadow of evil at bay.

When the sun finally began to rise and it was light enough to gather wood, Joshua felt no closer to God than he had the night before. He built a fire, then unrolled Isaiah's scroll and began to read.

"In the fourteenth year of King Hezekiah's reign, Sennacherib king of Assyria attacked all the fortified cities of Judah and captured them. Then the king of Assyria sent his field commander with a large army from Lachish to King Hezekiah at Jerusalem . . . Eliakim son of Hilkiah the palace administrator . . . went out to him. . . . Then Eliakim, son of Hilkiah . . . went to Hezekiah with clothes torn . . . Hezekiah sent Eliakim . . . to the prophet Isaiah."

Joshua read, fascinated, as Isaiah retold the story of the Assyrian invasion. Joshua read his grandfather's name with pride and pictured his father boldly confronting the Assyrians face-to-face. Both men had faithfully played the part God had given them.

When he finished that passage, Joshua scrolled backward, skimming the words, until he found a prophecy that halted him. In it Isaiah predicted Shebna's fall from power: *"He will roll you up tightly like a ball and throw you into a large country. There you will die."* Joshua recalled Hadad's story and shuddered at the accuracy of Isaiah's words. Then he read the familiar prophecy of his own father's rise to power: *"In that day I will summon my servant Eliakim, son of Hilkiah . . . I will drive him like a peg into a firm place . . . All the glory of his family will hang on him: its offspring and offshoots."* Joshua himself was one of those offshoots, resting on the weight of his father's glory.

But the words that came next stunned Joshua: *" 'In that day,' declares the Lord Almighty, 'the peg driven into the firm place will give way; it will be sheared off and will fall, and the load hanging on it will be cut down.' The Lord has spoken."*

The utter finality of Yahweh's decree astounded him. Yahweh had known that Abba would die! He had known that Joshua would fall, as well. Yahweh had willed it! Joshua dropped the scroll and fell prostrate before God in the desert sand as if stunned by a blow. He moaned aloud as he struggled to reconcile Yahweh's will with his own image of what God was like: Yahweh rewarded righteousness; He punished evil; He blessed those who served Him. Yet the Lord had spoken and his father had died.

"Yahweh had to destroy your limited image of Him," Rabbi Gershom had told him, *"so you would worship Him as the sovereign God."* Joshua's body trembled as he tried to dislodge his idol from its throne.

In Moab he had seen the superstitious pagans bringing endless offerings to their idols in order to stay in their gods' favor, to guarantee good crops and prosperous lives. Like them, Joshua had also obeyed all of God's laws, fulfilled all the sacred obligations, in order to continue his life of wealth and privilege. He had worshiped an idol, trying to bend his god to do his will through sacrifices and good deeds. Suddenly Joshua understood the difference between idolatry and true worship, and his unanswered questions vanished like stars at the sun's rising. True believers like his father and grandfather didn't try to bargain with Yahweh; instead, they were willing to bend to His sovereign will.

And now Joshua heard Yahweh asking him

a question: Was he willing to do the same? Would he submit to God's will whether or not he understood it?

The sun climbed higher, and soon the desert heat rivaled the bitter cold of the night before, bearing down on Joshua like a blast from a furnace. He imagined it melting all the golden images and idols he had formed and worshiped, turning them to ashes at his feet. Joshua shed his robe and draped it over a spindly broom tree, then took shelter beneath its canopy. His stomach ached with hunger, just as his spirit ached to discover the answer to a new question: If his father and grandfather had died for a reason, then what was the reason that Joshua himself had been spared?

He lifted Isaiah's scroll from the dirt where he had dropped it and began to read every word from the beginning.

18

Eight days after he left the caravan to go into the desert, Joshua knocked on the door of Rabbi Gershom's house shortly after sunset. All afternoon, as he had climbed the steep road to Jerusalem, he had worried about how he would get inside without revealing who he was; now he breathed a sigh of relief when Yael's brother Asher opened the door.

"Joshua! You came back?"

Joshua glanced around, hoping no one in the street had heard Asher speak his name. "May I come in?" Asher stood aside as Joshua touched his fingers to the mezuzah on the doorpost and entered the darkened passageway. He heard the mumble of men's voices in prayer, coming from the main room and the sound of women weeping in the distant part of the house. "Who else is here?" he asked.

"The rabbi's three sons, a few of the other

Levites —"

"I don't want them to know I'm here."

Anger flared in Asher's eyes. "Why not? Don't you trust us?"

"I don't trust anyone! Manasseh was my best friend, and he turned against me for no reason. Why should I trust strangers?"

"Because our lives are in as much danger as yours. One wrong word at the Temple, one stupid mistake, and Manasseh has threatened to slaughter all of us — and our families, as well. He has already filled the streets of Jerusalem with innocent blood. We hate him as much as you do."

A tall, burly man suddenly appeared in the doorway from the main room. "Asher? Who was at the — ?" He glared at Joshua. "What does this Moabite want?"

Joshua recognized Rabbi Gershom's oldest son. He returned the Levite's stare for several moments before deciding to answer. "I'm Joshua ben Eliakim. I need to speak with your father."

The Levite's brows arched in surprise. "I'm sorry, I didn't recognize you. My father said you would return. He was convinced that God would allow him to live until you did. Come in." He turned and led the way to Rabbi Gershom's bedchamber, then paused again at the door. "My father slipped into a coma this morning. It's only a matter of time now."

Joshua nodded and moved into the cramped room. Overheated by the blazing charcoal brazier, the stuffy air reeked of sickness and death. The rabbi lay beneath a pile of covers with his shriveled hands folded, corpselike, on his chest. Joshua would have thought him dead except for the whisper of his labored breaths and the occasional twitching of his limbs. A knot of grief and anger swelled in Joshua's throat. *Don't take him yet, Yahweh. I need him. I need to know if I've really heard your voice.*

Gershom's two younger sons sat on either side of the bed. They glared at Joshua as they would at any stranger who entered their father's bedroom, especially one who was a Moabite. "I'm Joshua, Lord Eliakim's son," he told them. "May I have a moment alone with your father?" They studied his face with curiosity and awe as they rose and left the room.

"Rabbi Gershom?" Joshua's hoarse voice sounded dull in the small room. "Rabbi, I need to talk to you."

He stood for a moment at the foot of the bed, praying that the rabbi's eyes would open, praying that he would sit up and roar in his booming voice, "Stop dawdling,

380

Joshua, and get on with it! Tell me what God said to you!" But Gershom never stirred. Joshua pulled Isaiah's scroll from the leather bag on his shoulder and sat down with it beside the rabbi's bed.

"Yahweh answered some of my questions, Rabbi. Some . . . but not all." Joshua found the prophecy he wanted and began to read: " 'The righteous perish, and no one ponders it in his heart; devout men are taken away, and no one understands that the righteous are taken away to be spared from evil. Those who walk uprightly enter into peace; they find rest as they lie in death.' "

Joshua's voice choked and he had to stop. He watched the rabbi's face but saw no sign that he had heard. *Please, Yahweh. I need him.* He cleared his throat.

"Rabbi, I asked God 'Why?' over and over again. And when He finally answered, He simply said, 'Because. Because I Am.' He is a sovereign God. I understand that now. Isaiah worded it better than I can: ' "For my thoughts are not your thoughts, neither are your ways my ways," declares the Lord. "As the heavens are higher than the earth, so are my ways higher than your ways and my thoughts than your thoughts." ' "

"After I read all of Isaiah's prophecies I saw that God's eternal plan is so much greater than I ever imagined, yet each of us — you, me, my father — we each have a part to play in His plan. We're here to serve Him, not the other way around. So I stopped asking 'Why?' and I began to ask 'What?' — what did Yahweh want from me? How do I fit into what He's doing?

"I remembered all of the things you taught me, Rabbi. I remembered who I was — part of His chosen people, redeemed from slavery, joined to Him by His covenant. I remembered my duty as His servant — to live in obedience to His laws, even in this fallen world, in order to help establish His kingdom on earth, until He redeems all of creation. Isaiah talks about that day, too: 'The Lord will lay bare his holy arm in the sight of all the nations and all the ends of the earth will see the salvation of our God.' "

Joshua stopped and gazed at the rabbi's pale face. He saw no change, no flicker of awareness. "Please, I need to know if I really heard — that I understand God's plan for my life. Isaiah says God is going to punish our nation for its wickedness, but that a remnant will cling to the truth. They will carry out God's plan by preserving the true path to salvation and to God. He says, 'Though your people, O Israel, be like the sand by the sea, only a remnant will return.

Destruction has been decreed, overwhelming and righteous.' And He also says, 'Go, my people, enter your rooms and shut the doors behind you; hide yourselves for a little while until his wrath has passed by.' "

Joshua knelt beside the bed and took the rabbi's lifeless hand in his. It felt cold and stiff, as if carved from wax. "Please, Rabbi. Is God asking me to lead that remnant?"

Rabbi Gershom drew a ragged breath, as if he was about to speak. He held it for a moment before exhaling with a long sigh. Then a deep stillness filled the room as the rabbi's spirit left his body. It was a holy moment, filled with Yahweh's presence, as if a curtain had parted and Joshua could watch the rabbi enter the eternal world of rest and peace. Joshua closed his eyes and bowed his head.

" 'Lord, you have been our dwelling place throughout all generations . . .' " he recited. " 'From everlasting to everlasting you are God. You turn men back to dust . . . For a thousand years in your sight are like a day that has just gone by, or like a watch in the night. . . .' "

When he opened his eyes again and looked at Gershom, Joshua knew that the lifeless body he saw wasn't the rabbi but rather a fragile husk that had once borne his spirit.

Grief for Gershom swelled inside Joshua and also a twinge of envy. He knew in that moment that his father and grandfather had passed through the same curtain, that they also lived in God's holy presence. " 'Teach us to number our days aright,' " Joshua murmured, " 'that we may gain a heart of wisdom. . . . Establish the work of our hands for us — yes, establish the work of our hands.' "

Joshua released Gershom's hand and rose to his feet. When he walked into the main room, the gathered Levites fell silent, staring at him. "The rabbi is dead," he said quietly. Gershom's oldest son moaned and tore his robes. The other men stirred from their places as they rose to go to his bedside.

"Wait," Joshua said. "The rabbi's death provides us with an excuse to gather all the priests and Levites together without arousing the king's suspicion. So before you prepare him for burial and begin the days of mourning, hear what I have to say."

Joshua was well aware that he was the youngest man in the room. The others had no reason to listen to him or to follow his leadership. He was also aware that any one of them could be a traitor who might betray him to the king for a price. But the enormous peace and certainty he had experienced at the moment of Gershom's death still surrounded him, canceling his fears. He studied their doubtful faces, unwavering in his conviction.

"I'm Joshua son of Eliakim, son of Hilkiah. I've come back to help you escape from Jerusalem — all of you, and your families, as well. We're going to rebuild a community of faithful believers outside of Judah and preserve the true faith. We must worship God and raise our families away from Manasseh's perversions and idolatry in order to remain obedient to His laws and to His covenant."

"How can we do that?" Asher asked. "His Holy Temple is here in Jerusalem. God's presence dwells here."

Joshua shook his head. "That building is no longer Yahweh's Temple. Not if idols are worshiped there. Not with an Asherah pole and altars to the starry hosts planted in its courts. We have to remove the holy ark to a place of safety."

Rabbi Gershom's son stared in disbelief. "The holy ark? But it was made during Moses' day! King David danced before that ark! It hasn't been moved since Solomon dedicated the Temple three hundred years ago!"

"I know," Joshua said. "That's why we

have to protect it from Manasseh."

"How can we be certain that God really spoke all of this to you?" one of the chief Levites asked.

Joshua drew a deep breath. "Ask Him. Use the Urim and Thummim in the high priest's breastpiece to seek divine guidance the way King David and our ancestors did. Ask God if this is really what He wants us to do."

While the women prepared Rabbi Gershom's body for burial at dawn, the men departed to summon all of the chief priests and Levites to the meeting. "We'll have to meet at the Temple," the rabbi's son told Joshua. "Priests aren't allowed to enter a house where someone has died."

"Won't we be watched if we meet in the Temple?" Joshua asked.

"We might be. Manasseh replaced all of our Temple guards with his own men. If they stay to supervise us, we'll simply pray for my father's soul as we said we were going to do. If they leave us in peace, we'll hold our meeting. The Urim and Thummim will be ready."

"What about me? My hair and beard haven't finished growing in yet. I still look like a Moabite."

Gershom's son held Joshua's chin and

turned his face from side to side, grimacing as he studied the foreign cut of his beard. "What a mess! No wonder Yahweh forbids this. Maybe we can blacken the stubble on the sides of your face with charcoal so it won't be so noticeable. You can wear my Levitical robes and cover your head with a prayer shawl. That's the best we can do. Just keep your head down."

For over an hour, four of Manasseh's Temple guards stayed inside the meeting hall with the assembled priests and Levites as they recited prayers for Rabbi Gershom. But when the first watch of the night ended and the guards left, Joshua finally had a few minutes to address the high council before the second shift of guards arrived. He spoke just loudly enough to be heard as the men continued to murmur their prayers.

"We don't have much time so listen carefully. You know from the words of the Torah that Yahweh's judgment must fall on our nation because of Manasseh's wickedness and unfaithfulness. Rabbi Isaiah saw this and he warned us to hide from God's wrath, promising that God would preserve a faithful remnant of His people. I've come back to help all of you and your families escape."

He saw fear and skepticism written on many faces and knew that the long months of Manasseh's brutal repression had ravaged their faith. One of the senior council members frowned as he stepped forward. "That's impossible. Manasseh has guards everywhere. Besides, where would we shelter so many people?"

"Yahweh revealed that to Isaiah, as well. He prophesied that 'in that day five cities in Egypt will . . . swear allegiance to the Lord Almighty' and 'in that day there will be an altar to the Lord in the heart of Egypt.' We'll escape with the ark of the covenant and build a new altar for Yahweh in Egypt."

His words were followed by an outburst of puzzled voices. Joshua had to shout above the noise, "Please, there's no time for this. The guards could return any minute. I've asked the council to seek guidance by Urim and Thummim. We'll allow Yahweh himself to tell us."

One of the chief priests, the senior member of the high council, came forward to stand in the center of the group. Chosen to wear the ephod in the high priest's place, he appeared nervous as he unwrapped the cloth in which it was hidden and slipped it over his head. The breastpiece, with the Urim and Thummim inside, was attached to the ephod by braided chains of gold.

Joshua gazed at the magnificent work of

art. Dating back to the time of Moses, its antiquity alone made it a priceless treasure.

The entire assembly knew they faced execution if Manasseh caught them seeking guidance with the high priest's breastpiece. They stood with their hands raised in prayer as the chief priest led them. "Blessed art Thou, Lord God Almighty, God of our father Abraham, God of Moses and David. We ask you to reveal to us by your Urim and Thummim if this is truly your will; if we are to leave this city which you have chosen for your dwelling place; if we are to take the holy ark of your covenant with us."

Every nerve in Joshua's body vibrated with fear. Had he really heard Yahweh speaking to him, or was he about to prove himself a fool? And what if God's answer was *yes?* Did he really want the lives of all these men and their families in his hands? He had trained for a position of responsibility and leadership beside Manasseh, but making decisions had been little more than mental exercises to Joshua, challenges to his intellect, intriguing puzzles to solve. He had never before grasped the fact that his decisions would affect the lives of innocent people. In his youthful arrogance, he had looked down on uneducated people like his servant Maki as part of the ignorant rabble who needed his guidance. In his pride, he would have governed the nation from his throne beside Manasseh instead of from his knees before God.

"O God, forgive my self-righteousness and arrogance," he whispered. "Help me to be even half the man that my servant Maki was."

The chief priest's prayer ended. The room fell silent. Joshua held his breath along with all the other men as the priest reached inside the pocket of the breastpiece.

"I've drawn Thummim. Yahweh's answer is *yes.*"

Immediately, everyone turned to Joshua, waiting. All the strength seemed to drain from his body at once. He felt utterly alone. He couldn't lead hundreds of priests and their families to safety past Manasseh's troops. He couldn't steal the ark of the covenant from the Temple.

Yahweh's answer is yes.

"Please . . . pray for me," Joshua said, then his knees gave way, and he fell prostrate before God. *Heavenly Father, I need you! I can't do this by myself. Help me! Please don't let any more innocent people die because of me. I need wisdom to know what to do. I need courage to face my enemies. Help me, Yahweh! Please, please help me!*

His prayers faded into the melodic murmur of the other men's voices as he cried out to God. When the room finally fell silent several minutes later, the chief priest helped him to his feet. This time Joshua was ready to face the waiting men.

"The guards may return any moment, so continue reciting prayers out loud while you listen to me. Passover week begins in a few days and hundreds of thousands of pilgrims will pour into Jerusalem. When they leave to return home after the final morning convocation, you and your families will leave with them. If you take only the bare essentials, you will never be noticed among such a huge crowd. Scatter in all directions like the other pilgrims and —"

"My wife is expecting a child soon. She shouldn't travel."

Joshua turned to see who had spoken and looked into the worried face of Yael's husband. Instantly, hatred rushed through Joshua's veins. Amos didn't deserve Yael. She belonged to him. As her beautiful face materialized in his mind, Joshua ached to hold her in his arms just once. Except for a brief moment when he'd taken her elbow to steady her after she'd stumbled over a loose stone in the street, he had never even touched her. Now she belonged to this stocky, balding Levite nearly twice her age.

Joshua's voice sounded hoarse when he answered. "Let those who can't travel far, and those with very young or very old family members, go north or east to the closest borders. If you're able to travel farther, go south or west. We'll rendezvous in Egypt later."

"That doesn't give us much time to sell our houses and other possessions," one of the Levites said.

"Don't even try to sell your goods. It will attract too much attention if every priest and Levite begins selling everything he owns."

The Levite pulled on his beard. "You mean I can't even sell my . . . ?"

Joshua shook his head. "Nothing. I'm sorry." He felt compassion for these men as he watched them slowly comprehend the truth; they were about to lose the accumulated wealth of their lifetimes and, in some cases, their ancestors' lifetimes. He couldn't condemn them for their struggle.

"I know what it is to mourn the loss of your home and your possessions," he told them. "But, believe me, your family's safety is far more important. Don't jeopardize their lives for a few pieces of silver. It's not worth the risk. Besides, if you stay here you'll lose everything when Yahweh's judgment falls on our nation." He saw heads nodding in agreement as the men chanted their prayers. Joshua drew another deep breath and continued.

"We must make sure we take a copy of the Torah with us — and all the other important books from the Temple library. Is it well guarded?"

The Levite in charge of the Temple scribes answered. "Manasseh's guards check on us regularly as they make their rounds, but for the most part they leave us alone. Still, they would certainly notice it if we emptied the shelves."

"You need to decide which books are the most important ones and leave the others," Joshua said. "Divide them among yourselves and put phony scrolls in their places. Then each of you can smuggle out one or two of them along with your personal possessions. Remove the scrolls gradually throughout Passover week, so the increased activity in the library won't arouse suspicion."

Joshua glanced at the door, aware that the new shift of guards might burst into the room any minute. He had to hurry. "What about the Temple vessels?" he asked. "Would Manasseh's priests miss one or two of the gold and silver vessels that you use every day for the sacrifices?"

"Do you have any idea what would happen to us if we're caught stealing gold from the Temple?" a Levite exclaimed.

"Yes. We would die," the elderly chief priest replied. He had taken off the ephod and breastpiece and hidden them beneath his cloak again, disguising them as part of his ample belly. "But this is a living death sentence, serving idols in a polluted temple."

Joshua's eyes swept the faces in the room. "The question is, do you trust God? No matter what happens to you? Whether you live or die? That's what each one of us has to decide. If we agree that preserving the ark and a remnant of the faithful is His will, then we should give ourselves to His work willingly and trust that if we die in the process, it is also His will. There's no shame in being afraid. I stand here tonight, terrified. But decide right now if you're willing to die. Don't wait until the moment you face death."

Joshua saw many heads nodding in agreement. Most of the men's faces revealed their resolve and their determination to follow God. "Good. Then we're agreed that we'll try to smuggle out as much gold and silver as we can."

"We should also bring one of the silver trumpets with us," Amos added.

Joshua nodded and quickly looked away as a shaft of jealousy pierced him once again. He couldn't help fantasizing that Manasseh's men would execute Amos for trying to smuggle out a trumpet, leaving Yael free to marry him. He shook himself to erase the vision before continuing.

"Hide the vessels in the bottom of the cart that carries the ashes and bones to the dump in the valley every day. Moses told our forefathers to plunder the Egyptians that first Passover night, and we will do the same thing. Is there a place in the valley where we can safely store the gold?"

"The area by the dump is riddled with caves of all sizes," one of the priests said. "Beggars and lunatics sometimes live in them."

"Good. Choose two reliable men from among you and declare them unclean the day before Passover. They'll be forced to live outside the city for seven days. Have them guard —"

Suddenly the door burst open and four new Temple guards stormed into the room. The steady mumble of prayers, which had continued while Joshua was speaking, stopped abruptly. The captain of the guards leaped onto the empty dais at the head of the room.

"What's going on in here? The other guards told me you were saying prayers for the dead, but they didn't tell me you were going to go at it all night!"

Joshua felt a runner of sweat trickle down his face from beneath the heavy prayer shawl on his head. He resisted the urge to wipe it, fearing he would smudge the charcoal he had rubbed on his face. The chief priest took charge.

"Rabbi Gershom was a very great man as well as a fellow colleague of ours," he said. "We mourn his loss deeply. As priests, we're forbidden to enter his house or attend his funeral at dawn, so —"

"How much longer do you intend to go on with this?"

Joshua couldn't allow the soldiers to disband the meeting before he'd outlined his plan for rescuing the holy ark. He stole a quick glance at the four soldiers to make certain he didn't know any of them, then stepped forward.

"If I'm not mistaken, Captain, King Manasseh himself was once a student of the honorable Rabbi Gershom. Has the king been informed of his death?"

"I don't know."

"Then perhaps you should inform him right away. His Majesty might be offended if he wasn't invited to pray along with us. Not to mention how great his anger might be if you were to forbid us to pray for his esteemed teacher."

Distrust battled fear on the captain's worried face. He opened his mouth to speak, then quickly closed it again. A moment later he stalked from the room, taking his three men with him.

"You were very foolish to call attention to yourself," the chief priest began, but Joshua cut him off with a wave of his hand.

"Start reciting prayers again. Hurry. We haven't much time." The mumble of voices began once more and Joshua matched his tone and pitch to the sound. "We must rescue the ark. Now, as long as the golden poles can be seen protruding past the holy veil it won't be missed for a while. Am I right?" He saw heads nodding. "I know that only the priests may touch it and that the Levites who are descendants of Kohath are assigned to carry it on their shoulders by the poles. How well do these false priests know the Passover rituals?"

"I don't know," the chief priest replied, shrugging. "This is the first Passover they'll celebrate with us. All of them are from the northern tribes, though. None of them are true sons of Aaron."

"Then we'll have to take a chance that they're ignorant of the rituals. We'll need to make a litter the same size and shape as the ark and also carried on poles. Tell the false priests that it is your custom during Passover to carry away the ashes and bones from the Temple altar on a cart without wheels. Tell them it's to commemorate our desert wanderings. Cover the litter with whatever you're required to cover the real ark with and use it throughout the seven days of the feast. If they lift the cover to inspect it the first day or two, they will see bones and ashes. On the last evening, have the priests remove the ark from the holiest place with wooden poles but leave the golden poles sticking out as usual. Then the sons of Kohath can carry it to the valley and hide it with the other vessels that you've smuggled out during the week. Can you see any problems with the plan so far?" He glanced at their nervous faces, then at the door.

"Good. I'm going to have my brother send a caravan of goods to Jerusalem during Passover. It will leave here empty on the final evening and meet up with the sons of Kohath in the valley. His caravan will escort the Kohathites and the treasure out of

Judah during the night. The next morning, after the final convocation, you and your families will follow.

"I'll need a few volunteers to remain behind to perform your usual duties at the Temple. Manasseh will know you've all fled as soon as you fail to conduct the sacrifices. But if the evening sacrifice proceeds as usual, you won't be missed until the following morning. That will give your families extra time to escape." Joshua saw several priests and Levites, including Asher, raise their hands to indicate that they were willing to stay behind.

"Good. One last thing. After that last evening sacrifice, one of you will draw Prince Amariah aside into the Temple side chambers where I'll be hiding. We're going to smuggle him out in the last ash cart and take him with us to Egypt."

"Does the prince want to escape?" Asher asked.

"It doesn't matter if he wants to or not. The line of David must continue, in exile."

The elderly chief priest stopped praying and stared at Joshua. "That's going too far. We won't have any part in kidnapping Prince Amariah. He's Manasseh's secretary of state. You said nothing about him when we sought Yahweh's will with Urim and

Thummim."

"He's right," Rabbi Gershom's son added. "As Levites, we have a sacred duty to preserve the ark and the other holy things, but we have no right to kidnap —"

Suddenly Manasseh's guards flung open the meeting room doors and flooded into the room. When Joshua saw the angry look on the captain's face, he inched backward to try to blend in with the other Levites.

"King Manasseh sends no regrets at the death of your Rabbi Gershom," the captain said. "The king called his former teacher a bully and a tyrant who tried to brainwash him with guilt and lies. This meeting is over!"

19

"Innkeeper! This wine tastes like camel water!" The Moabite pounded his fist on the table. "If you can't serve us something better than this, we'll have to look for another inn."

Hadad laughed along with the two other Moabites seated at his table, but it was a bluff. He liked this dingy inn. It had become his second home. He felt comfortable seated at his usual table in the darkest corner. But he wasn't so sure, at times, if he felt comfortable with his three Moabite friends.

It was early evening, and Hadad was still sober enough to wonder if they were using him. Ever since they'd sat down beside him three weeks earlier, he seemed to be paying for more than his share of the drinks. His drunken blackouts were becoming longer and more frequent, yet the three Moabites always appeared by his side no matter where, or when, he awoke. Hadad didn't quite trust them, and in his sober moments he suspected that if they ever learned where he hid his grandfather's gold, they would disappear with it.

The innkeeper hurried over to Hadad's table with a new skin of wine and refilled all their glasses. The Moabite who had complained took a drink, then smacked his lips. "Ah, much better. A toast, then, to our brother Hadad." His smile was broad and warm as he thumped Hadad on the back.

Hadad swallowed half of his drink in one gulp. As the wine's numbing warmth spread through him, he chided himself for being so suspicious. These were his friends, his dearest companions. They helped fill the aching loneliness in his life since his grandfather's death. They had been kind to befriend a stranger in a foreign city, so far from home.

Home.

Tears filled Hadad's eyes when he thought of Jerusalem. He still missed that golden city, and his privileged life in the king's palace. He finished his wine in another gulp and stared into the empty cup.

"Hello, Hadad."

It took him a minute to recognize the bearded stranger standing beside his table. "Jerimoth! Great to see you again. Hey, whatever happened to your crazy brother, Joshua?"

Jerimoth's somber expression didn't change. "That's why I'm here. May I have a word with you, please?"

One of Hadad's companions grabbed a nearby stool and dragged it over for Jerimoth. "Here, have a seat. Any friend of Hadad's is also our friend. Innkeeper, another glass over here."

Jerimoth didn't sit. "I don't want any wine," he said. "Please, I need to speak with Hadad alone."

The Moabite kicked Jerimoth's stool, sending it spinning across the room. "What's the matter, Jew? Think you're too good for our company? Tell him to be on his way, Hadad."

Hadad felt a tremor of fear when he saw the angry looks on his friends' faces. He knew that the little merchant would never survive a brawl with the three drunken, street-tough Moabites. Hadad smiled nervously and raised his empty glass. "The next round of drinks is on me, my friends. Please, give us five minutes alone, all right?"

The air was tense as the Moabites took their time draining their cups and rising from their places. Jerimoth waited to sit down until the men crossed the room to join the revelers at another table.

"You'll have to excuse my friends," Hadad said. "They're a little drunk."

"What about you, Hadad? Are you drunk?"

He shrugged. "Does it matter?"

"Yes. My brother's life might depend on it." Jerimoth's face was so somber, his gaze so intense, that Hadad's head cleared all at once. He pushed his empty cup aside and leaned closer to Jerimoth, resting his arms on the table.

"What happened?"

Jerimoth exhaled. "A while ago I received a letter from Joshua saying that his fiancée was married to someone else."

"I'm sorry. That's a tough break."

"Yes, Joshua took the news very hard. He decided to stay with the caravan instead of coming back to Moab. That was the last I heard from him — until yesterday. He's back in Jerusalem. He needs our help."

"*Our* help?"

Jerimoth nodded. "His letter was very vague — he was obviously worried that it would fall into the wrong hands — but the gist of it is that I'm supposed to send a caravan of goods to Jerusalem, arriving just before Passover week ends. I'm not to come with it."

"That's all?"

"He said that the caravan should include a pair of oxen and a cart, and litters, carried on poles by porters. And he asked me to give this to you — but only if you were sober." He pulled a folded square of parchment from his cloak but held the sealed message close to his chest as if debating whether or not to hand it over.

"I've had a few drinks, Jerimoth, but I'm not drunk. I admire your brother's guts for going back there. I won't betray him."

Jerimoth nodded and slid the message across the table. Hadad picked off the lump of sealing clay and unfolded the letter.

Hadad —
    For the sake of your grandfather's honor and good name, it's time to repay the debt you owe. My brother's caravan can deliver it to Jerusalem.

He read it through three times before handing it back to Jerimoth.

"He needs money?" Jerimoth asked after reading it.

"It's not about money," Hadad said. "The only debt I owe in Jerusalem is my life. Prince Amariah warned my grandfather and me to escape. Now I think Joshua wants me to help Amariah escape."

"That must be why he wants the caravan. But why the porters and litters?"

"I have no idea."

Jerimoth groaned and shook his head. "I never should have let him go back there. He's going to get himself killed." He sat with his head in his hands for several moments, staring at the tabletop, then he looked up again. "Are you going to help him, Hadad?"

"I don't know."

For the sake of your grandfather's honor and good name . . .

Hadad knew that he should help Joshua. But he was safe here in Moab. Why risk his life? He glanced over at his Moabite friends and suddenly saw them for the crude, worthless drunkards that they were. And he was no better.

Jerimoth's stool scraped on the stone floor as he stood. "You don't need to decide tonight, Hadad. I won't leave for Jerusalem until next week."

"You're going? But I thought Joshua said you weren't to come?"

"I know what he said, but I'm going just the same. Let me know when you make up your mind."

Miriam sat at the table with the others as they finished their evening meal, wondering why the atmosphere seemed so tense and strained tonight. Was it because Jerimoth was going away with one of his caravans tomorrow morning? Was he worried about leaving his wife, now that she was pregnant again? Jerimoth hadn't been his usual jovial self for days, and whenever he held Mattan or little Rachel on his lap he seemed to pull them a little closer to his heart. Jerusha was unusually quiet, as well. Miriam wondered if it was because her younger son had never returned from his caravan journey, and now her older son was leaving her, too.

When a knock on the front door echoed through the house, Miriam jumped to her feet. "I'll see who it is."

She didn't recognize Hadad at first. Not only was he clear-eyed and sober, but he had grown a beard and mustache. "Hello, Miriam. Is Jerimoth home?"

"Yes. Come in." She led him inside, surprised that he remembered her name.

The conversation halted when everyone saw Hadad. "I'm sorry," he said. "I didn't mean to interrupt your dinner."

Jerimoth appeared shaken. "No, no, we were just finishing. Won't you join us?" He stood and motioned to Joshua's empty place.

Hadad shuffled his feet. "I've already eaten."

Miriam watched them carefully, sensing something wrong in their awkwardness, then she saw a look of understanding pass wordlessly between them.

Joshua.

He was the only tie connecting Hadad and Jerimoth. Miriam's heart began to race. Hadad must have news that he didn't want to share in front of the others. She knelt beside the mat they used as a table and began gathering the dinner plates.

"If you're sure you're not hungry," Jerimoth said, "I was just about to step outside for some air. Will you join me?"

"All right."

Miriam watched the two men disappear through the back door into the courtyard. She had to find out why Hadad had come.

"Could I please be excused, Lady Jerusha? I need to wash out a few clothes down by the river. Please, I know I should have done it earlier today, but I ran out of time and now it will be dark soon, and . . ." She stopped, aware that she was babbling.

Worse, she was lying.

"Certainly, Miriam. Go ahead. We'll clean up the dishes."

Miriam tossed a few of her things into a bundle and hurried out the back door. Jerimoth stopped midsentence as she walked through the courtyard to the rear gate. She closed it behind her, then ducked behind the garden wall to listen as Jerimoth continued.

"What made you decide to come with me?" he asked Hadad.

"What difference does it make?"

"You and I are both safe here in Moab. We have new lives. I have a young family." Jerimoth spoke slowly, deliberately, as if measuring every word. "I'm putting my life at risk because Joshua is my brother. I love him. For my own peace of mind, I'd like to know what's motivating you." There was a long pause. When Hadad said nothing, Jerimoth spoke again. "It can't be money. I understand that Lord Shebna left you plenty of that. You said you owed Amariah your life. Is it gratitude, then?"

"Sure, gratitude. Does that ease your mind?"

"No. You might better show your gratitude by staying here where you're safe. If the prince cared enough to warn you, then that's obviously what he would want you to do."

There was another long silence. Miriam began to wonder if the men had gone inside. She was about to peer over the wall when she heard Hadad speak.

"I'm doing it for myself, all right? I admire courageous men — men of conviction like you and your brother — but I'm not one of them. I never worried much about it before all this happened." He gave a short laugh. "Until your stupid little serving girl started lecturing me."

"You mean Miriam?"

"My grandfather tried to give me the same speech dozens of times — what was I doing with my life, when was I going to amount to something. But he never got through to me like she did. Maybe it's because I saw myself in her — I don't know. Or maybe I'm just sick and tired of living like a drunk. Either way, I've decided to do something noble for a change. Something that would have made my grandfather proud." His voice had grown so soft Miriam barely heard his last sentence. There was another long pause. This time Miriam waited.

"We leave at dawn," Jerimoth finally said. "It will take us about two days to get to Jerusalem with the caravan load."

"How will we contact Joshua?"

"We'll wait for him to contact us. He'll be watching for a caravan from Moab."

"Well, I guess that's all I need to know," Hadad said, exhaling. "I'll meet you in the marketplace at dawn."

"Hadad, wait. Listen, my brother-in-law and I usually say evening prayers about this time. Will you join us?"

Miriam barely heard Hadad's reply. "Yeah . . . sure."

In the faint light before dawn Miriam shook her brother awake. "Nathan . . ." He bolted upright, as tense in sleep as he was awake. She stroked his head to soothe him, aware that she was the only person he would allow to make such a tender gesture. "Shh . . . It's me, Nathan."

"What's wrong?"

"Come outside. I don't want to wake Mattan." She waited for him to put on his robe and sandals, then led him outside. She heard Jerimoth stirring as they passed his door. "Master Jerimoth isn't going away on a trading venture," Miriam told her brother. "He's going back to Jerusalem. Joshua needs his help."

"He told you this?"

"No, I eavesdropped last night when

Hadad was here. The thing is . . . I'm going with them."

"Jerimoth will never let you —"

"I know. That's why I'm not going to tell him. I'm going to follow his caravan until he's too far from Moab to turn back."

"Miriam, no! It's too dangerous!"

"I promise I'll stay within shouting distance. Listen, Nathan. I need you to tell Lady Jerusha and the others where I've gone so they won't worry."

"Let's wake Mattan and we'll all go," Nathan said.

Miriam planted her hands on his thin shoulders. "Matt isn't the same boy he was a year ago — and neither are you. We have a new life here, a better life, with opportunities you boys would never have if you returned to Jerusalem. You can both read and write now. You have a future here."

"I don't care. I want to come with you."

"If you try to follow me, Nate, I'll tell Jerimoth that you're still stealing from the other vendors. He'll throw you and Mattan both in jail. Is that what you want?"

She saw his surprise and embarrassment, then his anger. "You're just like Mama! Always running off and leaving us! I knew you'd do the same thing someday! I knew it!"

"But I'll be back, Nathan, I swear it. Master Joshua promised to be a father to you. He needs help. I'm going to bring him back so he can do that — don't you understand?"

Nathan didn't reply. He stood with his wiry body rigid, his arms folded stubbornly across his chest. Miriam pulled him close, rocking him until his body sagged limply against her own. "I love you," she whispered. "I promise I'll be back."

Nathan's arms closed tightly around her.

Travelers crowded the road out of Heshbon for most of the morning, making it easy for Miriam to follow Jerimoth's caravan from a safe distance without being seen. Late that afternoon, when the road forked west into Samaritan territory, the traffic thinned out. In the plain below, the swollen Jordan River overflowed its banks from the early spring rains. Flatboats ferried passengers and cargo to the opposite bank. Since Miriam had no money to pay the fare, she would have to make herself known.

Jerimoth didn't notice her as he paced near the water's edge, issuing orders to his drivers and supervising them as they loaded the litters on board. So when Miriam saw Hadad sneaking off to a clump of bushes by

413

himself, she decided to follow him. She watched as he removed a small flask from inside his robe and turned his back to take a drink.

"Hadad . . ." Her sudden appearance startled him, and he whirled around to grab her by the shoulders. She smelled the fruity wine on his breath as he shook her slightly.

"Miriam! What in blazes are you doing here?"

"The same as you. Helping Joshua."

"Does Jerimoth know that you followed us?"

"No. Does Jerimoth know that isn't water you're drinking?" He released her with a curse. "Pay my fare across the river, Hadad, and he won't find out what you're drinking."

"You've got some nerve, you little . . ." Hadad cursed again. "You may as well show yourself. We've come too far for him to send you back now."

"Not until we stop for the night," Miriam said. "I want to cross the river first."

Hadad dug into his pouch and shoved a small piece of silver into her hand. "Here. I hope the blasted boat sinks, with you on it!" He took another long drink as Miriam disappeared into the crowd of travelers waiting to cross the river.

Once they reached the other side of the Jordan, they faced a long, slow climb up thousands of feet to Jerusalem. The men and animals were too weary to begin the journey before nightfall, so Jerimoth decided to spend the night in Jericho. Miriam knew that it wasn't safe to sleep alone in the caravansary. She saw Hadad standing apart from the others and went to him again. He shook his head in disgust.

"Well, if it isn't Miriam. Still tagging along, I see."

"And here's Hadad, still fortifying himself with wine. I want you to tell Jerimoth you found me."

"I hope he beats you senseless." He gripped her arm and towed her behind him. Jerimoth groaned when he saw Miriam and clutched his head.

"Miriam! Oh no! What are you doing here?"

"I came to help Master Joshua."

He groaned again and turned to Hadad. "Did you know about this?"

"Not until she popped up out of nowhere."

"But my mother will be worried sick. . . . Miriam, does my mother know you're here?"

"Nathan knows where I am. He'll tell her."

"No, I can't let you come with us. It's too dangerous. I'll have one of my men take you home in the morning."

"Wait," Hadad said. "She might come in handy. Didn't she help you escape the last time? Besides, I don't look like I belong with this caravan. Miriam and I can enter the city as two pilgrims, coming a few days late for Passover."

Miriam could scarcely believe that Hadad would defend her. She held her breath, waiting for Jerimoth's answer.

"Why have you done such a foolish thing, Miriam? You were safe in Heshbon."

Miriam blurted out the first answer that came into her head, too embarrassed to confess her love for Joshua. "You've been a father to Mattan. I didn't want him to lose you, Master Jerimoth."

"Joshua will be furious when he sees that I've come," Jerimoth told her. "I can't even imagine what he'll say when he sees you."

Miriam worried about what Joshua would say all the next morning as she made the steep climb to Jerusalem. She walked in front of the caravan with Hadad to avoid the dust, staying within sight of the lead driver. There were very few places where the road leveled off to give her legs a rest

416

and they ached from the strain of the continual ascent. Hadad said nothing until they stopped to eat lunch; then he shoved his canteen beneath her nose.

"Here, smell it! It's water." Miriam didn't reply. They walked all afternoon in silence.

Jerusalem looked beautiful to her after nearly a year in Moab — pristine and golden in the late afternoon sun. But the streets were so jammed with pilgrims for the Passover feast that the caravan could barely move through them. She watched Jerimoth's men unload the goods in the caravansary, then she sat with him and Hadad inside the vacant booth they'd rented, waiting for Joshua to find them. Even in the dim evening light, she could see the strain of worry etched on Jerimoth's face. When the Temple shofar announced the evening sacrifice, he didn't move. Hadad grew restless.

"I think I'll go and —"

"Sit down, Hadad!" Jerimoth ordered. Miriam had never heard him speak so forcefully. "You're staying right here!" No one spoke again as they waited in the growing darkness.

When Joshua finally arrived shortly before dawn, he crept up so silently that he seemed to materialize out of nowhere, startling them all from their sleep. His hair and beard had grown and except for his bronzed skin, he no longer looked like a Moabite. As soon as he saw his brother his temper flared.

"I thought I told you not to come, Jerimoth." He spoke in a whisper, but Miriam heard the anger in his tone and saw it in his rigid stance. Jerimoth stood and embraced his brother.

"We're family. We stick together. Your battles are my battles. . . . Thank God you're all right."

"I am for the moment, but who's going to take care of Mama if anything happens to us?"

"I'm trusting that Yahweh will."

Joshua exhaled and looked around the tiny booth, acknowledging Hadad's presence with a nod. Then Miriam stood and stepped out of the shadows. At first Joshua's mouth gaped in surprise, then his features quickly hardened in rage. "Are you out of your mind, Jerimoth? What did you bring her for?"

"I didn't bring her — she followed us. She wants to help."

Joshua walked toward Miriam, stopping just a few inches from where she stood. The muscles in his neck and arms tightened as his hands bunched into fists. Miriam backed against the wall, certain he would strike her.

"You foolish girl, this isn't a game! I don't need your help! I don't want you anywhere near me! You're not part of this family!"

His cruel words hurt Miriam more than any physical blow. Through a haze of tears, she saw Jerimoth step forward to defend her.

"Listen, Joshua, she —"

"Shut up, Jerimoth! You have no idea what's at stake!" Joshua grabbed Miriam's arm and propelled her toward the door, shoving her roughly into the street. "Go home and stay there! I don't want your help! You don't belong here!"

Miriam ran from the marketplace without looking back.

Joshua shook with the force of his anger. He felt as if he was suffocating as his lungs began to squeeze shut.

Hadad sprang to his feet. "I'm going after her. You can't let her run off alone like that!"

Joshua blocked the door. "Sit down! Both of you! She knows how to take care of herself."

"But you had no right to treat her that way," Jerimoth said.

"I had every right! Isn't it bad enough that Maki died helping us? Do you want to kill Miriam, too? Now sit down and listen to me." Joshua tried to take several deep breaths. He was wheezing as he battled against his rage and the panic that always accompanied his breathing attacks. He cursed Miriam for upsetting him and triggering his illness.

Jerimoth leaned against an empty crate. "What is this all about? What in heaven's name are you doing here, Joshua?"

"I don't want Miriam involved. This isn't a game." He ran his fingers through his hair as he drew another breath. "I can't begin to describe what Manasseh has done to this nation. Every evil thing you can think of . . . every abomination . . . Walk up the hill to the Temple and look at his filthy idols, right in the middle of the courtyard! There's an Asherah pole in the holy place and . . . and he sacrificed his own son!" He stopped, bending over double as he coughed, struggling for air. Jerimoth came to his side and rested his hand on his shoulder.

"Easy, Josh . . ." he said quietly. "I believe you. What do you want us to do?"

"Tonight, just before the gates close, take your empty caravan out of Jerusalem. Leave a pair of oxen and a cart outside the Sheep Gate with a reliable driver. Tell him someone will come for them after the final convocation tomorrow. Take the rest of your men to the Kidron Valley, where the priests dump the Temple ashes. I'll meet you there. As soon as everything is loaded, get the caravan across the nearest Egyptian border as quickly as possible."

Jerimoth gripped his arms. "What are we smuggling, Joshua?"

The air whistled through Joshua's lungs as he drew a deep breath. "The ark of the covenant."

Jerimoth sank down on the empty crate and closed his eyes. "God of Abraham!"

"You're out of your mind!" Hadad said. "The priests will never let you —"

"The priests and Levites are part of this. Their lives are already in jeopardy. We're smuggling all of them and their families out of Judah with the pilgrims, after the morning convocation."

"Are you sure you know what you're doing?" Hadad asked.

Joshua nodded. "The priests sought God's will with the Urim and Thummim."

"O God of Abraham," Jerimoth moaned again.

"Now do you understand why I didn't want you to have any part in this?" Joshua asked him. "If we're caught, we'll be executed — like Abba was."

Hadad sank down on his sleeping mat and

folded his legs in front of him. "And what do you want me to do?"

"Meet me at the south Temple gate the following morning, before the final convocation. I'll need you to get Prince Amariah's attention and draw him aside into one of the priests' rooms where I'll be waiting."

"Then what?"

"That's all. Your job will be finished. You'll be free to go home with the rest of the pilgrims."

"Wait a minute," Hadad said. "He saved my life. I have a right to know what you're planning to do to him."

"I'm going to get him out of the country so we can preserve the line of David." His outburst triggered another coughing spell. It was a moment before he could speak. He wiped his mouth with the back of his hand. "The prince will be subdued and restrained, then carried out in one of the ash carts."

"Swear to me you won't harm him," Hadad said.

"I'm trying to save his life, not kill him!" Joshua said. The Temple shofar suddenly sounded, startling Joshua. He hadn't realized it was dawn. "I have to go. Is there anything else you need?" Jerimoth shook his head. "Then don't leave this booth all day. Either of you. Don't take any chances that someone will see you and recognize you. There are too many innocent women and children involved in this." He opened the door.

"Joshua . . ." He turned to face his brother. "Be careful," Jerimoth whispered.

The sun was just beginning to rise above the Mount of Olives when Miriam reached the tiny shack that used to be her home. The first thing she noticed was the smell. The house stank of rotting garbage and human filth. She left the door open and unlatched both windows to air the place.

Someone had been living here since she and the boys left almost a year ago. The mound of ashes on the hearth was faintly warm. Stale bedding straw sprawled across the floor. A few meager food supplies — flour, oil, roasted grain — were scattered all over the shelf. Every pot and dish they owned was either piled on the table or stacked on the floor beside the hearth. Flies crawled all over them, attracted by the crumbs of food. Her mother must have returned.

Tears of shame filled Miriam's eyes. Even their poorest house in Moab had been clean and fresh-smelling compared to this. How had she ever lived this way? And how would she stand living like this again? No wonder Joshua wanted nothing to do with her. He had seen all of this. He knew exactly where she came from and what she was.

Miriam allowed her tears to fall as she bailed water from the cistern and carried it outside along with three armloads of dishes. She preferred to work outdoors, but even the tiny patch of bare earth behind the house stank with strewn litter — rotting vegetables and fish heads, more straw bedding crusted with vomit. A horde of flies buzzed near one corner of the house, which someone had used for a latrine.

She hauled wood to build a fire, then dug a hole to bury the garbage as the water heated. But even after soaking the dishes, Miriam couldn't scrape all the dried food off them. As she chipped at it with a wooden spoon, one of the bowls cracked into pieces in her hand. She covered her face and sobbed.

More than anything else, she longed to feel Lady Jerusha's arms surrounding her, comforting her. How she loved that gentle woman, and Miriam knew that she had been dearly loved in return. She felt it in Jerusha's touch, saw it reflected in her soft, green eyes, heard it in the tender words of praise and encouragement Jerusha lavished on her. Miriam had never experienced such love before. It was one of the reasons she had stayed in Moab. But now Miriam would never see Jerusha again. Joshua didn't want her as part of his family. He had made that very clear. Miriam wished she had said good-bye to Jerusha, but maybe it was better this way. What made her think she deserved Jerusha's love?

At last Miriam wiped her tears and plunged another load of dishes into the hot water to soak.

"Well, well, look who's finally come home to roost!"

Miriam turned to find her mother standing in the doorway with her hands on her hips. The familiar aloofness in her eyes hurt Miriam more than she ever imagined it would.

"Hello, Mama." Miriam made no move to embrace her, knowing her mother's arms would be stiff and unyielding in return.

"And where have you taken yourself off to all these months?"

Miriam hesitated, unsure if she could explain all that she had experienced. "Does it really matter?"

"I suppose not," she said, shrugging, "as long as you're not coming home pregnant."

Miriam turned back to the tub of dishes

to hide her sudden tears. She willed her voice not to shake. "I've never even slept with a man, Mama."

"Hah! You expect me to believe that? Just look at you with your fancy clothes and your shiny hair all piled up like a queen's. Where else would a girl like you get money to fix yourself up, if not from a man?"

From people who loved me, she wanted to say. *People who treated me like family.* "I earned my own way," she said, instead. "I worked for a rich family, doing their cooking and washing." She conquered her tears with stubbornness, rather than shed them in front of her mother.

Her mother walked the few steps into the backyard and took a corner of Miriam's robe between her fingers, feeling it to gauge the quality of the fabric. She sniffed as if it were beneath her notice. "Then why did you leave your rich family?"

A simple question with not such a simple answer. "They moved to Moab," Miriam said after a moment. "I didn't want to go with them." Miriam wondered when her mother would ask about Nathan and Mattan. Or if she would ask.

"So now you expect me to support you again, I suppose?"

"I'll find another job. I can —"

"Well, and who might this be, darling?" a man's voice boomed from the doorway. "You didn't tell me we'd hired a maid. And such a pretty one at that." The man swaggered into the yard and wrapped his arms and hands around Miriam's mother. He was made from the same mold as all her mother's other lovers — middle-aged, arrogant, and loud. His flabby body, ravaged by his lifestyle, was clothed in cheap, flashy robes. Miriam recognized the greedy look in his eye and knew she would have to get away from him and find another place to live.

"This is Miriam," her mother said. "She isn't the maid, but she is looking for work. Or so she says." Miriam knew her mother would never introduce her as "my daughter." It would make her mother seem old in her lover's eyes. The man released her mother and took a step toward Miriam. She sprang to her feet and backed away.

"Jittery little thing, aren't you." Miriam cowered under his gaze as he appraised her from head to toe. "She's your daughter, isn't she?" he asked. "I see the resemblance."

"She's a mistake I made before I learned how to take care of my mistakes."

"Well, she's a very attractive mistake, I'd say. Yes, she's her mother's daughter, all right. What kind of work are you looking for, darling?"

"I can cook and clean," Miriam said quickly. "I can wash clothes, tend babies . . ."

He grinned at her. "Can you, now. Well, it so happens a friend of mine runs an inn. He can always use another serving girl, especially a pretty one who'll draw in the customers."

Miriam saw a quick flash of jealousy in her mother's eyes before she wrapped her arms around her lover's ample waist and nuzzled his neck. "Do you think your friend could board her there, too? There's barely enough room for the two of us here as it is."

"Sure, I think he could probably find a place for her to bed down."

A voice inside Miriam urged her to run from them, knowing the life they were planning for her, knowing what she would inevitably become. But Miriam also knew that she had no other place to go. She could never travel back to Moab by herself, nor was Joshua likely to change his mind and take her back, even as his servant. His harsh words burned in her heart. *I don't need your help! I don't want you anywhere near me! You're not part of this family!*

Lady Jerusha would tell her to pray, to

trust Yahweh to take care of her. But why should Yahweh help her? She had nothing to offer Him in return. She was illegitimate, and Hadad had already explained what Miriam's life would be like: she would never find a respectable job or marry a decent man. In the end, she had no other choice than the one this man offered her. After all, she was her mother's daughter.

She met his gaze dry-eyed, grateful that her silly tears were no longer a threat. "When would your friend like me to start work?" she asked.

20

Joshua slipped his arms into one of Asher's Levitical robes and fastened the sash around his waist.

"Are you sure you're feeling up to this?" Asher asked. "You don't sound well."

"I'm fine." But Joshua wasn't fine. Every breath he took felt like a spear thrust through his chest. The breathing attack had worsened since that morning, aggravated by his mounting anxiety as he had spent the day waiting.

He tucked the sacrificial dagger into its sheath beneath his robes. "Let's go."

They left Asher's house through the rear door and stepped outside into a light rain. They couldn't have asked for a better night to remove the ark from the Temple. The dark clouds would help shield their movements, the rain would keep the guards inside, and the blanket of fog in the Kidron Valley would conceal Jerimoth's caravan from the view of the sentries on the wall. But the cool, damp air made it difficult for Joshua to breathe.

A cartload of wood stood waiting in the alley behind the house. Joshua had hidden one of his brother's empty litters beneath the cart, along with the wooden frame he had built.

"Let me show you how this goes together," he said. "I won't have time to explain it once we get to the Temple."

"What is that?"

"It's a phony replacement for the ark. The golden poles will rest in these grooves. I made it the same height as the real ark so it will look as if everything's still in place from outside."

"We'll never be able to sneak this past the guards. It's too bulky."

"It comes apart . . . see? And the pieces are small enough to fit beneath the priests' robes. Once you're inside the holy place you can fit the frame back together again like this. Here . . . you try it."

Asher quickly rebuilt the frame. "You're a genius, Joshua."

He managed a tired smile. "Now take it apart again and let's get this wood loaded."

"What's this carving on the side?" Asher held one of the frame's pieces close to his face, trying to see it in the dark. "What is this . . . a bull?"

Joshua yanked it out of his hand. "It's nothing. Come on, let's get this litter loaded."

Asher didn't move. "There are seven lamps inside the holy place, Joshua. The priests are going to see the carving. What am I supposed to tell them?"

Joshua wiped the rain out of his eyes and sighed. "It's my signature," he said quietly. "Manasseh used to call me 'Ox.' "

Asher threw down the piece of wood he was holding and sprang to his feet. "You're not doing this for our sakes, are you! You're staging all of this to get even with King Manasseh! You're using us, putting us all at risk, just so you can show him —"

"Shut up and listen to me. You were there the night the priest used the Urim and Thummim. Did I stage that, too? I could be safely out of the country by now, but instead I'm risking my life for you. Believe me, one lousy carving of an ox can't even begin to settle my score with Manasseh!"

"But stealing the ark of the covenant can."

They stared at each other in silence. Joshua shivered in the cold. "Do you have any idea what that man has done to my life, Asher? I have nothing left. Nothing. Is leaving my signature too much to ask?"

Asher kicked at a piece of firewood and sent it spinning down the alley. "What other little surprises aren't you telling us about?"

Joshua looked away. "After everyone else has left tomorrow I'm going to kidnap Amariah. The priests wanted no part of it, so I'm doing it without them."

Asher shook his head. "God help you, Joshua." He turned his back and began throwing wood onto the litter, his anger evident in the way he tossed down the logs. When the litter was nearly full, Joshua tucked the pieces of the frame among the firewood.

"Listen, Asher. Don't get distracted because you're angry with me. Save all your energy for what we're about to do. We need to stay calm." Asher didn't reply. Joshua bent to lift the rear poles as Asher picked up the front ones. They started walking toward the Temple. "Have the guards been suspicious because you've been using litters all week?"

"They inspected them once or twice in the beginning, but lately they haven't seemed to care. They have more interesting things to worry about."

"What do you mean?"

"Asherah's prostitutes. Women are thronging to the Temple to fulfill their service. There's hardly enough room for them all. And, of course, the men are lined up a mile long to do their part. The guards have their hands full keeping order."

Joshua shuddered. "I've heard about such things in pagan nations, but I never thought I'd see it in Yahweh's Temple."

The load of wood was heavy, and by the time they reached the top of the Temple Mount it was raining hard. Joshua could barely control his coughing. The guards didn't seem to notice them as they passed through the service gate. They set the litter down near the bronze altar and began unloading it. The two priests who had been chosen to remove the ark from the holiest place came out to help them.

"How many guards are there?" Joshua whispered.

"Two at each entrance, two patrolling the grounds. We're praying that the rain will keep them all inside."

Joshua quickly surveyed the courtyard for movement, then handed pieces of the frame to each priest. "Hide these inside your robe." The last priest's hands trembled so badly he fumbled the wood and it clattered to the ground. Joshua picked it up and handed it to him again. "Take it easy," he soothed. "You can do this." But Joshua's own nerves felt as tight as bowstrings. This was only the beginning. So much more could go wrong before he escaped with Amariah tomorrow night.

Asher and the priests moved toward the Temple doors to get the ark. As soon as they were inside the sanctuary, three Levites emerged from one of the side chambers carrying the wooden poles. Like Asher, they were also sons of Kohath, the tribe assigned to carry the ark. Joshua climbed the altar ramp with an armload of wood to watch for guards, pretending to feed the fire. Just as the Levites slipped inside the Temple doors, he saw two guards round the rear corner, walking toward him along the side of the Temple. He dropped the wood into the fire and hurried down the ramp to intercept them before they reached the front courtyard.

"I . . . I need to ask you something," he said in a whisper. "I don't want the others to hear." He motioned them into the shadows on the side of the Temple. He didn't need to pretend to be nervous. "Suppose I wanted to . . . you know . . . to be with one of Asherah's women. How would I do that?"

"Well, I'll be blessed! A pretty little Levite in his clean white robe wants to worship

Asherah!" The two guards laughed uproariously. One of them draped his arm around Joshua's shoulder. "It's easy, son. You just take your pick, toss her some silver, and she'll follow you into the booth."

The second guard thumped Joshua on the back. "After that you're on your own, kid!" They turned to go.

"No, wait. It's not that simple. I can't let the other Levites see me." Joshua glanced around as if afraid that someone might overhear him, but he was watching for the Levites to cross the courtyard with the litter.

"What do you care if they see you? It's a free country."

"You don't understand. I'm related to half of these men — they're my brothers, uncles, cousins, second-cousins. If I get caught, they'll murder me."

"Guess you'd better get yourself a woman the old-fashioned way, then — marry her!" They burst into laughter once again.

"But my wedding could be years away. Please, can't you help me somehow?" The two men looked at each other, and Joshua saw their expressions soften in sympathy. He knew he had their interest. One of them leaned against the wall, scratching his chin.

"What you need is a disguise of some sort."

"Yeah, that should fix you up, kid. A disguise."

"When would be the best time to . . . you know . . . take my pick?" Joshua's question started a debate between the two men that quickly escalated into an argument. He let them bicker. It kept them from noticing the figures moving across the courtyard with the covered litter. He waited until the Levites were almost to the outer gate, then pretended to see them for the first time.

"Oh, no! I'm supposed to be helping them carry the ashes! Please, go back the way you came! I don't want them to know I was talking to you."

"Calm down, kid, and take a deep breath. You're wheezing. We'll stay put until you're out of sight."

"Good luck with the ladies, son. Pick a good one!" He heard their laughter behind him as he jogged across the courtyard toward the gate.

When Joshua reached the guarded archway leading from the Temple grounds to the Kidron Valley, one of the gatekeepers stood in his path. "Where do you think you're going?"

"I'm supposed to be helping the others

dump the ashes."

"There were enough of them to do the job without your help. It doesn't take five men to dump a load of ashes."

"You're right, my lord, it doesn't. But I'm an apprentice in training. If I don't catch up with them, I'll never finish my apprenticeship in time to be ordained."

Joshua held his breath so he wouldn't cough. His heart leapt wildly as the guard appraised him. "All right, then. Get going."

Manasseh drained his wine glass and lay back against the cushions in his chambers. Zerah leaned toward him and refilled his glass. Manasseh felt peaceful, listening to the gentle drumming of rain against his shuttered window and the soft murmuring of Zerah's voice beside him. But the room was growing cold as the fire in his charcoal brazier slowly died away. He rang for his valet to rekindle it for the night.

"Your concubine sent this message to you, my lord." The servant handed him a sealed note before tending to the fire.

Manasseh waited for the valet to leave before opening it. *His concubine.* He hadn't thought about Dinah in several weeks. Zerah eyed him curiously.

"Dinah can read and write, you know,"

Manasseh said. "Her father taught her."

"How convenient."

He picked off the seal and unfolded the note. It contained only one sentence: *My days of purification have ended.* He handed it to Zerah.

"What do you make of this?"

Zerah read it and smiled. "You know, Your Majesty, it would be a very good omen to conceive an heir during Passover, under the sign of the ram. Then you wouldn't need to tolerate Prince Amariah's insubordination any longer."

"Will you wait here for me until I get back?"

"Of course, Your Majesty."

As he made his way down the hall to the harem, Manasseh realized that the strong pull he felt toward Dinah was more than a simple longing for an heir. Her message had been an invitation. Was it possible that she had missed him? That she cared for him?

She was only a woman, one among many who would live in his harem and bear his sons. Yet Dinah meant more to Manasseh than the others did. She was a link to Joshua and to Eliakim, a part of the innocence of his childhood that he could still cling to. Against his will, he found himself longing to hear her say that she loved him.

When he entered her room she stood waiting for him. The lamps in the room had been dimmed, but Dinah's dark eyes danced with fire. He had missed her. He moved toward her and reached up to unpin her hair. Then he gasped as a shaft of pain sliced through his gut.

"Die, you murderer!" she breathed. "Die and rot in Sheol!"

Manasseh staggered backward, clutching his stomach. He saw the shard of broken glass shining in Dinah's hand. It was covered with blood. His blood. She drew her arm back to stab him again.

"No, don't!"

He raised his hand as a shield as she lunged at him and the blade sliced across his forearm. He cried out in agony as blood pumped from the second wound, spurting everywhere. An alarming amount of blood was pouring from the jagged tear in his belly.

With a surge of desperate strength, Manasseh grabbed Dinah's wrist before she could stab him a third time, and he wrestled her to the floor. "Help me!" he cried. "Somebody get in here and help me!" She was stronger than he imagined. It was all he could do to keep her pinned beneath him as he struggled with her. The pain in his gut was agonizing. She managed to get one

440

hand free to claw at his face, and her nails tore into his skin. "Help me!" he shouted again.

By the time Manasseh's servants burst into the room he was dizzy from losing so much blood. He rolled off of Dinah as the guards grabbed her and he curled into a ball, holding his stomach.

"She tried to kill me," he moaned. "The little dog tried to kill me!" The shock of Dinah's betrayal hurt Manasseh nearly as much as his wounds. Zerah ran into the room and bent over him, his face white with fear.

"I don't want to die," Manasseh whispered to him. "Please help me!" Then Zerah's face disappeared as Manasseh lost consciousness.

Joshua caught up with the Levites before they reached the bottom of the hill. Asher turned to look at him, but none of the men spoke. Their somber faces and slow, careful steps testified to the enormity of what they were doing. This ark, symbol of their nation's covenant with Yahweh, had stood in the Temple since the time of King Solomon — until tonight.

The valley was so dark with clouds that Joshua never saw Jerimoth and the waiting caravan until they suddenly emerged from the fog in front of him. "Joshua! Thank God!"

"Did you have any trouble leaving the city?" Joshua asked.

"No. None at all."

Joshua saw the shadowy forms of men and animals in the mist behind his brother. "Do your porters know what they're hauling?"

"Only that the goods are stolen. And that they're being paid extra to be quiet about it."

"Are they armed?"

"Yes."

"Are you?"

Jerimoth nodded.

The Levites halted and lowered the ark to the ground with great care. Joshua saw the deep emotion in their troubled eyes; he couldn't tell if their faces were wet with rain or with tears. "Are you sure we're doing the right thing?" Asher asked him.

"We sought God's will with Urim and Thummim, remember? Let's get this stuff loaded."

The two Levites who had been guarding the cave helped Jerimoth's men load the hidden goods onto the caravan. The amount of gold and silver the Levites had managed to smuggle out amazed Joshua. Everything was proceeding smoothly, just as he'd planned.

Jerimoth didn't help his men with the loading. Instead, he stood to one side, staring at the covered litter. Joshua moved up beside him. "I can't believe what's hidden beneath that cover," Jerimoth whispered. "Dear God in heaven — the ark of the covenant! Who are we to carry out such an awesome responsibility!"

"We're our father's sons, Jerimoth. Yahweh entrusted His house and His nation to Abba's hands. Now the burden has been passed to us."

"This is God's mercy seat," Jerimoth breathed. "God's presence goes with this ark. Do you realize what that means? When this leaves Jerusalem, it's the end of our nation . . . the end of our people . . ."

"The people themselves made that choice — God didn't. And this isn't the end. It's only a new beginning." Joshua shivered in the damp, cold air and coughed. He saw Jerimoth appraise him with a worried frown.

"You're not well, are you?"

"I'll be fine."

Jerimoth gripped his arms. "Joshua, forget about Prince Amariah and come with me tonight. You've got the ark — now let's both get out of the country alive. Too many things can go wrong tomorrow. Hadad isn't strong-minded enough to help you. He'll fall to pieces at the first hint of trouble. Please, for Mama's sake —"

"The Levites need a leader. They have no one. It's what I've been trained to do."

"It's more than that, and you know it. You want to get even with Manasseh. I don't blame you, Josh, but revenge is a hunger that can never be satisfied. Even if you capture Prince Amariah, it still won't be enough."

"It will be a good start."

One of Jerimoth's porters approached them. "Everything is loaded, my lord. We're ready." Joshua gazed at the shrouded ark for the last time. The two Levites from the cave, along with two other Kohathites, traded places with Asher's men, lifting the ark onto their shoulders. They would carry it to safety in Egypt. Asher's men would carry one of Jerimoth's empty litters back up to the Temple.

Joshua turned to say good-bye to his brother but before he could speak, Jerimoth gripped him in his embrace. "Come back alive, brother," he whispered. "Please, God. Come back alive."

Hidden inside the entrance to another cave,

the beggar watched the shadowy forms moving in the mist near the dump. Something odd was going on over there. Ever since two strangers moved into one of the other caves, the beggar had been on the alert. It only took him a few days of watching to catch on to the fact that they were smuggling something out of the city along with their garbage and stashing it in that cave. But he hadn't quite decided what to do about it yet.

If the loot was valuable, the strangers would be armed. The beggar knew he would need help overpowering them before he could make off with their goods. He needed to consider all of his colleagues carefully, working out in his mind who to let in on his secret. If he blabbed to the wrong man about a heist this big, he could get himself killed.

But now it looked as though he had debated too long. There was a lot of movement over there tonight, and the loot was being hauled away by a dozen new men. He cursed himself for being too slow to act. He had missed his big chance to score. What if the smuggling operation didn't continue after tonight?

He watched the steady rain form huge puddles outside his cave as he debated what to do. The rain would turn all the roads out of Jerusalem into mud. The smugglers would leave a trail any child could follow. But once all the pilgrims left the city tomorrow morning, the trail would be wiped out. There wasn't enough time to gather a gang and waylay the smugglers. He couldn't even tell his fellow thieves what they were smuggling!

No, the only chance he saw to benefit from this whole escapade was to alert the authorities and hope for a reward. Let trained soldiers fight the battle, not him. A small payment was better than nothing at all, which is what he had at the moment.

As the beggar watched, the knot of men across the valley formed into a caravan and disappeared down the valley road into the fog. Another group of men, five of them, started climbing up the hill to the Temple again. The beggar pulled his cloak over his head and sprinted down the valley through the rain to the Water Gate.

"I want to report a smuggling ring," he told the sentries standing guard. His words were met with howls of laughter. "Take me to your captain, then," he shouted above the noise.

The raucous debate among the soldiers about what to do with him seemed to take forever. Meanwhile, the thieves were probably disappearing into the night along with his hopes for a reward. The beggar persisted, shouting wildly, until he was finally dragged up to the palace and brought before the captain of the guard.

The captain sat in his booth by the front entrance, cleaning his fingernails with a knife. The aroma of roasting meat drifted out from somewhere inside the palace, making the thief's mouth water. Maybe he'd settle for a leg of mutton instead of silver.

"What's your story, old man?" The captain wore an expression of boredom on his bland face.

"Those priests at the Temple are up to something, my lord. I've been watching them. They've been smuggling stuff out with their garbage and stashing it in a cave in the Kidron Valley. Tonight I saw a caravan down there, hauling it all away."

The captain looked up at him and sheathed his knife. "Which Temple priests are these?"

"I wouldn't know the difference, my lord. They're the ones who carry stuff to the dump every day."

"And how long have they been doing this?"

"All week, my lord."

"Can you prove your story?"

"I'll take you down there myself. You'll see all their footprints in the mud by the cave. I'm sure their pack animals left a trail, too. Your men could still catch them on horseback if they hurried."

The captain folded his arms across his chest. "Do you know what the penalty is for leading us on a wild goose chase?"

"Yes, my lord. But I'm telling you the truth. I could use the reward money, sir."

The captain stood. "Very well, I'll go down with you myself and —"

Suddenly the door flew open and one of the palace guards rushed in. "Captain, you must come right away! Someone just tried to assassinate King Manasseh!"

When Manasseh opened his eyes he was lying bare-chested on Dinah's bed. His blood-soaked tunic had been torn away and one of the royal physicians was pressing a thick wad of bloody cloths against his stomach. "Lie still, Your Majesty. Don't move."

Sweat rolled into Manasseh's eyes. "Where is she?"

"In the dungeon beneath the palace," Zerah answered. "In chains." He dipped another cloth in cold water and laid it on Manasseh's forehead.

"I want her executed! Tonight!"

Zerah turned to the doctors. "Is the bleeding under control?"

"Yes, my lord."

"Then leave us." Zerah waited until the physicians and servants left the room. Then he sat on the edge of the bed beside Manasseh. "When your bodyguards saw what she did to you, they beat her. I stopped them before they killed her. It isn't in your best interests to execute her just yet. You need an heir from this woman first."

Manasseh closed his eyes to make the dizziness stop. "The prophecy . . . the night of the equinox. The spirits warned me that I had another enemy. I just never imagined . . ."

"None of us did, Your Majesty. I'm sorry. We should have been more alert."

The pain in his gut was the worst Manasseh had ever known. He moaned in agony. "Am I going to die?"

Zerah wrung out another cloth and placed it on his brow. "Don't upset yourself. I'm seeking omens right now."

Manasseh glanced down at his arm. The wound was wrapped in a bandage with a strip of linen tied tightly above his elbow to stop the bleeding. "Untie this thing, Zerah. It's too tight. I can't feel my fingers."

Zerah shook his head. "The cut was very deep. Leave it for the doctors."

"Well, get them in here. I need something for the pain!"

"First, we must decide what to do about Dinah."

"I don't know . . . I can't think. What should I do?"

"Offer her to Asherah, Your Majesty. Make her fulfill her service. Then the goddess will bless you with an heir."

"But I'm the king. If another man has her . . ."

"Of course. You're right. When he's finished, the man who chooses her will be killed. And once she provides you with an heir, she will be killed."

21

By the time the captain returned to his guard booth, the beggar was curled up on the floor asleep, dreaming of roasted lamb. The captain shook him with his foot. "Old man! Wake up!"

The beggar sat up, rubbing the sleep from his eyes. It took him a moment to remember where he was. "King Manasseh . . . the assassin?"

"Everything is under control for the moment. Are you still sticking with your smuggling story?"

"I know what I saw, my lord. But surely the smugglers are long gone by now. It's almost dawn, isn't it?"

"Take me there just the same. I want to see for myself if there's any truth to your story. After tonight, I'm leaving nothing to chance."

The sky was growing light by the time they reached the Temple dump, but thick fog still hung like gauze over the valley. Even in the gloom, the muddy footprints in the cave and the caravan trail down the valley road were plain enough for any man to see. The beggar watched smugly as the soldiers inspected the evidence. When they finished, the captain walked over to him.

"I was telling the truth, wasn't I?"

"So it seems. How many times a day do the Levites come down to this dump?"

"Twice a day. A few hours or so after each sacrifice."

"And you didn't see what it was they were smuggling?"

"No, sir. Everything was wrapped up in cloths. But I figured it was all different things because they were all different sizes. Do I get my reward now?"

"Come back to the guardhouse with me, and I'll see that you're properly rewarded."

Rain clouds hung stubbornly over the city as Joshua watched thousands of pilgrims stream into the Temple courtyard for the final morning convocation. There would be a huge traffic jam when they all departed afterward. The guards couldn't possibly notice the Levites and their families among so many people.

Joshua pushed his way through the crowd

to the southwest corner of the Temple wall where the priests blew the shofars. Amos was the trumpeter who was sounding the call to worship this morning. Joshua waited at the bottom of the stairs for him to finish.

"You'll find a cart and a team of oxen outside the Sheep Gate," Joshua told him. "They're yours. For Yael."

Amos stared at him in surprise. "How can I thank you for this?"

"Understand me, Amos. I didn't do it for you. It's a gift for Yael."

"Then let me repay you —" He reached for his money pouch. Joshua grabbed his wrist. He wanted to break the fat little man's arm.

"You even try to pay me, and I'll throw your silver into the gutter and spit on it!" He let him go again. Amos rubbed his arm.

"You're in love with my wife, aren't you."

"The Torah tells me it's a sin to love another man's wife. But it doesn't tell me how I'm supposed to stop loving her. She was meant to be mine, not yours."

"I didn't marry her to spite you, Joshua. We didn't know you would return for her. I'm sorry —"

"You're not sorry, so don't insult me with your pity. I hate you enough as it is." Joshua felt the familiar pain swelling inside his chest, suffocating him.

"The Torah also says it's a sin to hate," Amos said quietly.

"Are you worried that I'll burn in Sheol for it, Amos? Do me a favor, then — when Yael is safe in Egypt, you can sacrifice the oxen as a sin offering for my soul."

Joshua knew he had to get away before he lost his temper. He could already hear the air whistling through his lungs as he strained to breathe. He had to stay calm. Getting upset only made his breathing attacks worse. But he turned to Amos one last time. "Take care of her," he said softly. Then he hurried away to the south gate to meet Hadad.

He found him already waiting outside the gate, glancing around nervously. Hadad's hands were trembling. "Are you all right?" Joshua asked him.

"A little nervous, that's all."

Joshua realized, too late, that his brother had been right. Hadad lacked the strength of character for such risky business as this. But Joshua had no time to change his plans.

"I, uh . . . I've been watching the royal walkway for a while," Hadad said. "Prince Amariah hasn't come up from the palace yet. No one has." When Hadad looked up at him, Joshua smelled the fruity odor of wine on his breath. He gripped the top of Hadad's arm from behind, where no one could see, and squeezed.

"You've been drinking, haven't you?"

"Ow! Just a little to calm my nerves, I swear! You're hurting me!"

"Then you can imagine what I'll do to you if you mess this up." After a moment he let him go again.

As the convocation began and the first strains of music floated toward them from inside the Temple enclosure, Joshua knew that his plan to kidnap Amariah was beginning to unravel.

"Now what?" Hadad asked. "The sacrifice is starting."

"We'll stay here and watch for Amariah."

"What if he doesn't come?"

Joshua closed his eyes. "He has to come," he whispered.

Dinah awoke with a blinding light shining in her eyes. She tried to sit up and found that her ankles and wrists were shackled. Her entire body ached from the beating the guards gave her. She wished they had killed her.

As her eyes adjusted to the light, she could see guards with torches unlocking her cell door. She crawled backward away from them until her back was against the rear wall. Only one man entered her cell, a tall man with a halo of bushy hair and startling, peaked brows. His eyes were set too close together, making him appear cross-eyed. The hatred she saw in them made her shiver. He was going to kill her. And he was going to enjoy doing it.

"Look at you! You're a mess!" he said. His voice sounded hollow in the tiny cell.

Dinah looked down at her robe, stained with Manasseh's blood. "I just pray that he dies," she murmured.

He took another step closer and slapped her face with the back of his hand. She felt his ring bite into her cheek. But when she looked at it closely she saw that it wasn't his ring — it was her father's. He was also wearing the palace administrator's sash — Abba's sash. And Abba's palace keys were fastened to his shoulder. She knew then that her father was dead, and she felt such a wellspring of grief that nothing else mattered to her anymore. She was ready to die.

"Get somebody in here to clean her up," the man shouted. "And get her a clean robe to wear. She can't go out like this."

Dinah sat numbly as they undid her shackles. Someone washed the blood off her face and hands. Someone else stripped off her clothes and dressed her in a clean robe. Then the man wearing Abba's ring put a garland of string on her head like a crown.

They led her out of the cell and up the steep stairs with a guard walking on either side of her. Dinah was surprised to see that it was already morning. The night in the cell had gone quickly. The cross-eyed man led the way through the palace hallways, past the throne room. The huge doors were closed. She would be given no trial before they executed her.

Dinah was still calm as they left the palace and walked into the rear courtyard, passing Ahaz's clock tower. But instead of leading her toward the Damascus Gate and the king's execution pit, they led her up the royal walkway toward the Temple. She could hear the distant strains of music as they drew nearer.

Above her head the sky was filled with billowing gray storm clouds, stained red from the dawning sun. The higher she climbed, the wider the vista of sky grew and the deeper the red that smudged the clouds like blood. Dinah knew it was a sign from God. The blood of Manasseh's victims had reached to the heavens. Her son's blood. Abba's blood. Her own. God had seen everything Manasseh had done. And God would pay back all his sins in full.

When Joshua saw the distant figures emerge through the palace doors and start up the royal walkway, he nudged Hadad. "Look. Here they come." He watched them draw closer and closer. Then frustration defeated him when he realized it wasn't Amariah but a woman. She passed just fifty feet from Joshua, and suddenly he felt the cold shock of viewing a ghost.

"God of Abraham — it can't be!" He leaned against the wall as his knees went weak.

"What is it, Joshua? What's wrong?" Hadad asked.

"That's my sister! That's Dinah!" The courtyard started to tilt in front of him. Hadad grabbed him to keep him from falling over.

"Joshua! Don't faint on me!" He pulled a flask of wine from inside his cloak and held it to Joshua's lips. "Here, take a drink."

Joshua swallowed one mouthful, then another and waited for the earth to stop spinning.

"Are you all right?"

"I think so." But he had to double over with his hands on his thighs, straining to pull air into his lungs. "Where are they taking her?"

"Are you strong enough to walk? We can follow them and see."

Joshua had no sensation of his feet touching the ground as they hurried into the Temple grounds behind the guards. Dinah was still alive! After all this time! It *was* her! He could tell by the way she walked and by the proud tilt of her head. But why was her hair unpinned? And why was she wearing a garland of string on her head?

Most of the assembly had crowded into the two main courtyards for the last Passover convocation, but the guards skirted the crowd, leading Dinah around to the other side of the Temple grounds.

"They're heading for Asherah's precinct," Hadad said.

"No, she would never . . . Dinah wouldn't . . ." Joshua stumbled and nearly fell. Hadad shook him.

"Joshua, look at her! She isn't here because she wants to be. They're making her do this."

Joshua forced himself to look and saw that Hadad was right. "We have to rescue her!"

"How? They're guarding her. And what about Prince Amariah?"

Joshua raked his fingers through his hair. "I don't know. . . . I have to think!" His mind raced in a dozen directions at once. He couldn't seem to focus it. He only knew that by some miracle his sister Dinah was still alive and that he had to save her. He struggled against panic to concentrate as an enormous weight settled on his chest, pushing the air from his lungs. "If you bought her, Hadad . . . you could take her into one of those booths, right?"

"Are you crazy? They're guarding her! I'd be trapped in there!"

"How long could you stay inside with her?"

"I don't know . . . a couple of hours. Why? What are you going to do? How will you get us out again?"

"I'm not sure, yet. Just stay in there until the next watch. I'll figure something out by the time the guard changes. Listen for it."

"This is insane!"

Joshua unsheathed his knife and slipped it to Hadad. "Could you use this if you had to?"

"I . . . I guess so."

"Don't *guess*, think! Your life depends on it! And Dinah's life! Are you prepared to use a weapon?"

Hadad exhaled. "Yes."

"Good. I'll create some sort of a diversion. That will be your signal to run. Get

Dinah out of the city and take her to Moab."

Hadad nodded, then turned and hurried away before Joshua could think to ask him if he needed money to buy her. He held his breath as he watched Hadad walk across the cobblestones and enter Asherah's sacred precinct. Hadad seemed to take his time weaving between the ropes, appraising the women as if he had all the time in the world. Then he stopped in front of Dinah. He reached into his money pouch in slow motion and threw something shiny into her lap. The guards grabbed her arms and hauled her to her feet. Hadad led the way inside the empty booth. The guards pushed Dinah into the booth behind him and slammed the door.

Just then a shout went up from the crowd in the courtyard as the priest laid the offering on the fire. The Levites began to sing the closing hymn. In a few more minutes the pilgrims would start their journey home, and the priests and their families would make their flight to safety.

Joshua leaned against the wall that surrounded the Temple Mount and closed his eyes. *O God, help me! Please! I don't know what to do!*

As the door to the booth slammed shut,

Hadad felt as if his heart would tear from his chest in fear. He was trapped! Then he saw Dinah backing away from him, whimpering in terror.

"No . . . no . . . please!"

"Dinah, listen to me," he whispered urgently. "I'm not going to hurt you. I'm here with your brother Joshua. We're going to help you escape." He could see that his words hadn't penetrated her terror, so he repeated them. "I'm not going to touch you, Dinah. Joshua and I have come to rescue you."

Dinah froze. He wondered if she had finally heard him. She trembled all over, as if she stood naked in a freezing gale. "Joshua's here?"

"Yes. He's outside in the courtyard." As his eyes adjusted to the dim light in the booth, Hadad saw that her face was bruised and swollen from a beating. But even disfigured, she was the most beautiful woman he had ever seen. She had her mother's thick sable hair, her father's dark, soulful eyes. Her slender body was as delicate as a fragile wildflower compared to his treelike frame. "I'm going to get you out of here," he said again.

"How?" she whispered. "They'll never let

you out of this booth alive. I tried to kill him."

"Kill who?"

"King Manasseh."

Hadad groped behind him for the edge of the bed and sat down. "What did you say?"

"Manasseh killed our son. He deserved to die!"

"You're King Manasseh's *wife?*"

"His concubine. And his prisoner."

Hadad closed his eyes. He had walked into a trap. Joshua would never be able to get them out of here alive. He had the sudden, panicky thought that his life was over already and he had wasted it. All those hours he couldn't account for, lying drunk in his own vomit — what had been the use of it all? The irony of his situation made him want to laugh and weep. This was the first noble deed he had ever attempted in his life, and now he was going to die for it.

He heard a noise and looked up. Dinah had covered her face. She was weeping. If he was terrified, how must she feel? Without thinking, he stood and drew her into his arms to comfort her. She leaned against him and sobbed. "Shh . . . it's all right, Dinah. It's all right."

"Abba is dead, isn't he?"

"Yes," he said softly. "Your father died a

year ago. But the others are all safe — your mother, your sister, and brothers. They're all living in Moab."

"Joshua came back . . . for me?"

Hadad didn't see how the lie could hurt anyone. "Yes," he said. "And he's going to get us both out of here. We just have to sit tight a little while, that's all."

Hadad could feel her entire body shivering against his own. He took off his outer robe and wrapped it around her, then he led her to the bed and sat down beside her. She looked so forlorn as she huddled next to him that he took her in his arms again. "Do you mind if I hold you?" he asked. "I think we need each other."

"I . . . I'm grateful," she said as she settled against his chest. "I don't even know your name."

His name. All his life, it had been so important to Hadad to have a name. Now he would die trying to earn one. But as he held Lord Eliakim's daughter in his arms, offering her comfort before she died, he knew that his grandfather would be proud of him. "My name is Hadad," he said. "I'm Lord Shebna's grandson."

Joshua fought his way through the crowd while they poured out of the Temple courtyard as if trying to swim upstream through a powerful current. The sacrifice was over. Neither Amariah nor King Manasseh had attended it. He would have to concoct a different plan. Joshua guessed from the angle of the sun that it was not quite the third hour. The guard would change at the sixth hour — noon. That didn't give him much time.

He found Asher and the Levites who had conducted the service in a Temple side chamber, changing into street clothes.

"Hey! You're not supposed to be in here!" Asher shouted when he saw him. "This is sacred —"

"Asher, it doesn't matter. None of this is sacred ground anymore, remember?" Joshua felt a rush of pity for these men as they vainly tried to cling to the only way of life they had ever known. He understood how difficult it was for them to let go of it — he had struggled with the changes in his life for almost a year. "Please, Asher, I need your help."

"I'll have nothing to do with kidnapping Amariah."

"That's not what I'm asking you to do. Look, I've run into a problem. None of you should stay until the evening sacrifice as we planned. You all need to get out of Jerusalem right away."

"Why? What happened?"

"I don't have time to explain. Please . . . *please* help me." He deliberately drew one deep breath then another, releasing them slowly. He had to remain calm. He was *not* suffocating.

"What do you want me to do?"

"Find one of the palace guards and lure him in here. Make sure you come through the door first."

"Then what?"

"Then all of you get out of here!"

Asher stared at him for a long moment, then hurried from the room. Joshua picked up the priest's heavy golden censer and stood beside the door with his back to the wall. When the other Levites realized what he was about to do they turned their backs on him and quickly finished dressing.

Joshua waited, his breathing audible. He heard footsteps approaching and Asher's voice. The door opened and Asher walked in, followed by a palace guard. Joshua swung the censer against the back of the guard's head as hard as he could. The man staggered forward, then toppled to the floor, knocking over a wooden bench. Joshua leaped on top of him and pinned his arms behind his back.

"You could have killed him with that thing!" Asher cried.

"But I didn't. Help me take his uniform off."

The guard's eyes rolled back in his head. He was groggy but still conscious enough to struggle. It took five of them to strip him and tie his hands and feet together. Joshua stuffed a wad of cloth in his mouth and tied a sash around his head to gag him. The look of fear in the young guard's eyes speared his conscience, reminding him of the young guard he had killed. Then he remembered the look of fear he had seen on Dinah's face.

"I'm sorry," he said simply, then he clubbed him again with the censer. The guard lost consciousness. Asher and the other Levites gaped in horror.

"Don't waste time," Joshua said. "Warn all the others to get out of the country. Now!"

Asher didn't move. "You're going for Prince Amariah alone, aren't you?"

"I have to."

"Joshua, let it go. He's not worth the risk."

"How can we reestablish our nation in exile without an heir to the throne? God promised King David that his kingdom would endure forever. Amariah is part of our identity as a people."

"And he's also Manasseh's brother. His rival. That's the real reason you want him, isn't it?"

White-hot anger raced through Joshua's veins as Asher's words struck their mark. He picked up the censer. "Get out! All of you — get out!"

When they were gone, Joshua dragged the soldier into the corner behind the door, concealing him from view beneath a table. Then he counted slowly to ten to clear his head, breathing deeply, ignoring the pain in his chest.

The leather uniform fit tightly across his chest and stank with the soldier's sweat. Joshua's hands shook, making it difficult to lace up the shin guards. There was a dark stain on the back of the leather headpiece where it was soaked with blood. Joshua pulled the visor as low over his eyes as he dared and strapped on the soldier's sword.

He decided against taking the royal walkway to the palace, even though it was the shortest route. Instead, he fell in with the last of the stragglers from the sacrifice and took the main street south from the Temple. Once he noted that Captain Micaiah was on duty in the guardhouse outside the palace, he doubled back toward the side entrance that led to the barracks. It was the door he and Manasseh had used every day as they left the palace for their military training.

He knew his way around the palace — it had been his second home — and he was counting on the fact that if he walked purposefully, without hesitation, no one would question him. He looked straight ahead as he strode through the palace door. The guard standing watch didn't stop him.

Inside, the palace swarmed with soldiers — dozens more than on any ordinary day. It made it that much easier for Joshua to blend in, but it would also make it much harder for him to escape again with Amariah. He pushed aside the fleeting thought that the presence of so many soldiers might mean that something was wrong.

Memories crowded around Joshua like ghosts as he walked through the familiar hallways. Memories of Abba. Of Manasseh. Memories from all of the years he had spent growing up in this palace, preparing to sit beside the king in the throne room one day, governing the nation. He shoved his distracting thoughts aside with the thought that Dinah and Hadad were waiting for him. Counting on him.

Amariah was Manasseh's secretary of state now. Joshua chose the most direct route to

Shebna's old office, hoping that he would find the prince there. Instead, he found Amariah's aide sitting in the outer chamber.

"Yes? May I help you?"

When the man looked up, Joshua almost lost his composure. He knew this man. He would hate to have to kill him.

"Prince Amariah sent for me." He forced himself to stand erect with his shoulders squared, remembering that as a youth he had been self-conscious about his height and had always slouched.

"He's in his chambers. I'll take you —"

"Don't trouble yourself. I know the way." He hurried away before the aide could rise from his seat.

A warning tried to sound in Joshua's brain when he saw the guards posted at either end of the hallway outside Amariah's chambers. He recognized both of them. They had consistently beat him in training exercises at the guard tower. And they both wore swords, just like his. He felt like a deer walking straight into a trap, moving closer and closer toward the hunters encircling him. He straightened his shoulders and walked past the first one.

"Just a minute. Where are you going?" the soldier asked.

"I have orders to guard the prince."

"That's what the two of us are doing."

Joshua knew that the longer he talked with them, the greater the risk that one of them would recognize him. "Captain Micaiah told me to go inside." He opened the door to Amariah's chambers and let himself in before they could argue further.

The prince sat slumped on his couch with his elbows on his knees, his face buried in his hands. He looked up when Joshua entered. "What is — ?"

"Don't make a sound or I'll kill you!" The blade flashed as Joshua drew his sword. Amariah leaped to his feet.

"Where are your servants?" Joshua asked him.

"A-at the convocation. I'm alone."

Joshua stepped closer and saw the prince swallow a lump of fear. "Take a good look at me, Amariah." He watched the prince study his face, then saw recognition dawn in his eyes.

"I don't believe it! *Joshua!*" Amariah staggered backward and sank down on his couch again. "Where . . . ? H-how did you get in here?"

"It doesn't matter. I'm leaving again. With you."

"You'll never make it out of here alive. Didn't you see all the guards?"

"I saw them. Why so many?"

"Dinah tried to kill my brother last night."

Joshua felt the floor rock beneath his feet. "*Dinah* did?"

"You don't know, do you? Manasseh has kept her here as his concubine. He sacrificed their son to his pagan gods a month ago. Last night she stabbed him in revenge."

Joshua needed to sit down, but he didn't dare. The sword was growing heavy in his shaking hand. Dinah was Manasseh's concubine? That meant Joshua had just sent Hadad to a certain death. There was no way that anyone could ever get Hadad or Dinah out alive. It was several moments before Joshua could speak.

"How badly did she hurt him?"

"Help came in time. He's weak from losing so much blood, but the doctors think he'll live."

"That's why you're under guard, isn't it?" Joshua asked. Amariah nodded. "O God of Abraham, help us." Joshua ran his hand over his face. He would never get them all out of this mess. He would be lucky if he got himself out.

"What in heaven's name are you doing here, Joshua?"

He sheathed his sword and sank into the nearest chair. "Last night we smuggled the ark of the covenant out of the country. This morning, all the priests and Levites are escaping with their families. We're setting up a community in exile to preserve God's Law and the sacrifices. I planned on abducting you when you came to the convocation this morning, but you never came."

"I would have gone with you willingly, Joshua. I hate what Manasseh's doing to this country. I don't want any part of it, but he's forcing me to work for him. He has people following me wherever I go, watching me. You never would have been able to get away with kidnapping me. And if you're smart, you'll walk out of here right now, while you still can."

Joshua knew that Amariah was right. It would be impossible to steal him out from under so many guards. He rose to go. Amariah stood, as well. When he did, there was something in the prince's stance and in the set of his broad shoulders that reminded Joshua of King Hezekiah. Amariah had grown several inches taller in the year since Joshua had seen him, and his newly grown beard was the same burnished bronze as his father's had been. The sudden realization astonished him — Amariah was Hezekiah's son. If Joshua left him behind, Manasseh would murder him as soon as his heir was born.

"I'm not leaving without Dinah. Or you," Joshua said.

"You're crazy," Amariah whispered.

"If I am, it's your brother's fault. He drove me to this. Do you want to leave the country with me or not, Amariah?"

"Yes . . . but the guards . . . I told you they follow me everywhere."

Joshua's mind raced ahead as he began to see a possible way out of this. But it would be an enormous risk.

"Wait one hour," he told the prince, "then come up to the Temple. Tell them you want to worship Asherah. Will they believe you?"

"I . . . I guess so . . ."

"Convince them. Put on a show. The woman you choose will really be working with me. Take her into one of the booths and wait. I'm going to create a distraction for the guards. When you hear a commotion, run! The girl knows her way around the back lanes of Jerusalem. Do whatever she tells you to do. She'll smuggle you out of the country into Moab."

"How will I recognize her?"

"She has a mole right here, under her left eye."

Amariah moaned. "How do you know she

can do this?"

"Because she smuggled me out of the city a year ago." Joshua watched several emotions play across Amariah's face as the prince considered the plan. At last a look of resolve settled over his features.

"All right," he said quietly. "One hour."

"If you have a weapon, bring it."

Joshua hesitated, unsure if he should ask one last favor of Amariah. If either of them were caught later on, it would link them together in conspiracy. "Will you do one thing for me? Leave this in your room where Manasseh will find it." He opened his silver pouch and took out a potsherd with his drawing of an ox.

"You really hate him, don't you," Amariah said.

Joshua shoved it into Amariah's hand. "If you don't want to leave it, you can crush it to dust. Now walk me to the door and let the guards see that I haven't harmed you."

"Joshua? I'll see you again, won't I . . . in Moab?"

"Of course."

22

Joshua knew that Miriam's house was somewhere in this northwestern section of the old city. Even though it had been dark the night Maki first led him here, he recognized the area of slums by its stench. He wandered, lost, through a jumble of houses that were clustered close together with no pattern of streets or lanes. He tried not to think about what he would do if she wasn't there. She had to be there. Where else would she go?

He pounded on the wrong door three times before he finally found the right one, recognizing it by the cracked stone watering trough that served as a front doorstep.

The man who answered Joshua's knock wore only a rumpled undertunic, stained with sweat. He had the stale smell and disheveled look of a lifelong drunkard. When he spoke, his words were slurred. "What do you want?"

"Is Miriam here?"

"Who wants to know?"

Joshua hesitated, then decided it was too dangerous to give his real name. "I'm . . . a friend."

The man grinned. "I'll wager you're a very good friend — a handsome young buck like yourself." Joshua resisted the urge to shove the man aside and force his way inside.

"Who's at the door?" a woman's voice called.

"Some young soldier looking for Miriam."

"Tell him she doesn't live here anymore. Send him on his way."

"You heard the lady. Get lost."

The man started to close the door but Joshua wedged himself inside the doorjamb. "Where is she?"

"Get out of our house before I bust your jaw!"

"You're in no condition to fight me or anyone else. Answer my question before I lose my patience." Joshua felt his anger billowing dangerously, and he struggled to stay calm. He knew what he was capable of doing if he lost his temper. He had no time for this. Too many lives were at stake.

A woman appeared in the shadows behind the man, and Joshua knew in an instant that she was Miriam's mother. "Where's your daughter?" he asked.

She folded her arms across her chest and stared back at him with a cool, hard gaze. "Who are you, soldier-boy?"

"Miriam worked for my family until a week ago. I've come to ask her to return."

"Well, she has a new job now. Be on your way."

"I'll offer you double whatever she's being paid."

The man turned to grin at the woman drunkenly. "Sounds to me like she's a lot more to him than a maidservant!"

Joshua grabbed the man by the front of his tunic and lifted him off the ground, swinging him sideways and smacking his head against the wooden door. Then he tossed him backward so that he tumbled to the floor inside the house.

"I don't have time for this!" Joshua said through clenched teeth. "Where is she?"

The woman stepped back. "You'll find her at the inn near the Dung Gate, across from the sheep market." Joshua took off at a run.

The inn was a low-slung, ramshackle building, jammed with the shiftless sort of men who rarely did an honest day of labor. He wasn't surprised that Miriam would choose to work in a place like this. She was her mother's daughter.

He spotted her immediately, weaving between the tables with a serving tray. She stopped beside a table where four ruffians were seated and carefully placed the bowls and wine cups in front of them. The moment she finished, one of the men grabbed her around the waist and pulled her onto his lap.

"Take your filthy hands off of me," she cried as she squirmed to break free. The man laughed. Joshua saw the hatred and humiliation written on Miriam's face as she struggled to her feet, and he knew he had misjudged her. She hadn't chosen to be here. It was his fault that she was.

"Miriam!" he called to her as he strode across the room. When she looked up and saw him she backed away, her cheeks bright with shame. "Miriam, I'm sorry that I sent you away like that. Please, I need your help."

She didn't reply. The inn grew quiet as everyone turned to watch the spectacle. Joshua reached behind her and untied her apron, then tossed it to the floor. "Please come with me, Miriam."

"Just a minute, mister!" The ruddy-faced proprietor hurried over to them, wiping his hands on a towel. "She works for me now. You're not taking her anywhere unless you pay me for her."

Miriam's head dropped lower between her trembling shoulders. Joshua longed to lift her chin high and tell her that the shame was all his, not hers. He had broken his promise to her father. He had driven her away because of his own guilty conscience. Instead, he reached for his money pouch.

"How much for her, then?" he asked the innkeeper.

"Well, to begin with she owes me a week's room and board in advance and —"

"But she already worked a couple of days, right?"

"Well, yes —"

Joshua's eyes never left the innkeeper's as he slammed a fistful of silver onto the table. It was part of the dowry money he had saved for Yael. "This should cover it."

Before the startled man could respond, Joshua took Miriam's hand. "Come on." He pulled her with him as he wove across the room between the tables and hurried from the inn.

By the time Joshua and Miriam got to the Temple, Amariah was already there, wandering through the roped-off lanes, surveying each woman carefully. The two guards from the palace hallway walked on either side of him.

"That's him with the reddish beard," Joshua whispered. "Do you remember what to do?"

Miriam nodded. "You didn't tell me he was a nobleman."

"Make sure he leaves his embroidered robe behind in the booth. It will give him away."

"Where will we meet up with you again?"

Joshua hesitated. "At our house."

"Our house?"

"Yes, in Moab. Now get going." He watched her walk calmly across the courtyard and enter Asherah's sacred precinct as if she did it every day of her life. Her courage and poise astonished him. She unpinned her hair as he'd told her to do and tossed it over her shoulder with a shake of her head. Then she put on a garland of string and sat down. Joshua saw several other men watching her, too. It surprised him to realize how young and pretty Miriam looked beside the other women. He held his breath, hoping that Amariah would get to her first.

It seemed to take the prince forever to reach Miriam's side and toss the silver into her lap. She stood and took his hand, leading him into an empty booth. It was close to the booth that Hadad and Dinah were in. The sun was almost directly overhead.

Joshua heard the new shift of guards marching up the hill from the barracks to relieve their comrades. It was time.

God of Abraham, please let this work!

Joshua strode around the side of the courtyard as if he had a right to be there and headed toward the storage silos behind the Temple. His father had built them for King Hezekiah before Joshua was born, when Abba was still the king's engineer. Joshua remembered coming here with Abba, holding his strong hand in his own small one and watching the golden rivers of grain pour into the silo. He also remembered the strict warning Abba had given the priests.

When Joshua reached the circular bin, he climbed the stairs that spiraled up the side and opened the small door halfway to the top. It was dark and cool inside the stone structure — the air vents allowed in only a little light — but Joshua knew that the silo would be nearly empty. The new grain harvest was two months away. He jumped into the bin, sinking to his knees, and quickly tied his handkerchief over his nose and mouth. Then he picked up the priests' measuring basket and began scooping up the grain and tossing it high in the air. He scooped faster and faster until his arms ached and the showering grain coated his clothes and hair. Five minutes later, the air in the silo was filled with grain dust and Joshua could scarcely breathe.

Gasping and choking, he climbed out of the silo again, leaving the door ajar, and ran into the building next to it where the olive oil was stored. The earthenware jars stood stacked on their sides like cordwood, a taller pile of empty ones on his right, the full ones on his left. He took a torch handle from its socket by the door and used it to smash the full jars, spilling oil in a slippery stream around his feet. Then he tied his handkerchief around the handle and soaked it in oil.

It seemed to take forever to kindle a flame with his shaking hands, but the spark from his flint finally ignited the torch. He ran to the doorway and touched it to the tongue of oil flowing behind him. He could feel the heat on his face as the storehouse erupted in flames with a loud *whoosh.*

Joshua ran back to the silo and took aim at the open door halfway up the side. He would only get one shot at it, so he would have to make it count. He drew his arm back and threw the torch through the door into the bin, then he turned to run. A second later the force of the deafening blast lifted Joshua into the air, then smashed him into the pavement. He was already unconscious when the hail of bricks and grain showered down on top of him.

Twenty yards away inside the booth, Hadad was knocked to the floor by the explosion. Dinah tumbled down on top of him. It was a moment before he realized from the screams and shouts outside the door that this was the diversion he had been waiting for. He scrambled to his feet, pulling Dinah with him.

"Come on. We've got to run!" He had to force the door open.

Outside, the Temple courtyards were in chaos. Most of the people were lying on the ground, stunned, as bricks rained from the sky. Hadad stepped over a guard who lay moaning beside the booth and ran toward the burning storehouse.

"Hold your breath!" he shouted to Dinah. "There's a gate leading out of the city on the other side!" He pushed her ahead of him into the blinding cloud of smoke.

Hadad's ears still rang from the blast, so he wasn't sure if he really heard footsteps behind him or not. He glanced over his shoulder, his eyes stinging from the smoke, and saw a Temple guard quickly gaining on them.

"Run, Dinah! Keep running and don't stop!" he told her. Then he turned to face their pursuer. His own short dagger was no match for the guard's double-edged sword, but Hadad took a defensive stance, praying that he could buy Dinah a few extra minutes of time to escape.

As the guard charged, Hadad feinted to the left, then ducked right, anticipating the thrust of his sword. He heard the blade whiz past his head. The guard stumbled forward with his own momentum but quickly regained his footing to turn on him again. Hadad was ready for him. Quick on his feet, he dodged the sword a second time, infuriating his adversary. The third swing grazed Hadad's shoulder as he dove to the ground and rolled away from him. But he could see the soldier coming toward him again and he realized he would never be able to scramble to his feet in time. Hadad knew he was about to die.

Suddenly a darker shadow emerged from the dense smoke behind the advancing guard's back. The man never heard Dinah as she ran up behind him and smashed the brick into his skull. His sword clattered to the ground, and he toppled to the pavement beside it a moment later.

Hadad slumped back, weak with relief. "I

thought I told you to run," he said, grinning.

Dinah smiled in return. "I couldn't leave you, Hadad. I don't know the way to Moab."

"What on earth was that?" Amariah cried as the explosion rocked the booth.

"It was Joshua, distracting the guards." There was no doubt in Miriam's mind. "Come on, we've got to get out of here!"

"That was one powerful distraction!" he murmured.

"Take off your robe and leave it here."

"Why?"

"Are you going to question everything I say, or are you going to live through this? Take it off!"

Miriam opened the door and peered out. The courtyard was littered with bodies, most of them moaning and bleeding, some of them dead.

Joshua. Was he among them? Had he survived the blast he'd created?

People ran in all directions, screaming in panic as a dense cloud of smoke billowed toward Miriam from the priests' storehouses. Most of the guards were running to extinguish the flames before the fire could spread to the Temple. She grabbed the nobleman's hand and took off toward the southern Temple gate as Joshua had instructed. She didn't waste time looking back to see if anyone was following them. She could lose their pursuers in the maze of alleyways near her home. Within moments they were running down the hill into the city, leaving the Temple Mount far behind.

"Wait . . . I can't run anymore," the man panted. He was dragging on Miriam's arm, slowing her down.

"Don't stop now, we're almost there," she told him.

"Almost where?"

"Listen, my mother might be home, so just go along with whatever I say, all right? Do you have any money with you?"

"Money? Yes, I —"

"Get ready to part with some of it." Miriam drew a deep breath, bracing herself, then opened the door to her house.

Her mother sat at the table alone, with a skin of wine in front of her. Miriam could tell she was drunk. "What are you doing back here?" her mother asked. "And who is this?"

"He's my lover." Miriam hadn't thought to ask the man his name. She slipped her arm around his waist as she had seen her mother do with her lovers countless times. The man jumped, as if she had surprised him, then a moment later he gingerly draped his arm around Miriam's shoulder. Her mother grinned.

"My, my, you're a busy girl, aren't you? What happened to your soldier-boy?"

"Mama, we need to use the house for a couple of hours, all right?"

"I thought you had a room at the inn for that?"

"The innkeeper wants too much of my pay. Wouldn't you rather have the profit?"

"Who is this lover of yours? He looks familiar. . . ."

"Do you want the money or not, Mama?"

She hauled herself to her feet, swaying, and held out her hand. "Sure, sure. Let's have it, then."

Miriam had to nudge him. "Pay her."

The man fumbled in his silver pouch and laid two huge pieces in her mother's hand. She closed her fist around them. "Hang on to him, honey. He's a generous one."

Miriam pushed her mother out of the door and closed it behind her. Then she turned back to the man and took a really good look at him for the first time. He was as tall as Joshua but about three or four years younger, with curly reddish-brown hair and wide brown eyes. She could tell by his posture and bearing, and by the expensive linen tunic he wore, that he came from a very wealthy family. But as he gazed around the one-room house he had a dazed look about him, as if he had never imagined that people lived like this. And he seemed genuinely stunned by the transaction that had just taken place.

"That's the second time I bought you in the last hour," he said.

"And you paid way too much for me both times. Who are you, anyway?"

"Didn't Joshua tell you?"

"There wasn't time."

He looked a little embarrassed. "I'm Prince Amariah."

"Prince? You mean King Manasseh's brother?"

"Yes."

"Oh no!" Miriam remembered how she had been ordering him around and she dropped to her knees to bow to him. "I'm sorry, my lord. I'm so sorry. . . ."

"Don't do that, Miriam, stand up. I'm counting on you to smuggle me out of here. What do we do next?"

She struggled to gather her scattered wits. "We're supposed to take the road north to the Samaritan border."

"How will I get past the guards at the city gates?"

Joshua's instructions seemed ludicrous to Miriam now that she knew who Amariah was. She was almost afraid to tell him. "My lord . . . Master Joshua said you must shave off your beard."

"Why?"

"I . . . I'm supposed to dress you in my clothes . . . and smuggle you out as a woman."

Amariah stared at her, then burst into laughter. "It took me a year to grow this beard!"

"I'm sorry, my lord. It wasn't my idea."

"Oh well, never mind. Where's the razor?"

"All we have is a flint blade."

"Ouch! Do you have any soap?"

"Just the kind we wash clothes with."

"Great. How about a mirror?" She shook her head. "Well, if I don't bleed to death, I should be ready to go in a few minutes." He sat down at the table while Miriam brought the blade, soap and a basin of water. Then she dropped to her knees in front of him again.

"My lord, I need to ask you something. Please don't be angry with me. . . ."

"What's wrong, Miriam?"

"It's Master Joshua. I'm so worried about him, my lord. The explosion was terrible . . . so many people were injured . . ."

"I know," he said. "I've been wondering about him, as well."

"May I please go back and look for him? You can shave while I'm gone and change your clothes. I promise to hurry, and —"

"Yes, go. I'll wait here for you."

"Thank you, my lord."

Miriam never stopped running until she reached the top of the Temple Mount. Then she wove through the tangle of groaning bodies, turning over the ones that were lying facedown, searching for Joshua. The sight of so much blood made her stomach heave. This was taking too long. She had to find him. She had to get back to Prince Amariah. God in heaven, why didn't Joshua tell her he was the prince?

Miriam remembered that the blast had come from near the storehouses and decided to search there, first. She ran through Asherah's courtyard, passing the toppled booths, and saw what was left of the grain silo. The roof and the upper two-thirds of it were gone, leaving only a low circular wall topped by a jagged ring of stones, like broken teeth. Beyond it, a relay team of Temple guards worked feverishly, bailing water from the brazen laver, trying to extinguish the burning row of storehouses. The ground was littered with fallen bricks and grain.

Then, beneath the rubble, Miriam saw a man's body sprawled across the pavement. His arms and legs were limp and twisted, like a straw man's. He wore a military tunic and had black tousled hair, just like Joshua's.

Oh, God, please! I won't ask you for anything else as long as I live if you, please, please, just let this be him! Let him be all right!

She knelt beside the body and turned it over with shaking hands. He was limp and heavy, a dead weight.

Joshua.

Miriam recognized him, even though the right side of his face was destroyed, leaving nothing but blood and pulp where he had smashed it against the pavement. She couldn't hear him breathing, nor could she see his chest moving beneath the tattered leather tunic. Fighting tears, she held her fingers to his throat and felt for his heartbeat.

His life pulsed faintly.

"Oh, God, thank you, thank you!" she wept. In that moment Miriam knew that Jerusha's God was with both of them.

Joshua moaned and tried to open his eyes. For some reason, he could only see out of one of them. His blurred vision was surrounded by stinging sparkles of light. A dark shadow bent over him. He tried to focus on it, and when he did, the pain in his head was so excruciating that he retched. The shadowy figure cradled his head, murmuring something he couldn't hear. A loud roaring noise rang in Joshua's ears, making all the sounds around him muffled, as if he were lying at the bottom of the sea. He didn't know where he was or what had happened to him. His body felt both numb and pain-wracked at the same time, and his limbs seemed to vibrate as if a gigantic hand had slapped him. The last thing he could remember was trying to light a torch with his flint, but the reason he had been lighting it was a mystery to him.

Someone pushed him into a sitting position. The shock of the sudden movement and the soaring pain he felt as he raised his head made him vomit again. He moaned and closed his eye, wanting nothing more than to lie down and sleep until the agony ended. But his tormentor hauled him to his feet, forcing him to stand on deadened legs, as weak as willow branches. He leaned against the shadow, nearly knocking both of them to the ground.

"No . . . I can't walk. . . ." he tried to say,

but his swollen mouth wouldn't work properly and his words came out in a jumble of sounds that even he couldn't understand. The ground started to move — or else he started to move, he couldn't tell which. He felt as if he was on board a ship in a wildly tossing sea. He wanted to stop, but on and on he plunged, with shapes and shadows he couldn't recognize, whirling past him, sickeningly.

Now the deck sloped sharply downhill. After a few steps, Joshua lost his balance and tumbled to the ground, pulling the shadow with him. He seemed to roll forever and his lifeless limbs and throbbing head came alive with pain. The agony didn't stop when he struck a wall at the bottom and stopped rolling. He lay facedown on the ground unable to move, tasting dirt and blood in his mouth. *Oh, God, end this,* he prayed.

But the torment didn't end. Instead, his adversary rolled him onto his back and lifted him beneath his armpits, dragging him along the cobblestones. He lacked the strength to raise his head, and it bounced helplessly from side to side as he was pulled along.

"Stop . . ." he groaned. "Stop . . ." He was going to be sick again. But the noise he uttered didn't sound like words. It didn't even sound like his voice.

Finally the movement stopped and he was rolled onto his side and shoved into a depression in the street. It was dark inside and cool. The shadow hovered over him for a moment, then vanished.

Joshua couldn't move. The pain in his head was trying to crush him, extinguish him. He wondered where his torch was and what had happened to his flint. He had to light the torch. He remembered that it was important, but he couldn't recall why. Maybe if he went back to sleep he would remember. Or maybe he would wake up in paradise and the pain would be gone. Joshua closed his eyes, welcoming unconsciousness.

When Miriam burst into the house, out of breath, it took her a moment to recognize the tall woman standing beside the hearth. Prince Amariah's disguise was perfect. He wore her mother's old, tattered robe with her own blue-and-white shawl over his head. A lock of his curly brown hair fell across his forehead. He had swaddled one end of the scarf around the lower part of his face to help hide all the nicks and scrapes on his chin.

"I found Master Joshua!" Miriam blurted. "But he's hurt, and I can't carry him by myself."

"Where is he?"

"I hid him in a drainage ditch at the bottom of the Temple Mount — not far from here."

"Let's go."

"Wait, my lord . . . I think I know of a way we can all get out of the city. If you give me some money, I can buy a shroud and rent a funeral cart. We can wrap Master Joshua up and carry him out of the city as if he were dead."

"That's an excellent idea, Miriam. Joshua told me you were good at this."

"He did?"

"Here's my silver pouch. But hurry, before the guards spread the word that I'm missing."

Miriam didn't bother to haggle with the cloth merchant over the price of a shroud or bargain with the owner of the donkey and hearse. She simply paid the first price they named and hurried on her way. Joshua lay in the ditch where she had hidden him, unconscious.

Prince Amariah paled when he saw him. "Are you certain he's still alive?"

"I made him walk part of the way. And he

was moaning."

"He needs a physician, Miriam."

"I know, but there's no time. Help me take his uniform off."

"It's fortunate he was wearing it, or his whole body would look like his face does." Amariah removed the flint blade from under his robe and cut the leather guard's tunic and leggings off Joshua's body. Then he lifted him up so Miriam could wind the shroud around him.

"Can you weep, my lord?" she asked the prince.

"Can I *what?*"

"You should be weeping when we get to the gate, like women in mourning do."

Amariah smiled. "You think of everything, don't you? Very well, I shall do my best to weep."

She let Amariah carry the weight of Joshua's upper body, while she lifted his legs and feet. Together, they loaded him on the cart and headed toward the graveyard across the valley near the Mount of Olives. But first they would have to pass the guards at the Water Gate. When Miriam pictured Joshua's ravaged face, genuine tears sprang to her eyes. She wept softly. The noise Amariah made behind her sounded fairly convincing.

The guards stopped them at the gate. "Who's inside the shroud?" one of them asked.

Miriam wiped her tears. "Our brother, my lord. He died in the accident at the Temple."

"What was his name?"

"Nathan, son of Maki."

"Let's see him."

"He's dead, my lord. Have you no respect for the dead?"

"I need to look at his face."

Miriam turned Joshua's head to the left, praying he wouldn't moan or move, and parted the shroud to reveal the mangled right side of his face.

"I'm sorry," the guard said in a hushed voice. "You may go."

She covered his face again and hurried down the ramp out of Jerusalem.

23

"Please . . . I need to rest," Dinah said. "I'm sorry." She collapsed on the grass alongside the road. The steady downhill descent for the past hour had made her knees shaky. She saw the concern in Hadad's eyes as he knelt beside her.

"When did you eat last?" he asked.

"I don't know. . . . Yesterday, I guess."

"I need to find you some food. And another pair of shoes. I don't think yours were made for walking very far."

"Are we almost to the border?"

"Dinah," he said gently, "it's twenty-four miles from Jerusalem to the ford of the Jordan River."

Her eyes filled with tears. "I'll never make it that far." She was so exhausted, physically and emotionally, that she wept at the impossibility of it all.

"I have a better idea," Hadad said. "We'll head north to Michmash at the next crossroads. The Samaritan border is only five or six miles from here. We can rest and spend the night there."

"Where are we supposed to meet Joshua?"

She saw him hesitate. "He'll probably meet us at your family's house in Heshbon."

They had talked all morning as they'd waited inside the booth, and Dinah had described her year spent in fear and isolation. He'd listened with compassion and even reached to take her hand in his own when she told him how her son had died. Hadad had filled in the missing pieces for her about her family, assuring her that they were safe, telling her of Jerimoth's growing cloth business and the reputation Joshua was earning in the building trade. He told her how he had traveled to Jerusalem with Jerimoth's caravan and how Joshua helped the Levite families escape. But Hadad had said little about himself.

He was very good-looking, Dinah thought. His Egyptian heritage showed in his broad face, his straight black hair and brows, his dusky skin. And when he flashed his dazzling smile, he revealed a perfect row of even white teeth. He had been so gentle with her, so patient, that she felt as if she had always known him. Yet she knew nothing about him.

"Who are you, Hadad?" she asked. She saw a look of sadness cross his features.

"I'm not really sure," he said softly. "That's one of the reasons I came back to Jerusalem. To find out."

She reached for his hand. "Then I'll tell you who you are — you're an answer to prayer."

"I am?" She thought she saw tears in his eyes.

"You have no idea how hard I prayed for God to deliver me from Manasseh. There were so many times when I thought it would never happen, that God didn't hear my cries. But He did, Hadad. He heard. And He sent you. He *is* the God of the impossible, just as Abba always said He was."

"Your family has a lot of faith in God, don't they?"

"If you had known my grandfather, you would understand why. He loved Yahweh the way the Torah tells us to — with all his heart and all his soul and all his strength. He lived his faith every day of his life, and he taught Abba to believe by his example. Abba passed his faith on to all of us. I always knew that if my earthly father loved me that much, then my Heavenly Father must love me even more."

Hadad reached to gently wipe her tears

with his fingertips. "I envy you for that. My grandfather didn't know God. And I've never really known what it means to be loved."

"Do you know God, Hadad?"

"I'd like to."

"Someday when I teach my children about Yahweh, I'll tell them how He sent an angel named Hadad to rescue me."

He pulled her into his arms and rested his cheek against her hair before releasing her again. "We should go, Dinah. Do you think you can make it the last couple of miles to the border?"

"I think so."

"I'll try to buy us a ride on the next cart that comes our way, all right?"

As they walked on for another hour, Hadad's promise of finding a ride kept Dinah going. But when she finally saw a cart coming up the road behind them she changed her mind about hitching a ride. It was a funeral cart, bearing a shrouded body. Two women walked beside it, leading a sway-backed donkey.

"Hadad, I don't think we should —"

"Miriam!" he shouted. "Dinah, that's Miriam!" Hadad started running down the road toward the cart before Dinah could ask who Miriam was. Dinah watched as he lifted one of the women into his arms and whirled her around, laughing. "Am I ever glad to see you!" he said.

As Dinah walked toward the cart, the other woman suddenly pulled the scarf off of her head. Dinah stared in astonishment. It was Prince Amariah. Hadad saw him too.

"Amariah? I can't believe it!" Hadad cried. "That crazy fool said he was going to rescue you, but I didn't think Joshua would actually —" Hadad stopped suddenly, a look of horror on his face as he turned his gaze to the shrouded body. "Oh, please . . . no . . ."

Dinah's legs collapsed beneath her as she fit all the pieces together. The corpse on the funeral cart was Joshua.

Amariah caught her before she hit the ground. But it took a few moments for his words to penetrate her shock.

"It's all right, Dinah. It's all right. He isn't dead; he's alive. Joshua is alive!"

"The omens all promise that you will live, Your Majesty. Your enemy has not prevailed."

Zerah's words should have reassured Manasseh, but they didn't. His body still felt violated, vulnerable. He ached from lying in the same position, yet he was afraid to move, afraid he would rip himself open again, spilling his insides.

"Where's Amariah? I thought I told you to send him in here? Is my brother refusing to cooperate again?" He saw Zerah and one of his bodyguards exchange glances. "Tell me what's going on!" Manasseh ordered.

"I'd like everyone to leave the room, please," Zerah said.

Manasseh lay back and waited, bracing himself for bad news. Zerah paced at the foot of his bed, cracking his knuckles. Manasseh knew him well — the priest was extremely upset.

"Your body needs time to heal, Your Majesty. You must not let this news upset you and start the bleeding again."

"Tell me where Amariah is."

"He's gone, my lord. He disappeared. I had men following him, but he slipped away from them. We're searching the city."

"Well, he couldn't have gone far. Where would he go? Surely he'll come back when —"

"He won't be back. We found this in his room." Zerah held up a potsherd. Manasseh knew without looking at it that there would be an ox scratched on one side. He shuddered with the same impotent rage he'd felt after Dinah stabbed him. Joshua, his enemy, had been here, inside his own palace, conspiring with his brother.

"They won't get away with this!"

"There's more," Zerah said quietly. "Dinah is gone, too."

"How? How is that possible? Where were the guards? Don't tell me Joshua took her, too?"

"It appears so, Your Majesty. He and his forces must have stolen into Jerusalem with the Passover crowds. They created a huge disturbance at the Temple this morning. The explosion you heard a while ago was a grain silo. Eight people were killed, including three guards. Dozens more were injured. In all the confusion, Amariah and Dinah both disappeared."

"It's your fault, Zerah! I told you to execute her, but no! It was your idea to take her up to the Temple!"

"I take full responsibility, Your Majesty. I'm sorry."

"Meaningless words! Get out of here and leave me alone!" Manasseh's anger and frustration had him close to tears. Joshua had beaten him. He had always beaten him.

"Before I leave there is something else you should know." Zerah spoke rapidly now, as if spilling the bad news quickly might soften the blow. "In the aftermath of the explosion, once the fires were extinguished, my priests realized that none of the Levites had helped them. My men began a search, and it seems the Levites have disappeared, as well, along with their families. Their houses are filled with possessions but no inhabitants."

"They were all against me anyway. Good riddance to them!" But in spite of his words, a terrible emptiness and dread filled Manasseh.

"Your Majesty, when I learned that a witness reported a smuggling operation down by the Temple dump, I decided to see what else had been stolen."

Manasseh closed his eyes. He didn't want to hear any more. He was the king, yet he felt horribly impotent. How had Joshua stolen his wife, his brother, his treasures, and all the priests and Levites right out from under him?

"How much did they take?"

"It's not a matter of how much, Your Majesty . . . it's *what* they've taken. The ark of the covenant is gone."

Joshua's audacity stunned Manasseh. It also terrified him. It was a moment before he could speak. "*Joshua* stole it, didn't he?"

"We found his signature inside the holy place." Zerah's voice had grown more hushed with each new revelation.

Manasseh understood what a powerful national symbol the ark was and how his enemy might use it against him. As all the pieces of Joshua's plan fell into place, Manasseh suddenly cried out.

"He's going to challenge my throne! That's why he took Amariah. And that's why he took all the priests. They have the authority to anoint the king of Judah. And thanks to you, he has Dinah, as well. If Amariah marries her, it will strengthen his claim to my throne!"

He could tell by the look of astonishment on Zerah's face that he hadn't fit all the clues together until now. Zerah sank onto a chair, his face unnaturally pale. "I had no idea how truly powerful your enemy was."

But Manasseh knew. "I was warned a long time ago," he murmured. "When Joshua and I were children, a beggar-woman once read our palms. She told me that Joshua would be too powerful for me . . . and that he would try to destroy me."

"You should have told me."

"I never wanted to believe it. But now that I finally understand what I'm up against, I'll be ready for him the next time. This isn't over between Joshua and me. This is far from over."

■ ■ ■ ■

The cool, wet cloth bathing his face nudged Joshua into consciousness. He ached. Every inch of him ached. His body felt heavy and dull, but his pounding head felt heavier still. Where was he? And what had happened to immobilize him this way?

He heard a woman's garbled voice, but he couldn't make out what she was saying above the ringing in his ears. It took an enormous effort to open one eye. There was nothing but pain and darkness where his other eye should have been. He saw a woman hovering over him, but her image danced and wavered like a mirage.

Someone helped him sit up, and the woman put a cup to his mouth. His lips felt tender and swollen, but he drank the water greedily.

"What happened?" he mumbled.

"You blew up half the Temple Mount, that's what! And you almost blew yourself to paradise along with it." The man's voice sounded muffled and far away, yet familiar. Joshua searched his memory to place it.

"Hadad?"

"Yes! I'm glad you can still remember something!"

"I remember . . ." He groaned and closed his eye again. His head hurt so much when he tried to think. He remembered trying to light the torch. His hands had been shaking, and he couldn't get the flint to work. But he must have gotten it lit because he remembered flames afterward. And heat. "Where am I?"

"In Samaritan territory. We're all safe, Joshua. We crossed the border a little while ago."

"Who did?"

"Miriam and I . . . Prince Amariah . . . and your sister Dinah."

"Dinah?"

"Yes, Joshua. I'm right here." She took him gently in her arms and pressed her cheek to his. He felt her tears on his face. "Thank you for coming back for me. Thank you for saving me."

Then he felt his own tears as the memory of what he had done finally returned. He wrapped his arms around her and hugged her fiercely, ignoring the pain.

"Dinah! All this time . . . we thought you were dead."

"And I thought you were dead when I saw you lying on this funeral cart."

"How did I get here? Hadad, did you . . . ?"

"It wasn't me; it was Miriam. She went back to the Temple for you."

"And it was her idea to hire the funeral cart," Amariah added. "She saved your life, Joshua."

"Where is she?"

"She's watering the donkey," Hadad said, laughing. "She's the only one of us who knows how to handle the cursed thing."

"Get her for me."

Joshua slowly took stock of his body while he waited. He was glad to see that he could move his legs and feet as well as his arms. Nothing seemed to be broken, just terribly sore. When he gingerly touched his face and swollen right eye it brought needles of sharp pain. But once his head stopped aching and his vision cleared, he would probably be fine.

"You wanted to see me, Master Joshua?"

He groped for her hand. When he found it, he held it between his. "I've treated you badly, Miriam. And yet you still saved my life. I'll never be able to thank you."

"All those stories Lady Jerusha told me about God are true, Master Joshua. I didn't save you; He did. Yahweh saved all of us."

Yahweh had done it.

The ark of the covenant; the holy books; the priests and Levites and their families;

Yael; Prince Amariah; Dinah — they were all safe from Manasseh.

They were safe.

Joshua imagined Manasseh's astonishment when he discovered all that he had lost. And his rage when he realized who had stolen it from him.

But then Joshua recalled Jerimoth's words and he knew that his brother had been right — Joshua's hunger for revenge wasn't satisfied. What he had accomplished could never bring Abba back. Or his grandfather.

"It isn't enough . . ." he mumbled.

As long as Manasseh was alive, it would never be enough.

Epilogue

Joshua stood in the doorway to the court-yard of his house in Moab and watched his mother as she bent over the kneading trough. The aroma of baking bread drifted from the outdoor oven.

"Mama . . ."

Jerusha turned and saw him. "Oh!" she breathed. "Oh, praise God!"

Joshua hurried across the yard on stiff legs and clasped his mother in his arms. Her hands, white with flour, left trails of dust in his hair and on his tunic as she ran them over him as if to see if he was real.

"Joshua . . . your face!" she cried.

"It's healing, Mama." He was glad that Dinah had convinced him to hide the dam-aged side beneath a bandage. "Listen, I have a surprise for you. Sit here on the bench and close your eyes."

"One surprise is more than enough. I can't believe you're finally home!"

"Close them. And no peeking." He waited until Dinah stood in the doorway, her eyes already shining with tears, then said, "All right, Mama, you can open them."

Jerusha cried out as Dinah raced across the yard. They fell into each other's arms, weeping.

"Dinah! It can't be! Is it really you?"

"I never thought I would see you again, Mama."

"Oh, my precious daughter!"

Joshua's voice was hoarse with emotion when he finally spoke. "And don't worry about Jerimoth either, Mama. He's in Egypt, probably buying and selling the pyramids by now."

"But he'll be home soon?"

"Well, I hate to spring too much on you at once, but he's not coming back to Moab — we're moving to Egypt."

"What?" Jerusha was laughing and weeping at the same time as she stroked Dinah's face and hair.

"We're going to build a community of believers there, and an altar for Yahweh," Joshua told her. "Prince Amariah will serve as our leader, and I'll be his second in command. The priests and Levites are already in Egypt, too, with their families."

"I can't comprehend this, Joshua! It's

enough for me to have my children back. I don't care where we live as long as we're all together." She hugged Dinah close and Joshua surrounded both of them with his arms. His mother sighed. "Now if only . . ."

"What, Mama?"

"I'm still missing my other daughter . . . Miriam."

Joshua stared at her in astonishment. "Miriam?"

"I've missed her so much."

"But . . . she's here, Mama. She came back with us. I'll get her." He hurried inside and found Miriam watching them through the window like an outsider. "You're part of this family, too," he said gently. "Come on, Mama's asking for you."

"She . . . she is?"

Jerusha's eyes lit with joy when she saw Miriam. She drew her into her arms. "Miriam . . . my daughter. You're home!"

"Yes," she wept. "I'm home."

A NOTE TO THE READER

People often ask me which portions of my stories are based on fact and which are products of my imagination. While my principal source of factual information is always the Bible, I also supplement it with non-conflicting accounts from other sources such as the Greek historian Herodotus, the Jewish historian Josephus, Jewish oral traditions, Assyrian annals, and archaeological evidence.

The Bible records the depth of Manasseh's sin and apostasy. According to Jewish tradition, he martyred Isaiah by sawing him in half (Hebrews 11:37 might refer to this). Hezekiah did have a second son, Amariah. Zephaniah 1:1 reveals that Prince Amariah was one of the prophet Zephaniah's ancestors.

In 1961 archaeologists uncovered the ruins of a temple on the island of Elephantine in Egypt. Aligned to face Jerusalem, it was identical in size and construction to the Jerusalem Temple and had been built by Jewish priests and Levites fleeing the persecution of King Manasseh's reign. Records unearthed with it revealed that a full schedule of sacrifices and feast days had been celebrated there. Since no other temple was ever built by exiled priests or Jews, some scholars have concluded that the ark of the covenant might have been rescued from Manasseh and housed there, as well.

In his book *Temples and Temple Service in Ancient Israel,* Professor Menahem Haran says, "I am certain the ark was removed in Manasseh's time . . . the orthodox priests of Yahweh would under no circumstance have permitted the ark of Yahweh to stay in the same place as the idol of Asherah." *Faith of My Fathers* and its sequel, *Among the Gods,* are based on this premise.

If the pagan rituals I've described seem contemporary, it's because the so-called New Age movement is centuries old. Practices such as astrology, channeling, voodoo, crystals, divination, and witchcraft date back to ancient Canaanite and Babylonian beliefs. These pagan beliefs are rooted in the four lies used by Satan in the Garden of Eden and were condemned by God in ancient times, just as they are now. There is truly "nothing new under the sun."

I expose them in my novel not to glorify them, but to warn readers of their dangers and to reveal some of the lies that lure people into practicing them. One of the marks of a cult is that it twists Scripture or uses it out of context. As believers, we must cling to and protect the purity of the faith entrusted to us while proclaiming the fact that all other religious practices are false. Jesus said it best: "I am the way and the truth and the life. No one comes to the Father except through me" (John 14:6).

Interested readers are encouraged to research the full accounts of the events in this book in the Bible as they enjoy this fourth book in the CHRONICLES OF THE KINGS series.

Scripture references for *Faith of My Fathers:*

2 Kings 21:1–18
2 Chronicles 33

See also:

Isaiah 10:22; 19:19; 22:18–25; 26:20; 36;
40:27–31; and 41:9–13

Psalm 22; 35; 37; 90; and 103
Ecclesiastes 1:1–3

ABOUT THE AUTHOR

Lynn Austin is a three-time Christy Award winner for her historical novels *Hidden Places, Candle in the Darkness,* and *Fire by Night.* In addition to writing, Lynn is a popular speaker at conferences, retreats, and various church and school events. She and her husband have three children and make their home in Illinois.

The employees of Thorndike Press hope you have enjoyed this Large Print book. All our Thorndike and Wheeler Large Print titles are designed for easy reading, and all our books are made to last. Other Thorndike Press Large Print books are available at your library, through selected bookstores, or directly from us.

For information about titles, please call:
(800) 223-1244

or visit our Web site at:
http://gale.cengage.com/thorndike

To share your comments, please write:
Publisher
Thorndike Press
295 Kennedy Memorial Drive
Waterville, ME 04901